Reviews from Readers Who Have Found

The Klamath Treasure

"*The Klamath Treasure* a real treasure of a book."

-- Bill Duncan, *The News-Review*

"I just finished the book last night and it was wonderful. Extremely well written. I can't say enough good things about it and will recommend it to everyone I know! I bought two copies and am so glad I did! It brought back lots of wonderful memories, and of course a few tears along the way for the fictional hero whom I fell in love with! Anyone 8-80 would enjoy this book."

-- Deanna Fisher, Reader Review (Tumwater, Washington)

"I was a bit surprised how fast I read the 400-plus page book, but I was concerned about the main character and the adventure that was unfolding in front of him. It's so well written it's hard to remember that it is historical fiction -- and be ready to laugh and remember your own childhood and even shed a few tears as you read this book."

-- Estelle Ribero, Reader Review (Los Angeles, California)

The Klamath Treasure

The Adventure of Euclid Plutarch Hammarsen

Mike

Here's to fishing stories!
Good luck on your next
trip to the Klamath,

My best,

Josha Burnes

The Klamath Treasure

The Adventure of Euclid Plutarch Hammarsen

Trisha Barnes

River
Canyon
Press

EUGENE, OREGON
www.RiverCanyonPress.com

ISBN-13: 978-0-9815914-0-7
ISBN-10: 0-9815914-0-X
LCCN: 2008931378
ASIN: B001EHEBK8

Edited by Nida Lawson Johnson, Earl Johnson, Benjamin Barnes, Jr. and Nicholas Barnes. Cover, layout, interior graphics and manuscript design by Trisha Barnes.

Ten percent of the net proceeds from this book will be donated to non-profit organizations in Siskiyou County, California.

ATTENTION CORPORATIONS, UNIVERSITIES, COLLEGES AND PROFESSIONAL ORGANIZATIONS: Quantity discounts are available on bulk purchases of this book for educational, gift purposes, or as premiums for increasing magazine subscriptions or renewals. Special books or book excerpts can also be created to fit specific needs. For information, please contact River Canyon Press, P. O. Box 70643, Eugene, Oregon 97401.

Euclid P. Hammarsen

In Memory and Honor Of

Mrs. June Lawson

Table of Contents

A Note to Readers of

My Journal

There are times, even now, when the thought strikes me to walk from my home to the rocky cliff that skirts this bend of the mighty Klamath-*Ishke'esh*. Each time I consider that daredevil adventure, I can imagine myself perching at the top of the highest rock, standing straight, and curling my legs under as I jump into the river water. Something I've done a thousand times, but now it seems like a thousand years ago. I might be able to pull it off, but my ninety-one year old body may not.

Or maybe I'll venture out a little further on my walk today and search out some of the arimantus trees that are still standing over a hundred years after the Celestial men placed their seeds in the river soil. I wonder if I could make it all the way to the top of one of those deep green spires – what we all used to call the Trees of Heaven – before my old and tired heart just stopped beating altogether.

I grew up here, in the Klamath River valley, near the mining and logging town of Happy Camp. You can find it on most newer California State maps – look for the Oregon-California border, trace Interstate 5 south, follow the winding Klamath River to the west, and look really, really hard and our little town will be right there.

This stubborn community has been here longer than California has been a State, but it's only been a recent development that anyone's paid much attention to our River Canyon.

Believe you me that us locals still aren't too sure what to make out of this latest gold rush, what with all the folks coming in on the weekends or just for a summer – panning and dredging – and then leaving. We don't really get a chance to get acquainted, like we did when folks used to stay and work their claims for a living – not just a vacation.

Although I was away from the place from time to time during my life, I always considered it my home and no one was very surprised when I finally moved back to stay. In all of the hours and days that have made my life this long, the best ones happened in this land when I was a boy and a young man.

In these parts I've worked as a miner, a logger, a trapper, a river guide in my old drift boat, and a timber feller – sometimes all in the same year.

I am an old man now, but I am not too old to remember the exploits and escapades that my friends and I used to have. Someone said once that the young boy lives in the old man. Now, nearing the end of my life's journey, I spend a lot of time thinking about the young boy that I was. I spend a lot of time thinking about the friends I had here, back then, and the adventures that we had together.

I'm the last one – of all of us. If I don't get some of these stories down the rich history may be lost forever.

I've been using this old brain for quite some time now, and I don't fault it much for getting a few things mixed up now and then. I guess my faculties have naturally been slipping a bit. More than once lately I've set out to go to Ben's house, to ask his Mother if Ben could come along fishing – only to remember as I reached my garden gate that I hadn't seen my buddy Ben in over seventy-nine years. I wonder to this day if he ever sailed to Spain like he was so fond of talking about. I'd like to think that he did.

I still read Sir Walter Scott and the Greek and Roman masters of adventure as much as my old eyes will let me. I still say *Crick* instead of *Creek*, *clum* instead of *climbed*, and regardless of my education and knowledge of grammar and language and syntax I probably always will. I can still recall most of the Latin and the art history and the old dramas and tragedies that my Mother had taught to me by lamp-light over our little worn kitchen table. Searching my old brain nowadays for words, I often frustratingly come up with their Chinese, Latin, hay-seed or native equivalents instead. I've had lethogical tendencies for so long, that at times I tire of looking for the right word and just set to make up my own.

I still carry my worn and ancient-looking library card to the little book house next to the Cemetery and insist on showing it to the librarian even though she's assured me all their records are electronic now. Out of practicality and responsibility and knowing that it's just a matter of time before I'm going to be hauled out of my house toes first – and because I take my library borrowing privileges very seriously – I've let the Library Lady know that I generally keep my books on the kitchen counter near the back door. I figure it'll be easier for her to retrieve them that way. Some other folks may have thought my announcement a bit macabre or in poor taste but all she said was, "I wish more of our senior patrons were as considerate as you."

Almost every time I visit, before I head for home, I bother her with my same complaint – asking her to make a call to see if the County folks could bring back the good old card catalog so I could browse through the little bibliographies to find just what I wanted. They haint set it back up yet, and I figure they never will.

I almost expect to see the Running Indian padding down the road, or see the wild horses of the valley once again crest the mountain to the south. My elderly mind wanders, during these times, since I do still know in my heart that neither the Running Indian nor the wild horses will ever be seen in these parts again.

I bought this handsome leather journal way back in early 1920 or so on my first leave in San Pedro de Macoris in the Dominican Republic, while serving on the *USS New Hampshire*. I spent a lot of time in that bookseller's shop near the Higuamo River, where the little old man hand tooled the leather book covers and repaired our baseball gloves on the same ancient workbench his family had used for centuries to make riding saddles, shoes, and tack.

My shipmates and I also spent a lot of time playing baseball – whenever we could get away to it – with the local boys who had got the game from some Cuban sugar cane workers dozens of years before we showed up. We tried to play us against them, but after being beat too long we decided to pick mixed teams – at least that way some of us Navy boys could win now and then. I look real hard now at the baseball on the television at the strong fellas coming out of that tropical baseball paradise to see if any look familiar, as I am sure I rounded the bases and fielded hits with many of their grandfathers back then. A few years after we left their country in our ships, they got so serious about the sport that at one point in the 1930's folks like Satchel Paige, Josh Gibson, and Cool Papa Bell were kidnapped from one team by a Dominican General and forced to play for him instead. The time I spent on those hot dusty fields in Dominica was unfortunately the closest I ever really got to playing in The Big Show.

This book that the leather-tooler made for me long ago is large and heavy and the pages are unlined. I remember that when the book trader finished the last stitch in the spine of my journal, he laughed as I remarked at the beauty of his work. "No one," he modestly replied, "admired the quality of the canvas brought to Henri Rosseau, only what he made of it after with his paints." The workman and I both knew that someday when everything slowed down I'd fill his handmade journal front to back with all of my stories. The leather embellishments on the remarkable cover show grand horses parading through a forest – and every time I look at the detail I light on to something I've missed before. To date, I've actually spent more time looking at the front of this tome than I've spent writing in it.

Is it better to have lived a life that books could have been written about, or to have written a book about lives we wished we could have lived? I carried this neglected journal during most of my travels – from the Caribbean, to Eastern and Western Europe, across Australia, down the Yukon River, and even to the top of Mount Olympus in Greece – and failed to ever write in it. It was my constant reminder of my plans to become a novelist, and a quiet companion that did not argue or fuss at its lonely unutilized existence when I chose to sail or hike or climb a tree or wrangle a fish to the bank instead of exercising my pen. The closest I got to using it was around 1928 or so in what was then a United States territory, wedging it under a broken door to keep it propped open in my ocean-side *hale*. That lasted for almost the entire two wonderful and exciting years I spent on the Maui Island.

I've dusted it off. It's been waiting for me on this bookshelf for many years.

Under my aged hat I have some fish stories, one love story, tales of adventure, details of legendary exploits, historical accounts of local events, and one really incredible treasure hunt. I'm sure I'll also have occasion to add a few of my scratchy pencil illustrations here and there when I can.

As I begin to write this, I will for the moment forego the urge to jump into the river or to climb any of the Trees of Heaven. Instead, with the warm Siskiyou morning sun on my back and my journal in hand, I will set to getting at least some of these stories written down.

Chapter One

How We Came To Be Here

"Back before the whole mess over the Spotted Owl, I had the unfortunate occasion to eat a few. Even just eating them they're more trouble than they're worth."
— Cade McKetter, Resident

I suppose that if any of these stories are to make sense, you'll need to know a little about where we are and why any of us were here to begin with. A starting point, if you will.

This whole area – *ab ovo*, or in the beginning as it were – was called Murderer's Bar. Like many community names, it was the imperfect blending of an historical event and a place. The event was a low-handed murder of one fellow by another, and the place being the sandy river bar that used to be near where the Klamath River and Indian Crick met. Most folks agree that the fight was over a claim, and local talk has it that the murdering coward cut the other fella after sneaking up behind him. That day our land and our river were christened in a dying man's blood. One of them fellows lost his life there and another lost his soul, if it wasn't already missing before he committed his crime. Probably not the best and luckiest way to start a community.

Murderer's Bar grew as a rag-tag mining and lumber camp. Heard tell that the mining came first, though – way back in 1850 or so. Sutter's Mill – down south – had started to pay out really daisy in 1849, and it didn't take long at all for all manner of folks to weave their way up to our canyon.

The rail brought the Southern Pacific line into Montague, and round about 1889 or so the shortline was built into Shasta Butte City proper. Due to a bakery-tent sign mix up pretty near that time, that town was mistakenly called Yreka after that.

Before the rail had been put into whatever you wanted to call that city, it was no argument that it had been a bit of a wagon ride or a long walk to get to it. Outfitters, blacksmiths, farriers, and saloon owners prospered from the steady flow of *greenhorns* as well as *old sourdoughs* that were let off by the regular train.

Almost every miner and miner-to-be coming off the rail first played his pick and shovel at the aptly-named Thompson's Dry Diggin's – our very own Gold Rush area – where a fellow named Thompson had struck it rich around 1851. It was a famous place, written up in newspapers around the country and around the world. Finding the Dry Diggin's really dry of any color, the newcomers directly made other plans.

Tiring of the overworked infamous Diggin's, fellows would strike out in all directions – some burrowing tunnels into the high desert mountains in what would later become Northern Siskiyou County, and still others, used to mining placer claims or panning, would seek out water sources like rivers and cricks.

Us river folks have always known that some of the abandoned high tunnel mines are still pretty rich since the fellas that worked them so long ago were only interested in the fist-sized pieces. Everything else was too little and a bothahrayshun. A heap of today's *greenhorns* strike out in the high desert mountains to survey the old claims, and to look for lost gold treasure that some poor miner may have holed up somewhere. A few words of advice, if you happen to be one of those expectant interlopers – it's a land chock-full of six-foot-long rattlesnakes, mountain lions that may kill a man just for the sport of hunting him, murderous bears that can run uphill as fast as downhill, and vacant of any help for you if you happen along any of the three terrors I just mentioned.

Remember – you are welcome here – just don't get one of *us* killed trying to fish your fool dead body out of one of the sets of Klamath-*Ishke'esh* rapids or hauling your broken self out of one of the thousand dark, wet, and slippery old mining tunnel shafts. One unfortunate visiting fella we found was considerate, having written his name and address with a water-proof marker on his chest and his leg – which was a great idea, because even though the mountain lion had chewed him up pretty good in both areas we were able to piece together the information, so to speak.

Back in the beginning most folks came west from Yreka. Many of the early miners would traverse the seventy-odd miles along the Klamath River to the

Murderer's Bar encampment – hiking, on horseback, or even with pack trains of mules or donkeys. They would often work their pans along the way, resting from the long walk under their heavy gear or watering their animals – sometimes even taking the entire summer season for the journey with plans to winter over at the tent camp at Murderer's Bar – or The Bar, as it was often referred to. The high desert landscape would change before them as they followed the river while it wound like a snake atwixt the steep green mountains and through canyons and valleys.

Early articles about our Golden Canyon mentioned how quaint it was that the Klamath and the famous Thames River were exactly the same length – 268 miles. I can tell you after seeing every mile of both of those tributaries, that just about the only thing they had in common aside of their length was that they were both wet.

To give our beginning timeframe a little perspective, it's important to remember that in 1850 Smith and Wesson hadn't yet invented their revolver, Millard Fillmore was President, and the Oregon Territory wouldn't become part of the Union for about another decade. It would be twenty-six years before Custer's Last Stand would happen at Little Big Horn, Montana, and thirty-six years would pass before the dedication ceremony for the verdigris Statue of Liberty in New York harbor. Those first folks in the River Canyon would see about eleven years of panning and rock breaking before the Pony Express would be made obsolete by the completed national telegraph line, and about that same amount of time before our countrymen in the South and North would start to wage a war on each other. Heck, it'd be over sixteen years from the time those first few fellas made camp at Murderer's Bar before Nobel created the miner's best friend – dynamite.

There's no limit to the strength and perseverance of determined miners, and given the luck of good health and the ability to accurately land a true rifle shot more and more fellas had started to finish the trek. Some folks would make it to The Bar the back way – through the Scott Valley and down the wild Salmon River to where it met up with the Klamath to the south of us. If on the slim chance they made it out of that hard country alive, they usually forged their way up the Klamath the forty miles or so into our community. In those wild and terrible beginning days, not many folks who chose the Salmon River option were ever seen alive again.

Regardless of how the miners got to The Bar, the fellas that were already established here soon separated the new wheat from the chaff, so to speak. They had their own code and their own sense of law, and their own sense of justice too. Most of them were good men – the kind who would stop and take time to bury you if they happened across you dead somewhere – not just commandeer your gear and horse and leave you out in the sun for the birds and the bears. Real decent folk, who just wanted to peaceably make their way through and hopefully make some money from their hard work.

On their travels toward The Bar, open pine forests would merge into stands of oak and madrone, returning to pine forests again around the next bend. The musty, green smell of the river accompanied all of those men on their journey from the high desert and down into our river valley. You can still see some of the original track across the Klamath if you're traveling on Highway 96.

I've made that hard trek a few times on my feet,

and once on my back in a wagon when my folks thought I was sick with scarlet fever – but all of that happened a coon's age ago before the fancy new curvy two-lane highway was even thought of.

Somewhere along the way, as the local history goes, the men in the camps were tired of their lonely existence. A community celebration was held in July of 1852 – perhaps to celebrate the Nation's Independence or even the late news that California had been admitted to the Union two years previous. The area was purely a man's paradise – legendary hunting and fishing, with nigh unto every pan swish showing great color – but the celebration and the town lacked something very important. With over twenty men still standing after the whiskey and the Chinese wine had been disposed of, it was decided that to attract marryable women to the area they would have to change the name of the town. Two letters of proposal had been refused, so far, sent from local men asking their intended to marry and live happily ever after in Murderer's Bar. No respectable or even semi-respectable mid-west mother would send her daughter knowingly to a community named after a place where a killing had occurred.

It was agreed, by a majority of those still able to stand at the miner's celebration, that the new attractive name would be Happy Camp. Accordingly the river valley was filled with loud exclamations of "Huzzah, huzzah!" It has been widely reported that at the passing of the vote someone declared, "It's true that everyone here is happy, but it would be right descriptive instead to name the place Drunkardsville." The proposal letters were rewritten and sent, and by the next year the rough canvas tents were starting to be replaced by small cabins large enough to house beginning families.

Shivarees were held about every other week to celebrate the nuptials and broom-jumpings and it wasn't uncommon to see the newly married folks being carried through town in sitting chairs on the shoulders of rowdy miners and serenaded with bells, rough songs and banging kettles far into the night. I've often heard it said that with the wives came the churches, table manners, moderate temperance, and later, schools. Many a hen-pecked man – or a John Tamson man as we used to call them – remarked after the town name change that they were not so sure those original jackdaws may have thought their plans out very well at all when they had asked some of those ladies to stay on.

The town naming story has always interested me and I wonder sometimes if the Camp brothers, settlers at that time, didn't have something to do with the ending title of our community. There are several versions of the stories, and like most folks always do – we just pick the one we like the best and run with it.

Soon after we became a proper burg, the local ladies had planted rosebushes and lilacs in their yards and the vegetable gardens also flourished under their care. A store and inn had been constructed in the middle of town. It was the only two-story building in the area at that time, and it was so well built that it would withstand three floods. Originally named the American Inn, perhaps the glorious national name protected it through the years the same as that name has protected all of us to this very day. As I write I can see the old girl standing tall, surrounded by trees and still holding down the corner of Second Street and Indian Crick Road. It's a shame that someone tried to paint it recently because the deep brown look of the oiled wood sure was beautiful. Perhaps she'll last long enough for all of those garish colors to fade or wear away. Lord knows that building has been through much worse.

When I was a boy there had been a man named Meamber who ran an irregular pack string through, and we'd get mail from him once in a while and buy or trade provisions right off the backs of his mules. He liked to stop off here and there on his way down the river or on his return trip and no one could ever know when to expect the fella. At some point his name turned into a poor verb – even today when most of us talk of wandering semi-aimlessly through the forest from one point to the other, we'll be caught saying Meamber instead of meander.

The Camp brother's old storehouse, which resembled an iron-doored prison more than a goods shop still stands across from The American. Not quite sure when the new Mercantile was put in, but I recall that the business hopped around on that same little corner of our town until it finally came to rest opposite the American to the south. To the east of both of those a bit is where the Del Rio Theater used to be, before it burned down. I've spent many evenings since then wishing it hadn't. Also missing is Bert's Super Service Gas Station, where a lot of folks would gather for good talk before heading out fishing or up to their loggin' work. There have been so many changes to our community over the last hundred-fifty years or so it's hard for anyone to keep track of.

It seems like there's always been a Hammarscn in this area of the Better Part of California, but there had to be a beginning to that story too. My Father, eighteen years old and fresh from two years of duty in the Spanish-American War had left behind all of his ties to his large Minnesotan family and eventually rambled his way down this river canyon. I can imagine the prospect of rejoining his twelve brothers and sisters on the swampy family farm didn't look too good after his adventures defeating Linares and Cervera and helping Mr. Roosevelt take San Juan Hill.

My Father arrived in this area shortly after being mustered out of the Kansas Volunteers 20th Infantry Regiment, in San Francisco, purt near the end of 1899. He prospected, milled lumber, and eventually built a proper home when his marriage proposal letter was finally answered in the affirmative by his childhood sweetheart Miss Elanora June Swensen – with the permission of her parents. She arrived in Yreka via the Southern Pacific on March 12, 1901, and was promptly walked to the nearby courthouse by my Father to be officially married. I was born in late 1902. My little brother, named Thorin Hjalmer, arrived in December of 1904 – but he only lived for two weeks before he fell to an illness. Even though the death of an infant child was common then, burying Thorin broke my Mother's heart, and my parents had no more children.

My Mother and my Father were both very intelligent and well-read folks, who in their youth had to rely on the dinner-table book learnin' common in large Midwestern families. Both had been lucky enough to have books to borrow and lend in their respective communities, and they read whatever they could get their hands on to pass the closed-in winters they had to suffer through as children. They both were very religious but often argued the finer points of the church doctrines and rules each had been raised in – the compromise, for my learning, was a Sunday morning lay-service in our front room that included the three of us reading and discussing passages from the Old and

New Testaments. I was given a wonderful history lesson of the Holy Lands as well as a tutorial in interpreting meaning and substance in lengthy passages. I was also, while very young, the owner of a large and oddly-old vocabulary filled with 'thee' and 'thou' as well as an enhanced reading ability for my age.

Throughout my life I've often wondered how everything would have been different if little Thorin had lived. I'm fairly jealous of the old folks around here who never have to call around for a fishing or hunting partner, 'cause they have a brother always on the ready to take with them.

My childhood consisted of the revolving cycle of waiting for winter to end so that I could get outside to play, and then hoping that spring and summer would stretch out a little bit so that the next winter wouldn't be so long. I also, of course, got into a bit of trouble here and there – but for the most part nothing really big or that I couldn't try to talk my way out of.

In the summer of 1913, I was almost eleven years old. My family and I lived up Elk Crick in the house that my Father had built. Miles of mountains were laid out atwixt us and anyone else. Our modest home stood to the west and south of Happy Camp proper. We managed to make it to the town two to three times a week during the summer, and every day when school was running. The whole place was still wild and rough, but there were obvious changes from the days of the mining camp. A ferry had been built to cross the Klamath at the aptly named Ferry Point to the south and then later one was installed at the mouth of Indian Crick.

During the surrounding settlement period, folks were becoming more civilized and another progressive addition to the community was the Schoolhouse. Now, of course, the locals call it the Old Log Schoolhouse and the ancient rooms now host community meetings and bingo games and such. Built from big, sturdy, local logs, it originally held one large classroom. Over the years walls have been framed in inside and a kitchen has been added. The woodstove still helps heat the place, as it did when I was a young boy. I can't count the number of hours I spent chopping wood and kindling in the gully washin' rain and in snow drifts outside of that building – but always with a smile on my face, since I was excused from classes for the chore.

The window panes on the east side of the building still hold the original bubbled glass from over ninety years ago. Boy, if I had a nickel for every minute I spent staring out of that window, daydreaming about being away from school instead of paying attention to the lessons at hand.

Like every boy who suffered through the rigors of a school day back then, I practiced holding my breath and counting in my head or seeing how close I could get to sleeping with my eyes open, instead of paying attention to the teacher. I got real good at saying, "Yes, Ma'am," along with the class in my self-induced meditative state wherein I'd be traveling the game trails and climbing trees in my mind's eye. The only time I'd regain full consciousness was when she'd proudly share her overdue newspaper with us. Mrs. Hudson had moved to our River Canyon from the city of San Francisco, and by the way she talked and carried on about that place a lot of us wondered why she had ever left it.

I had drug myself away from my daydreaming one mid-morning as she read from her pride and joy. Her lesson started with an overview of current events as she longingly and lovingly relayed to us details from her delayed Bay broadsheets. I often thought that the term "current events" must not be quite accurate, for happenings that had long since passed.

I recall that on that day she recounted to all of us an article about a Professor Ashbury Balboa Hayes who had translated the works of my favorite author – Sir Walter Scott – into one of the Chinese dialects. I said a silent "thank you" to the far away Professor – knowing in my heart that the world would only be a better place as Scott's works spread through it. She also railed on about how important the man's translation work of the New Testament was, but that comment really confused me since I knew that the Celestial folks didn't need the Bible or Jesus because they seemed to be doing just fine worshipping the Buddha. I also felt bad that no one had told the Professor about that, and he had toiled so long by mistake.

During our whole history in the River Canyon, folks worked hard – from the timber fellers to the hands at the mills built much later. There are so many old men, like me, who had worked in our river valley and who are scattered around the Western United States now. What a grist of good men. You can't chuck a stick into a group of retired log truck drivers without hitting a few fellas that used to make the daredevil runs through our truck-killing-steep mountains. If you ever meet one, ask him if he remembers any close calls coming down loaded off of Independence Crick or if he ever hung a few tires off of Elk Crick Road on his way to the mill. And if you really do chuck that stick, you better move on fast – log truck drivers are slow runners but they're persistent, and if they catch you you'll be quick to wish they hadn't.

Now, since someone decided that we were lacking trees about twenty years ago, the mills are gone and no one has to get out of bed at 4 a.m. anymore. The truck drivers and most of the loggers moved their families to far-off places like Winnemucca, and Sitka, and Idaho Falls, and Springfield. Heck, now some otherwise productive and healthy folks in our little town may never voluntarily see this side of noon. Whoever thought the trees were gone should've probably looked out a window around here. We have so many that we can afford to let thousands of acres of them go to wildfires each year – allowing the scorched trees to rot where they stand – with what we've been told is no real impact on the rest of the forest. I guess the hundreds of deer and rabbits and foxes and bear and all of the other animals we find burnt to death after those fires may have had a different opinion about that – probably the same one the fish choking to death in the ash-clogged mountain steams had as well.

Worse yet, the lack of cutting and logging have eliminated most of the fire breaks those opened areas used to provide. The lack of logging activity has also allowed the understory to become clogged with debris and brush and diseased snags, primed and ready for the fires that the August lighting storms always bring. I've held my hat and bowed my head at many firefighter funerals – victims of the raging flames and unbearable heat our canyons produce when lit. Try telling one of the wildland firefighting fellas that the new policies have a minimal effect on us humans, after he's carried a dead coworker and friend out of our steep and dangerous mountains.

Those jackdaw protestors and spineless

politicians who pushed for those fashionable-yet-empty changes to our forest use laws have blood on their hands, and I hope they never forget it.

We'd been dealing with environmentalist folks in our own way for several decades. As loggers we tried to draw a line in the landing-dirt several times, and rallied together against the interlopers on many occasions. We struggled to defend our livelihood. We were pushed real hard by outside folks who didn't understand that we had always been the first ones in line to take care of the forests we lived in.

We all had a story of a clash with a protester or two, believe you me. Some of the run-ins were a bit more humorous and creative than others, though. One company owner fella set to greasing up his heavy equipment on his logging show, so that when the protesting folks showed up to put sugar in his diesel tanks they'd only make it about half-way up the machinery before heading back to earth real quick. I also understand that on one weekend when a lot of the out-of-town jackdaws were wandering through our forest, a group of local fellas happened upon their hidden vehicle parking area. In the deep summer heat of the River Canyon, the owners of those expensive cars and station wagons had all rolled their windows down just a bit to let the super-heated air out. One of our fellas had a great idea, and returned with the back of his truck filled with horse and pig manure. The local boys set out to make a non-violent protest of their own, pushing handful after handful of the horse and pig droppings through those window openings and sealing it all up with some duct tape. I'd have liked to been a fly on the windshield of one of those rigs when their owners came back from their own protesting idyll. One of the local ladies at the Café opined that the unwashed folks may not have even noticed the smell.

The longest I ever laughed at one of those stories was when Old Man Henry told us about the day that he and his logging crew took action against some out-of-town jackdaws up at one of the Poker Flat timber sales in the early 1980's. To get the whole effect, you'd have had to have listened to him tell it – his matter-of-fact deadpan delivery with perfectly timed eyebrow raises made the story even better.

I was a front row spectator to his story, as I sat across from him at the table at the Café one morning not but a year ago – just about the only social event us old men are involved in on a regular basis. He was in unlikely form that day – in the talking mood – and I motioned the nice waitress for another cup of coffee and settled in for a good yarn.

Henry finished up his hot food, and got hisself another cup of coffee and then started to tell those of us assembled what really happened that day at the Poker Flat sale.

There had been thousands of protesting events that Henry had patiently waited through – most of the time just shutting the show down for a couple of days to go fishin', knowing the protestors would leave soon without an audience. He'd leave a couple of fellas to watch over the equipment, and schedule the crew to work a few extra days on the back end of the month to get the job done and make sure their paychecks came out regular. He was one of the only bosses that paid his boys for their travel time to and from the logging show, and that endeared him to his crew and ensured he had the best and most loyal employees.

There came the fateful and overdue day when he

couldn't take any more of the foolishness without fighting back. Old Man Henry had been pushed to the edge of his limits – usually a good natured fella with a ready smile and a slow temper – but that day his good nature was replaced by anger. It was his logging show, and you can imagine his surprise when he parked the crummy to open the gate and found that a greasy and dirty looking fellow had chained his very own neck to the bar crossing the road, hoping to try to stop the loggers from passing through. I have tried to imagine how that chained-up fellow felt all lit up in the headlights of that rumbling diesel rig at about 4:30 that morning – must've been the bravest thing that the little antiestablishment chucklehead had ever worked himself into doin'. He must've heard new words and descriptions coming from those loggers that he still wouldn't fully understand even after he returned to his university that fall and tried to look them up in the fancy library full of books. There's no official etymology for some of those clever and well-worn phrases.

The self-chained fellow who called himself Spirit Man or Timber Warrior or Rainbow Arrow or some dang thing had made a shaky-voiced announcement deriding the loggers, and showing all the logging fellas the key to the chain around his neck he made a little speech about how his life was nothing compared to the trees and then he tossed the key into the brush down the hill. Timber Warrior's efforts were for naught, since Old Man Henry just stepped over him and unlocked the barrier. Without even a glance at the discourteous objector, Henry pushed the gate as he moved it on its pivot to secure it open. The hebetudinous fool attached to it was simply drug to the side of the road by the chain he had placed around his own neck and finally ended up out of everyone's way in a sprouting of poison oak bushes. I figure he had a lot of time to rethink throwing the key away and whether or not he had chosen a comfortable place to protect, since he sat there for about five hours before the Highway Patrolman pulled in to cut him free and issue him a trespassing ticket.

The funniest thing that happened that day was Old Man Henry's response when he found about ten of the self-described Saviors Of The Forest perched and tied in the canopies of tall timber marked for cutting. He had thought the gate boy's Katie-bar-the-door tactics were amusing, but facing a cutting deadline and with log trucks already heading in to the landings Henry took direct action to free the trees of their human ticks.

His cutting foreman came up to him and asked, "We goin' fishing today?"

Henry was quiet and thoughtful for a minute, shoving his clenched hands in his pockets and looking at the faces of all the men – and hearing the log trucks rumbling up the hill to the job site – he simply set his jaw, sighed, and said, "Not today."

He said to all of us assembled in the Café that every time he had looked at those working men around him – from his logging crew to the contracted truck drivers – he couldn't help but think of their wives, their kids in the school, and the old folks that lived with some of them. He was proud that his show could provide a chance at a living for so many folks for so long, and he was protective of the whole group because he cared about each family and the community where he lived as well. We all knew he had been one of the local logging show owners that folks could count on to help the high school clubs with their autumn woodcutting fundraiser, to donate money to help a sick community member, or even offer second chance employment to family men a bit down on their luck.

He said that he thought about all of those things the morning the protesters showed up, and it got him fumin' mad on the inside. He hollered up to the enlightened folks that after he had his coffee he was going to start cutting. No arguments or name-calling came from the quiet and thoughtful logging man, just a matter-of-fact statement that he figured gave all of the tree-trespassers fair warning of what was about to happen.

I figure many nervous looks were exchanged high above the forest floor as the sun began to peek itself over the tall mountains. One tree-girl started hollering and chanting something, and Henry and the boys just sipped their hot coffee on the tailgate of his work rig and went over the logging plan for the day. Then the working fellas split just like usual – the cat side went over the hill to the north and the yarder side went to the south. The timber fellers all grabbed their saws and their swamping gear, and headed off the landing and out to their cutting lines. A few hung back with Old Man Henry – in case there was any trouble – and some of the early log truck drivers had gathered around the base of Henry's first cutter of the day to watch the outcome.

He filed his saw chain, checked the fuel, and shouldered his saw for the short hike to the first tree in his line.

All of the tree-top chanting stopped when the saws started, and I suppose some of those little dirt-worshippin' atheists started right in praying to God Almighty. The saws bit into the giant trees, spewing fine curls of sweet-smelling sawdust into the morning air in a rough chorus of sharp chain and two-stroke engine noise. By that time six of the trespassers were already heading out of their perches, and three more were fumbling with their ropes and harnesses trying to get down as well. One jackdaw was so motivated to get back on the ground that he got tipped around and ended up rope-sliding down the trunk of the cedar he had been in – skinning his back all up with the slightly-poisonous bark slivers. I had just one of those kind of slivers in my arm once and it had bothered me for about three months – I couldn't imagine what that fellow was in for with his skin all spurred up with the stuff. The cedar tree hadn't even been marked for cutting – that jackdaw could have stayed up there for weeks and no one would have cared.

The brave matted-haired Butterfly Defender in Old Man Henry's tree had decided to stick it out. The trespassing method had worked well for tree-defense groups like theirs in the past at other logging sites, and I suppose the misguided young fella figured that it would work again. The difference was that Henry wasn't fooling around, and more important – he was at a point where he didn't give a dang about anything except paying his fellas and feeding his own family.

It only takes a good timber feller about five minutes at the most to down a tree, and it only took Old Man Henry about half of that before he paused his saw to place his wedges on the back side cut. He took that opportunity to holler up and inform the fella in the tree his best chances for surviving the ride down would be to move around to the uphill face of the timber and unhook his harness, so he would have better luck to be thrown free of the thousand pound crown when it bounced and rolled. Henry added in, almost as an afterthought, "You know, this is supposed to be a hardhat area."

The defiant lofted knucklehead unfortunately stayed in his perch – but he did move a bit and drop his harness as he was beginning to finally understand that the timber feller was about to make his last cut. It was the proverbial day of reckoning for the thin and dirty man in the tree who was forced to contemplate the wiseness of some of the decisions he had made that brought him on his path to the logging protest.

Using his hammering maul end on his timber axe, Old Man Henry tapped the center wedge and without fanfare or commotion the old big tree began to edge over – snapping and creaking – and he watched while it and its passenger slowly gained speed as both tipped toward the downhill slope below.

Now I know a lot of fellers – some have to run for their lives after each cut they make and then there are professionals like Henry who could lay even a twisted and snarled snag easy-as-you-please in any direction that he wanted. Knowing Henry like I do, I figured that even in his anger he had picked the best lie for the cut tree and its rider.

As Old Man Henry told it, when the jackdaw in the tree felt it start to go over he instantly dropped his defiant attitude and started caterwauling. Some say at that point the tree rider raised his little freckled fist in the air for a bit as a sign of solidarity with the forest conifers and hardwoods, and some others say he was just giving a California wave to the onlookers. Everyone on the site stopped and watched his carryin' on. The men there that day had seen fellas ride up dangerous yarder lines to get out of dark timber sale holes at quittin' time, seen cat skinners climb hillsides so steep they couldn't be hiked, and seen Big Harvey Turner carry twenty-one coiled chokers from one end of the landing to the other – but no one had ever seen a fool bronc-ride a falling tree like that.

For a moment it looked like he was saddle-riding the log monster, with his little leather sandals flapping around on the bark as he was trying to get a foothold. He screamed loud and high-pitched, like a woman, and when the felled tree was about twenty feet from bouncing on the ground the Butterfly Defender made his best attempt at soaring himself – launching like an ugly and wingless flying squirrel toward the branches of a nearby pine. As the first log settled gently on the slope below – bouncing a bit and shaking the ground – the self-flung trespasser fell through the dozens of branches of the second tree. He flailed his little protesting arms wildly on his way down until he brained himself on a thick branch which quieted him considerably – finally landing on the ground in a heap.

Old Man Henry hollered, "Let that be a lesson to you! Git!" The felled man leapt up and limped off as fast as he could toward his misanthropic co-conspirators. They all wandered off down the road to whine about the morning's events, escaping into the brush.

One of the truck drivers called the Highway Patrol on his CB radio and all of the protesting folks were picked up and charged with trespass. When the lame tree-sitter complained about how the logger had tried to murder him, the Patrolman laughed and explained that they were all luckier than they knew – that if the loggers had a mind to, there was no trying only doing. He reassured them all that Old Man Henry had probably laid down the cut timber as precise and as gentle as he could, noting that he could just as easily dropped the tree sidehill into the poky-yarded decks or even in the rock field to the other side. The officer also mentioned to the trespassers that if he felt a mind to search them, and found a tree spike in the mix of their ragged possessions – that they would all be thrown into the county jail to face real attempted murder charges with a great possibility of a jury of twelve of Siskiyou County's finest unemployed loggers deciding their fate.

I wish I could have seen the look on the Butterfly Defender's face as he sailed through the crisp and clean Siskiyou mountain air and turned himself into a human pine cone that day. I wish I could have seen the log truck drivers, hats in hand, ribaldry temporarily suspended while reverently watching Old Man Henry like he was a prophet finally sent to part the Reds from the trees and lead them all to the promised landing. It was almost a Holy Story to us river folk.

Spurred by the famous philosophy question, some folks around town made up their own: If a tree-sitter screams as his tree falls in the forest, and no one listening really cares, does he still make a sound? After that day, I've noticed that some folks refer to Poker Flat as Joker Splat and I smile every time I hear it.

On the heels of that dispute came the spotted owl debate, which didn't ever really seem like a debate at all since only one side got to do all of the jawing and the deciding. That whole mess only further goes to prove what most of us around here have known for a long time – that essential critical thinking skills are gone up the flume when folks don't wash their hair for months on end and are constantly running around the forest giving trees hugs. George at the gas station summed it up well when he said, "They call it dope for a reason."

When all the government folks went on their big owl survey some time back, no one told us. We could have helped, since we knew where a lot of those little spotted devils were. I don't figure that any one of us would have believed that there was true interest in the little rats with wings.

I had a couple pair of those owls living in an old tractor on my property. Joe, down the street had at least one residing in an old dog house that had slipped off his back porch toward the crick. McClendon, up the hill had dozens of them nesting in the old tire pile he had out back. There had been a flock of them seen rummaging around at the dump and the high school janitor had been setting mousetraps to kill off the twenty or so that plagued the football bleacher area and the eaves above the band room – but he had only limited success because they kept breeding. In fact, if you look around town, it seems like many of us are doing our best to help with the Spotted Owl habitat – we don't really want to keep all the broken washing machines, rusted out trucks, tire piles and old logging equipment in our backyards or in the empty lots in town, but we're leaving them there for the benefit of the little winged mouse-eaters. Apparently, those owls weren't as tender and sensitive as most outside learned folk were led to believe.

I have heard, though, from a couple of the fellas that the little flying terrors can be very tender when plucked, rubbed with butter, and roasted slowly in a 325 degree oven until the internal temperature reaches 160 or so. Personally, I think they're too small and too much work for good eating. And forget trying to stuff a homemade down pillow with their feathers – it'd probably take about a thousand of them to make a proper cushion.

The social semi-decline in our community rose as the timber industry fall continued – Old Man Henry's efforts or his masterful sawmanship couldn't touch baseless politically-fueled decisions made by an uninformed elected fella who, as it turned out, happened to be making other poor decisions in our Oval Office at that time as well. After he had to leave that elected position, the damage here was already done to our economy and our workforce and our schools and our children and nothing could set it right again.

Our fine-tuned knowledge base of professional woodsmen and sawyers and fellers had moved on to other parts of the country where federal and private timber sales were still rolling on. They moved to places where working folks and government folks both understood the theories of sustainability and had local elected officials with spines strong enough to back their timber economy.

I saw the list that was published by one of the leaders of the local anti-logging efforts. It had thirty or forty "threatened" animals on it, which they were prepared to use as challenges in court to stop the logging in The Better Part of The State. It was disheartening to look at it – we were fighting an uphill battle against many folks who drew government welfare checks while they were volunteering for their protesting efforts. I was sickened after my neighbor's brother explained to all of us how he just had finished carpentering a giant wood deck – about 2000 square feet – at a beautiful home in Scott Valley. He was asked to make it out of long and clear redwood for the very same man who had published the threatened animals protesting list. In California, *"environmental hypocrites"* have been on a different Threatened List since about 1978 but despite the best efforts of some local folks they unfortunately have never made it to Endangered status.

I wonder how it all could have been different if the State of Jefferson split from the State of California had gone through. I think the schoolbooks still have something about an important protest in Boston Harbor – some time back – where other folks were sick and tired of being taxed without representation too. I don't figure the folks around here are willing to put up with much more, and their protest would include dropping much more than tea into the Klamath.

Our dismay with our official State goes way, way back.

Today some houses stand empty, and the school classes are smaller and smaller every year. There are entire families of people living here now who have never had to do for themselves, relying on the State or the County to feed and clothe them. It has always been such an irony to me that in such a rich and abundant place so many are satisfied with the hand-outs. My Father would have said they were just lazy – and unfortunately our County isn't the only one with that problem.

I'm gaining too much elevation up here standing on my rickety old soap box. I believe I better get down before I fall off.

My little two-story house is just feet from Indian Crick – or *Athithu'uf,* as it was sometimes called – about a good ten miles from where my Mother, Father, and I started out up Elk Crick. Talking about the old days one morning over breakfast and too much coffee at the restaurant, my friend laughed when he mentioned how far I've made it in life. He said, "Euclid, most folks are lucky if they make it five miles."

Painted white with dark green trim, my home blends into the working-man construction along this side of the road. It's where I carried my Amelia over the threshold, and later where our son was born. It seems small compared to some of the houses I've seen built lately, but it's all that I need. It certainly seems small when I think of all of the memories and love that it has held over the years.

In the long standing local tradition my wife had also planted roses in the flowerbeds and the lilacs in the front yard, and I've kept the weeding, trimming, and watering up since she's been gone. There's also a little vegetable garden that I've planted and cared for religiously every year, but now it seems that the deer get to eat more of it than I do.

Some of the rosebushes in my yard are probably a little older than me. About four of them are survivors from the first move of being dug up from the Elk Crick house dooryard, and then their next move of being dug up from my Mother and Father's second house after they both were gone. I'm not sure how long rose bushes are supposed to live, but they and I both are still standing after all of this time.

The thick, flower-filled beds that line the walls of the house and the fences would seem more appropriate at an old woman's cottage – and that's what it was supposed to eventually be. It was natural for us to assume that I'd be the first to go, and that Amelia would live out the rest of her days here, gardening and fussing with her shrubbery. Planting all of the flowers in the world wouldn't have stopped the awful sickness that took my wife. I've kept all of the color in the yard because it keeps her memory close to me – it's something I can see every day that reminds me of all the goodness in my life when she was here. Mnemosyne has at least thankfully left me those memories intact – even if I question everything else my old mind brings to my thoughts.

The brick-lined patio is a home to two old wooden chairs that look like they may have seen service in the American Civil War, accompanied with a nearby table that I built when young Kennedy was the President. The table bears the stains of backyard life – drops of different colored paint from birdhouses Amelia and our son made one summer, a few burn marks from where once I foolishly tipped the barbecue coals over, and a ringed spot where I've been setting my coffee cup for more years than I care to mention. I carved a heart into the old table wood in the side closest to the house, where Amelia used to like to sit – and in it, the initials A. H. and E. H. She had laughed when I knifed it and called me a destructive chucklehead, but she would always absent-mindedly run her fingers over it when we used to sit out here. I think it meant something to her, because even after she forgot my name she remembered that special piece of the table. Funny how things – simple things – become so important to us when it seems that they are all that we have left as touchable proof to remind us that someone was alive.

This backyard and the side yards are somewhat private, and the small deck that faces the crick is my favorite room in the house – even if it is outside.

My face and my body show the wear of years and years of hard work and of a life spent mostly outdoors. At each check-up the doctor shaves off a few more melanomas from my neck or face or even my ears. He always looks surprised to see me – like he thought each previous appointment was obviously my last – and I have to admit that is not a very comforting quality in a supposed medical professional. I knew I was truly an old man when people stopped asking about bandages I sported on my neck and face – which had, after all, become a regular part of my attire.

That same doctor warns me that I drink too much coffee, that the occasional pipe I enjoy will ruin my lungs, and that I should take every precaution to stay out of the sunlight. I've often wondered if those educated and over-priced fools – looking at a man who has lived as long as I have – would ever chuck caution to the wind and actually suggest that I live it up while I still can.

Amelia used to say I had rugged good looks, but I never thought that a bean-pole Swede with squinty-green eyes and scar across his jaw and neck would be attractive to anyone, let alone a stunning beauty like her. She loved me, and I suppose that if she could see me today – my bent frame, my shock-white hair, the missing fingers on my left hand, my withered muscles, the deep lines and wrinkles mapping across my face, and above it all my drooping and faded Navy tattoo on my forearm – she would still say the same thing about me. I learned a coon's age ago that love doesn't just see what is, but also all of the possibilities of what can be. Of course, she would justifiably have to give me a sound what for about the unruly look of my hairstyle – I've never gotten a good haircut since the last one she gave me round about 1975 or so.

I suppose it won't be too long before I find out what she thinks of this old man, as I am sure hoping that after I'm gone I'll see her again. While I can't seem to talk myself into making it to any of the local church services – except maybe the sunrise service that's held every Easter up at our tiny airport – I'd still like to think that I may have half a chance on getting through the Pearly Gates on a special dispensation. I will hash that I spent purt near every day of my life in awe of God's natural creations and that I tried really, really hard most of the time to treat others like I would like to have been treated. I'll also mention that I think I'm fairly qualified to attend Heaven – after all, I'm already really good at climbing the Trees.

A family of otters has been residing on this crick side about as long as I have, and although I curse at them at times when the fishing is poor I think that by now they know that my threats are empty. They have to eat too, and I'm confident that they appreciate the trout and the steelhead just as much as I do.

I know that it is the natural regression of mind and social ability of aged folks like me to create fond familial relationships with critters, so I make no excuses about my concern for the welfare of my river otter family and the generations of these playful and smart animals who have terrorized the fish nearby. I talk to them like they can understand me, and I give them nicknames like Speedy, Scar, Whiskers, and Momma. I'm not yet to the point where I can imagine they're speaking back to me – I'm just to the point where I am certain that I know what they *would* say if they *could* talk. There's a big difference.

I've had an emergency bag packed for some time – ever since I had a minor stroke about three years ago. I've told most folks who visit that I've packed it to take to the hospital on my next stay, but it's really filled with items necessary for my belly-through-the-brush escape if I ever hear anyone's coming to take me to an Old

Folk's Home. I figure I can grab the bag, wriggle out the bathroom window, and be headed for the Marbles before anyone discovered that I lit out. I'd rather die tomorrow trying to make it up the trailhead near Johnson's Hunting Grounds than be locked away with smelly, slow-dying people for the next ten years. I'm staying put for now but I'm keeping a watchful eye. I've been on the *qui vive* for a spell now.

I never get tired of looking at the crick flow by, and over the many years here I've gotten used to the sound of the water pushing the tumbling round rocks from one place to the other. Thousands of nights have passed as I've leaned on the railing peering into the darkness at the moving water, lighted only by the starry skies. When the moon is full, that light ripples on the surface and illuminates the rocks and bending tree limbs. I can always count on the crick's breeze to flow downstream in the morning, fade off in the afternoon, and then bluster upstream in the early evening. I'm sure that there's some explanation for that, but I just took it for granted years and years ago.

There's really no way to describe the sweetness of the air as the breezes boil past and gust about – racing through the rosebushes, the wild sweet peas, and the fresh-cut grass and at the same time bringing the fragrant notes of river foam, rich earth, and dry dust along with it.

Chapter Two

The River Chinese

"In this River Canyon, I never once
met a hard-working man that I
didn't like."
— Leif Nordheimer, Resident

From my side yard I can see where the Chinese
settlement used to be. It's been years since I thought of
that place. The bridge that crosses the Klamath has one
of its feet square in the middle of where one of the old
trading houses had been. The river's path has covered
up some of it too. A lot can change in almost a hundred
years.

Now and then you can still find some of the
strange coins that had been left behind. Almost every
year I uncover a few in the flowerbeds or in the
vegetable garden. I've got a mason jar full of the trading
pieces with cut-out center holes and that
undecipherable script. My jar of Chinese coins resides
nobly next to my wood axe and my gardening shears —

handy and closeby waiting for my next deposit. I used to joke with the Running Indian that I wished I could grow U. S. dollar coins in my garden instead.

There used to be a little museum up at the old drug store where folks would take the odd whatnot that was found. I myself placed an oak and pearl Chinese abacus, some medicinal pouches, and a few other historical lookin' items there at one time. I figure after the store closed up all those pieces went out to the county museum in Yreka, but I don't know that for sure.

The hard-working foreign folk – now long gone from our valley – have been referred to by many names in the past. There are a few that shouldn't be said, leaving only terms like Chinaman, Oriental, and Celestial. I was taught that it was proper to refer to them as Chinamen or Celestials only, and I preferred Celestial because it was such a perfect word. It reminded me of stars, and the flawlessly bright full moon on a clear night, and it seemed to fit the indescribable peacefulness that most of those folks worked so hard to display. The word also had a melody to it, reminding me of the guqin zither musicians on the riverbanks playing songs about their Chinese homeland.

I've seen those fellas, long ago now – rough and dirty and tired from a whole day of workin' in their mines – take those strange looking instruments and play them with a delicateness that in their calloused and broken hands belied their respect for the songs of their far-away homes. Men with blistered and bent fingers, plucking out the sounds of home which to us were both foreign and right at the same time. The music they made on those neckless, many-stringed guitars never rose above the sound of the river flowing past, or the otters playing nearby. The musical timbre and melody of our land and flowing waters didn't compete with their plucked sounds – instead they seemed to be playing the same unknown song together.

The Chinese men who made their homes here carved a community out of the riverbank and the hill to our south. I recall that roughly sixty huts and cabins had covered the riverside back when those coins' owners lived in these parts. They built a meeting hall, two or three trading houses, and planted large vegetable and herb gardens in the loamy river dirt. The Celestial district accounted for half of our entire population for many years in the beginning.

The Chinese workers, like my Father's dear friend who many called War Sing, had long been part of the history of the area and to this day something seems missing in our community. We used to enjoy exotic festivals and celebrations, fireworks and different foods, and became used to those men wearing red jackets to weddings and white jackets to funerals. If you happen to be in or around Happy Camp on New Year's Eve, to this day you can still hear one legacy that the Celestials left with us – the smashing together of pots and pans and wood blocks from one end of our River Canyon to the other, just at the stroke of midnight as was done for many of their celebrations.

At one time several hundred of the foreign-born men lived in the Klamath River valley, and today you can still see some of their methodical handiwork in the rock walls and road supports on the old mining claims.

Sadly, some of the lost souls are still buried in the California earth. One of the biggest and oldermost Chinese pioneer graveyards can still be found in Forks of Salmon, down the river from Happy Camp. They remain there today, patiently waiting for almost a century to be taken back to their homeland for a proper burial in their sacred earth. They must have been overlooked as the last of the Celestials left our River Canyon. It's unlikely, after all of this time that their bones will ever return to the land of their youth as was their custom.

If you're lucky, or if you know where they are, you can see some of the trees that the Chinese folk planted. The deep green, spire-like arimantus trees continue on through days and nights nigh unto a hundred years after foreign gardeners planted their seeds in the earth. Local folks opined that they were so beautiful that they called them Trees of Heaven.

I've always thought that it must have comforted those Celestial fellas, so far away from home, to see that familiar greenery. Starting as a seed across the ocean, surviving a voyage in a damp and over-crowded ship, carried in a pocket or a parcel for hundreds of miles, placed to grow in a foreign soil to eventually outlive everyone from the community that had cherished you – if there was a tree that ever needed to be hugged, I suppose that those would indeed be the ones. I feel that I have a lot in common with those trees – I hope they don't feel as alone as I do sometimes.

Many folks think that those exotic trees held some religious significance or marked burial areas, when in fact they were mostly grown for their medicinal properties – a tea of their needle-like leaves was much like the willow-bark remedies used by some Native American groups with the same results as the aspirin we use today. There are a few stands, though, that have a different meaning – but once again, I'm getting ahead of my story a bit too soon.

Aside from the coins, the rockwork, the graveyards, and the arimantus trees, not much evidence of the residence of the Chinese in this part of California can be found. What men did not destroy nature took care of, with fires and floods, and what remained was stolen by the biggest thief of all – time. It is possible, too, that in true Buddhist fashion their footprint in our valley was never meant to stay forever.

There are a few Buddhist Temples that still stand today, like the ones in Weaverville and Oroville but they are the exception. Many were burned down – including the one that had been in Yreka – by rioting folks trying to drive the Celestials out and limit the competition for the dwindling gold returns.

Most of the Chinese came to this canyon in search of gold after having worked on building projects in the West. The Central Pacific railroad company had employed quite a few of the Chinese Nationals to carve a line through the rocky Sierra Nevada Mountains and through the arid Nevada landscape. When their work for the Central Pacific was finally over, they went to labor for themselves with a pan and determination.

Some had also been involved in cigar manufacturing and wine making further south, until laws were passed that limited their ownership of businesses and property in California. In 1880 the Chinese Exclusion Act was signed into law, but it didn't really have an effect on our River Canyon Chinese brethren. They had heard of the Land of the Golden Mountains – Gum Shun – and our community was high on their word-of-mouth list of places to rake and scrape the elusive metal. Quite a few who ended up spending time working in our area were from Kwangtung, a southern province of the Chinese Kingdom that also shared much of our same geographical qualities.

Our community was a refuge from many of the laws that muddled up the workings of the rest of the State – we were so remote and so free-willed that when the outside news finally got to us, often we didn't pay it nevermind or it had taken so long to get to us that it wasn't even relevant anymore. We had been our own authority and government, and did a right fine job by all accounts. I'm proud to say that our folks never forced the Celestial workers to pay the Foreign Miner's Tax of four dollars a month – we saw that unfair practice right away for what it was.

Aside from the school teacher's irregular receipt of the San Francisco newspaper, I cannot recall any other source of outside news or politics that made its way to use. Heck, it wasn't until about 1985 that we got FM radio signals to bounce their way into our valley from outside.

A general disdain for outside politics and the sensibilities of those in the rest of Our Great State seemed to surround us back then. My Father used to joke that it must be in the water, because those feelings sure haint lessened to this very day. We were *lex non scripta*, disregarding any of the laws that we had no power to set.

It took our community purt near a hundred years – from the time of the naming ceremony – to launch an actual revolt against California proper. In 1941 we voted to secede from the State, elected our own Governor, and manned roadblocks with loaded rifles in hand. The State of Jefferson was created out of what I call The Better Part of California, but all of us tabled the Statehood business as news spread of the underhanded

Japanese attack on Pearl Harbor and our entry into World War II not long after. We knew that the last thing our country needed was a quarrel in the kitchen when somebody outside was trying to burn down the house.

Today, our Governor has to bully folks to volunteer to represent our interests in Sacramento's State House and Senate. I've heard that our entire population – from the Oregon border down to about Red Bluff – is the equivalent to about three square miles of folks in San Diego. I suppose it would probably be best if they'd just forget us altogether, just the same as we've done with them. We've made a culture out of always being separate from The Other Part of The State, and are happy to remain among the willows, so to speak.

Like everyone who was prospecting in The Better Part of California in those daisy old days before The Wars, the Chinese miners also found that the Murderer's Bar area was rich in color. The country was thick with streams and cricks that carved the high mountain gold out of the steep hillsides, tumbling it down, and down, and down to a turbulent meeting with the Klamath River far below. The townsfolk were friendly enough to those outsiders, since local folks had been accustomed to a transitioning population since the beginning of the settlement. The auric industry of our area was well-known and growing.

Clear Crick, Elk Crick, Indian Crick, and thousands of other streams and waterways caressed the gold out of its mysterious home. For years prospecting flourished, and the Celestial, the Indian, and the white folks got along well together.

When the findings became more difficult, so did the interactions atwixt people. Greed and gold fever forced the hands of many men in those days, and they did crimes to each other that they never would have thought of doing before. Houses were burned. People disappeared. Neighbors stole from each other. Some men even leapt that great moral gap and became killers of other men.

A revolution, far away in their homeland of China, called for many of the foreign-born to also return. In 1912, the boy-king P'u Yi stepped away from the Dragon Throne of Manchu and effectively ended the Qing Dynasty rule of China – leaving all manner of thieves, noblemen, and warriors to fight for the power to be appointed as the ruler of the people. Gold was also beginning to be scarcer then. There came a time when many of the locals thought that if the Chinese were gone, that there would be more claims and color available for the rest of us. Needless to say, my Father never took part in any of that rubbish.

Acts against the Celestial folks were started to drive them out, I suppose. Most of the violence around here was done by folks from other places moving in to try their hand at mining. Nairn of the respectable folks we knew would ever have lifted a hand in greed or tried to take another man's claim – it just simply was not tolerated among our own. Enough of the trouble for the Chinese was caused, though, for them to begin leaving in large groups from about 1908, with the last local folks moving on in 1914. I was there as our Chinese folks moved on from our River Canyon, and I'll never forget the night they left.

There I go getting ahead of myself in this journal again. My apologies, Dear Reader.

With what may have eventually forced out many of the last Celestial in the eastern part of our county, the great Buddhist Temple in Yreka was burned. It may have been an accidental fire, but we all figured that it was set on purpose to drive those folks away from our hills and river.

We knew that the Temple House was an important place for our Celestial brethren. It wasn't just a sacred place where Buddha was revered and worshipped – it was a meeting place and a community center. In many of the surviving Temples in California, there are great boards set aside where travelers could post and read messages from each other. Imagine, being so far away from home, how wonderful it would have been to know that another person from your village had made it this far and was well? How invaluable would it have been to read a message card, from an older brother or a cousin or even your Father, stating that they were still above snakes?

It was odd to us, back then, that our River Chinese lacked a Temple in their community. It was mentioned occasionally in our local banter. All of us folks went through the Chinese District all of the time – to trade or to visit a friend or to arrange the hire of a group of fellas for special mining projects – and we were familiar with their buildings and homes just as they were familiar with ours. Rumors swirled now and then that either they had foregone building a Temple to avoid harassment from us folks – which was ridiculous, as we didn't treat folks that way – with the other more intriguing rumor stating that a hidden and private worship house had been constructed somewhere in our deep mountains. I heard one fella say that he was certain that was where they were caching all of their gold bullion – stacking it up in a safe place before their return to China.

I would find out much later that a Temple was in

fact built – a Secret Temple, made of carved Indian Crick jade, decorated in hand-hammered gold, and housing an ancient Buddha crafted well before Alexander the Great was born.

The path to that discovery would become one of the greatest adventures of my life, but would first involve a horrible accident, an unbelievably long footrace, me lying to my Father, and a restless ghostly revelation in my dreams as I perched high above the River Canyon floor in an ancient cave.

Chapter Three

War Sing

"The Buddhist monks taught me that the way to Nirvana is right faith, right judgment, right language, right purpose, right practice, right obedience, right memory and right meditation. The man from Yreka taught me the way to Happy Camp is right down the Klamath about eighty hard miles."

– Cho Si Lin, Celestial Miner

My Father had left a large family of twelve brothers and sisters in Gatzke, Minnesota – atwixt Thief and Mud Lakes – when he turned fifteen and signed on with the Kansas 20th Infantry to fight in the Spanish-American War. Not sure how he got all of the way from Minnesota to sign on with the Kansas 20th, or how he convinced them when he got there that he was old enough to be scripted into the Infantry. I can imagine that even at fifteen he was plenty old enough to set out on his own, and for the two years he spent in Cuba and South America he had no news or contact with his Mother or his Father. Back then it was difficult to stay in touch with folks so far away. Later, when he settled in the Klamath River canyon, he received occasional letters from his large Minnesotan family – but fewer and fewer as time went on. They tried to update him on the doin's of the Hammarsen clan, but I often heard him comment to my Mother that it saddened him that so much time had passed since he had seen any of them that he may not even recognize one of his brothers or sisters if he met them on the street. Traveling back to visit them would have been such a tremendous undertaking that it wasn't even thought of as a possibility.

It may have been from a natural extension of my Father's sense of family that he included War Sing in our lives. They had met working elbow to elbow panning in the local streams back in the early days, and my Father – being a just and reasonable man – did not decline War Sing's offered friendship merely because the two were from different backgrounds. My Father's Norwegian family had suffered the same scrutiny and derision when they had first moved to the Midwest, and he understood what it felt like to try to overcome stereotypes and language barriers.

We knew War Sing was a leader in his community. Although he was a young man, the other Chinese folks treated him with an air of deference – and I had thought that it was because he had been elected as Mayor of the Celestial Men or something equally important. He was very gracious to all who approached him, and I had seen him hundreds of times give council to feuding Chinese miners. My Father and I just accepted his leadership in his community and didn't question it at all. Even when I overheard some of the Chinese miners referring in hushed and secretive tones to War Sing as Yong-Li Jun I figured it was a nickname or one of his other ten last names I could never remember well.

He was tall – almost as tall as my Father – and he was nigh unto as strong as my Father, too. Together, they were a reckoning force with a list of accomplishments to prove it. They were always doing something, from hunting to mining to setting trap lines to building houses and fences and woodsheds and as soon as I knew how to walk I wasn't far behind.

War Sing was almost a constant figure in our home for many years when I was a child – he was my Father's best friend and his mining partner – and I looked to him much like he was my Father's brother because my Father did too.

War Sing was a hardworking, well-mannered man who helped our family on many occasions, with the last help he gave us being the most important gift anyone had ever given us. He gave my Mother and me the life of my Father.

I grew up spending so much time at his side – listening to his stories and tales of adventure in far-away lands – that at one point I complained to my Mother that she had to quit cutting my hair so often if my braid was ever going to get a chance to grow. I wanted to be just like War Sing, devil may care what my friends thought of my hairstyle choices.

When they weren't working their claims, or working hired out as loggers or mill hands, they roamed the river valley and spent a lot of time fishing and hunting. War Sing worked a claim with two of his countrymen and still found time to help my Father when he needed it. They hunted deer and bear together, sharing the kills. My Father remembered late into his life that War Sing always had insisted that our family got the biggest share, as my Father was responsible for a growing family.

War Sing would take me aside after my Mother's dinners, and tell me countless stories of China and where he was a boy. He would also tell me tales of temples carved of jade and boxes and boxes of gold that he planned to send back to China, where later he would return as a wealthy man and build his own family. I was enthralled by his stories – hanging on every word – and I longed to see his homeland for myself one day.

I was certain that War Sing's accounts of hidden gold were true, and I spent a lot of time thinking about his hidden fortune and his exotic homeland while I was doing my chores. I also thought a heap about Pirates and Giant Whales and Indian Ghosts and the Fabled Da Yao Yu – just like most adventurous boys did, growing up in the River Canyon with plenty of mind-wandering time to be filled while stacking wood or pressing apples or picking blackberries.

War Sing often teased me about the Da Yao Yu – a mysterious often-seen but never-caught giant fish – that supposedly roamed our River Canyon waters. He would update me on sightings of the presumed monster he had heard from members of his community. He entertained me with tales of close calls by the other Chinese with that giant fish, and even when he regaled stories that sounded made up or embellished I believed every word – hook, line, and sinker – because I wanted to. Pushing the boundaries of my belief only once, he told me how seven of his friends had lassoed the scaly behemoth and rode on it's back for three days and nights – up and down the Klamath – until they were so hungry and thirsty that they had to jump off, one by one, and swim for the shore. I didn't question him directly about the details when he told me the happenings, but after thinking about it for some time I was a bit suspect since I figured those fellas could have just reached down and scooped up a drink from the Klamath itself, and had a chance to ride a little longer. I never called him on that detail, though.

I remember one afternoon when we went into town for some groceries and nails, some fellows passing through to the coast jeered at War Sing's long braided hair. My Father took them aside and kindly and firmly explained to them that in War Sing's country, he should not return with his hair cut. It would have been a shameful thing to do. When the outsiders insisted on taunting War Sing some more, threatening to cut off his "pig tail," my Father and a few others showed those men the trail out of town to the south. My Father didn't have to even raise his voice at the travelers for them to understand how serious he was about his friend.

My Father wasn't much for making a big deal about birthdays – especially his own. My Mother figured his attitudes were from his childhood, where it would have been impractical for their poor family to celebrate so many birthdays in grand fashion. When my Father was approaching his 33rd birthday, he requested that Ma make him a boggy top blackberry pie – his very most favorite – for after-dinner dessert. War Sing was invited to our little party, and we spent that evening like so many others – laughing, among those we cared about and who cared about us, enjoying my Mother's wonderful cooking.

After supper was cleared off and the pie had been cut, my Mother and I readied to give Dad his present, and War Sing looked like he was up to something too. When the conversation subsided a bit, War Sing retreated outside and came back in with something hidden under his jacket. He was able to avoid my Fathers' protests and finally was able to hand him the gift.

Opening the bundle carefully, my Father had a strange look on his face – and having completely freed the gift from the package he finally held up the contents. The bright pink and yellow and red and green silk was bordered by golden and black embroidery, outlining the traditional Chinese tunic and pants. It was, by far, the most outlandish set of britches I had ever seen, and by the look on my Father's face he thought so too.

My Mother and I snuck a glance at each other – we knew that Father was a man who, everyday, preferred to have his work pants, shirt, and belt just so. I'd never seen him wear anything else, except when he took off his shirt and belt to go swimming. My Father's forced smile was almost painfully funny to watch.

"You had spoken how much you liked my clothing during the last celebration," War Sing said, "so I had these made for you." War Sing looked as if he was enjoying making my Father a jot uncomfortable – we all knew that in front of my Mother we were all expected to be painfully polite to houseguests, and War Sing's gift almost pushed those limits to break.

On Mother's urging, Father went to the back of the house and changed into the silky attire. When he returned to our front room I can best describe him looking a lot like the Norecross' fluffy cat after it fell – briefly – into Elk Crick. Always respectful to his friend, my Father wore the silks for the rest of the evening, giving his thanks to War Sing and commenting that it was unfortunate that five of War Sing's countrymen had to go naked so he could have that one suit. We all laughed some more.

Next, it was finally time for our gift. My Mother and I were nigh unto beside ourselves with excitement and nervousness to see Father open our present. We had conspired – first by scrimping and saving a penny here and a penny there, and second by sending the money months before to Grandmother and Grandfather Hammarsen back in Minnesota. There, they used the money we had mailed them to make something very special to send back to the son who hadn't seen them in over eighteen years. My Father opened the package slowly, and even slower once he started to figure out what it was.

The color drained from his face. He slumped over a bit, kind of like if he was punched in the stomach by someone really hard. A whispered, "Oh, my," escaped his mouth right before he set his jaw. He held our gift quite gently in his big, rough hands – like as if it was made of glass. He looked to my Mother and me and with a break in his voice said, "Thank you. I thought that I'd never look upon them again." He couldn't finish the rest of what he was saying.

Believe you me we all sat motionless and quiet for a few minutes as he studied on the picture. Tears were streaming down my Mother's face, and I felt the stinging hotness in my eyes as well.

My rock of a Father almost cried in front of me – not crying like a girl, or like me the time when I fell off the roof onto the shovel – but the tear that was forming in his eye was rubbed quick into his bright silk shirt sleeve and was gone forever. Fumbling an excuse Dad stood to walk outside and away from us, but my Mother met him at the door and brought him back into the room. We all passed around the daguerreotype, and after a bit my Father rolled the stories of his youth at us one after another. War Sing held the picture to the lamp, looking closely, and commenting on the beauty of my Father's Mother.

"You are a lucky man, Jack," War Sing said, "to have a likeness of your family. After time passes, it's hard to remember faces of those separated by distance and time."

We knew that at that point, War Sing was thinking again about his own family. My Father stood and put his arm around War Sing, and said, "What do you mean? We're standing right here!"

We laughed and laughed, knowing that changing the subject didn't really change the fact that War Sing's people were so far away. He knew, though, that we were trying to make him feel welcome and a part of our family and shortly War Sing's blue mood was brightened.

We would have made quite a peculiar sight, if someone had been looking through the front window at us that night – with War Sing carrying me around on his shoulders while I whipped his braids like a horses bridle, my faithful dog jumping around and playfully nipping at War Sing's legs, and my Mother being held in the arms of the biggest, blondish and most brightly dressed Celestial ever to walk the valley.

I wonder, now, where that picture is that Mother and I gave Father for his birthday. I'm sure – except for crows and maybe an especially bright woodland pack rat – that people are the only beings on earth that ascribe and inlay emotions in objects. I'm especially guilty of that, since I've lost so many people over my long life. Just on my mantle alone I've got several possessions that are much more valuable than what they should be – a smooth white heart-shaped piece of quartz rock that Amelia had found by the crick, a carved ivory bear that I got on my second trip to Denali, a silver-colored little bell I had given to my Mother to use to call for me when she had been too sick to speak out, and just one of the dozens of athletic awards that my boy had won in high school. I'm sure I must have got that sentimentality from my Father, who surprised me years and years after his birthday night by occasionally wearing those old Chinese silks around his house and yard.

As a child I had learned a lot by being a keen observer of the folks I was around. I recall that when I wasn't underfoot my Father, I was War Sing's shadow. My Mother used to enjoy telling the story of the first and last day she heard me cursing, and she was always careful to quickly add that it really didn't count because no one could understand it.

Apparently, I had been a very precocious three-year old with an affinity for climbing. Left alone for a moment near the pantry I scaled the cupboard shelves and in my clumsy exploration for some crackers or a bite of one of my Mother's sweet cakes, I knocked down some airtights and the tin that held the ground flour. It hit the floor so hard that the top came off and a dusting of the flour settled on most everything in the kitchen area. Investigating the noise, my Ma said she came around the corner just in time to see the white flour cloud put down and spy me descending the pantry cupboard. She was about to rush in to scold me, but stopped as she saw me stand over the tin, kick it, and holler something she said sounded like, "Eee-kwar, lou-din swee-high ett!" Later when she told my Father and War Sing what had happened, they had laughed right until the end of the story. When my Mother repeated what I had said after I kicked the tin, and asked War Sing what it had meant, he turned deep red with embarrassment and fled the house in a flurry of apologies. My Father pretended not to know, either, and busied himself outside at his tool bench for the rest of the day.

The two men were smart enough to know that if my Mother ever found out the translation to what poor War Sing had inadvertently taught me, that the both of them having their mouths washed out was the least of their troubles.

I always remember War Sing as a pleasant-faced smiling man. Although only a titch shorter than my Father, his arms were just as long and his shoulders just as wide. He was a hard worker and my Father always talked of him as a top hand. My Father often said that War Sing was as strong as any other two men, and that he worked twice as hard as four.

As that stubbornly observant young fella and I noticed quickly that War Sing looked different from the rest of us. His eyes were the shaped in quite a wonderful fashion. They shined in his tanned face, and they twinkled when he smiled. I had near often most seen his hair braided like a girl's hair, but I did not find the style unusual as some of my Indian friends also wore their hair that way.

Any doubts I had regarding War Sing were quickly

erased one spring morning when I was about four years old. He showed up at our house with six or seven mountain quail that he had taken in one of his handmade woven traps. Before long my Mother had them simmering over the woodstove, and War Sing and I set to move to the yard to get out from underfoot in the small kitchen.

He had a funny look on his face, and kept holding at his stomach. I became more and more concerned – inasmuch as a little fella can be concerned about anything – as he continued to wrench up his face and grasp his own middle. When the squeaky noises started spilling from his jacket, I ran into the house for my Momma certain that War Sing was sick. From the commotion going on in his middle section, I figured it wouldn't be long until he burst wide open.

I ran into the house yelling like I was on fire, "Momma, War Sing's got the Fever! Look Momma, his face is all funny and he's squeaking and growling from his tummy!"

When we returned to the dooryard, he sat laughing on the ground, with the cause of his disease wriggling in his hands. I fetched up in my tracks, in full amazement and wonder – eyes wide and unbelieving.

It was a little black puppy dog. I fell in love with her immediately.

War Sing's gift – made after my Mother's approval, of course – was amazing to me. From the first day I set eyes on that dog, to the day I laid her in mountainside grave, she was my best friend, my protector, and company on my varied adventures.

He set the thick little puppy on the ground, and she raced right to me. She bounded and hopped clumsily around me until I had the sense to pick her up, and then she wriggled and licked at me so much that I actually thought about putting her back down. War Sing delighted in my joy at the puppy, and for a moment he looked like he was thinking far away – if I would have known more at that age, I would have supposed he was thinking about a dog that he had owned, back in his homeland.

"It looks like you have a friend," War Sing laughed. I didn't know if he was talking to me or the dog, but he was right either way.

He came up to me, with my little arms chock-full of wiggling dog, and grabbed us both up. The dog and I were both startled a bit, and we each looked at War Sing with the best solemn regard that a four year old boy and a puppy dog could muster as he began to speak.

"You both have found each other today. I hope that your friendship will be long and your adventures are many." He paused as he searched for more of our words. "You will both take care of each other in these woods, and you will love each other."

Looking straight at me then, he asked, "Will you promise me that you will take care of this dog?"

With a furrow on my brow, and in my most serious little boy voice, I answered, "Yes, of course!"

He watched us running about the dooryard, and Mother came out to the porch to see how the dog and I were getting along.

I raced around the back corner of the house after her – she'd run ahead and stop to see if I was coming along – and I heard War Sing ask, "What will you name her?"

Right then, the dog leapt at me and I tripped and we both went end over teakettle into the ash pan laid out nearby the vegetable garden. Ash and soot flew around us, and on us, and over us. Unchanged in her drive to finish our chasing game, she raced back to the dooryard and I was right behind. I suppose we were a sight – a black dog and a blackened boy emerging from behind the house. I grabbed the dog up just in time to see War Sing doubled over in laughter, murmuring something about all he could see was my eyes and my teeth.

"Cinder," I said. "I'm gonna name her Cinder – 'cause she's black like coal but she's got a burning ember in her."

The dog and I played together in the front yard for most of the day, and later I almost talked my Mother into letting the animal eat dinner at the table with us. It was a discussion we'd have thousands of times, but each time my sweet dog got to take her meals on the front porch. Mother also prohibited the dog from sleeping in the house at night, for a while.

After finding me away from my bed on several early mornings, having spent the whole night outside on the porch sleeping next to my dog, my Mother compromised and allowed Cinder instead to sleep on the end of my bed. In most all other manners, she was treated like a part of our family – included in on purt nearly every picnic or workday outing we took. From the beginning to the very end we were as close as two friends could ever have been.

Later in my life as I served in the Navy, not knowing any better, I tried to compliment an officer. I do not recall the circumstances, only that when I said, "Sir, that's very heathen of you," I was put on the duty roster for cleaning the ship's head twice as much as the rest of my buddies. In my limited exposure to the world,

I had in the river valley at times heard of the Celestial folks referred to as "heathens" by some townfolk – and knowing what a right-good people they were, and unfamiliar with the meaning of the word, I had assumed that it had meant something kind.

Through my talks with War Sing, I found out a lot about him – but only a little bit at a time. At first, I figured he held his past close because he did not trust anyone with his secrets, and then later, as his language skills grew and his trust for our family increased he told us fabulous tales of the land where he had come from and about the people he had known there. I always figured my Father knew just a little bit more about him than I did, but I was used to accepting the mysteries that adults had in their lives that they kept from young folks. It was the way it had always been.

I knew that War Sing was born in China and was brought to America on a large boat to work in the Sierra Nevadas for the railroads, and when that was over, he moved on to the Gold Fields of California.

I asked him about the journey on the boat quite a lot, and each time he would change the subject. I later learned that his older brother somehow died on that ship, and that War Sing was made to finish the journey in cuffs and leg irons for a fight with part of the English crew.

Searching for the golden and famous land of Gum Shun he eventually worked his way up to Yreka, and then to the Chinese enclaves at Indian Crick and Elk Crick near what would someday become Happy Camp.

There he and my Father had met and were fast friends.

I enjoyed his tales of adventure and of fighting dragons and of princes that faced riddles and doom.

They sounded like stories or legends that maybe his Mother or Father had told him when he was a child. As over eight decades have passed since I heard War Sing's voice, many of the details of those stories have faded from my aging mind – but one I will never forget.

Of his homeland tales my favorite had been the Temple Story. It was beautiful and when he spoke it, his voice had peace and calm in it. Here it is, best as I can remember:

"In the days of the men, a great challenge was to be held. The King decreed that the winner of the challenge would be made a great Prince of the province. The King wanted a new grand temple to honor the great Buddha. The contestants would travel the Kingdom to choose the most beautiful places to build the new temples. The contest would last for three years. Three young men answered the challenge, and stood before the King in the courtyard of his castle home. They were Henshi, Penchee, and Berhai. The king stated that the winning temple would be the one with the most beauty and decorous gilding befitting the Buddha and his teachings. The King gave each of the three men ancient carvings of the Buddha to place in the new temples. Henshi chose to build his temple next to the King's home, and labored for three years to place waterfalls and trees and songbirds within the temple grounds. His workmen hammered expensive imported gold and metals into the temple as decoration, and Henshi was certain his temple would be chosen because of the rich embellishments. Penchee chose to build his temple in the center of the grandest city in the kingdom, and he labored for three years to carve waterfalls and trees and songbirds into the walls and grounds of the temple. His workmen placed diamonds, rubies, and carved jade and ivory on the temple as decoration, and Penchee was certain that his temple would be chosen because of the expense of the adornments and how well it represented a natural theme. Berhai took a mule, laden with lumber and paint and a tapestry woven by his wife, and traveled to the deep countryside of north Zhaoqing where he had been a boy. He traveled to the long-forgotten Star Lake, and began to climb the Seven Star Crags. He entered a little valley through a break in the mountain rocks. "This will be my Mountain Gate," he said. He moved further into the valley, and walked past a waterfall coming from a spring in the rocks. "This will be my Temple Screen," he said. He walked up a treeless hill, and began building a simple structure to keep the wind, rain, and mountain snows off of the grand Buddha. Rocks were placed in the center of the structure to serve as an altar. He placed his wife's tapestry on the rock altar to protect the Buddha from the cold of the rock. Wildflowers grew in great carpets throughout the little valley, and the songbirds perched on the beams of the temple structure in the tinctures of rubies, emeralds and garnets. At night, the starlight ringed the temple roof like diamonds set into the richest dark velvet, and the Crags towering above were topped by a grand constellation with the Lodestar prominent. Berhai was certain that his temple would be chosen because he could think of no other place more beautiful and befitting of the Buddha than the wild lands where he had grown up. For the rest of the allotted time, Berhai traveled throughout the kingdom, building houses for the poor farmers and structures for their field animals to rest in. At the end of the three years, the three men met back at the Emperor's castle to finish the contest. Henshi and Penchee arrived dressed in their richest robes and were surrounded by their well-appointed attendants and slaves. Berhai, dirty and tired, arrived at the last moment on the back of his tired old mule. Penchee and Henshi laughed and pointed at the third man, even as the king approached. The King, his court, his guards, and the three builders then began their journey to see each of the temples. The King admired the gilding of the temple that Penchee had built. He noted that the Buddha would be well protected in that temple. The King commented on the adornments of the temple that Henshi had built, and noted that, in the city, it would be well attended by the people. On the way to the temple built by Berhai, the King was deep in thought about what he had seen, and he noticed along the way that the homes of the villagers were solidly built and beautiful in a simple way. The villagers all bowed to the King as he passed, but they hailed Berhai with their respectful thanks as they saw him go by. Berhai motioned to the guard when they were close to the mountain trail to the temple that he had built, and all in attendance began the winding journey to Berhai's Temple. For most of the morning the party hiked, with loud complaints from Penchee and Henshi, who had gotten very fat during their service to the King. The King motioned them onward. When they passed Star Lake, only the King and Berhai looked up and paused to admire the lakewater's life beauty. The group traveled onward until Berhai stopped, almost reverently, at the opening in the mountainside. The rest of the party lumbered past, looking at their feet, and complaining of the tiring walk. The King stopped walking when he reached Berhai, and looked at the Mountain Gate with him. The King nodded his approval at Berhai – for both men knew the true teachings of Buddha. The King and Berhai continued on the trail, through the Mountain Gate to the Temple Screen waterfall, and again the King understood. When they finally arrived at the simple altar and the beautiful carved Buddha, the King kneeled before it and wept with joy. In all of his life he had longed for a perfect temple, and it took the peasant builder Berhai to help him find the one that was there all along. Berhai was made the Royal Temple Builder of the Kingdom, but spent most of the rest of his long and happy life helping others see the beauty that was already around them."

I had asked War Sing about his religion and his churches. He was quick to point out to me that there was a bit of a difference from the churches that he had seen here in America and the temples that he had visited. He had noticed that here there were many styles of churches – one that he had seen in Virginia City was painted white and its spires were so tall that they almost seemed to touch the desert sky. Another one he had seen in California was made of packed mud and clay tiles, and from the outside it looked like an army garrison fort. He admitted that the temples were each different, too, in their own ways, but regardless of the adornments of the temple or the lack thereof, a true temple would contain four important items. First, the Mountain Gate was the door to pass through to reach the sacred part of the temple, or a defined entrance that was distinctly different than that of the common rooms and the meeting house areas. Second, the Temple Screen was usually a hand-woven partition that shielded the inner workings of the temple from the outside world. Third was the altar that lay behind the Temple Screen – which held offerings and was adorned at times with incenses, or flowers, or candle-lit lanterns depending on the season or the ceremony. The fourth and most important part of the temple was the carved Buddha at the center of it all, resting also upon the altar.

He told of many beautiful temples he had seen in his homeland – many-roomed palaces for the Buddha with lodges attached for lesser gods or for special ceremonies. He said that he had liked the Berhai story the best, because as a child he never understood why a richly adorned temple would lie in a countryside where just outside the doors people were dying of hunger. I had agreed with him that it was wrong. He added that while all of the special adornments were placed there out of respect for the god, the teachings held nothing about requiring riches in the temples. I remember trying to explain to him about our religion, and that Jesus seemed to have had that same problem with some of the goings-on in our churches a long time ago, too.

One of my first mining memories was of panning for gold with my Dad and War Sing, near what is today called Gordon's Ferry. The river was still cold, and my fingers hurt, but I swished and turned the tin pie pan my Mother had given me like I was an old sourdough. I had crawled around the bedrock outcroppings on the upriver-ka'am side of that outside bend of the Klamath, keeping a keen eye on my Father and his friend as I filled my pan. They kept a keen eye on me too, as they investigated the hillside for placer mining opportunities and the bedrock field we were in for gold movement from the winter river waters. I wondered why they were so busy making little piles of rocks here and there, and I remember thinking that they were never going to light on to any gold by building stone towers everywhere.

Over the course of the morning, I panned and explored – every once in a while standing to holler to the fellas in my best copy-cat of the miner's lingo, "This color is a huckleberry above a persimmon," "Aces-high, gents," or, my Father's favorite, "Big find, sound on the goose." My announcements were met with a smile or a nod, and I'm sure that they were both glad that I was playing with the tin pie pan instead of getting under their feet all morning.

I was busy with my industrious venture, and they were busy with theirs and when the morning turned to the afternoon they were ready to move on to another area.

My Father and War Sing walked down to where I was crouched, moving the pan in the dirty Adam's Ale.

"Time to go, son," my Father said as he reached down for my hand.

"Yeah, this pan's about played out," I said in my most serious four-year old voice, tipping the sand and little rocks back into the cold water. Impatiently, with a strained smile that showed he had nigh unto enough of my pretending for the day, my Father encouraged me once again to get going with a pat on my behind.

I remember that I began to throw a conniption fit, and then my Father started to holler at me, and he picked me up by my jacket collar and hauled me kicking and screaming to the wagon. When he pitched me into the back and I noticed that my tin pie plate was missing I turned and yelled at him – with amazing bravado, after the extrication I had just received – as loud as I possibly could, "Can I please have my gold pan?"

War Sing was an amused by-stander to the whole event, and when he heard my bellowed request he went to retrieve the pan for us, probably hoping to spare me a bigger fit and a bigger whoopin'.

I heard him laughing from where I had been with my pan, loudly, even over the noise of my stomping and hollering. "Jack", he called to my Father, "come down here."

War Sing and my Father returned to where I sat shortly. War Sing's face was still scrunched in a half-laugh, and my Father's face was bright red and he was carrying my pan in one hand as well as a handful of something in the other. They both clum into the wagon and my Father turned to me.

"Sorry I didn't believe you son. You must have found at least two ounces of little nuggets down there today."

I sat back down, crossed my arms and made sure that when I said, "I told you so," that I spoke so quietly that no one would hear me.

Later when my Dad got over being upset at himself for being so impatient with me he told Mother the story.

I still remember how he told her, if not all of the words. I remember that when he told her about what had happened he sounded *proud*.

Chapter Four

The Flood

"I lassoed the smallest coffin and
started to pull it to shore, but
when I saw the others floating
behind it I untied the little box and
pushed it back out to the river. I
know it sounds funny, but it
seemed wrong to keep it apart from
the rest of them."
                    – Red Callahan, Resident

Living in a river valley, we were all pretty used to
the whole area flooding about every ten years or so.
Invariably, a heavy snow pack would grow in the high
mountains around us in late spring just to be melted by
a fluke warm gully washin' rain from the Pacific. The
ground, already holding as much water as it could from
a whole season of precipitation, would shed the melted
snow water away and down stream after stream until it

finally reached the Klamath.

The canyon walls would become churning and crashing funnels of the thick and dirty water, and the valleys would become depositories of the muddy offal. Trees were uprooted, landslides caused, and all manner of objects stowed far above the normal high water lines were carried away down to the river.

During these floods, I've seen hundreds of items unintentionally set adrift from the thievin' high maelstrom. From my kitchen window I've seen many pilotless boats, millions of board feet of timber, two cars, an outhouse, a chicken coop with its residents inside, cows, one drowned horse, and six coffins. The coffins floated by about eight years ago. A little later it was discovered that a family cemetery up the river had partially fallen into the roiling, cold water. The coffins were never recovered.

Right before I turned twelve, all of the conditions were in place for a flood. We had suffered through a big forest fire in the surrounding canyons late in the last summer, and it was still smoldering here and there despite the fall and winter rains and snows. The ground was already unstable with so many tree roots rotted and burnt away. The old men at the woodstove in Scully's Cook Tent seemed in high alert, and their usual musings were replaced by their loud coffee-fueled reports regarding the nearby hillside's inevitable rearrangement. From their birds-eye view at the Cook Tent table they were a wealth of knowledge for all within earshot.

Folks who lived waterside had moved their belongings and selves further from the streams and rivers in anticipation of an early spring flood – but no one could have expected what was about to happen.

The Indian Crick drainage collects most all of the water that runs out of the Greyback Mountain range, and it is walled in by the Dillon Peak range and the Cade Mountain range on either side as it nears Happy Camp and the Klamath. Many times in the past Indian Crick has turned into a temporary but murderously giant river fed by those three groups of mountains.

After Indian Crick makes its way almost to the Klamath, it first travels through the center of Happy Camp. If the Crick makes it past the town, it empties into the already swollen Klamath and continues eventually to the Pacific Ocean.

Several home-made bridges had been constructed across Indian Crick, with at least two solidly built crossings reaching over those troubled waters. The biggest bridge up the crick was a log tie and girder affair, while the one town bridge was made of an amalgam of girders, steel rail posts, Portland cement and a few original wood crossbeams.

Like any tragedy, smaller events lined up to contribute to the ending mess. The mill pond, at the workin's up Indian Crick, had just been loaded in with about five hundred twenty foot chute-fed timbers to soak the bark off. Right below the mill, downstream, a slide fell into the crick leaving a thirty-foot pile of rock, dirt, and root-balled trees that the unending flow just couldn't get past. The water rose from behind that point in the little valley where the mill was, eventually covering the roof of the eighteen-foot-tall sawyer's shed. The impromptu dam, built by nature on that Friday night, went unnoticed till Sunday evening when the force of the walled in water behind it pushed it out of the way – bringing all of the mill pond timbers, a few buildings, livestock, and the shingled roof of the sawyer's shed down the crick canyon with it.

From where some of the debris was found, townsfolk figured that at certain points in the rocky and narrow parts of the v-shaped bedrock-lined canyon the water wall must have got as high as forty feet over the normal stream run.

The crashing timbers and the rest of the water-borne objects made their way the eight miles to town – picking up other objects and more speed as the water rushed downhill toward the Klamath. Many folks later told stories of just escaping with their lives and the lives of their children as the water coldly and steadily began filling their homes in the middle of the dark night.

All of the little home-made bridges and catwalks over the crick were taken away by the flooding stream, leaving some folks stranded on the other side of the muddy run for a few days after.

The wall of water almost made its way to the Klamath, but when it reached the last bridge in its path, somehow, the girders began to hold the whole mess back. That lasted long enough for the logs to jam up the stream, lodging as if they were pile-driven into the muddy ground and hillsides where the bridge stood. The whole structure would have probably boiled over – creating a mess of logs here and there – but when the shingled roof of the sawyer's shed met the log jam at the bridge, it was pushed into the logs and stopped up any water at all that had been trickling through.

The crick, still delivering thousands of gallons of Adam's Ale each second, was stopped in its natural path and was forced to take another. The water began to fill the entire lower part of the town, and got to about five feet deep or so before someone decided to clear the log jam with explosives.

Either they used too much dynamite or not enough – the jam in the crick was cleared, but the log pieces and debris were still so big that the entire mess just moved into the river, floated downstream about a quarter-mile and settled just above Lewis' Riffle.

The water damage caused by the backed up run was nothing compared to what the mighty Klamath brought upon our community as it was forced to pour over its banks and reach into far more homes and businesses that the crick ever would have.

Folks nigh unto died that night, and some of them lost everything they had ever owned. For some, it was all gone – pictures, cradles, books, clothing, food, horses, silverware – never to be seen again. What was left was covered in mud, leaving a marking line on the walls in the remaining homes and buildings that can still be seen today.

Some buildings, like the good old American Inn, were spared of any damage at all. Depending on who you asked, folks answered that it was luck, divine intervention, or good living by the occupants or owners that spared the unharmed buildings – my Father, in his practical manner, explained later that all of the buildings left standing were those that had been painted with heavy oil to preserve the wood after they were built. It had worked.

At our home so far from town we had no idea that the floods had occurred, until the fellas blew the second jam with enough dynamite to make toothpicks out of the timbers. To Mother and I the explosion sounded like thunder, but my Dad knew better and soon he was off on the good horse to give his help.

I worried about my school friends and all of their families. I was worried about War Sing, and all of his friends who lived so close to the river. I sure hoped that no one had gotten hurt. I had got myself so upset about everything that I almost couldn't eat the supper my Mother had made. I'm sure she had the same trouble, but made it look like she had eaten something by pushing her food around her plate. I couldn't ever get away with that, but I let her be.

When I went up to bed Mother was setting in the front room staring out the dark window, wrapped in a heavy shawl and waiting for my Father to return. I laid awake upstairs for hours, until I heard him come in. I listened to his details of the two floods, and about all of the upset that the water had caused. One phrase that stuck in my head all of these years, was my Dad saying, "No one is missing."

Relieved, my thoughts wandered. What would be left of our town? How would we get to the Indian Crick claims if the road was washed out? Was there any good that could have come out of the horrible events of the weekend?

That night I dreamed that the buoyant Log Schoolhouse was lifted by the flooding and was bobbing along the Klamath – getting caught in an eddy or two here or there – as it slowly floated its way out of our lives forever. I imagined the clutter inside of the Schoolhouse, as books tumbled from their shelves as the log building nosed in to rocks or timbers on its long and winding path toward the open sea. I wondered, as I drifted off into a blissful slumber, that if that structure could make it past Dragon's Tooth and over Ishi Pishi Falls – what the unlucky South Pacific tribe or Australian family would think upon finding that prisonous building washed up on their shore.

After everything was said and done – all of the

houses mucked out and the chickens put back in their coops – I got the worst news of any of it. The Norecross' from down the road came by and told us, that by the grace of God, the Schoolhouse had been spared after all.

Chapter Five

The State of Jefferson

"No one could answer us when we asked if we could just volunteer out of the State government. I'm sure they didn't want us as much as we didn't want them, but no one knew where to start."
– Dirt Hat Collins, Resident

After the last near-yearly forest fire and then the flood, folks around here were pretty much wore out. Some of the sparks from that year-old fire still continued to smolder in the duff under the winter snows, and most of us weren't even close to fixing all of the damage from the high water. Along about May, when the snows began to melt from the high peaks the landslides began.

A couple of the buildings rebuilt by the Chinese folks were taken again by the falling mud and timbers from the steep slopes behind them.

The hillside trees – firs and cedars and sugar pines – dying from the burn could no longer keep their hold on the steep mountainsides. They fell, one by one, like wounded soldiers. Their long and deep roots, weakened by the fire damage, broke their last tenuous grasp on the cliffs and promontories. Exhausted by their battles and weary of their wounds they crashed to the ground.

Without the latticed network of roots encasing the steep hillsides, the mountains became pregnant with tons and tons of water-filled dirt. It didn't take long for these heavy deposits to start to slip toward the bottoms of the canyons or drainages. Some only moved inches every week, while others quickly slid in earthen avalanches wherever the fires had touched.

That oily, viny, and bushy enemy of man – poison oak – crept up in every spot in our River Canyon newly opened to the sunlight from the tragedies of the past fall. There was hardly a place you could go where the cat-paw shaped leaves didn't reach out to brush off their itchy poison. I saw more swollen-eyed, scratched-up folks that next spring and summer than I ever had before. There even became quite a revolving group of folks near our house, who had sought out the sulfur-infused hot springs up the crick a bit to give them temporary relief. I myself, when rarely afflicted with the awful rashes, preferred to use a remedy I had accidentally come across – I stripped naked and rolled in the mud, and laid out in the sun until the mud dried to me drawing the poisons out. After a dip in the cold run to wash off I was usually doing just fine. Although I've been tempted to use that remedy later in my life, I haint – folks don't take too kindly to old muddy naked men sunning themselves next to our local waterways. In fact, there are a lot of things I used to be able to get away with when I was a kid that I wouldn't even consider considering now.

At that time we were all a puffy, itchy, scratched-up, and intolerable group of folks. Everything was pretty much in a muddled state, and by the hour was getting worse and worse.

When the river breezes would pick up in the afternoon we'd all take cover. You could see the yellow clouds of that sticky and itchy powder born aloft by the wind from the acres and acres of shiny Poison Oak bushes and vines. Fingers crossed we'd be hoping that the dusty airborne menace would find a landing spot far from any townfolk.

There was no hiding forever, and we all eventually got it. It was manageable, still, at that point – until someone had the bright idea to light the giant patches of the evil vegetation close to town on fire to get rid of it. Folks who were just mildly affected by the miserable itching were almost killed after unavoidably breathing in the smoke from those well-meant clearing fires. Folks who had been suffering the miserable rashes only on their arms and legs and faces, woke up the next day to find it in their ears, up their nose, inside their eyelids, and even in their throats – causing a fearsome swelling that hampered breathing.

We held a town meeting, and folks still able to attend voiced their concerns about the lack of medicine and how some of our community folks were hungry since they were unable to get out and work their gardens or hunt for food. Some of the kids had gotten infections in their skin that weren't clearing up, and those injuries were leading to fevers and other malaise.

In a marked air of defeat, and unlike our community spirit would ever have allowed under normal circumstances – we drafted a letter to the Governor's office and asked him for some help. We figured that if we got medicines for the itching and the infections we'd right ourselves soon enough, and laid our plan out. We didn't stoop to ask for food or anything of the like, as we were proud and still able to take care of each other with our canned preserves and what a hunting party of fellas brought into town to divvy up. The letter was very respectful, and held no hint of our disdain for the government or the State. The school teacher checked it for spelling and grammar errors, and after righting our writing she addressed it and sent it on with the next outgoing packer. It was marked important, and the pack-train letter handlers got it as quick as they could all of the way to the coast and then it was specially borne on a southerly ship, eventually ending up at the big white building in Sacramento with the help of a few fast riders.

Within a quick two weeks we got our response, and a second town meeting was called to deliver the news in the letter. By that afternoon almost everyone who could was assembled, and someone whose name I have long ago forgotten stood in front of us all and opened the official envelope.

"From the Governor's office," the man said as he held up the delivered papers. Huzzahs and clapping erupted here and there in the crowd, with hands freed for a moment from the constant scratching we all had come used to. He carefully opened the thick and expensive-looking envelope, and drew from it our original post as well as a letter written out on a grand and shiny letterhead.

The man cleared his throat, and began to read the words to all assembled.

"Dear Residents of Happy Camp," he began with his best orator's voice. "Thank you for your well-written letter." More huzzahs and clapping. He continued to read.

"Unfortunately, our records show that your community is not in the State of California, but in Oregon instead." We all sat in a stunned silence. Could it be true that we didn't know where our community was? Could it be true – instead – that our Governor didn't know where our community was? Expletives and concerned voices began to rise in the crowd, and then someone urged us to quiet down for the telling of the rest of the letter.

The confused looking man continued reading, "We Californians are sympathetic to your plight, but our resources must be used for the residents of our State. We recommend sending your request to your state capitol in Salem, Oregon. Our best wishes for the recovery of your community. Sincerely, H. M. Samuels, Executive Secretary for the Governor's Office of Correspondence."

That letter pretty much summed up our contact with our State government for years. Heck, we didn't even rate notice by the Governor hisself.

We did take care of ourselves, and we took care of each other – like we always had. Folks got better and we didn't lose anyone, although several children got pretty close with high fevers caused by the skin infections. We used mud poultices, old cures, drank the Chinese arimantus teas, and many of us consulted one of the medicine women for her remedies.

Chapter Six

Hard Work and the High Claims

"I must've wandered around that area for a whole day, checking my maps and my compass. It's not often that a mountain has been misplaced."
– Scotty O'Neil, Surveyor

Our life back then, believe you me, was difficult. My Father worked at times for the mills and for local logging operations, but we also had several mining claims of our own in the area. Although the claims never really produced much while I was real young, over the years it must have added up. Hear tell that when the doctor presented the bill for my complicated birth to my Father, he paid it in full with placer gold. Until I was about twelve, I naively thought my Pa had coined the phrase "worth your weight in gold" because I had heard him say it so many times.

To be prosperous then a family had to be very

enterprising as well as thrifty. A trap line provided a jot extra money for us. We gleaned what we could from the land. Rabbit and venison and fish were the food staples in our household. I've also been fed rattlesnake, raccoon, and river eel when times got especially lean. Even though we always seemed to be poor, my Mother reminded me often that we were actually very rich in spirit. We had food, a home, a woodstove, horses and a mule, a rickety old wagon, and of course, each other. I was always daydreaming about a big gold strike on one of the claims, so that my parents wouldn't have to work so hard.

We mostly had placer mines which we worked for most of the year – even though my Father hired out a few times for some of the local big patent mine operations. I remember the Reeve's nearby *China Creek* operation, *The Brusse* float-find process, Wheeler's *Classic Hill*, San Francisco based Dunnigan Consolodated's big works south of town run by Mr. Stickel, the dramatically-named *Grey Eagle* owned by a chuckleheaded bunch of stuffy New York fellows who paraded through town on occasion, and Compton's dry works at *Colby-Stern*.

My Father had decided that the March rain had washed away enough snow for us to be able to make it to one of our higher claims. After months of being away from the Indian Crick claims – aptly named the *High Mountains #1* through *#4* – we were both anxious and curious about what the winter had left us. I helped my Father place his trunk of tools and hardware in the front of our old cart, curiously on top of some straw to cushion the trunks' ride. I thought about kidding my Dad about how much care his tools received when all I got was the hard seat plank under my rear, but I was soon on to other tasks that needed to be done before we set out. We loaded our pickaxes and shovels, bivouac supplies, our lunches and some spare clothes and set out with Jenny pulling the cart with our good horse tethered and following behind. Cinder jumped in as we pulled away, and I was glad for her curled up warmth at my feet. We stopped at our old lumber pile and threw some milled pieces in the back in case we had to repair a sluice box or two. War Sing was busy on his own claims, so the two of us set off ready for a cold campout and three days hard labor and required improvements.

On the long trip up I was thinkin' on all of the hard work we had sunk into those claims the season before. I knew that no one had ever drowned in his own sweat before, but believe you me I felt like I had got pretty close a time or two. We had in the past successfully planted a thirty foot horizontal shaft that held dozens of exploratory arterial tunnels – each angled just so to catch an ore line or gold vein running through the area. Our work in the last year had extended the arterials and by the end of the season we had been seeing excellent results from the deepest excavations in the back. The snow and the wet earth had finally forced us out for the season, and purt near every day or so that winter my Father and I would bring up the spring plans for the *High Mountain* claims.

We had heard some scuttle about a slide or two on the hill, and while neither my Father nor I put any real stock in the idle talk of folks who spread bad news we had loaded the wagon prepared for the worst.

The ride seemed to take forever, and I bolted out of my seat as soon as we got close with Cinder right in behind me. Running up the trail and trying real hard not to trip on my dog, I had visions of giant boulders of gold uncovered by the swollen winter stream. I recall now that a bit of snow still lay about the forest floor, and the cold early spring wind chilled my neck and exposed hands. All winter long I had daydreamed that this next season would bring us the big one – a nugget big enough to ease the constant financial hardship that we seemed to always be facing. As I neared the top and looked into the ravine where the stream and the tunnel were, I lost almost all of my breath. I was still standing there with my mouth wide open and shocked beyond words when my Father stopped beside me. He looked at the giant landslide that had covered the entire claim. Fallen trees were strewn across the mass of dirt and rocks. Water trickled over and through the whole mess.

Above the roar of the felonious and angry stream nearby, my Father simply said, "Well, son, I'm sure glad that we weren't in there when all of that came down." He put his hand on my shoulder, patted me on the head, and finished by saying, "Looks like we have a heap of work to do." I knew that he was upset, and that he was trying to ease my disappointment – even though his face couldn't hide his own feelings. He had faced much bigger setbacks in his life.

I couldn't help but think of the months of work we had already done to build the tunnel and the exterior sluice system. I could see another year of fish and venison, wood cutting and hard work, without a baseball bat and glove for me, and without any fine things for my Mother.

As that day progressed and my arms and my back grew tired my anger got the better of me and I had a few conniption fits. It's a little funny now, thinking about the trees I kicked and the rocks I heaved down the bank in my boyish tirade since my anger toward the mountain didn't really seem to concern the mountain at all. At one point my dog was so disgusted at my attitude she just returned to the wagon and curled up in the corner. My Father calmed me down each time I started hollering, but I wasn't quite convinced by his shoulder-patting and his words. As the morning wore on, it seemed like my Father was just putting up a good front for me and I began to see that his anger about the slide coursed through his veins too. At one point, as his eyes searched over the slide area it looked like someone had lit him on fire. After all, I had got my anger-ability from somewhere, and it sure wasn't my Ma.

The spring claim improvements started in earnest that day as we began the back-breaking work of clearing some of the moveable rocks and salvaging what was left of our old sluice box system. We'd make a little progress, just in time for more water-logged earth to slide back into its place and erase the progress we had just made. Over, and over, and over again the same frustrating chain of events played out in front of us.

The blue streak, which had lain below the surface of my Father's vocabulary for the entire morning, was at one point unleashed. As they say, it's hard to get the horses back in the barn after the door is opened.

The general understanding that my Father and I had about his cursing was stretched to the boundaries that day, until there came a point where I began to hum a song to myself lest his logger-talking corrupted my own language skills. I didn't mind him cursing that much – in all honestly I felt like doing it too – but I was afraid that if I grew too accustomed to it, that at some unfortunate mishap I may utter one of those words in the presence of my Mother. That would have been a truly disastrous slip-up, both for me and for the seat of my pants. I had made that long felon's walk to the wood shed before for a lesser violation, and I wanted to try to avoid it in the future.

After lunch and four more hours of futile labor, I looked up to see my Father standing again on top of the whole mess. It was more than a whole crew of men could get through in two seasons of full work. I recall he had his hands placed on his hips, and was facing the giant sliding mountain of soil. From where I sat I could see that his ears were a bright red – what I later learned the hard way was a sure warning sign to stay clear of my usually well-behaved Father. He looked almost like he was challenging the hillside to a fight.

Stomping down the dirty mess toward me, he murmured something about fixing that mountain once and for all. In what seemed like an afterthought, he told me to get out of the way and to keep behind the rock ledge until he said different. My Father's own tirade against the mountain that day was bigger and stronger than my little fit had been, and while I did no lasting damage to the eternal forest, my Father sure did.

He went about digging through the box that had been hay-cushioned in the wagon. When he came back he was walking a jot more carefully. I can't tell you how my eyes lit up when I saw the pile of dynamite sticks he was carrying in his arms. I was always surprised at what the local fellas had been allowed to take home from their service to America – he would forever be digging around for something in his shed or toolbox, and come out with the perfect mechanical solution in the form of some contraption or gadget he'd been discharged with. I never asked him where he got the dangerously sweaty sticks marked "U. S. Army" on their labels – but I think I knew.

Passing where I was perched behind the wall, he only glared at me and said "Git!" I scurried further back down the wall, and against advice I inched back to watch him as he progressed up the mountainside of rubble.

We'd used selective explosive strikes in the past – but only half or quarter stick charges we'd bought in town. I had always enjoyed the blasts and had annoyed the heck out of my Dad on the blasting days. That afternoon, though, I steered clear and kept to the safe area after seeing the amount of explosive he planned on setting. It never once occurred to me that day that what we were setting about doing would be dangerous – maybe because I trusted my Dad so much, and maybe because at that time in my life I believed that nothing ever would go wrong as long as he was there.

People in town still jaw about Hammarsen's Earthquake. It took Dad over two hours to place the dynamite in the tangled mess of the slide. You'd think that it would have been enough time for him to cool off and take a second look at what he was about to do, but it actually seemed like he was growing consistently madder as he went along. Since he was usually a relatively even-mannered person, it was a rare event to see my Father in that state of fury and I stayed the h-e-double-hockey-sticks out of his way.

He finally appeared above me, on the ledge of the rock wall, and called for me to grab the fuse when he dropped it down. I carefully caught the waxy funny-smelling rope, and stood stock-still until my Dad was able to scramble down the ledge to relieve me of my post.

He instructed me to crouch low, beside him, and cover my ears. I had blocked in my dog between me and a rock corner, and I warned her to stay put. Then my Father and I had the regular little discussion on what to do if everything went south – meaning, if he was killed or injured and was unable to take me home – which was by that time an old hat lecture to me.

I crouched as instructed, and glanced back and forth between my dog and my Father as he lit the fuse rope. I studied his face – his anger had turned into determination, and I thought I could see a little hope glimmer in his eyes too. It was a strong remedy for what had befallen our claim, but it fit the problem.

The spark burned full chisel on the fuse, and the acrid smoke lingered in our little hiding area and stung at my throat and my eyes. As the spark crested past our view, over the ledge and up the hillside toward the charges, my Father stayed crouched next to me and somewhat over me – as if he could shield me from a stray boulder or one of the twenty or so pieces of thousand-pound timber lying on the ground above us. My hands were, as instructed, over my own ears, and he placed his hands over mine to give me an extra layer of protection from the giant pending explosion.

My Father was back to the thoughtful, strong demeanor that marked most of his time on earth. The rock was cold behind us, and my legs ached in the crouch after a while. I was thrilled beyond words to be a witness to the grand event that was about to occur. I never once opined that we were in any danger, because my Father was there to protect me.

All of the thoughts that usually raced through my head constantly were quieted, one by one, in anticipation of the event. My breathing slowed and was shallow, as I listened hard through two sets of hands for a hint of ignition.

Just when I started to think that the fuse must have been a dud, I heard a sound and felt the earth move in ways that I've only heard the preacher talk about when referencing the onset of the end of the world.

With the blast set off, I looked in wide-eyed wonderment at the tons and tons of earth as well as the giant rocks and pieces of wood that sailed up and past us – knocking into other trees, bouncing down the hillsides, or settling in unusual places. It was the end-all be-all super-wonderous explosive eruption that most boys could only daydream about. When the dust settled, Cinder shook the dirt and pebbles out of her black coat and left us as she returned to the wagon. On her way she turned and barked at both of us in a scolding manner, and for a minute I was glad that Mother couldn't speak Dog like Dad and I could – because if Cinder let on to mother what had happened that day Dad and I would've probably had to find a new place to live.

On many older maps of our area, you can find Threadneedle Mountain to the northeast of the junction of Indian Crick and Scorpion Crick. On those maps published after that day in 1912, the place of Threadneedle Mountain is taken by a newer geographical formation, aptly named Hammarsen's Hole. Months after the detonation, the brass U. S. Geographical Survey marker that had once resided near the top of what had been Threadneedle was found by a placer miner several miles from where our destructive eruption had occurred. It was given to my Father as a novelty, but being a former Navy man he felt it was his duty to officially notify U. S. G. S. – so he sent the medallion away to them, along with a simple letter that read, "The Mountain isn't there anymore."

The rest of our bivouac there and the remainder of the spring when we worked on those claims, my Father set about to build an enormous structure at the base of the hill. I helped him when I could, but I knew not to ask many questions about what he was doing. At first I thought that he was building a new sluice box, but as I saw the size of what he was assembling grow, I lost all ability to recognize it. The mouth of the box was over thirty feet wide, and by the time it was almost finished, it ran in length for almost a hundred feet. We used all of the timbers that we had salvaged from the mess, and then moved on to the planks and timbers from a long-abandoned cabin and barn that was nearby.

War Sing came up with us to help build the structure when he could. He had a puzzling smile on his face as he hammered away. At one point, I figured that my Father had surely told him what the structure was to be used for, so I approached War Sing with curious caution. He gave me no information, only an all-knowing wink and a big smile.

The next week found us back to the high claim, placing pieces of heavy metal railroad track across the mouth of the structure about a foot apart. We repeated that effort along the stair-stepping behemoth, placing metal closer and closer, until screens could be used instead of track.

Standing back, amazed, I realized that may Father had indeed built a giant monster of a sluice box – only it was so much bigger than anything I had ever seen or even heard of. Instantly, practical questions filled my mind – but the most glaring one kept surfacing to the top. How would we get enough water to move dirt through the giant box?

I understood that the ground we had tunneled through was in the giant balded mound of exploded dirt in front of us, and the veins we had discovered were in there somewhere too. I figured that my Father planned to get all that dirt over the giant sluice, but I couldn't imagine how.

Leaving the house on our next trip to the *High Mountains*, my Father had a look in his eye that reminded me of a picture of a high seas marauder I had seen in a book once. In those illustrations, the pirate had his sword in one hand and was preparing to face thirty hostile mariners. I imagined that is what my Dad felt like, only that it was him, once again, against a mountain.

Somehow the word had spread around the town about my Father's monstrous sluice box. I'm sure the rumors were fettered by the tall tales of the mountain-moving explosion that had occurred earlier at the mine. We had quite a few passers-by on that little stretch of out-of-the-way mountain road that day, and after a while some of them even parked their rigs or tethered their horses and watched as we worked. Along about lunchtime another set of carts and mules came puffing up the hill, apparently under quite a load. They stopped and the driver put rocks under all of the cart wheels to be doubly sure that they would not roll away. He proceeded to bark orders at the looky-loos standing around. Before long, they were shamed into lending a hand carrying the heavy devices from wagons on the road to our perch at the top of the box.

Now, the work of those two months had shown me sides of my Father that I had not previously seen, and unfortunately taught me words I had not previously heard.

Watching the progress of the delivered item as the bystanders carried it to us, I almost became faint with worry about my Fathers' brain. I understood his anger, and I understood his frustration. I did not understand what I saw being carried up the hillside, or how it would take a part in the whole tragic play.

It looked like the bystanders, from where I was perched above all the workings, were bringing up a giant blackened cannon. Incredulous, I looked at my Father – with the wind blowing his hair, his shoulders thrown back, his hands once again on his hips, and the look on his face, in another time he could have easily been mistaken for that marauding pirate of the High Seas or even the deranged Don Quixote.

He directed the volunteers to place the pieces, and with a large wrench and lifting help, he began to assemble the giant thing, with confidence, just like it was something that he did twice every day. All at once I remembered a story about a man in Oregon who had tried mining with a water cannon. Instantly all of the pieces fit – in my mind and on the device – and my concern for my Father's addling mind was quickly replaced with excited anticipation for what I was about to see.

The cannon was a specialized device, and by the inscription on the side it had been forged and made about a thousand miles away in Illinois. A local man was currently, somehow, in possession of it although he had never had the courage or the means to use it. Later I found out that he bartered the lease of it that day to my Father, for a percentage of the color at the end of the excavation. Now I think he would have brought it for free, just to watch the spectacle of its use and its mountain-moving power.

The cannon itself was odd-looking. The nose opening was about ten inches across, and each piece attached to it widened out further so that the intake area was nigh unto two feet in diameter. A hush went over the crowd that had gathered, as my Father directed someone to place the intake mouth of the device into the diverted stream. Looking to see that I was clear of any danger, my Father took his place next to the other men who were holding the cannon's direction.

On my Father's signal, the water from the heavy stream was diverted into the cannon by lifting a wooden gate. With the force of gravity as well as the water behind it pushing it forward, the liquid was thrust down a narrowing earthen and wooden sluicework and then into the barrel of the cannon. Since the size of the walls of the cannon decreased in a taper to the front, the pressure and force were multiplied several times – until the resulting stream of water shot violently out of the other end of the cannon.

The water flew forth from the cannon with an intensity that I cannot explain here. I had never seen water move that way, and the fact that we had a hand in creating that forceful tool was a bit overwhelming. I believe we all were taken aback by the whole affair, but the fellas manning the cannon quickly gave more focus to their duties as the cannon began moving under it's own power. They were able to regain the aim of the cannon after wetting down us all and knocking a few birds out of the sky. They paid better attention after that.

It took five men to aim the cannon proper – two on each side and one near the front. The fellas had to take turns because most could only last an hour before they tuckered out. A line of folks formed to take a shift – more for bragging rights, I suppose, than out of any interest in the end of the day color.

I was fascinated how the whole process worked. When the men aimed the cannon at the slide, the stream of water forced the boulders and soil to move toward the mouth of the waiting sluice box. While the boulders and large rocks had been kept out of the works by large bars placed across the top, the smaller rocks and dirt would rush through the box, finishing on one of the screens. The rushing water carried the dirt, rocks, and hopefully gold down over and through the whole progression – from a big-holed guard to smaller and smaller-holed guards in the bottom of the box. We pried the boulders out of the top boxes with long rods. The gold, being so heavy, would lodge itself in the smaller screens and sluice ribs and the dirt and rocks would keep on going out of the end into the tailings pile carried and bounced along by the muddy water.

The timber in that giant dirt pile was freed up enough that we could hitch the team to most of the downed logs and move them out of the way of the whole works.

Tons and tons of slide dirt that would have taken a hundred men several weeks to clear, was taken care of over the course of seven hours that afternoon using the water cannon.

We got about thirty ounces of gold that day, and shared part of it with the owner of the water cannon – as agreed – and we even gave some to the folks who had ended up helping. We had a pretty good haul on that site, and after ten good mining days we were sure that whatever was left of Threadneedle Mountain would never be a trouble to anyone ever again.

The water cannon event firmly placed my Father in the lore of the town. We all had heard that with determination a man could move mountains. They all saw firsthand that day that the saying was actually true – but I had known that about my Father for quite some time already.

Chapter Seven

My Gravemarker

"Ever heard that joke, about why they had to build a fence around the cemetery? 'Cause people were just dyin' to get in? Not here – we're just trying to keep the deer and the cows out."
                                    – Big Ross Tollsen, Resident

Billy McKetter and I were the kind of friends that got each other in trouble, usually a result of some great idea one or the other of us had. Each of us were cursed with the same defiant independent nature and wildness, so the time we didn't spend arguing we spent hatching plans for adventure, constructing treetop hideaways, or shooting at indefensible targets like apple trees, loamy hillsides, and our favorite – an abandoned outhouse. Usually as long as our chores were done, we were given free reign to run about the town and the county-side – after all, we were "good boys."

One of our favorite games was "driving the nail" wherein we'd act as if we were making dead-aim shots at an imaginary spike – mostly we were pleased when we hit somewhere close. We'd try some pretty awful shooting stances with our wore out old .22's – one-armed standing, belly-style, or even from the hip – finding that regardless of the cowboy or Infantry styles we chose our aim was generally poor.

We took some of our inspiration from some boys in a book that Billy had read, and would trade off pretty regular on who we "were" during our adventures. Something about some hoodlum fellas and a raft and the Mississippi River and such, but Billy explained it so poorly that I didn't know where Billy was making up pieces of it and what was from the real book. He suggested I read it, and I laughed so hard that I almost split my sides. He knew from dozens of our conversations that I had no stock in any contemporary authors, as I had told him a thousand times that the last good book to ever be written featured a misunderstood and crazy fella fond of tilting his joust-stick at windmills – and that all learned men knew that nothing after it's publication in 1605 ever measured to it's mark. "Except anything written by Sir Walter Scott," I would quickly add.

We tried to build a raft – and it went pretty daisy until it broke up in the rapids at Lewis' Riffle and we had to swim for our lives – and we hiked several times to our very own real and actual Hidden Fort up Dillon Crick a ways and even considered creating our own troupe of high binding marauders. We reconsidered becoming marauders after we decided we didn't have enough fellas under us to boss around 'cause we sure weren't about to take direction from each other.

Later that same week we created the Elk Crick Regulars, and charged ourselves with monitoring the lawfulness of all the travelers and residents therein. When Billy got hit in the head with a hard-thrown apple, launched from the able arm of the oldest Norecross boy we'd caught trespassing in the orchard, we quickly reconsidered being self-appointed law men and set to minding our own business again – at least for a little while.

We next played at being opposite the law – from a book I had read – and I was Clym of the Clough and Billy was supposed to be Adam Bell on our legendary arching and outlawing adventures. Billy tried for a little while, and then admitted that he was fairly suspicious of any story written by a man named Percy. Just wasn't right, he said. We had an awful rough time bringing together his poor reenactments of the short-sighted contemporary literature stories and my interests in only classic and sometimes ancient tales.

We set about to make our own legendary adventures, and I promised Billy that a day would come when I'd set aside the writing of my world-exploration novels for a bit and put down all of our heroic acts to paper. He brought up my well-worn objections to contemporary authors and their irrelevant works, and I figured he had a good point. I countered with the fact that I planned on writing about the adventures simply as a courtesy to him, not reading them myself.

We captured critters and planned to make the first River Circus, but regardless of what we tried we could not train the lizards or snakes to do any tricks besides bite us – and we both knew that wasn't really a trick if it's what the animal does anyway. Our plans of touring the countryside, dazzling folks with our velvet-red tailored suit coats and high-stepping horses – and bull-whips, Billy added – were soon forgotten with the premature demise of our beloved enterprise.

We spent quite a bit of time laying in the area roads, acting as if we were dying or wounded. We waited for the wagons or horse riders to slow down, then we'd light up and run away as fast as we could go – laughing all the way to a hiding spot. I don't really think we fooled anyone, and it's a wonder we weren't killed by getting ourselves run over.

On a rainy summer afternoon, we cornered the cart-mule in our barn and fixed a wood and cloth contraption to its back – doing our best to transform the sad-faced creature into the warrior Bellerophon's flying steed, Pegasus. It played along well enough, but looked even sadder-faced as Billy and I argued whether or not we should try to run her off the cliff to get her aloft. When Billy suggested that we nail a broken-ended milled board to her forehead to make her into a unicorn, she set square and kicked at us both – missing my fool head by an inch. She shook the wings off her back and made her escape to the hillside a-braying as she went – just like she could understand our words. I wouldn't have let him nail wood to the head of that poor animal – since I was thinking that glue or a head-harness was better suited instead to horn-placing and subsequent removal. She didn't come out of the woods until nightfall – I figured it was a close contest for her, between the wild coyotes out there or Billy and I in the barn.

Of course we spent hours and hours swimming, and then when the cricks would dwindle down in the late summer we'd become industrious engineers, building rock dams across all manners of waterways near our favorite swimming holes – creating deeper pools and inadvertently making it much more difficult for the returning spawning steelhead to swim to their egg-laying beds upstream. We were probably responsible for the single-handed biggest reduction of the Indian Crick and Elk Crick fisheries, but Billy always argued after that we were like the hand of God – only letting the strongest and the best fish make it up to their home-waters to lay their eggs. He spinned the whole theory, until he almost had me convinced we were doing nature a service when all we really wanted to do was keep our swimming holes deep enough so that when you jumped off one of the rocky ledges you wouldn't have to break a leg in the process.

We pulled the large, broad leaves off of the crick-side plants that we had always called "elephant ears" – and placed them upside down on our heads to resemble the hats of the local Chinese. That was mostly done out of poking fun at the strange, wide hats those folks wore, as well as out of necessity when we were toiling in the great heat of late summer, building our own Great Walls stone by stone across the stream beds.

When we tired of the river damming project, upon my urging we set to go about on building our very own imitation of the Colossus of Rhodes. Billy went along, but seemed a jot mad that it wasn't his idea so he held back working his hardest. With handfuls of red clay from the crick bank we set reproduce Chares' giant warrior statue straddling the crick. We got as far as the boots and the shins on each side of the stream and tired of the hard labor – especially as we figured there was really no way to finish the statue after it got over about five feet tall.

We gave each other courtesy titles, like marquis,

earl, and viscount as we set about our games – and that lasted only a jot longer than our attempt at building the Colossus of Elk Crick.

He and I caught the deep-red crick crawdads by hand, daring each other to bite the heads off – although we never did. We did, however, try to roast some one afternoon using some matches Billy "found" in his Mother's kitchen and we almost started a forest fire when the dry afternoon wind whipped the flames into a nearby tree. We got away scot-free on that one – with only about seven or eight bushes lighting up – but I suppose that after eighty years no one is after us for that crime anymore.

About once a week we'd give a scare to our mothers in one horrible fashion or another. Billy was tired of our "I got my teeth all knocked out" ruse, wherein we'd get a mouthful of blackberries and some chewed up apple and show the proof of the injury to any available relative or parent, and I admit it had lost it's scarefulness after five or six times – so Billy came up with another bothahrayshun. Starting by mashing a poultice of ripe and semi-ripe blackberries together, we'd decorate a sharp stick placed tight up under one arm making it look bloody and awful. Charging into the dooryard, the fake wounded boy would fall to his knees bellowing up a storm, and the other boy would announce, "Quick, quick, I think he's been run through like Hamlet." After the near running through we both really did get from my Mother the last time we pulled that one, we decidedly moved on to other activities.

We enjoyed playing at Ned Kelly – one of us being the desperado and the other being the sheriff. I upset Billy every time we played that game, since I ended the game too soon – I wanted Ned Kelly's fame but I didn't want his hanging end.

Billy showed me how to pull the Helgrimites – little crick water bugs – out of their delicately built tube-shaped protective shells. Then we would put the shells in our noses to pretend to be a couple of ocean walrus. I can't imagine how long it took those little bugs to make those shells, but in short time we had destroyed their work and their homes and were on to the next adventure.

We liked playing pranks and usually they were harmless. There was an occasional missing cookie from ladies' cooking racks, but we didn't try to pull that one very often. When we found dead snakes in the road, we'd usually pick them up with a stick and leave them in places for folks to find – like on gates, front porches, and even once on a carriage bench. I still feel bad about that one, because it scared a Mrs. Lerley so bad that it actually made her cry – and even worse she could have been killed or broke something when she leapt from that coach to the rough ground below.

I learned a lot during my friendship with Billy. Like how alibis and excuses work. And practical things, too – like the fact that if one rattlesnake dies, its' mate searches it out. That hard-learned lesson nigh unto worked against us when we placed a squished rattler in Hank Boyd's lunch can and were all very surprised to find an accompanying killer-snake wound about that very same can when we returned.

The worst prank that we ever pulled scared me silly and put an end to most of my free-wheeling devil-may-care nonsense. For quite a long time we had dared each other to find a way into the caretakers shack at the Cemetery. We had figured that there were no end to the number of intriguing items that could be found in there, which were of great interest – of course – to a couple of 11-year-old boys. I had finally gotten tired of Billy's derision of my character and my moral fiber, and his near-remarks that I was a coward to go into what we called the Grave Shed.

As we were headed on some adventure or the other that fateful day, we found ourselves walking on the road toward the shady mountain Cemetery. Our regular verbal jousts and challenges ensued like clockwork. The predictability of our banter was secondary as long as Billy was bringing into question my courage.

Over those years when we had dared each other to enter the spooky Grave Shed we talked about it often, even during our other various adventures. It was a subject we used to posture our strength and courage to each other, and I'm pretty sure neither one of us ever planned to really step foot in that forbidden hut.

As we had almost walked to the corner of the resting property, Billy got off the first volley.

"You know, Nancy-Boy, I expected more from you," he said with an air of challenge in his voice. "Of all the people I've ever heard jawing up their courage and their strength of bein', I was sure you was the only one telling the truth."

Frustrated by his backhanded challenge, as well as being referred to with a girls name – a real verbal slap in the face – I replied, "Looks like you were wrong again Billy, since you and I both know that I've promised a hundred times that if the shed was open, I'd walk right in – head held high. I am not," I continued, "a common thief or burglar who would break through a lock or upset someone's belongings."

I was really taking advantage of the situation, and

peppering my vocabulary with spectacular flourishes and using dramatic arm gestures as I spoke.

"You'll just have to wait for Providence to intervene," I added with more and more embellishment, "and that day I will prove to you that I am not afraid of what the Grave Shed holds."

I suppose I should have looked at the shed before I spoke, since I saw soon enough when I turned my head that the door was swung wide open. At that time, the Cemetery didn't have a fence around it – only a lawn that ran straight to Buckhorn Road – with an arch and a gate in the front, standing by itself. I said some select Celestial words to myself, and then – because I was only as good as my word – I marched right up the gravelly roadway, through the front gates of the Cemetery and right up to the Grave Shed with Billy right behind me. I could have just walked across the Cemetery grass, instead of walking up the road to go through the main gate – but even as I was fixin' to trespass and snoop in the Grave Shed I still acted kind of respectful of the passed folks that were near.

I turned around to look for my dog, and as if she knew what I was up to she gave me a scornful look and sat down next to the road with her back towards me. It was like she was telling me that if I was chuckleheaded enough to go in there, that I was on my own. I've gotten a few disapproving looks over the course of my life, but the worst ones always came from that dog.

I looked around quick for the awful caretaker. He was an evil-looking dirty man with foul breath and stringy hair who seemed to enjoy his job just a bit too much. He and his horse and wagon were gone. I figured he must have forgot to shut the Grave Shed before he left for the day.

I stood outside of the place for a minute. Looking at my feet, I had the toe-ends of my shoes just barely on the sunny side of the line between the grass covered Cemetery lawn and the shady damp darkness of the Grave Shed proper. Prodded by Billy behind me, whispering, "Nancy-boy, Nancy-boy," in my ear and tapping me in the ribs I helplessly watched my feet enter the restricted Shed.

The dark little shack smelled like dirt and lime. As Billy and I inched inside we first spied all manner of blades and trimming tools and scythes and shovels that were lined up against the wall. I figured that if I scared Billy we could cut stick quicker, so I tried to point out a dark spot on one of the shovels. "Look. Billy, there's the blood of the last kid who came in this shed – still on the shovel."

He laughed and said, "Good try, coward, that's just rust from the shovel being wet," pushing me further into the darkness.

Hanging from the rafters, all around us was dirt-moving gear such as I had never seen. Some items probably were for digging corners or shoring up the walls of graves so they didn't fall in before the work was done – but our young, fertile imaginations were set abuzz with the possible uses for all the interesting implements above our trespassing little heads. To this day, I'm not sure why there were a few hay-hook-looking handles in there and maybe I don't want to know.

In all of our posturing and road-side speculating we would have never come close to the veritable richness of mystery and doom that the shed held. Never once could we have imagined how much more interesting it all was with the element of impending being-found-out thick in the dank air around us.

The light filtered in, barely, through a dim and dirty little window. Not enough light to really see what was all in the shed, but enough for dark shadows to be cast in the corners – perfect places, I thought, for a Zombie-Man or Restless Ghoul to hide in before it jumped out on us.

We came across a work bench, with little iron letters scattered about and around a rectangular metal form. It took us a jot bit to figure out what the letters and the rectangle was for, but after we saw the metal letters spelled out in a name, backwards in the form, we said at the same time with amazed awe in our voices, "It's a headstone maker."

Chilled by the coincidence of our words, I'm sure we were both ready to really cut stick at that time although neither one of us wanted to be the first one to say so. I grabbed the bull by the horns and announced to Billy that I was fixin' to pull the prank of the century, but that then we'd have to hightail it so no one would know we had been there. I told him that I had decided to change the name in the headstone form, so that when the caretaker came back to pour the cement in, another name would be made.

By the revered look in Billy's eyes, I knew that I had won the widely-disputed Courage Contest and the Prank Of All Time Contest as well. He tipped his imaginary hat to me, and bowed a little at my royal idea. Trying to gain some prank fame hisself, he suggested that we change the name to Mrs. Elizabeth Hudson – our new school ma'am and quite the irritating Blue Stocking – and I was forced by my self-pride to agree.

As I began to lay the letters of her name down, I

got a real unlucky and cold touch on my soul that made me feel really sad – and I suddenly didn't want to do the prank anymore. It was almost like I was asking Death to make a visit to Mrs. Hudson's house – although it was no secret I didn't much care for being cooped up in school, I sure didn't want to harm the poor old lady. I felt that if I put her name down, it'd be like pushing her toward the Big Jump.

I knew it was just a matter of time before we were found out, and I was getting more and more nervous. While Billy was distracted by a scythe hanging near us, I reassembled the letters and the numbers below quickly – told him I was done – and we ran out as fast as our trespassing little feet could take us. I figured that I'd come back after Billy went home and clean up what I had placed in the metal form.

Later that day, when I finally was able to return by myself to the scene of our crime I found the shed locked tight, the curtained window drawn shut, and an empty and crumbled Portland cement bag outside of the door.

With nothing I could do save breaking the door down I hung my head and continued home. I tried to forget about the Grave Shed prank, and I spent the next few days at my house and away from Billy and his wayward influences.

I was the best and kindest child ever during those days right after. I figured that helping without complaint in any manner needed without prompting by my folks might magically stay the inevitable trouble I had got myself in. After a while, I just waited for the proverbial axe to fall.

After dinner on Saturday, there was a loud and slow knock on the door – and when my Mother looked out the side window all of the color drained out of her face as she recognized the Cemetery caretaker. I found out later that he was also often the man in town that delivered the news to folks that someone in their family had died. That day, though, I just wrote up her reaction to the fact that the man was so scary looking.

My Father asked him in, but he declined politely, asking instead that my Father come out to the front. I wished myself invisible, but it didn't work. My Mother was about to faint at that point, and sat in one of the kitchen chairs as my Father walked outside with the old man. I began to clean up the dinner dishes and put our victuals away, but my Ma grabbed me up short and began to pray with a fierceness that I had never heard before. I was praying too, but for a different reason.

I peeked up from those fierce prayers to see my Father and the old man, standing near the back of the Cemetery wagon just in time for my Father to put his hands up to head in an exhibition of grief or anger. I thought about trying to pray harder. I was sure that my trespass had brought terrible bad luck to our family, and that at that moment the two men stood looking at an entire cart-bed full of friends of ours – all dead and stacked like cordwood in the back – and that it was my fault.

My Father charged into the house, and grabbed my weakened Mother to take her to see what the old man had brought – and turning for a moment toward me to say, "Git out there," in a deep and scary voice I had never heard from him before.

My Mother made it to the planked wagon bed before me, and she purt nearly fainted at what she saw. My Father had to hold her up or she would have fallen on the ground. She screamed and looked at me like I was a ghost as I reluctantly walked toward her, one heavy footstep at a time. Looking up to the Cemetery caretaker I thought I saw a little smile on his face, directed right to me. He sure was enjoying my agony, and was getting his so-called pound of flesh right out of my insides.

I saw directly enough that the prank that I had thought of to get me out of the Grave Shed had most definitely secured me a place in our wood shed. Propped up against the side of the bed of the caretaker's rig was a cement, two-and-a-half foot tall gravestone that read, "Euclid P. Hammarsen, Born 1902 Died 2002."

I was forced to tell the whole story to my folks and to the caretaker. I was so ashamed that I didn't even protest when my Ma uncharacteristically slapped my face. My Father drug me to the side of the house and gave me a logger-talkin' what-for likes of which I had never been given. When we came back, the old man was still there – and my Mother was paying him with our precious money for the wasted cement and for his work on the headstone.

As the old man turned to go, he picked up that blamed headstone and before he handed it to my Father, he looked to me and said very matter-of-factly words that haunted me my whole life, "May as well save it since there's no use to make another with this one already done. You – or I guess I should say, your folks – can always have the date recast."

He leaned down toward me, then, and I could see the thin dusting of grave dirt on his mean face and in his hair. His whiskey-soured breath pressed down on me through his brown and broken teeth, as he winked one of his yellowed eyes at me and whispered, "See you soon."

He backed off as my dog began to growl at him, and he got into his wagon and headed back towards town. I recall thinking that if I did die prematurely, in the height and glory of my youth, that I'd most rather have bears and the mountain lions take care of my final disposition than that dirty, foul-breathed man.

After the wagon was out of sight, I headed immediately to the wood shed without any prompting at all. It was the first whoopin' that I got that I didn't seem to mind too much. I deserved it. I was embarrassed of what I had done, and most of all I was sorry that I had made my Mother cry.

I never played much with Billy after that, and I spent a heap of time working off the money that my Ma had paid the caretaker for the cement. My Dad tossed the headstone into the bowels of our barn – intending on destroying the thing as soon as possible – but it was forgotten for years and years.

Chapter Eight

The Dancing Boats

"All fishermen are storytellers, but
not all storytellers are fisherman."
– Lois Totten, Resident

Deep in the river valley, past where the fiddler's
boy was found lays a mountain said to be the center of
creation for some of the local Indian tribes. The warm
waters of the Klamath, heated all day by the summer
sun, flow softly by the shady banks where the people
gather for their festival.

The water winds through the tall, mysterious
mountains, slowing as it comes near their holy grounds,
seemingly in reverence and tribute. There's a mess of
places on those sacred mountains where the Indians
worship their god during a festival that celebrates the
renewal of their world. It is a time and a place where
their secret names are spoken, where boats dance, and
where the women wear shells and the men wear nigh
unto nothing at all and dance like their Fathers and
grandfathers have danced through the ages.

My interest in the area was merely limited to the

humongous fish that were said to swim in the deep green pool. From upstream and avoiding the current on the one side, with a small weight on my hook, I had in the past let out over one hundred feet of my precious line and still hadn't touched the bottom. I just knew that those depths held some braggable fish, just like I knew the sun would set over Preston Peak each evening.

I had spent the entire afternoon fishing, and between navigating the game trail thoroughfares and climbing over riverside rocks I had made several miles on the south bank of the river without realizing that the day was slipping away from me. My dog lay sleeping on the warm rocks in the late afternoon sunlight. I, of course, was under the spell of the Klamath and my sport when I found myself opposite one of the most solemn Indian religious festivities – which also happened to be in that deepest pool of the river I had previously explained. Being a boy and curious by nature, I sat in the long, reedy brush and watched for a while. I recognized some of my school mates and people from the town. Although I thought that it was probably not true that the Great Master lived in a down-river mountain, and that the continuance of the world did not depend on the dances of those folks, I did respect their choice to believe it. I had also felt that awesome power in the river, and in the mountain, and in the trees that I climbed. I remember thinking that I wished that I had a church to go to with warm river rocks for pews and a roof of the sweet afternoon sky.

I was very naive about their religious ceremonies – I still am a jot, I suppose – as it was only around my 85th birthday that I finally figured out that the famous Pikyavish Ceremony I'd heard about all my life was not pronounced "pick-yer-wish" like I'd been mistakenly saying and thinking for so long. My apologies, brothers.

My pole, forgotten during my lookin'-in, rested on the rock nearest my foot. The bobber floated gently in the lapping waters. The drums began to beat, and the sound floated over the river to my hideaway. Across the Klamath I could see the participants lining up, and the leaders of the tribe started their boat dance. Cinder seemed oblivious to the sounds, sleeping off the dozens of miles she had crawled over and around rocks earlier that day.

It briefly occurred to me that apparently I was able to get myself into trouble without Billy McKetter's help – but like the budding genius that I was, I figured I'd avoid any trouble at all if no one saw me.

Paddling out towards where I was hiding, one man turned his ceremonial boat just in time to miss my fishing line, which had floated out farther than I had noticed. I grabbed my pole, and began to slowly pull in my line. I hoped that my cover would remain, so that I could continue to watch the ceremony. I also hoped that I wouldn't get caught. I stopped my line mid-pull, in awe, as the men began to sing in time with the drums. Was it the heartbeat of the land? Were those people right all along about our connection to the earth, river, and sky? The goosey-bumps sprung up on my arms.

The boats began to move across the water. They would fetch up, turn, spin, and charge away. Every movement was planned and seemed to tell part of a story that was unknown to me. The men's arms flexed and bowed as the weight of the boats as the current pulled at them. The drumbeats and low singing became louder and louder, until the heated air seemed to pulse and push in the rhythm.

As I watched all of that, in the settling dusk, a woman screamed and pointed in my direction. I was caught. I was ashamed. My Dad was gonna whip me extra fine for sure. I was found watching a ritual that I had no business being at.

Purt near every person at the ceremony turned and looked my way, but to my relief they were not pointing at me or my clandestine viewing area. They were pointing at the biggest, hugest, most beautiful fish I had ever seen. Jumping out of the Klamath waters, it twisted and turned, its' steely silver spine reaching toward the mountainous walls and its long tusks nearly piercing the sky. I stood and moved closer to the water, amazed at the giant fish and its' watery dance.

In that instant, I realized several things at once – that I had revealed myself of trespassing during the solemn and secret ceremony, that I was certainly going to be in sore trouble, that I was tangled in my fishing line, and that the line, now taut, was pulling me into one of the deepest holes in the mighty Klamath. Cinder had leapt up, and had pulled and grabbed my clothes in her teeth best she could while I struggled to kick loose of the line – but the fish was winning that tug-of-war. Frantically trying to free myself, my last thought before being pulled under the river water was a strange one. That I had finally hooked the Fabled Da Yao Yu.

My lungs began to burn at a killing pace, since I hadn't had much of a chance to take a breath before being dragged under the water. I could still hear Cinder barking above me, and I thought I saw her diving down for me once or twice. I'm pretty sure I heard her say, in Dog, that she'd get some help. It hurt to be under the water for so long, and I was awful frightened. I wanted to close my eyes and make it all go away, but I knew that I had only a short time to free myself from the line cat-tangle and the giant fish on the other end.

The greenish water became darker and darker as I was pulled deeper and deeper. I thought of all the times I had silently prayed for my line not to break when I got a big one on, and opined that I finally truly knew the school ma'am's definition of irony. I pulled at the line with all of my strength, and getting nowhere, I entertained the notion that it was, in fact, the horrible and tragic end of my life. All of those old ladies had been right, warning of the danger of drowning. All of the good deeds I had done in my young life would be forgotten, and I would forever be remembered as the Boy Who Liked To Catch Fish But Died When He Was Caught By A Fish. I would become a story, and a warning to other children who dared to go near the danger-filled river.

As the stabbing pain in my ears continued, and my lungs screamed for air I nearly became resigned to my fate and thought that if I just stopped fighting that the horrible pain would be over soon.

Still being dragged lower into the water, I gave surviving another shot. Who would take care of my parents and my dog if I just gave up and died like the big chicken Billy McKetter always said I was? I put my right hand over my mouth and with my left I pinched my nose. Looking down into the blackness where the fish had gone, I saw a few flashes of its' silver body. I started to black out a little, and then almost fatally gasped in that thick Klamath water when the giant fish made a swift turn and then began swimming at full speed upward – right towards me.

I found out later that above the water, during my whole drowning affair, the ceremony was turned upside down. After the initial shock of the whole scene wore off, many of the men who had been performing the boat dance had drifted too far down river to help me. People on the shore were yelling in all manner of languages, and some were simply just screaming. My dog was barking and yapping like a wild animal, running up and down the opposite bank – trying to get someone to help. I heard later that because my tragedy occurred during the middle of the ritual, many in the crowd thought that no one should enter the water to retrieve me – as the river spirit or some such thing had deliberately taken me as a sign to all and was not to be fooled with. Others gathered alongside the river were urging the boat dancers to return to the shore for their own safety. The women of the tribe, who had been placed a safe ways from the river and the male ceremony, were keening and chanting – except for one.

Adal Oak Bottom was as old as the river and the mountains. She had trouble walking without her cane, and was almost hopelessly lost trying to move over the round rocks near the river. Common thought was that she was purt nearly blind and deaf, and perhaps a jot touched by the spirits. She was rumored to be the cousin of the hanged Modoc Kintpuash – locally known as Captain Jack – and had grown up in the Lost River area as a child. She was the mother of fourteen children, the grandmother of forty, and the great-grandmother of a hundred. She always had a baby in her arms and children at her feet. Even people who weren't related to her called her Gram Adal. I had met her the year before, in school, when she came each week to teach the Indian kids about their language. Not knowing that I wasn't really invited, I tagged along to all of the special classes that were given. She had made me feel welcome, and she seemed to enjoy having me in her lessons. She had even made us some bitter acorn stew and brought some dried eel meat to taste.

Now, as I was drowning, the aged woman leapt into action. Deftly maneuvering around the women and the men that stood in her way, she bounded like a light-footed deer from round river rock to round river rock. The ancient tumbled granite seemed to have been placed on the river side for her exact purposes. Onlookers, unsure of what to do before, stood with mouths agape at Gram Adal's incredible response.

As the old woman dashed onward, her ceremonial dress of white and light-tan buckskin and sewn-on sea shells barely kept up with her. People said later that she seemed to be scanning the water *ka'am* and *yu'ruk* for any evidence of me as she ran, like a river osprey looking for a steelhead. Seeing bubbles of air that had just left my lungs rise to the water's surface, she planted both feet at the river's edge, and with all of her built-up momentum from her incredible run she launched herself into the air and over the river just like she had gone off a fancy springed diving board. Reaching the apex of her flight, she drew her arms out and for one brief part of a second, the sun shone one of its descending last beams perfectly on her and the beaded shells on her dress, and many swore afterward that she had turned into a giant white falcon.

Apparently, unknown to me as I prepared to drown under the Klamath's waters, the fish had also caught sight of her. My Father gently said in private to my Mother and me, when later speaking of the events, that the giant watery beast must have thought she was the end-all be-all fishing lure of all time.

I had thought that the fish had turned and was

swimming right up toward me as fast as it could – probably to gore me with it's tusks or at least run me through with it's sharp spines – but in fact he was swimming up to make a jump for Gram Adal's shiny dress.

As she dove into the river to get me, the fish breeched out of the water to get her and missed. I can just imagine the startled look on each of their faces as they passed each other midair. Gram Adal continued in to save me, and in my state of near death in the darkened water I looked up to see a beautiful ethereal woman swimming toward me. Her long gray hair had become unbraided and trailed behind her and around her, and her shell-beaded dress floated about her as if she was a mermaid or an angel. In those brief moments, the darkness of the water took the wrinkles from her face and the gray from her hair, and I moved my hand toward the outstretched arms of that beautiful and strong Indian girl. My fingertips brushed hers, and I smiled in spite of my closeness to a watery death because I was so happy to see her rescuing arms reaching out for me.

The fish had other plans for me, though. Perhaps he was irritated at the whole affair, and missing the beaded dress made him that much madder. He wriggled and twisted and flung himself so far into the air, that just as I was almost safely in Gram Adal's arms, the line attached to my legs grew taut once again and I was pulled away by the fish.

Believe you me it must have been called a fish story, every time it was retold. I was there, and a part of it and even after all of these years I cannot say for sure exactly what happened next. Somehow, when the giant fish leapt higher in the air out of spite it also pulled me from the water, courtesy of the ten pound test line that was wrapped around my leg. The murderous fish jumped so high that the line that attached both of us got caught in a single tall snag leaning over the river. With the fish hanging in the tree and unable to go anywhere, I continued my momentum after him and landed in a tangle in the tree as well, ending up sitting easy-as-you-please on the branch above him.

The evil fish thrashed and moved about below me, and I grabbed a tight hold on the tree branch just in case it got free and tried to drag me somewhere else. I took so many deep breaths of that sweet late summer riverside air that I thought I was going to get sick.

A cheer went up from the crowd, and Gram Adal had slowly pulled herself from the river just in time to see me land in the tree. Later my mom explained to me about the old lady's amazing rescue attempt – that some women who are true and unselfish mothers would do anything to try to save a child from death – even if the child wasn't her own.

I am still grateful to Gram Adal for trying to save me. If it hadn't been for her dress shining during her heroic flight, the fish probably would have pulled me deeper to my watery grave. I would have missed so much if I had indeed died that day.

My faithful dog, seeing me finally out of the water, leapt in from where she had been and crossed the wide Klamath in moments – hardly getting wet in the course. She was at the base of the snag, waiting for me and keeping a watchful eye on the Monster Fish even before I was undone and let down.

Now I've been on both ends of a ten-pound-test line during my life – more often on the fishing pole end – but I've never seen line act that strong before or after that day. For some reason, I still prefer to use the National Trout Catcher brand ten-pound-test made in Gary, Indiana – with the packaging that proudly states, "Guaranteed to land the fishing excitement of your life." Well, if those folks only knew. I have to also say that I take great care, since that day, where my line is laying and where my feet may be.

The chanting began again as the fish and I were both pulled down from the tree. Someone sent for my folks. I looked that giant and ancient fish right in one of the black fishy eyes and told it, "Seems like I won, Da Yao Yu – your days of trying to drown children are over," right before I whacked it in the noggin with a piece of wood. It was a bit of a dramatic statement, but I had recently been without air for over two-hundred elephants and I was pretty scared as well.

My brush with death only a short jot behind me, I recall thinking that I couldn't wait to tell War Sing of my fight with the infamous monster.

The women prepared the giant fish, and half of it was roasted on a hot fire made from two twelve-foot fir logs. Everyone ate until they were chock-full, and then had a jot bit more, and even had some left for one and all to take a quantity of fish meat home. That half of fish fed over two hundred hungry people. The other half of the fish was smoked over the fire on sticks for the next few days, and provided food for the Indian folk and my family for a while. It has been said that the fish was as big as three wagons, tied end to end. That is a pure exaggeration – I'm quite sure that it was only as big as two wagons, and maybe adding the length of a horse.

War Sing arrived first, told by a passing man on the road that the child called "Jack's Boy" had drowned. I found out later that War Sing nigh unto killed his beautiful horse that day, riding it so hard and so fast without stopping to get to where the Boat Dance was held. When he saw me, he ran up to me and purt nearly crushed me in his strong arms. All I remember him saying, over and over in his funny misinterpretation of our talk, was, "You're trout, you're trout!" Meaning, of course, that I was out of the water – but that nickname stuck to me for a good eighty years or so. Some folks don't know me by anything but Trout to this day. The handle also seemed appropriate to some, since I had been able to stay under the water for so long without drowning. I attributed that to all of the days in school, where – bored senseless – I'd resort to holding my breath and counting. I'd counted as high as one-hundred-fifty elephants in my prime, during one especially long lesson about past participles.

Needless to say, when my Mother and Father arrived at the fish feast I got a rough talking to. My Ma only could look at me and cry. Gram Adal, back to hobbling and meandering over the rocks, took them both aside after my Father was done yelling at me.

Through my tears, sitting on a rock that my Mother had forbid me to move from, I tried to watch Gram Adal's animated speech to my parents – one moment wagging her fingers in their faces and the next hugging the stuffing out of them. When they returned to me at my rock of exile, all of the anger was gone from their voices and they held me until all of our tears were dry.

Years later, my Mother told me that during the talk Gram Adal had slowly and patiently explained to them about each one of her sisters, brothers, children, grandchildren, and great-grandchildren that she had helped bury with her own hands because they had lost their battle with the Klamath. She told them also of others whom she could never bury, as the river forever held them in a watery grave instead. She commanded my Father and Mother to leave their anger and fear and appreciate the fact that the Spirit had allowed their wonderfully defiant and curious son – me – to be drawn forth from a certain and horrible death. She was sure that I had some great task yet to do for the world, and had to stay until it was done.

A picture of that day showed up in a local historical journal about sixty years after it had happened, and the question was raised in that elite and rarefied academic community regarding the authenticity of the likeness. On its face, it does look like it should be a made-up thing, what with the amazing size of the fish and all. Apparently, an enlightened jackdaw from some University in the Eureka area looked at the photo for a coon's age, and determined by it's markings that the fish was more than likely a 300-year-old river sturgeon – or *Ish'xikih'ar* – with a snout-horn to tail-fin measurement of over twenty-six feet. He wrote some kind of scholarly paper about the whole thing, and caused quite a stir with all of his fellow learned folks.

I'm not sure about all of that Academic Work. I do recall that we ate the fish in question with the Indian folks and as we feasted the story of the day was retold several times. With my parents' permission, I was given a secret name and became an adopted member of Gram Adals' extended family. I won't tell here what that secret name is – I never will – but it adds to this tale to hint to you that the main words in it are not noble sounding like "Eagle" or "Warrior" but can be loosely translated, instead, to the words like "bait" and "fish-hook".

Chapter Nine

The Fall of a Great Man

"It's a rough life and a rough land, and more than not – it's a rough death."
– Carter Matthews, Resident

There are many local treasure tales about the Chinaman's Lost Fortune. Some buried boxes of gold have been found that probably were left by those departed miners, and about two years ago an ivory carving of a Buddha was unearthed during a road construction project near the Ferry Point. I'm hopeful that most of the lost treasure will never be unearthed or stumbled upon, but once again I find I'm getting ahead of myself in that story.

I've taken great pains in these pages to obscure certain locations that I'm referring to, in hopes that the treasures that are described in this journal are not widely found out. There will be those folks, who have grown up in this area like me, who will know straight away the places I'm mentioning – but of course, they're not the folks I'm worried about.

As a boy, I didn't recognize any of the historical problems atwixt the white man, the Chinese, and the Indians. My Father was a white man, and he had several friends that were white, Chinese, and Indian. Decades before I had heard of the teachings of Dr. King, my Father taught me about judging men by their actions and their character and by how they put in a days work. My Father had no use for a lazy man, and was not afraid to tell a man he needed to hold up his end of the saw, if you know what I mean.

In a mining and logging community, folks were really close. You learned who you could depend on. You learned which man on the work crew you could trust with your life. To my Father, the color of their skin wasn't important. Even then, in the river valley, along about August, every man was the same deep bronze color from the searing workday sun.

My Father knew that War Sing was one of those people that could be counted on. Their friendship had grown steadily over the years they had known each other, and my Mother and I had been told by my Father in a very matter of fact and practical fashion that if something was to happen to him that War Sing would be the one to look to for help to button up our little farm before Ma and I took leave and went east to family. We didn't like to talk about tragic possibilities like that, but then it was the necessary and responsible thing to do.

On that day in early June, when the river was still swollen and dirty from the snow pack run off from the high country War Sing and my Father decided to finally move a giant rock on *Hard Luck #3*. War Sing ate breakfast with us – like he often did – before he and my

Father planned to head to the mine and meet up with some other fellas who had agreed to give them a hand.

We had a full table of oatmeal and chicken eggs and some fried pork from the spring hog that had been salted away, and we talked and laughed and carried on just like we always had. I was even able to slip Cinder nearly a full plate of food under the table without getting caught once. School was out and the sun was shining and my head was swimming with all of the possibilities that the summer held.

Then War Sing announced, in the midst of our breakfast banter and my daydreaming something that made us all stop in our tracks.

"I'm going home to China soon, and I will never be able to return."

My Father and Mother looked at each other, and then they both looked at me, and then at the very same exact moment we all started asking questions of War Sing at the same time. My dog even came out from under the table to see what had happened, like she sensed that all of our hearts had just been broken in one fell swoop.

"I'm needed by my family," he said, and then looking at our faces, he added with a smile, "by my Chinese family." We started talking at the same time again, making an uproar that he had to almost yell over.

"I've known this day would come, and I've been preparing for it. I don't want to leave the River Canyon, but I have a larger obligation in my country." Clapping his hands together and trying his best smile, he said, "Enough of the long faces! We'll have plenty of time to talk about this after the work is done today."

My Father agreed, and gave a funny look to my

Mother – like they already knew more about War Sing's move than I did. I just stared at the table top in front of me, wondering why and how War Sing would ever consider leaving us – effectively taking away my Father's best friend and leaving me uncle-less.

I had planned to go along to help with the rock-moving effort, but I was conscripted into garden service by my Mother instead. I was a little sore that my Dad didn't override her request, so I just gave him and War Sing a little wave as they left our dooryard. I learned that day what a mistake it could be to part like that, and since then I've tried real hard to remember that lesson when ever taking leave of someone I cared for.

I recall that for two years before that awful day my Father and War Sing had talked about the possible riches that the river had deposited beneath the mammoth rock. Anyone who has read the river and the banks while mining could tell that it was a money rock – for hundreds, or maybe thousands of years before the river path changed, heavy winter currents had slammed into the bank where it sat. The placer gold, flaky and free-formed, would have been knocked loose from its high mountain home by erosion or a higher winter stream to eventually rake and scrape its way to the Klamath. There, it was rolled by the waters into the popular nugget form as the winter flows moved it down stream. This bend in the river, where that rock sat, was one of the many points on the Klamath that the river failed to be strong enough to keep its treasure moving. I imagined that water had slammed into the bedrock wall, all those years ago, curled over a bit, and smashed full force into the boulder. The newly-born shape-changing nuggets of gold, heavier than the other rocks and gravel that it traveled with, would be wedged into the nooks and crannies washed out by the river. This rock was perfect for prospecting.

My Father and War Sing had been very optimistic about the color that may lie beneath the *Hard Luck #3* obstacle, but they both knew that it would be very dangerous.

In their anticipation, they had made and revised several plans to move the giant boulder from its footings. Placed on the bedrock, but not attached to it, they figured that with the use of several pulleys and ropes, as well as the two strongest mules, they would be able to move the heavy rock. Dynamite was crossed of the list quickly, as it would only blow the whole works to the sky – erasing any chance of retrieving the hidden color.

As the story goes, it was in the morning that the accident happened. Like many River Canyon mornings, by nine o'clock it was already over a hundred degrees. On the way to the job, War Sing and my Father happened upon the Running Indian and asked him if he wanted a ride. The man grunted "No, the heat is good for me if I want to win the race."

They grinned and waved and moved on through towards their claim, used to not paying too much attention to certain eccentricities folks showed now and again.

Soon the men had assembled the required mules, ropes, and pulleys and extra help to move the big rock. War Sing had asked several of the other Celestial to come along and lend a hand. My Father had said that he was glad that morning to see them all, since it was common knowledge that each one of these select workers could do the work of three other men.

They placed bars under one side of the rock, and

began to pry and inch the big boulder loose. The water had become just barely low enough at that time of the year that the men could walk most of the way around it without having to get into the cold river. After about two hours they stopped for a lunch break, and sat in the shade of a grove of tall firs as they ate. My Father always says that he began to get a funny feeling along about then. Something that he couldn't quite put his finger on. While all of the other men laughed and ate, he said he sat and studied the lines and tie offs and pulleys that crisscrossed the small work area. His Father had at one time been a sailor, and had taught my Father all about ropes and knots. He was still studying the layout when War Sing called everyone back to the job.

It was decided that each man would work a rope, pulling and adjusting the lines as my Father and War Sing pried the rock. Some of the men were joking about the riches that lay beneath the stone, but most of them just wanted to get the job done and get out of the hot sun.

On War Sings' signal, the men were ready and the work started. Little by little, the rock moved. Progress was good, and everything was going well. The ropes creaked and the men groaned, but they had all done this type of rock moving before. The huge boulder got closer and closer to revealing its hidden treasures.

That was where the problems started. Like most tragedies, people will talk about them afterwards and some will place blame. The common opinion about that tragedy was an observation that the equipment failed the men. For the rest of his life, my Father's opinion was that he failed the men. He never forgave himself, and carried that heavy burden to his end.

The workers found themselves at an impasse, and even with the ropes taut and the full complement of men pulling with all of their strength the huge rock held. After some conversation, my Father made his way around the underside of the rock to find out what was keeping them from pulling the reluctant boulder all the way over. He found that a small group of stones, fitted like a puzzle, were in the way and would need to be removed before they could progress. Shouting instructions to those above, he was handed down a pry bar and some wood. With the boards he quickly placed a makeshift safety brace so that if the boulder was inclined to roll toward him, the brace would push the boulder another direction. War Sing directed the operation above and below at the same time. The men stood ready for the call to pull. My Father stood ready to pry the rocks out of the way.

War Sing looked down to my Father, and said, "Are you ready, friend?" My Father nodded and yelled, "Yes!" War Sing gave the signal and the men above pulled as my Father pried at the rocks. One large rock in the puzzle work below came tumbling out, revealing another behind it. Angry and tired he reached in closer and pushed more of the obstructions out of the way. Above, the men pulled and groaned. The rock began to inch its way over. My Father pulled back his pry bar and began to move to safety.

Even though the river was low, the little rapids near the mine were still chock-full with water. The tumbling and churning of the river was loud, especially behind the boulder, and my Father never heard the men yelling.

In the span of seconds, several things happened. One of the pulleys fell, and the rope in it went slack.

That affected the dynamics of the whole operation, and the boulder began to ease back into its former spot. War Sing yelled for my Father, and for the men to hold steady. Ropes were beginning to slip, and men – knowing what was likely to happen – were holding their places even though their hands were starting to bleed.

That part of the story I pieced together from what I heard in the town and from the little that my Father told me directly about it. The rest of what happened that day I know from hearing my Mother and Father speak of it as they were sitting on the front porch. They thought I was asleep.

Apparently, the men only held the ropes that way for seconds, as it was impossible for them to keep the rock from moving back. In fact, with the absence of the one rope and pulley, some of the men were unknowingly pulling the rock back into its old position. My Father moved to the safety area, behind the brace board. He said that at that time he had no idea that anything was wrong.

War Sing looked for my Father, and could not see him. Without concern for himself, he scrambled down and around the boulder to get my Father out. At that point, another one of the overloaded pulleys broke, sending the whole operation closer to disaster.

The broken pulley flew through the air at the same time War Sing found my Father. He motioned that they needed to get up and away, and both started climbing. My Father didn't understand what was wrong, but he trusted War Sing. The Celestial reached down a hand for my Father, and right then the heavy pulley hit my Father behind the left ear. Stunned and hurt, my Father fell into the path of the boulder. Instantly, War Sing jumped down and pushed my Father out of the way.

The men, knowing that something had happened as they saw the boulder move backwards and settle, ran to help. They found my Father, aware after purt nearly being put away by the flying pulley, holding tight the unmoving hand of his friend while trying to push the impossibly heavy boulder off of him. War Sing's chest had been pinned and crushed.

War Sing was dying and nothing could be done. My Father brushed his hair aside and told him to hold strong – that the men were going quick for another pry bar and it'd be real soon that he'd be got out of the whole mess. War Sing looked up at my Father with what was later referred to by several onlookers as a gentle peace on his face and in his final words he said, "Jack, I finally found the treasure under the temple."

Blood began to pool out then from under the giant boulder, into the wet dark sand and flowing over the bits of river gravel before running through the bedrock crevices. My Father pushed and pushed on the rock with all that he had, and even with others jumping down to try to move the killing stone it did not give at all. I was told later that my Father did not break his right hand in the accident, but after – trying to push that rock off of his friend.

And then War Sing was gone – lifeless and pinned in that hot and deadly place, having given his life for his friend. War Sing was trapped and killed instead of my Father.

He was buried on a hillside overlooking his beloved Klamath River. My Mother and Father stood quietly holding my hands as we watched the ancient ceremony. A carved stone was placed above War Sing's head and marked his resting place. Although I could not read the inscriptions, I knew that they were characters from his land and his family name. Each picture was a set of words, but to me some looked like flowing water or the starry skies or the treed mountainside and even one resembled a mother holding a child. It was so achingly sad for me to think that this man, our friend, was to be forever so far away from his family and from the land where he grew up. Were the hills of his youth like these? Were the waters of his rivers greener or clearer than the Klamath? I was simply crestfallen for his Mother and Father, who would never again see their son.

To make it all worse, if that was possible at all, I kept thinking on how he had only been weeks away from seeing them again when he had died. I felt ashamed and selfish, thinking on how I had wanted him to stay with us.

My sweet dog, who had jumped from the wagon and nudged in behind me at some time during the ceremony, sat respectfully listening to the words that I couldn't understand either. When the Chinese words were done, I saw her look up at me with a true sadness. She watched my tears welling up in my eyes, where they'd pool and overflow out and down my sad face. She stepped toward the fresh-dirt grave as respectfully as I suppose a dog could – and looking over her shoulder just once at my Father, my Mother and I – she sat where I figured War Sing's feet ought to be and let out a lonely and long wolf-like call that brought shivers to my spine. Her kind had been out of the wild for thousands of years, but she showed that the wild was still in her. She bowed her head, after, and walking past me toward the wagon she looked up and I swear I saw tears in my friend's eyes. Not one of the Chinese folks batted an eye at Cinder's display of grief, so we didn't say anything either.

The two Chinese fellas that War Sing had worked with quite a lot were the last of his folk to begin to leave the grave site. They stood over his headstone in quiet mourning before they paid their respects to my Father, bowing with tear-filled eyes of their own. War Sing had often called them Cho and Jin – shortening their given names for our ease. I don't figure they expected the thick bear hugs that my Father laid upon them, as their faces turned so red as a result I was afraid my Father had removed their ability to breathe altogether. I had been on the business end of those hugs several times, and the two men had my double sympathies.

They were let go after a bit, and when they regained their breath they marched down the hill a ways before they began what sounded like an argument with each other. I overheard several words that I almost could place from my years of being underfoot War Sing, but the meanings were just above my bend. Their argument continued into the distance, and as they raised their voices to each other as they went along eventually they were far enough away that we couldn't hear them anymore. I was so sad that I hardly paid attention to them, and my Father and Mother seemed to ignore them as well.

Looking around, I noticed other Celestial burial sites were not marked well. I remember thinking that it was a shame that no one seemed to care for those other men. I didn't know at the time that the resting places were intended to be temporary, as the Chinese belief mandated that the bones had to be returned to their homeland of China before the owner could ascend to his Heavenly Reward.

About the same time War Sing died, a country-wide conflict in China began and many of the young men were called home. The thirty-year-old Chinese Exclusion Act was finally being enforced in our little river valley by some new miners that were looking to take over the local Celestial holdings and claims – ensuring that the remaining hold-out Chinese left directly.

Later that evening a small procession of the Chinese folks showed up at our house, led by his two friends, Cho and Jin. They had gathered up War Sing's belongings from their shared bunkhouse in the little Chinese-town where War Sing had stayed. According to custom, as War Sing's closest family, they presented my Father with a small trunk and a few boxes. When Cho handed one heavy box to my Father I saw a definite glare and anger in Jin's eyes. A few words followed from Jin to Cho, but I only understood brief pieces like "duty" and "wrong path." With the last piece delivered, and the last bows made, wordlessly Cho and Jin walked away in separate directions from each other and we never saw either of them in the river valley again.

At that time, we mistook their anger toward each other for grief. There was no way for us to know at that time what their argument was about.

Later that evening, sitting at the kitchen table, my Father looked through the papers and belongings intending of course to send them all home to his friend's real family in China. We tried to make heads and tails of the beautiful writing, but we could not tell the difference atwixt a supplies list and an address. Over the next month or so, we asked quite a lot of the Chinese workers whom War Sing had trusted to translate the papers for us, but nairn of them knew how to read or write the fancy script War Sing had used. They explained that in their homeland, there were thousands of different languages and ways to write. One fella who had worked with my Father and War Sing on several occasions got a few words out of one of the papers, and then abruptly stopped – with his apologies – telling my Father that he just couldn't make out the symbols. The way he acted made me think he wasn't telling the whole truth, and my Father noticed it as well.

I could tell that my Father was very sad and frustrated that we could not understand the writing, and he spoke several times of the need to contact War Sing's family.

We set back into the routine of our lives, the best we could. Almost every time we turned around there was another reminder that War Sing was gone – I recall that my Mother set out four breakfast plates, by habit, for the longest time.

I remember that it was not long after when I stumbled across my Father in the barn. He was standing in front of the box that held War Sings papers, and was leaned forward with his shoulders slumped and his head nodded down. I was about to ask him what he was doing, when I heard him start to sob. I immediately hid – knowing that what was happening I was not meant to see – and having seen it, I knew that it would have embarrassed my Father to know that I saw him cry.

His wrenching sobs only continued for a while, and then I heard his voice whispering through the still barn. He was talking to War Sing, one last time.

"You spoke so often of your family. I know that you loved them and you planned to return to them.

"Your people are leaving here, more and more

every day. No one can or will tell me how to find where your family was, and no way for me to get your belongings to your kin."

Holding all of War Sing's papers – envelopes with red wax seals, scrolls with golden writing, what looked like letters or journal writings, and even a curious map with no recognizable markings – my Father must have known that all of the answers that he looked for were at the tips of his fingers but that the distance atwixt War Sing's language and ours was farther than could be bridged.

"I wish that there was a way for me to let your family know where you are now, but I can't read this damnable chicken scratch."

I was unaware of all of the reasons – and the most important reason – why my Father needed to know where War Sing's family was. I just assumed that he wanted to send the box to them out of respect, with the main goal to let them know the tragic fate of their son. Looking back at my knowledge of the situation, I didn't know a hill of beans about what really may have been going on. I never would have believed, then, that it was possible that the fate of thousands of people lay in the letters in my Father's hands.

I had assumed a lot about War Sing, and in my limited perspective of him and the world and my place in it – I was sure I had understood the situation pretty daisy. I was mistaken.

Closing the box, my Father slid it against the wall and it became part of the landscape of the tool bench. The bench was the only part of our house or property that my Mother and I were not allowed to freely use.

As he left the barn, I heard him say, "I'm sorry, friend." I continued to hide for several more minutes, and then ran like heck around the back of the barn and up the hill so I could make a great show of having been above the house the whole time. During my evasive maneuvers I began to hatch a plan to resolve the problem for my heart-sore Father. I figured out a course of action that had no real chance of working, but I was naive enough to think that it would.

It took almost a month but I worked like the devil to complete all of the steps necessary for my plan to get off the ground. My first move was to go to War Sing's gravesite, where I transferred the carvings on to paper I had brought by rubbing the paper, placed over the headstone, with a small piece of charcoal. Then, when my Father was gone from the house and my Mother was busy with the laundry chores, I snuck to the off-limits tool bench where my Father kept War Sing's papers and belongings. I had learned in school, watching Albert Flemming forge a note to the school ma'am, that if you held up something to a bright window and put another piece of paper over it that you could closely copy what was on the paper underneath. Unfortunately for Albert that day, his copy wasn't nearly good enough and I'm sure his seat still smarts from the whoopin' Mrs. Hudson gave him, and from the additional whoopin' his Ma and Pa administered later when they found out. From talking to Howard, and remembering something from one of the San Francisco papers, my plan began to come together fully. I knew I had to be done before August 1st, when the Running Indian was lighting out.

Since I had already resigned myself to the fact I was probably fixin' to get my own whoopin' for sneaking through War Sing's papers and such I figured that the window method was good enough for my secret purposes, and with the daylight shining through the shed window I could almost exactly copy the strange characters onto my paper.

At one point in my copying travails, I was almost caught by my Father. He walked in just as I had finished putting everything back in order – the papers just so in the box, the wood adze just so leaning against it, and the whole mess exactly like my Dad had left it. I had forgotten to push War Sing's box all the way to the wall, like it had been. My Father noticed instantly that it was out of place and he walked right past me to look it over. He turned to me with anger on his face, and bellowed, "Boy, have you gotten into that box?"

His brows were furrowed, and his ears were red, and I saw his hands tightened into fists like he was fixin' to tear down the barn – or me.

Not being a natural liar, or having much practice with it, I blurted out five words that baptized me into the dark world of deceit and would haunt me and my conscience for countless hours.

Looking into his angry face, I stood up as straight as I could and put my hands on my hips and heard myself say, "Absolutely not, Dad." And then to seal my fate as a doomed sinner, before I could stop it my mouth added, "I swear."

He took me at my word and calmed down a bit, pushing the box back into its proper place. As he walked out of the barn, he turned to me and said, "Sorry, Uke, that I thought you may have been messing with that box. I know you better than that."

And there it was, my first lie to my Father hanging heavy around my neck and dragging my steps wherever I would go. It was a strangling feeling to carry that with me, and even though I tried to rationalize what I had done and what I had said to him it was no matter – I had betrayed a trust that I had worked hard my whole life to deserve.

I quit off the copying for a while. Looking back, I know that was my only attempt to redeem myself and be shut of the whole thing. I'd like to say that I did the right thing, and confessed and learned and moved on. But I didn't. I recall arguing with myself over the whole thing – a fight was had between my good reason and my poor judgment each of those days. I had faced the fact that I'd started out with the copying for a good reason – to help my Father. I also knew that when I took it up again about a week later – when my good reason finally lost out – it was because I was selfishly intrigued with the mystery of the whole business and the excitement of finding the treasure that War Sing had mentioned when he was dying. I am ashamed to even put those words on this journal paper, now. The eighty or so years between this day and that one have done nothing to erase my embarrassment at talking myself into being a liar and risking my Father's respect for me.

After a few weeks of this secret tracing – and almost being caught on several more occasions – I added two letters to the stack of copied papers. From my recollection of the newspaper article and the teacher's speech about it I knew I needed to contact Professor Hayes of Chinese Studies or some such thing who resided in the great university in San Francisco. The first letter was addressed to him – and I felt I could trust him solely because he was a fellow Ivanhoe enthusiast. The other letter was to the parents or family of War Sing, wherever they were and whoever they were. I put the whole mess of copied documents and my letters in a large envelope, and went to the roadway to wait for the Running Indian to come by.

Chapter Ten

The Misery Whip

"Wood is the only fuel that warms you twice."
– Beans Goff, Resident

Most mornings I could be found in the kitchen sitting next to the wood stove. Cinder would always be close by, enjoying the stove heat as much as I did.

My Mother took a cotton to build a scorching fire early in the morning to warm up the house, and she would dampen it down later on to keep the house warm for the rest of the day. She was a very frugal woman in all aspects of her life, except for wood use. My Father would laugh and shake his head with every armload of wood he'd bring up to the back porch. It seemed amusing to him as well that the woman who would cut the send-away store catalog into small pieces for use in the privy – with a two page usage limit rule – would freely load the woodstove day after day like the wood walked itself out of the forest and into the woodshed just as easy as you please. But we didn't mind much, even though we pretended to give her ribbings about it. She didn't like to be cold. Neither did we.

The only months that we didn't have a morning fire were July and August. There were many June mornings, where we lived, where the frost was silver on the ground in the same day that later would sport temperatures over a hundred degrees. For us, wood cutting and splitting and hauling was a banausic and year-long chore.

Every spring my Father would size me up and measure my arms on his saw. When I had turned ten he said that I was almost long enough and strong enough for the misery whip. For the next month I refused to eat any vegetables at supper time. Angering my Father, he questioned me strongly about my waste of food. Eventually I admitted to him that I didn't want to eat the vegetables or greens because they were supposed to make me grow, and that I didn't want to be long and strong enough for the misery whip. I knew I was going to get a spanking, for being stubborn and for shirking work, but my folks' reaction surprised me. Both of my reserved parents were holding their sides in bellowing laughter. My Father, after composing himself, mentioned something like, "Son, if it was that easy to escape the whip, I wouldn't eat greens either."

By the time I was twelve, I was indeed long and strong enough. Years of hard work at home and at the mines had given my child's body man's muscles. My attitude had also changed about the whip, after watching my Mother and Father struggle with it just a few days after War Sing was buried. Sometimes, we had traded game or eggs for help from some of the Norecross boys to cut our logs into rounds, but most often War

Sing had helped work the handle opposite my Father.

At that time I wanted very much to be treated like a man, and I knew that the only way to be considered one was to work like one. I also had spent a lot of time daydreaming about being in the logging contest at the Jamboree. My Father and War Sing always had competed as a team in the whip saw event, and they had no equals on the river. I wanted to feel that glory, and the joy of winning. Most of all, I thought that if I started to do some of the mining, hunting, and adventurin' that War Sing had done with my Father, that maybe his sadness would be lifted a little.

I had watched several Jack of The Woods competitions in the past. I was enthralled by the level of skill that most of the men in the competition presented. There were events like the axe throw, the pole climb, the log chop, and of course my favorite, the whip saw event.

When those loggin' fellas came through at the start of the competitions us kids would gather around like somebody famous just walked by. It was strange to see them in their logging gear, but with clean faces and clean hands. Usually those fellas were dirty, greasy, and grimy real soon after they put those clothes on.

Today they have chainsaw competitions as well, but at the start of it all of the events were powered by men.

I spent the rest of the spring and that summer jumping on the other end of the misery whip every time I got a chance to. Without being asked, I would be a quick and ready hand any time one was needed. I still spent a lot of time daydreaming about my Father and I being the fastest whip sawyer team in the River Canyon. After a full afternoon on one of the ends of the saw, though, I would put off those daydreams for about a week or until my back was less sore. I figure that pulled muscles are the best reminder of how tough something is to do.

Nowadays I figure most folks don't realize what a godsend chainsaws were. On a good day, we may have been able to fell three or four large trees – almost more than we could buck up and split for firewood in a week. We knew a fella that had a team of pulling horses, and sometimes we'd trade him some gold to pull our logs down the hill towards our house so we could work on them a little at the time. My Father always said that there was no such thing as too much firewood, and knowing how my Mother liked to burn it I had to agree.

When I started to take over the saw duties, in War Sing's absence, I could tell by the look on my Father's face that I wasn't doing a very good job. Round about the end of that summer I was keeping up pretty well. I don't think that my increasing skills had anything to do with natural talent or ability – just the fact that I'd had so much darned practice.

One afternoon we had been working above our house, trying to take down a giant sized sugar pine that looked like it was ready to fall anyway. It was quite a tree – it looked like it had been hit by lightning on several occasions. On the outside, spiraling sections of bark were missing, probably from where the lightning had raced down the tree to the ground. I figured, by the way was leaning, that some of the roots must be killed off under the electrocuted side and over time they had lost their hold due to rot or decay. The damage of the tree was a factor in our choice to cut it, but equally important was the fact that it posed quite a risk to our home and to all of the other trees around it. We had to take special care while cutting, watching out for pockets of decay that could send the whole thing a tumbling down on our heads.

Previous to that day my Mother had never seen us fall a tree with the whip saw. I figure she assumed that there wasn't a lot to it because it was done all the time. Believe you me, it was one of the most dangerous things that we could ever have been involved with. There were about only one or two ways to bring down a tree, but there were about six hundred different ways that it could kill you as it fell.

We lit into that tree at about 10 a.m., and it only took me a little while to get my rhythm down. My Mother was looking at us from our dooryard, and I sure had a proud feeling about me with her watching us work. We sawed on and on that morning and after about two hours we only got about halfway through. It was a lot bigger tree than I thought it was when we started. At around noon time Mother called us down for a little bit of lunch, and we were luckily at the spot where we could stop for a jot.

Being a well taught fella, I took my boots off before going into the house. We were just eating our first helping of my Mother's wonderful supper when we heard a crack that sounded like the world was being opened up. There was a crash, and then there was a shaking of the ground so terrible that I thought for sure we were done for. To top it all off I heard a strange noise that seemed to fly over the top of our house and toward the crick. Still with our sandwiches in our hands and in our stocking feet, my Father and I lit outside to see what happened.

We couldn't believe what we saw. It was amazing that no one had got killed.

The hundred foot tall sugar pine, with our

whipsaw having only gone halfway through its base, had give up the ghost and decided just to lay down and be done with it. While we were eating our lunch supper, a gust of wind must have helped it finish the job we started.

There were branches and downed trees everywhere. Many of the trees that were still able to stand next to where the sugar pine fell had suffered quite a bit of limb damage from the big tree coming down. I gulped at my sandwich, and quickly laced up my boots. I clum over a lot of branches, and under a few as well, helping my Dad look for our missing whipsaw. We looked, and looked, and looked and it was nowhere to be found. Then I recalled the strange sound I've heard that seemed to move from where the tree had been and progressed over our house and toward the crick.

My Father just looked at me funny when I abandoned the mess of tree limbs and started walking towards the crick. I figured he thought I was up to some prank or that I had possibly just decided to quit for a bit and go for a swim. I hollered up to him when I found what I had been looking for. Right off I spotted it – our treasured whipsaw – lodged sharp side in about sixty feet up a stately cedar tree below our house.

I figure we both stood there for about twenty minutes, looking up at where that ten foot blade had finally rested. I could not imagine how fast or how hard that sugar pine must have buckled up to have thrown that whipsaw into the other tree so far. We were simply amazed at what had happened, but my Mother had a different reaction.

I could tell that when she started talking to us by using our full Christian names that she was pretty upset. I figure that she was thinking just like we were, that instead of the saw being stuck into a cedar tree it could have very well been sticking into one of us instead. Standing in the shadow that giant cedar, that day, she vowed that our whipsaw cutting privileges had been permanently revoked. She went on a tirade like I had never heard, except for the time I had put about three dozen water snakes and a couple of frogs into the kitchen sink without telling her first. My Father and I were smart enough just to stay quiet – we knew that she was scared and upset, but more than likely she was just blowing off steam instead of really and actually banning us from using a saw ever again. Matter of fact, we were never able to use that saw again as it was forever lodged high above us in that cedar. I figure that if a person knew the right place to look, that rusty old saw would still be there today.

Eventually we saved up enough money for a new saw, and I can't tell you how many blisters I got on my hands working those handles in. The good that came from that day was that every time I looked up from our dooryard, I had a constant reminder of the terrible forces at play during the act of felling a tree. I'm pretty sure that cautious lesson and reminder may have helped me stay alive during my logging career.

Once in a while we got a question about the cedar-lodged saw from an observant visitor, and my dad's favorite answer would vary a little but always contained a reference to the legendary logger, Paul Bunyan.

I continued to daydream about the glory and fame that would naturally follow my Father and me after we won the whip saw event at the next Jack of the Woods competition. My brain could always be counted on for some type of fantastic distraction, especially when I had time on my hands. And believe you me, clearing that downed sugar pine and its branches and the branches of all the trees that it skinned up, gave me plenty of opportunities to think on other things.

Every time I approached that felled mess, I glanced back towards our house and saw my Mother standing there, looking out the window at me, making sure that I was safe. After that day, it seemed like she burned the firewood just a bit more conservatively.

During those long weeks cleaning that mess, I took some time aside from daydreaming to think about the practical side of becoming a River Canyon logging contest sensation and near-celebrity, especially when the blisters started to cover both my hands.

I knew, though, at the sage old age of twelve that just because I daydreamed about something happening didn't mean that it would. I knew I'd have a better chance of being graduated out of the school at twelve because they found out I was a hidden genius, and that wasn't likely to happen anytime soon.

I thought on how to ask my Father if I could be his partner in the Jamboree events that year. Was there any way to approach the subject without mentioning the passing of War Sing? On that, I didn't much mind accidentally saying something stupid enough to warrant a good wood shed whoopin', my only concern was avoiding hurting my Father's feelings any more than had been done already. I decided to try to have some patience, and be ready with my Jamboree whip-saw proposal when the right opportunity presented itself.

Euclid P. Hammarsen

Chapter Eleven

The Running Indian

"I find it peculiar that folks were racing to San Francisco, instead of running away from it."
– Martin Mulebridge Grider,
Reporter

I heard the padding of his feet long before I saw him. I know his name now as Samuel, but at that time I couldn't tell you what his given name was – I had only heard him referred to as the Running Indian. You have to understand, Dear Reader, that I am aware now that some people consider the word Indian to be derogatory. I do not. I have worked and lived alongside the Indian peoples for several years of my life, and I consider the word Indian to be a compliment. My friend Samuel proved to be a man of the first water in my opinion, for what he did for our family and the family of a man he had never met.

In 1913 it was announced in the newspapers of the great State of California that a footrace of grand proportions was to be held. The runners would cut stick from the northern California sea town of Crescent City and would follow the coastline south until they made it to the city proper. Along the way they would cross log bridges, ford streams, and light upon ferries at times to cross larger rivers and bay inlets where no bridges or roads could be placed. The likes of that race had never before been attempted, and newsmen from as far away as France and Germany were said to be covering the story for their readers. It was in preparation for the next year's Word Fair in San Francisco, and an even bigger point-to-point footrace that would run from the Exposition Park all the way across the United States to New York City. Since the only person in the town that took the San Francisco paper was our homesick school ma'am, nairn of us had any clue about the race or most of what happened in the Other Part of California.

Apparently, the local man had overheard the details of the race from a fella passing though to Oregon the season before. When the visiting man spoke of the thousand-dollar winner's purse, Samuel set his mind on being the winner. To ready himself for the competition, he decided to forego walking as much as possible – choosing instead to sprint everywhere he needed to go.

You've probably met folks with incredible natural talents before. I've met such people – from singers to painters to musicians. I'm convinced there are some of us who are just born able to do things real good just from the get go – and Samuel had the natural gift of running. He had won every local footrace that he had ever entered.

Later, after the State-long footrace and events that occurred as a result of his entry in it, he and I became great friends. Destiny had pushed our lives together because of his desire to run, each of our curious natures, and the letter package that I desperately needed delivered.

I can remember that the other townsfolk called him the Running Indian – because he ran *everywhere*. At that time, it was merely a descriptive term that was used to talk about him. Those kinds of titles weren't uncommon in our community.

We had our share of nicknamed townsfolk, just like any place, and we still do. I used to be Jack's Boy. Then I was called Trout for years – an obvious result of The Boat Dance Incident – and now I'm just referred to as That Old Man Who Fishes A Lot. Not a lot of folks were too keen on calling me my given name, Euclid Plutarch – and I only have my quite-learned Mother to blame for that high-falutin' handle. I spent a great deal of time over my life explaining my odd name to folks, but my Father used to remind me that it could have been worse – that my Mother had considered "Ptolemy" for my middle name, and I would have had to forever be explaining the silent "p". My Amelia called me Uke when she felt fond of me and she would break out all three of my names when I was in the doghouse – mostly used when I was still breaking my habit of muddying up our floor with my dirty old boots or trying to gut my fish in the kitchen sink. My logging crews called me whatever they felt like – much of those terms can't be put down here. It's been a long time, but early in my life my folks took to calling me *Resenar* – Swedish for traveler – since as soon as I could walk I was often hard to find. Since my hair turned white no one ever calls me

Axva'htaahkoo anymore either.

For almost a year preceding the big competition –
that most none of us knew about – the Running Indian
was often found racing throughout the community and
even in the mountains that surrounded us in the
canyon. I was startled the first time that he trotted by
as my Father and I were hunting one afternoon about
four miles south of the town proper, but we all seemed
to get used to his eccentric behavior quick enough. We
minded our own business, back then, and it never
occurred to anyone to ask him why he was running
around everywhere. No one had a clue that he was
training his body for the long distances he'd have to
cover. The common idea at that time was that he was a
bit touched.

I asked him decades later why no one had known
that he had been practicing for the race. "Trout," he
said to me, pausing in the cast of his fishing pole,
smiling, "no one asked."

Renowned now as an Olympian and Native
American statesman, the Running Indian also had
helped pioneer a racing style that gave critics and
writers much to ponder. Like many other Indian
athletes of the time, the Running Indian ran on his bare
feet. Lengthy articles had been written about the
possible reasons why this athletic boy from Northern
California chose to run without shoes on. Was it a
native ritual? Was it a secret technique to increase
stamina and strength? Was it all a ploy to gain
recognition and glory?

As old men do, he and I often met decades and
decades after all of it at the river to fish in the late
afternoon. We enjoyed the long friendship that we had
shared over the years – one that allowed us to be

comfortable in the quietness of our conversations, and the knowledge that if something is needin' to be said, it will. If something isn't needin' to be said, it won't.

I knew, just by growing up here, what all of the writers and historians did not. I knew why the Running Indian ran without shoes. It wasn't a ritual, or a secret technique, or a ploy for glory.

It was, simply, that growing up, he had no shoes.

He's passed on now, like so many have. He was one of the last ones that had been there, back in the beginning of all of this. I can't imagine how my life would have turned out if he hadn't finished that race. He and I became such good friends after it was all over, and we spent many afternoons in our elder years fishing in the River Canyon together. Even after he was forced by age and his last stroke to be in a wheelchair, he still joked that he could run faster than me.

When he was younger – about eighty or so – he wrote a book about the strange adventures he had after that race was over. It's pretty good, and I'm still a jot jealous that he got published before me – but I'm awful proud of him, too.

I recall that like most other occasions in my life back then, one coincidence led to another one – forming an almost unbelievable chain of events. I had found out about Samuel's race while at school.

One of my classmates, Howard, was the cousin of the Running Indian. Several months before the great footrace we were seated in our classroom during our writing assignments wishing that we were outside. While the school ma'am was out of the room, we began to talk and joke about.

I told Howard that I was thinkin' on building a raft and floating it down the Klamath to the Pacific

Ocean and then hoist a sail and head for Burma. Howard mentioned that he had been working on a tunnel that he hoped would eventually open up around that area, and that maybe we could meet up there when he finished it. He figured he had a ways to go, but he had already dug in about ten feet or so – figuring it was only a matter of time before he finished and his shovel broke through. I brought up the fact that I had been engineering a flying machine in the barn, and after the mule-testing phase was complete I was going to be famous. Howard then told me that his cousin was fixin' to run to San Francisco on August 1st, and that he knew it because his Auntie had told him so. Howard had been known to stretch the truth a bit, but mostly only about fishing – which we all did. I gave him the standard ribbing about what he had said, and I ended my comments with something like, "Yeah, and on Christmas Day I'm going to jump in my flying machine and head to the moon." A coincidental conversation that I'd remember months later, out of sheer necessity, hoping all the while that the one part of our schoolboy banter was true.

I don't remember how many of those late July evenings I spent waiting for the man to run by. I always had the precious copied bundle nearby, hidden in the grasses or behind a log or something. I worried that the package would be too heavy, or that it may be lost on the way to the city in the Other Part of California. I never once thought that the Running Indian would refuse to take it – a lifelong problem I have had of naively overlooking certain obvious risks due to my ninety-year streak of blind, dumb luck. Sitting there, cooling my heels, I had plenty of time to ponder why it was that it seemed that everywhere I had been in the last year I could have been assured that the man would at some point come a running past. Not seeing him for several days, I actually thought that maybe some tragic event had befallen the runner.

At one point in my despair of boredom I took a pile of rocks and began to formulate a plan to build an Egyptian pyramid out of the rounded oval river stones. Lord knows we had enough of them around to build almost anything we would have wanted out of 'em. My namesake would have known immediately how big the base of the pyramid would have to be so that I could make it fifty feet tall, but all I could do was scribble out figures of algebra and geometry – my Ma had been learnin' me at home – in the dusty road dirt with a stick. I got to the point where I supposed each of the four sides of the base would have had to be about sixty feet long, and the upright measurements about the same. Trying to find the volume, I did some more figuring and estimated each face of the pyramid would have to be over 1500 square feet, making the tons and tons of rocks needed for the project a bit daunting for just myself to load and stack. A little lizard ran by then, and he stopped and looked at me, my figurin' stick, and my scribbles on the ground. He shook his little green head at me, and with a flick of his tongue and his tail he was gone. The lizard was right in his unvoiced disapproval of my activities – I could not believe it myself that I had fallen so far in my ability to find something to do as I waited for the man to run by. I was ashamed of myself that I had resorted to math to occupy my time.

I retreated to my roadside perch, and worked on my pitching arm instead – reverting to the normal activity of throwing rocks at trees, other lizards, and bigger rocks instead.

I was about to give up hope, but at dusk on one of the last days of July of 1913, I saw the Running Indian come padding his way down the road where I had been waiting for nigh unto a week.

He looked startled as I leapt out of the grassy hillside at him with what must have been a wild look in my eyes. I grabbed at his arm, hollered out my introduction in my best remembrance of my language lessons, "*Nanithvuny uun* Trout." I pleaded with him to talk to me, and without an answer from him, I ran beside him and began at the beginning and told him the whole story as fast as I could. I ended with my request – explaining how I needed the papers to go to the University man from the newspaper article.

The Running Indian finally slowed to a stop and looked at the road under his feet and then at me for the longest time, and then over me at the sky and at the tree line behind me. He finally replied to my request, "The package is not small and will weigh heavy on each step I take in the race."

Years later he told me that he hadn't stopped that day to speak to me, but he slowed down instead to look at all the figurin' someone had scribed into the dusty roadside. He laughed his old man laugh, and I laughed mine, as I explained what all those figures and diagrams had been for. His only response to that was, "I should have known, with you involved, it had to be for something fantastic like that."

I recall that after waiting for him so long, and then having the man stop – for whatever reason – I was afraid that I could almost hear the rejection of my request already coming in his voice, and I started to have a heavy feeling about ever getting the War Sing problems resolved for my Father.

He asked, "Why don't you send it on the pack train?" I must've had a funny look on my face as I quickly tried to formulate yet another lie – I was sure that if I let on to him that my Father had no idea of what I had done, and that I was afraid that Meamber would talk to my Father about any post I sent my whole plan would have been ruined. Not being a very practiced fibber, all that I could come up with was, "Oh, you'll be much, much faster. With the pack train, who knows if it'd even get there this year!"

He just looked at me – sensing something was awry. I nervously tried to grin and put on my best angelic please-do-this-for-me face and worked my best to look him in the eyes like an honest boy would have done.

The Running Indian must have mistook my juvenile attempt at subterfuge as increasing concern on my face, and patted me on the head with a smile on his face. "I will do this for you, sun-hair-*axva'htaahkoo* but only because you are my brother," he said with that same smile in his voice. "When Gram Adal saved you from the giant fish, I understand that she brought you into our family."

Thinking quickly, I blurted out, "There's nothing that I can give you now, but one day there will be." He still had looked very skeptical, so I searched for something more to say and all I found was, "I'll be grateful to you forever."

He looked at me in the strangest way as he set to move on, then stopped and turned and questioned me.

"What could you give to me that would be better than knowing I helped a family know the fate of their loved son?"

It was a question that had no answer, besides my weakly uttered, "Not a thing."

We talked for a while about what good medicine would come from such a noble deed, and how I truly did believe that War Sing's spirit would pick up Samuel and carry him when his feet became dragged out or weakness hindered his progress on his journey.

We spoke our secret names, clasped arms, and with War Sing's only chance of spiritual restoration finally secured firmly in the hands of the long-distance runner, I could only cross my fingers as he raced away and was gone – quickly fading out of sight as he left our River Canyon for The World.

Euclid P. Hammarsen

Chapter Twelve

Old Epharim, The Bear Man

"Goldilocks would've never made it out of the bear's house in one piece, if they had been river bears."
– Sarah Buckner, Resident

Only just a day after giving the Running Indian the package I had started to worry as to his progress. I also started to feel really guilty that I had done so much in secret from my folks. I was glad when my Father asked me to go visiting with him – not so I could finally lighten my conscience and tell him what I had done – but instead to take my mind off of my guiltiness and the all of the events I had put into motion.

We used to make time to visit others much more than is done today. Stopping by for a friendly get-together was almost expected then, and we looked forward to time spent with friends. We had no phone, no radios nor televisions to pass our social time. My Father enjoyed those visits – I often imagined that being at our home with just Mother and I was lonely for him, as he had been raised in such a large family. With War Sing gone, my Father and I spent a lot more time together – but he and I both knew that I would never fill the shoes of his friend. I had my own shoes to fill, and I was trying, but walking the tight-rope atwixt childhood and manhood I figure I messed up a few times.

My Father especially enjoyed visiting with a fellow nicknamed Old Epharim. His Christian name had been lost to all of us by then, although I did hear him referred to by some of the townsfolk as Grizzly or The Bear Man. He and my Father both had relatives from the same area in Lemland in the Aland Islands near Finland or some such place, and had a lot of the same upbringing even though Epharim was much older than my Father. Sometimes they would speak Dutch or Swedish or Finnish together and I would see a distance on my Dad's face.

His other language was mostly a mystery to me, even then – he insisted that as Americans, we would embrace the country and the language and the culture and many of the laws.

We mostly visited with Old Epharim at our house, on my Mother's insistence. I didn't understand why she seemed scared of where the old man lived – and I didn't appreciate her hesitancy until the first time I stepped foot on his property. All told I only visited Epharim at his home three times with my Father, and for obvious reasons my Mother was absent on those trips. It was also one of only a few places I ever went where I had to leave my dog at home.

Epharim seemed old even when I was a boy. He was almost as tall as my Dad, and perhaps would have been if he wasn't hunkered over with a curved back and a bum leg. He always wore olive green or slate gray work pants and a matching long-sleeve button down work shirt. He had gray eyes, and when I met him he lived alone. Unlike some bachelor men that lived in the river valley, Old Epharim always was presentable and wore clean, mended clothes. I think that his children were grown and moved away by the time I met him, and that his wife had died – but my knowledge of his past is blurred due to the screen that was provided by adults to children where grown-up information was concerned.

I had been brought up to always consider bears natural enemies – our family seemed to have story after story about how those black beasts had crossed our paths and then crossed us. Perhaps our clan was marked in some way – destined to battle those terrible creatures forever for some wrong done to them long, long, ago by one of our ancestors.

My Mother had been mauled by a bear when she was a girl in Nebraska, and she took great pains all of her life to cover the horrible scars on her legs. My Father had also been set upon by a murderous black bear as a boy, and if it hadn't been for his true aim and the last shell in the shotgun, he would have been surely killed.

The black bears of our River Canyon were crazy and mean. They were powerful beyond belief, and the most unpredictable of their species that I had ever seen. They were much more than the bothahrayshun garbage-eaters that many folk think of – they were man killers and hunters and still are today.

Old Epharim, I had overheard, lived smack in the middle of a hive of the black bears – feeding them like they were a yard full of farm animals instead of ruthless wild killers. I was immediately intrigued.

Going to Old Epharim's house was, for me, much like I imagined walking the plank on a pirate schooner with the sharks circling below. Only those black and furry sharks could chase a kid and eat him, in or out of the water. The dozens of black bears that he fed everyday roamed his property and perched in his trees like it was perfectly natural for beasts to be littered about the yard. I was justifiably afraid of the arrangements that Epharim had with those critters but drawn to the whole situation just the same.

We made our way up Indian Crick to his house. Long about the early afternoon we found ourselves sitting in his driveway, with our horses nervously stomping and whinnying a bit. We may have sat there for half an hour, peering from our perch in the wagon and sneaking glances at each other. The trees outside of the man's dooryard were decorated with bears, and one large beast even laid lazily sunning itself not more than twenty feet from the front door.

Spotting the old man through his living room window, my Father bolted out of the wagon directly toward his house door and I followed his example. We placed our backs to the door, eyes peering into the wooded darkness surrounding the house, and knocked as loud and as fast as we could trying not to sound frantic. We could hear him inside the house shuffle toward us, and when he opened the door and greeted us we dispensed with the usual formalities as quick as possible and found ourselves inside the house faster than a 30-pound steelhead breaks a ten-pound line.

We stood holding hats in hand while he rummaged around in back. We could have stood there forever, glad not to have been eaten by the walking black death that circled outside of his house. While waiting for Old Epharim to grab his hat and walking stick I looked around, and saw a giant book sitting on a pedestal by the front door. I immediately imagined that it was a magical spell book of some sorts, that let the Bear Man live safely in the midst of those awful beasts. How else could he survive such a terrible curse?

I figured that a magic to direct the will of animals would be a very good magic to have. My thoughts briefly rested on Merlin and Tarzan and soon enough I began to daydream of the power I could amass as a twelve-year-old King of the Beasts of the Forest. I found myself inching toward the mysterious tome.

He came back into the room then, and saw me looking toward his book. I saw that I was found out. Dejected, it seemed to me that someone was always finding me doing something I wasn't supposed to. It took years to occur to me that I had something to do with it.

Walking to me, he put his hand on my shoulder and asked, "Son, would you like to look?" He pointed at the old book, and I muttered, "Yes, sir," without really meeting his eyes with mine.

He took me to the book and opened it. It had a large, hardbound leather cover with gold-colored gilding on the edges of the pages. He opened the dusty tome, and its spine creaked and popped like an old man's. His weathered and lined hands moved through the pages. A big, thick, red velvet ribbon curled out of the bottom of the book, apparently holding the place of some child shrinking spell or maybe even one that would turn us all into bears to add to the group outside. I started to feel really hinky about the book, and then I saw what it really was.

It was a guest book. Hundreds and hundreds of pages were filled with the names, dates, and hometowns of visitors that had come to see the Bear Man.

"Sir," I said, "this can't be right." Pointing to one of the pages, I said, "This one here says he's from Italy, I think. This one says that she's from New York City."

He just smiled and reveled in my awe. "They're correct, son," he finally said, "I've had a lot of visitors from all over the world. They come to see the bears, between seeing other things."

I couldn't imagine that someone from Italy, on holiday in the United States, would ever in a million years trek to Happy Camp, then up Indian Crick road, then cross the little bridge to travel another ten miles on what was little more than a washboarded path cut out of the forest to end up at the Bear Man's house, standing exactly where I stood then.

That very moment was when my wanderlust was born. My eyes to the world were opened, looking into that book. Sure, I had daydreamed quite a bit about traveling but it had never occurred to me before that it was really possible to leave our little river valley, and go Out Into The World for any length of time.

Standing in that house, surrounded by the bears outside, I came to the realization that if, in fact, someone from New York or Russia or Sacramento had stood where I was standing – well then, of course there was a road that went to their cities or countries. The road they took to get here would have to run both ways.

The world lay open before me.

While we visited, I watched the bears outside.

After a while, we all ventured out to the yard and spent about an hour among the enemy. We tried to be good guests, but I think that our predisposition to bear hatred was just too great for us to overcome in that afternoon.

As we readied to cut stick, the Bear Man put his hand on my shoulder and talked to me about never trusting the bears of the forest just because the ones he had around his house looked like they were friendly. I assured him that he needn't worry since I planned to never make friends with any bears, ever.

He laughed at my words, and turned back to his house after our goodbyes were said. He fetched up after a few steps, turned, and said something that truly cemented my destiny to leave our little river valley.

"Young man," he called, "I forgot to ask if you'd like to sign the guestbook."

I was out of the wagon and up the walk and into his house quick enough to dodge any truant bear and also quick enough that he couldn't change his mind. My Father followed me back to the house, and chided me along the way for bounding around like a billy goat.

Savoring the moment, I weighed the heavy pen in my small hands – my mind wandered to those who held it before me, and who now were lounging in their villas or fighting in revolutions or carrying on in steamers headed for Morocco.

I signed my name below the exotic signatures of Mr. and Mrs. Nathanial Spooresbridge of Bruseburg, Kentucky, and above that of my Father, Mr. Hjalmer Carl Hammarsen of Elk Crick, California.

Years later – as I actually was Out Into The World – before touring my grandfather's homeland of Lemland in the Aland Islands atwixt Finland and Sweden I found myself with a few days on my hands in Northern Latvia. I stopped for a bit in a harbor city whose name I have forgotten, waiting for the ship *Cedric* to land from its stormy tour and take me to the north. I spent most of those two days walking the old city seawalls and adventuring into the town proper to see the beautiful old buildings and courtyards. Since I looked like I should have lived there – with my shock of blonde hair and my squinty green eyes – when folks spoke more than a hello to me I was unable to respond. I'll bet they must have thought I was addled, as I stammered only a few understandable words in my best mix of the German and Russian and Swedish that I had picked up in other places.

In my last evening in that quay town, I came upon an old, old man casting his fishing line from the weather-worn wharf into the sea. Always interested by any sort of fishing, I tried to speak to him about what he had in his creel, again trying my best German-Russian-Swedish. He replied first with a kind laugh at my language problems, and then in broken English he described his catch and the preferred local bait to use. He offered a pole to me, and we spent the rest of the afternoon there – talking and fishing.

The sun was beginning to set, and the late summer afternoon began to carry a little breeze off the ocean. I pulled in my line, and said, "Sir, I've enjoyed fishing with you. The folks back home never will believe that I put a line in the Baltic Sea."

"We call it the West Sea," the old man gently corrected me. "And the Finns call it the East Sea. Others call it the White. Only the English and the Americans call it the Baltic, really. Where then," the old man asked, "is home, young man?"

"Oh, far away in America. It's in California, way to the north," I replied. I was trying to decide if it would be worth it to attempt a description of the place where I was raised, when the old man began talking again.

"Son, I have been to California." For a moment, his eyes were far away and looking to the horizon. It seemed like he wasn't just gazing into distance, but also into time as well.

"You have, sir?" I answered with more enthusiasm and gaining more interest in following that leg of the conversation. "Well, where I'm from is almost in Oregon it's so far north."

Still looking far away, the old man responded, "Yes, I was briefly there with my Father around 1860. He had been a part of the diplomatic attaché for the esteemed Russian diplomat Prince Alexsandr Gorchakov." The old man still looked at the sea, but it looked like he was a million miles away in his thoughts – or, rather, about seventy years away from the places and names and adventures he was trying to remember.

He continued. "My Father was always very busy when I was a boy. I once was able to accompany him to the United States, where we traveled from San Francisco, California to Seattle, Washington. Along the way we stopped many wonderful places.

"The journey took us all summer, but it was an unbelievable time for me. I saw things that I had only read about. I saw Yosemite Valley, and I swam in the cold and clear waters of the Lake of Tahoe. I ate salmon with the Modoc Indians in a feast given in honor of Prince Gorchakov and my Father. I rode a horse to the top of Mount Mazama, where I saw the great volcano filled like a deep cup by rain of hundreds of years. I saw mountains, prairies, streams, and waterfalls all along our long path.

"I made friends with cowboys and Indians and best of all, my Father, on that journey."

Night fell on our seaside roost as he continued to tell me about his great childhood adventure. I think the old man mistook the incredulous look on my face for disbelief. He frowned a little and then said that there was proof in America that he had been in California. I nigh unto fell off the wharf and into the ocean when he started to talk about my little river valley. A chill went up my spine despite the warm evening sea breeze.

"We went to a small place called Happy Camp," he said, "and I was asked by a young man to write my name in his book. His name was Old Epharim, which I recall that I thought was odd since he was barely older than me."

Laughing a bit, he continued, "I couldn't write my name very well, because my hand was shaking so much as I thought the bears outside of his house were going to eat me."

I laughed then too, so hard that I almost hooked myself with my own line. We continued to talk until the stars came out in the black night. We talked about coincidences, fathers, the magic of being young, and times long past.

Two truths have held firm for me during all of my travels. The first is that the art and skill and act of fishing is an international constant – I've seen racial, political and economic differences melt on river banks and wharves across the world. The second is that the world is much, much smaller than we generally think that it is.

Chapter Thirteen

The Haunted Lake

"I was hiking up by Ukonom Falls, and I could swear I heard my grandpa call out my name and then I saw him wave at me before disappearing behind a pine. I looked for him, even though I know he's been dead for twenty years or better."

— Mike Cedarline, Resident

I will never forget the first time that I hiked into the Marble Mountains proper. Sure, I had been all over a section of what would later become the official Wilderness Area — for goodness sakes our first house was planted firmly in one part of it. I had always wanted to go higher and deeper into the mountains above our home, where there were places that no one had even walked before in the whole entire history of the world.

It was, even at that time, a forest area filled thick with legends and mystery — featured as a backdrop in many popular local ghost stories and schoolyard creative narratives and accounts. Many of our tales began with, "I heard my Dad's friend say that once up in the Marbles he saw a ..." or "My brother told me that they chased the beast up into the Marbles and ..." There were all manner of combinations of that same story, usually ending in some bloody attack by some kind of beast or monster on unsuspecting ten-to-twelve-year-old boys. The Ghostly Indian Chief – spirit resident of the Marble Mountains proper – was prominent in many of those fantastic stories.

Billy McKetter swore up and down that he had seen the infamous Ghostly Chief of the Marble Mountians one night as he happened to peer out of his window at the road that passed by his house. He said that he had looked out after hearing a scraping and dragging noise – and rubbed his eyes at the sight of the Chief dragging eight or ten fallen men down the middle of the gravelly thoroughfare. He said he got a chill when the Ghostly Man looked up at him and held up his war axe in the moonlight right before he vanished into the darkness. My friend Howard explained to me several times that he had been told by his uncles that the Ghostly Chief wove tight magical baskets during the day to hold the blood and spirits of the men he captured each night. He would use the blood from the baskets to fuel his Council Fire in the darkness.

I figured it was all a bunch of malarkey, but I always daydreamed about finding out for myself. I was beside myself in boyhood joyfulness when my Father announced his plans for our hike into the trout lakes high above our home.

My Father had planned our simple fishing trip for quite some time, and since the mill was retooling the saw he announced that he had several days to take me to the best trout fishing that could be found in the world. I was also determined to try to take my Father's thoughts from the horrible death of War Sing, if only for a few days, and I tried real hard to put the hobgoblin stories out of my mind.

The July morning was being born in front of us when we left our house way before dawn. I was loaded down with my pack and my pole and kept close by my dog. The cold morning air and the star-thick skies really woke me up, and I watched the heavy moon follow us on our hike to the trailhead. We passed by the Hunting Ground, climbing and hiking along the road as the sun began to rise.

Under the filled old Army pack and a bedroll the first few miles of the trail seemed longer than they were. In my mind I kept going over all of the essential items that I had insisted to take along – and I realized that my Father had been right when he had tried to convince me to pare down my packing.

Our old dog had new life in her, running ahead of my Dad and me and waiting for us in the bend of the trail. We may have walked five miles that day, but that sweet old lab must have walked ten.

As we climbed higher, the stream got smaller and clearer and colder. The trees looked a little different too, changing from the forests of sugar pine and cedar to other species like noble fir and lacy-leafed alpine evergreens. Granite rock pinnacles rose up out of the mountains around us like castle towers, and we hiked though lush valleys of mountain grass and yellow and purple sweet-smelling wildflowers. Even the sky looked different – changing from the deep blue I was used to, to a lighter-colored hue as the day grew on. I wondered, practically, how high we could climb in those mountains before the air just gave out entirely. After a bit, I really started to worry when I had to take two breaths to get one lung full of air – but my Father just laughed at my concerns, reminding me that my heavy pack I was lugging around assuredly was adding to my breathing difficulty.

As we hiked on and the novelty of the changing landscape wore off as my pack seemed to be getting heavier, I began to think on my favorite Marble Mountain story – which of course was the well-worn camp fire yarn featured the Ghostly Indian Chief of Spirit Lake. I tried to recall all of the details I had heard about the Long Dead Spirit who was said to hold Council around an ever burning blaze made of emeralds and blood of his enemies under the magic Marble Mountain lake water.

With my legs dragged out and my back stretched, I was glad when we finally made camp nearby the trail on the ridgeline that first night. I must've drank ten gallons of sweet Adam's Ale from the spring there, and I recall that it was so cold it made my teeth hurt.

Knowing my constant curiosity about stories and mysteries, my Father had piqued my interest for years with his versions of the tales of the strange goings-on in the mountains around us, so I knew as we made camp that day that we were about half a mile from the real Spirit Lake mentioned in most of the narratives. I must have asked my Dad if he would take me there about a thousand times that afternoon. Each time, he'd smile and answer, "Not yet, son."

We set to gathering up wood for the campfire and taking care of some general housekeeping items – like making sure there were no anthills near where we planned to sleep – and settled in to the quiet activities all of us wood folk know to do between fishin' and eatin' and sleepin'. I played with Cinder when she wasn't chasing chipmunks through the camp. It made me laugh how ticked off she got when a couple of those little things stood up on a nearby log and barked at her in voices too loud for their size. She didn't catch one that afternoon, but she sure tried real hard.

The good part of the day was almost gone, and I had about given up hope of the Sprit Lake jaunt. Believe you me no one in their right mind would consider a night trip to that ghostly and enchanted hollow. Resigned to the prospect of having to cool my heels until the next day, I finished my supper and began to whittle on a funny looking stick I had found.

A light breeze began to move through the camp, and the evening sounds were beginning to stir in the dark understory of the forest.

When I heard an owl call, I fully gave up on seeing Spirit Lake for that day.

A little while later, Dad came over to where I was stabbing at the stick. He picked up one too, and showed me how to go about carving a whistle out of a small piece of wood. We were having a great time, and as my Father was looking around at the sky and hills he said, "Let's go for a little walk."

I gathered up my things, and headed out of camp behind my Dad. I turned back for a second, then, running for my fishing gear. Visions of the famous high-stream trout fishing were racing through my head, making me near delirious.

My Father hollered, "Trout, what are you up to?"

"Nothing," I replied, "just getting my pole."

My interest was increased, especially so, when he said, "You won't be needin' that tonight." And then he said the words I'd been hoping to hear for two years, "We're going to Spirit Lake."

Then he added, with a smile and eyebrow raise, "Just be sure that you have your knife, and tell that old dog that it needs to stay at camp."

I gave Cinder direct instructions to wait for me to return, and I lit out after my Father. She did what I said, but by the look on her face and the disapproving gait in her walk she wasn't too happy about it.

I finally caught up with my Dad. Each time he made a step I had to make four, so I was usually pretty busy any time we hiked anywhere.

We followed an old trail for about fifteen minutes, barely making out the path in the lessening light of evening. We came to the top of a ridge, and the mountain seemed to slope away before us, save for a dark basin down and to our right.

We continued on, over the side of the hill and into the trees that hid the mysterious and legend-thick water.

The lake laid in the bottom of the bowl of land, with the tall pines and firs growing right to the pool's edge. The forest was dark, even in the early afternoon, and unusually quiet. I saw no real evidence of any animal activity. It looked like the whole world had forgotten that lake and the secret that it held. Even our footsteps seemed to have a different sound to them as we made our way to the boggy bank. Several times on our hike I had to fetch up and look back over my shoulder, as I was sure that some terrifying monster of the mountains was tracking me through the forest.

Night fell quickly in that dark little corner of the mountains. My Father and I had sat down together on the same fallen log near the side of the lake. We had a clear view of the small body of water and of the eastern sky, where later the full moon would rise to light our way back to camp.

By the time that dusk was upon us, I had somehow scooted from my seat several feet away from my Father to find myself stuck right next to him.

He put his arm around me, and looking down at me with a smile on his face, he said, "You know I'll never let anything happen to you."

I nodded in the approaching darkness, and tried my best courageous smile. I'm pretty sure he knew that I was still scared of what I was about to see. It's possible that my shivering body in the warm summer air gave it away.

As far as secret mysteries went – looking around – I figured the lake was somewhat of a disappointment. There were no Ghostly Campfires. There were no Mermaids, Monsters, Spies, Dark Knights, or Generally Nasty Villains anywhere to be found.

Another owl, far away, broke the silence of the descending darkness. Startled, I jumped in my seat and tried to coolly shrug it off with a grin and a smile. I moved even closer to my dad, and he kept his arm around me. Looking up at him, I saw peace on his face and I could feel no fear in his hold of me.

Then I looked again at the mysterious lake.

From the center of the body of water, I thought that I could see a light. I felt like someone who had stumbled on to a warm bowl of spaghetti and a baseball on the ridge of a mountain – it just didn't fit.

The light was a greenish glow, and it ebbed and grew as the minutes passed and as the sky grew darker. My imagination was running wild. Was the ghostly Indian Chief holding council with his braves around his magical, underwater campfire? Were the lights guiding Lancelot du Lac's false-mother, The Lady of The Lake – the legendary Vivienne and the wife of Merlin – up through the depths so she could once again see the starlight that surrounded this world? Was Elroy Feeney from school right, when he told all of us that men lived on Mars and they were coming to Earth to attack us? Was it a Mars-man, coming from his hiding place to begin his take over of Earth by gnawing on me and my Dad?

I remembered to breathe, then, and felt better after having done it. The center of the pool continued to glow, and the glowing spread until eventually all of the lake was luminous.

From the light of the green glowing lake, I could once again see my Father's face. He looked at me, too, and smiling he whispered, "Trout, I think you may have eaten something bad. You look a little green."

"Real funny, Dad," I replied. With that joke, I felt a jot more at ease in that strange place.

A small breeze found us, and moved the surface gently. My head felt like it was on a swivel. I looked up at the trees. I looked at my hands. I looked across the water. I looked, and looked, and looked. I even looked behind me, into the dark forest, quite a bit as I was not fully convinced that the terrifying monster of the mountains wasn't waiting behind a tree about to pounce on me.

I jumped about four feet, and immediately brought my full attention back to the lake when I heard a big splash nearby.

The lake's fish, enticed by the surface-top hatch of gnats, were leaping from the magic-laden waters hoping for some supper. I could actually make out, through the depths of the deep pool, the paths that the fish had taken by the greenish trails that followed them as they darted through the water. When they raced toward the surface, and broke through into our air after their prey, the sprayed droplets that surrounded them shot into the night sky like emeralds. The water emeralds and the diamond stars floated together for seconds, then the emeralds fell back to the lake and the diamonds stayed in the sky. The stars reflected their ancient light in the green pool, which looked covered in little floating green fires.

A question crossed my mind, then, and I wondered how many miles that the starlight had to come to sparkle in this Spirit pool – and for how long the pool had been changing the diamond sparkle to emerald fire.

The glowing gnats, perhaps trying to escape the leaping fish, began to fly higher and soon they were surrounding my Father and me. I imagined that they were little faeries of the forest, small and magical. Some landed on me, and I didn't squish them.

We sat there until the moon rose over the mountain, casting its reflection into the green pool. The lake and the woods were gradually transformed back to a moonlit scene, as the glowing subsided in the bright night.

We made our way back to the camp. When we got there, I was glad that Dad decided to build up the campfire. My faithful dog was waiting by the tent, just where I had left her. The soreness she had shown me before I went to Spirit Lake without her was soon gone as we shared some late dinner together.

It wasn't very cold out, but I was chilled through and through by what I had seen at the lake. I rolled out my shakedown near the fire, but still close enough to my Father's bedroll that I could alert him if a cougar came into camp to eat me or if a Bigfoot was setting to pack me off into the night. I shared my sleeping space with my dog, who started out laying at my feet but who would soon compete for legroom with me all night long.

I fell asleep that night thinking of the magic around us. I dreamt that night of the Ghostly Indian Chief, concerning myself mostly with where he got the blood to fuel his ever burning campfire. Atwixt the bedroll leg-room war with the dog and the imagined hatcheting by the Chief, I did not sleep well.

I think that we are lucky if, when remembering back on our long lives, us old folks can recall four or five times in our past exactly as they happened. Smelling the smells. Feeling the breezes in the air. Knowing the sounds. Most important, remembering the feelings of a time – a day or a moment. I have a few of those, and most of them are wonderful memories. The fourth day of July in 1936 when Amelia jumped the broom with me. The 15th day of March way back in 1942 when my son was born. Other times are there too, and one was that night at Spirit Lake with my Dad when I was just a boy.

I had figured out, years after that night, the logical reasons that Spirit Lake glows a beautiful green on certain summer nights. The naturally occurring phosphorous and other chemicals in the nearby soil, as well as temperature and the extreme darkness of the area at night, come together to create the scientific phenomenon.

One of the legends that I had heard about that enchanted lake stated that an Indian brave suffering life-threatening wounds could jump into the deep pool and live forever at the campfire of the Ghostly Indian Chief. I wasn't sure about that, but dozens of years later when my Father lost his brave battle with cancer, I brought his ashes back to Spirit Lake.

By myself, I hiked in, carrying him in my pack. I was there with him, one last time, on the same downed log on the side of that magical water. I quietly sat and thought about how much he had cared for me and my Mother, and the good and simple times before the wild horses were burned. I could almost see him there, next to me in the dimness of the mountain evening. I missed his arm on my shoulder, and the security his presence had brought to me, but I wasn't afraid in that darkness which years before had terrified me.

After the fish had jumped and before the full moon rose, I let what was left of his physical being go into the lake – he was then fully forever a part of the land that he loved. He mixed with the diamonds of the sky and the ethereal fiery emeralds of the water as well as the tears that fell from my eyes – in his Western Valhalla – as he was finally gone.

Instead of remembering my Father small and weak in that hospital bed, I choose to remember him as a proud and strong Viking warrior sharing his hunting stories with the other braves, forever sitting council around the Ghostly Indian Chief's campfire under the depths of Spirit Lake.

Chapter Fourteen

The Race

"Dear Brother: If a messenger has delivered these papers to you, the worst has happened to me..."
– Yong-Li Jun, From a Letter to His
Family

While my Father and I were avoiding the black furry death at Old Ephraim's house and traipsing around the Marbles spying on ghostly lakes and getting in some supreme world-class trout fishing, the Running Indian faced his own adventures. It was a long journey for the man who had never been out of Siskiyou County prior to the race, and his efforts changed the lives of many people.

Each night when I drifted off to sleep I tried to figure in my mind how far that Samuel had run. I had no frame of reference for my suppositions, and after just about a week I was starting to wonder when he was ever going to return. I'd fall asleep most nights imagining the sound of the man's tired and thick footsteps padding down the road.

On one of the evenings we spent fishing together – many, many years after his incredible race – Samuel and I talked at length about the details of the famous competition. He explained the odd newspaper story that eventually reached our little river valley – showing a picture of him standing in a horse trough at the Fisherman's Wharf – and all of the details of why he didn't return to our River Canyon for over a year after he set out to be the first runner to cross that finish line.

He told me that after he had left me on the road side he made his way to Crescent City hitching a ride in a supply wagon for most of the route. About twenty miles out from the ocean-side town and the start of the race, he was let off as the wagon's axle broke. He jogged the rest of the distance – stopping for a bit to stare in amazement at the shocking size and beauty of the Redwood trees – and arrived in the City with several hours to spare before the start of the competition.

Before the official start of the footrace bands played and folks made speeches and all manner of official hoorah was conducted. Instead of watching all of the nonsense, Samuel explored around a bit and, approaching the ocean, he found himself for the second time that day standing in awe of a natural wonder. He recalled hearing a story about salty water, and he confirmed it when a big gulping mouthful of the cold ocean water almost did him in.

Making his way back to the footrace he made his way through the entrance form – with its lengthy questions regarding colleges attended and membership in athletic associations – while he listened carefully to all of the race instructions. Racers were to leave from the starting line, there in Crescent City and race by foot down the length of most of the coast of California to the Fisherman's Wharf in the quay of San Francisco. The first runner to cross the finish line, who had abided by all of the race rules, would be confirmed as the winner. Competitors were able to race on the road or on the road-side, but were not allowed to take any short-cuts off of the marked route. There were food stops marked out on their little maps, and places to rest if needed. There would be no official nightly breaks, but the runners were encouraged to rest and avoid straining themselves to death as had befallen overeager folks in other races.

Race stewards would be placed along the route, and would forward race information by rider or telegraph as they could to the headquarters in San Francisco. The winner would receive fame and glory and $1000 and the second-place man would receive $500.

While he listened he secured my package to his back, under his shirt, by wrapping it tightly in an oilcloth and tying it to him like a bunting. It was the same type of bunting he'd used to carry fresh meat and game and parcels that would ruin otherwise as he forged deep streams or had to swim to cross the Klamath during his travels. He said later that the oilcloth was scratchy and rough, but he was trying to protect the letters from the rain and the fog and his own sweat that he anticipated along the race.

Newspaper reporters hounded around the runners as they finally were able to assemble for the contest, and soon one and all was weary and red-eyed from the camera men and their flash-smoke in the air.

The field of competition consisted of the Running Indian and roughly fifty other fellows. Most of the men were white folks and sported giant moustaches. Another fellow walked to the line, and drew many long stares and jeers from the crowd. Samuel recalled that it was the first time he had ever heard that kind of meanness and hatred from folks – and he went to investigate who the racer was that was receiving the derision. He figured the man must have been an outlaw or a murderer or something equally as bad, with how the folks were treating him. Making his way around the side of the crowd, the Running Indian – for the third time that day – stopped and stared at something he had never seen before. Standing in front of him, ignoring all of the awful words and yells from the crowd, was a curious fellow whose skin had turned black like the night. Samuel had never seen or heard of that condition, and trying to strike up a conversation with the dark fellow, pointed at the man's arm and innocently asked him, "What happened?"

The black man laughed then, part at the absurdity of the comment and half out of surprise. After more of the Indian's curious questions, including a request to be able to touch the black skin, the man understood that the Indian fella had never seen anyone like him before. He responded to each innocent inquiry and assured Samuel that he was not a murderer or an outlaw, and that he didn't know the folks who were making the awful comments. He explained to the wide-eyed Indian that the folks were probably only hollering at him because of the color of his skin.

On that river bank all those years later, I could still see the hurt on Samuel's face when he told that part of the story. "Friend," he explained to me, "that day I saw so many new wonders. I was so glad to see the Redwoods and the mighty ocean – but it broke my heart just a little to see how ugly people were to other folks, for no good reason." I understood him, as at my advanced age and in my worldly travels I had even seen that ugliness reach past the comments and jeers and manifest itself with beatings and killings. Coming from our River Canyon, I could understand how the young Samuel was confused by that irrational and unfounded hatred he saw that day because we hadn't had any of it in our community.

He and the blackened man, named Nestor Oaks – over the course of the long race – became friends.

In a volley of huzzah's and pistol shots, the race was begun and the field of men set upon their journey. Samuel said later that at the starting guns he had looked for Nestor, certain that he'd been finally shot by one of the jeering fellas – and he said that by the look on Nestor's face he had thought so as well. They both ran like the dickens for a bit, and then backed off into a fast jog when the crowd was far enough behind not to pose a shooting threat.

They set in to the style of running each man would keep for the remainder of the race – Nestor loping along with his long legs and stride on the ocean-most edge of the road path so he could keep a conversation with Samuel, who naturally chose to run with his quick and well-placed short steps in the weedy road bank and occasionally over the beaches they came across. Long about twenty miles after they started, Samuel told Nestor that they were soon to cross the Klamath River – and a mile later the waters streamed out in their path. Samuel had known the smell of his river a ways back, and didn't need the little hand-painted road sign to tell him what the waters were. Racing ahead a little faster, Samuel jumped down off the roadside and drank the thick, foamy green water – above Nestor's voiced concerns. The Running Indian sipped his fill and caught back up quickly with the other runner, and for about the next seventy miles he explained to the other man why that water was Life and Family and Home to him. He did warn Nestor not to drink the ocean water, though, and recounted to him how it had made him sick but Nestor just laughed at the simple and refreshing innocence of his new friend.

The two men continued on like that for the next three days and nights. They talked to each other about their respective corners of the world – about their families and their favorite foods and what plans they had for the prize money if lucky enough to win it.

Nestor talked about how his Father had fought in the American Civil War, and Samuel talked about how his Father had stood with Captain Jack when the Army came for the Indian leader near around that same time. Each man recognized the history of struggle they both shared, albeit different types of struggles at opposite ends of the country.

The six-hundred-mile race dwindled in front of them to five-hundred and three-hundred and then down to one-hundred. By the time they crossed the hundred mile marker they were comfortable like friends who had known each other all of their lives. They had both outpaced the entire field of other competitors hundreds of miles before – instead of sleeping for four of five hours and suffering cold and sore legs and backs, they chose to rest for a few minutes every couple of hours. Looking at the map on one of their stops, both of the men agreed that at the top of the last hill – Mount Tamalpais – they would set in to really race each other.

At times the mist clinging low to the seaside cliffs

made it difficult to see to run, and at night they were at the will of the rising moon to set their speed. When the road became too dark, they made their way down the beaches as they could – listening to the waves rush to the shore and following their glowing crests southward.

The newspaper article that I would read several years after the end of the race described a finish line unprepared for the quickness of those two runners. Sentries had telegraphed ahead about the two men, but most of the fellas at the San Francisco finish line thought it was some kind of a joke.

The wagons of the Official Race Committee were being unpacked of musical instruments and banners and all manner of huzzah-bellowing contraptions on the grassy spot in the center of the Fisherman's Wharf finish line area when they were all surprised by a breathless rider on a frothy black-tailed bay. The rider and the horse rushed so quickly toward them that some in attendance swore they saw sparks flying from the horse's metal-shod hooves on the cobble-stone roadway.

The message rider had just enough breath available to announce that he'd gotten the signal that two runners – further describing them in the vulgar terms of those times – were only five miles from the Golden Gate Ferry Company's transport across the bay. All the folks must've still thought it was a joke, since no man had ever run six-hundred miles in under seven days – let alone just over four. The rider reassured the Committee that the men were on the way and then fell, exhausted, off of his horse right on to the ground.

Nestor and Samuel stopped for a moment at the top of the last ridge of Tamalpais with what they both figured was but ten or twelve miles to go to the finish line, and shook hands. They agreed to meet again after the race was over – with no boasting or challenges about the last leg of the race that faced them, each man just fixed to get to the finish ribbon first. Samuel drew a line in the dirty road with a stick and with his winning River Canyon spirited smile, invited the other man to a little race into the San Francisco City. Both men laughed, and after they had lined up behind the drawn line Nestor counted backwards from five and then they were off.

Samuel was gone quick like the lightning that split the August Klamath skies of his home. He darted among the roadside weeds and over rocks like a buck mixed with a billy-goat, just as quick and nimble-footed. He laid his eyes only on the path ahead, and forgot the noises and sights except for what was right in front of his feet. He began to weaken and tire, stumbling a bit and dragging a foot on occasion.

He said that was when he remembered again the package I had given to him. He had felt the brush of it against his back under his shirt for the whole journey, thinking of it often as a bother and quietly wondering if the papers were going to weigh on him – but it wasn't until that silent and focused time where he made quiet everything else that he began to think of young War Sing – of his Mother and Father. Did his Mother look out of her dooryard every day, wondering when her son would return? Did his Father search the faces of men returning to their village to find a glimpse of the face of his son?

Samuel told me much later that it was in those few miles nearing the end of the race when he decided that he would travel away from the River Canyon – exploring the country and maybe even the world. He had been embarrassed that he had not known to drink the ocean water, and that he had not known there were peoples colored differently than him – like his new friend, Nestor. An intelligent and bright man, Samuel knew that there had to be more to learn and know about the giant world that was veiled to him by the apartness of the River Canyon. He was spurred on by the package of letters reminding him on every step that other countries and entire populations of folks were out there, over the sea he ran next to as well as in the land he lived.

Coming down off Mount Tamalpais on his quick feet, he passed another race sentry who had an extremely surprised look on his face. He could hear Nestor running in behind him, about a hundred yards back. The Running Indian's lead was increasing, bit by bit as they continued on. He said later that at that point he figured he was roughly ten miles away from the finish, and barring any injuries or accidents he would be the first to cross the line.

The race sentry hollered to them as both men passed. "No reason to run full out boys, since the ferry across the bay to Fort Point won't be back to this side for another twenty minutes. You'll both be on the same boat!"

Samuel looked back at Nestor and thought he saw a grin on the man's face. They had both overlooked that last ferry on their little worn maps. It hadn't been a problem before to wait together for the only passage over some of the rivers and the inlets that had blocked their path, but Samuel figured that if he was to maintain his short lead – the only way he would win against the other strong runner – that he'd have to come up with another plan by the time he reached the bottom of the hill and the ferry stop.

After all of the time he had spent in the race, and with the win within his reach he forced himself to run a little faster and harder to the surprise of his competitor, Nestor, as well as the on-looking race steward.

Samuel reached the ferry dock almost a mile ahead of Nestor, and found the ferry attendant straightaway. He questioned the little man real quick, and then walked down the sea wall and stopped for about a minute to think.

He remembered, as he told me about that day years later as we sat fishing, that he figured at that time there had been only one option left. The ferry man had told him that the boat was due to arrive in twenty minutes, and that it took about forty to cross the bay to connect up with the rest of the road. Samuel had looked at that mile-long stretch of the water – glassy flat in the absence of the late-morning winds – and figured he had only one option.

He quickly rewrapped the package of letters tightly in his oiled bunting, watched the flow of the waters in front of him for a moment – and then taking his bearings of landmarks at the ferry landing on the other side, he dove into the salty and surprisingly cold ocean inlet intent on swimming across instead of riding.

The ferry man couldn't believe his eyes as the Running Indian leapt into the ocean. He hollered after him and warned him but the swimming man did not hear what he was trying to tell him. Later when asked by a reporter about the event, the little man replied, "I knew he was a goner. I tried to stop him. If the channel's cold water didn't get him I knew that the sharks would. Or maybe both."

Commenting on that man's statement in the old article as we sat fishing so long after it all happened,

Samuel cast out his line again and laughed, "Trout, I didn't know what a shark was! If I did, I would have never jumped into that bay."

Now, everyone who's ever attempted a long swim knows that once you're in the water the distance seems to triple. From the dock, Samuel had thought of the mile in his running terms – six to ten minutes, and mentally added about thirty to it for good measure. If everything worked out right, he'd be on the other side about twenty minutes ahead of the other man.

He had crossed a few lakes before, and was confident in his swimming strength. He was about four hundred feet from the dock when he thought he heard Nestor's voice carried across the waves – and turning he saw the man reaching the dock and waving. The Running Indian thrust one arm up to wave back and then continued on his way – misunderstanding Nestor's waves as encouragement and not understanding the warnings that they actually were. Nestor told the reporters, later, that there was no way he was set to swim across that mile of open ocean, and he figured that second place was a preferable substitute for the great possibility of drowning or getting devoured and not finishing at all.

The Klamath boy prevailed. He judged the changing currents and reworked his swim path as he went along. He angled his charge forward to compensate for the swells and drifts, and after a bit the cold water stopped hurting and he swam on and on and on. It felt like he was crossing a thousand Klamaths, each one trying to turn him this-away or that-away, pushing him toward his goal or pulling him from it. He swam on and on, keeping Fort Point on the opposite bank as his immediate and only goal.

He felt for his bundle now and again, still tied tightly to his middle. It had lifted slightly, turned into a crude buoyant belt that helped keep the tired and purt near-frozen man above the surface of the sea. He told me later that it was at that time he remembered my words, and smiled knowing that in fact the floating oiled belt full of the Chinaman's papers was indeed lifting him and helping him finish his journey.

Along about halfway across he swam past the ferry that was headed in the opposite direction to the north dock to pick up Nestor and some other folks needing to make the long crossing. The fellas and ladies on board the north-bound boat leaned over the railings cheering on the lone swimmer – never having seen anything like that craziness before. Samuel waived at them, swimming on his back for a few feet, and then turned round to keep moving in the right direction.

At one point he felt something brush below him, and figured he ought to see if he could stand – maybe a shelf of rocks were just under his feet that he had no knowledge of. The floor moved under him when he tried, so he continued to swim on dismissing the false floor as a big fish or some sand bar that fell away. He could have never known that the true floor of the channel was some four hundred feet below him, or that the false floor he had felt had probably been either the playful ocean dolphins or even the terrible Great White sharks that frequented the mouth of that bay.

All in all, when he drug himself from those freezing waters – oilcloth package and papers intact – he found the first of the cheering crowds urging him onward. Word had spread from the announcement carried by the rider on the hard-run black tail bay horse, and folks were coming out to see history being made.

Looking back over his shoulder, briefly, he saw the ferry had turned and was about thirty or twenty minutes out – and he thought that he saw Nestor, on the top deck, hollerin' and cheering him on. He lit out, knowing that even though his new friend was happy for him making it across the inlet alive, as soon as that ferry docked Nestor would be running like the devil to catch up with him – and Samuel expected no less.

Dozens of photographers were ready at the finish line beside the wharf, and there was no end to the quickly assembled finery of the ladies and city gentlemen in attendance. Bands were playing all along the last few miles of the race way, and roustabouts and cowboys were even showing off their trick riding a bit and letting a little celebratory lead fly here and there.

The Running Indian began to limp a little, as the grassy and edged roadside began to disappear and he was forced to run on the cobbled or rocked streets. He later talked about the physical pain he endured in those last few miles, as his sweat and the salt from the drying ocean water on his skin met in his cut and bleeding bare feet to sear pain into his body on each step he took. Nestor would later remark that unsure of the exact way to the finish line, he followed the bloody footprints of his friend to the end of the race.

The Running Indian crossed the finish line of the race at 11:05 a.m. on August 4th, 1913 and was met by a flurry of photographs and back-patting. Catching his breath, he asked for a tub of water and finding none available he limped across the street and stood in the horse trough to soothe his hurt and wounded feet. Quite a few of the photographs of that day – including the one I had seen in the newspaper – showed him perched in that somewhat dirty watering trough, shaking hands with all manner of politicians and other seemingly important men.

He endured the start of a speech by one of those individuals, and not understanding the protocol of politely listening to self-inflated buffoons bluster on, he took advantage of a brief pause in the man's words and asked if anyone in the crowd knew the way to the University as he had a parcel to deliver there. That comment set off a few chuckles and guffaws in the folks, and one fella came forward. He wore British Naval attire and introduced himself as Captain Reginald Burlingame in the command of the *HMS Widgeon*, and the explained that later in the afternoon he had been planning to go toward the University himself. He invited the Running Indian to travel with him, through the city to the University, in his carriage.

With that detail set and out of the way, Samuel felt better about answering questions from reporters and folks. The red-faced politician had given up on the rest of his speech after several more interruptions from Samuel and the reporters.

When Samuel heard clapping and huzzahs coming up from down the road, he ignored everyone and hobbled to the race finish line. He waited there until Nestor came into view and applauded and urged his friend to finish the race strong. A blurry photo from one of the news stories shows a smiling Samuel reaching over the finish line to congratulate his friend. They both laughed and laughed at the end, talking over some of the adventures they had both been through, together, in the previous four days. They were awarded their prizes and ribbons and laughed again at the giant sums of money they had received that beforc would have been impossible to imagine possessing in a lifetime.

Nestor eventually said his goodbyes to Samuel later that morning, leaving for the train station. He was headed back to Missouri where he planned to open a store and maybe eventually a restaurant – and find a wife. Samuel had no immediate plans other than making it to the University, and like happens so many times in the lives of folks those two friends shook hands and went their separate ways.

After a few hours the Race Dignitaries put away their banners and buntings and let the band go home – by all telegraphed sentry accounts, the next runner wasn't expected for several more days if not a week. Soon after the last photograph was taken of Samuel, the *Widgeon* captain collected him to ride along to the University.

On the hour-long carriage tour through the bustling and giant city, Samuel and the Captain talked about the race and where Samuel had come from. The Captain smiled when Samuel talked about the Klamath River Canyon, as he had only a few years previous married a beautiful Yurok girl from near Trinidad, California. His wife had spent some time up the Klamath, as a child, with her Aunt Adal. Samuel nearly fell out of his carriage seat and explained his surprised reaction to the Captain. The Captain's wife, being a niece to Aunt Adal was most assuredly his cousin as Adal was his Aunt as well. Both men said the name, "Requa Threepony" at the same time and laughed again at the coincidence.

Arriving at the group of learning buildings, the Captain held the carriage and waited while Samuel – with garments wrapped around his sore and still-bleeding feet – limped into the University office.

He announced, "I'm looking for Professor Ashbury Balboa Hayes. I have an important delivery of letters and documents for him to translate."

The gentleman secretary behind the great desk gave Samuel the only bad news that he would receive that day – that the Professor had passed away several months before in a tragic locomotive and steam car accident. Samuel was crestfallen at the news, and slumped down in a nearby chair. After everything he had gone through to get the papers to the Professor, he couldn't believe that he wasn't going to be able to finish his agreed task.

The secretary came around the mammoth desk, and in the spirit of charity and kindness, he put his hand on Samuel's shoulder and expressed his condolences at his loss.

Samuel looked up with the tears of frustration in his eyes, and stood to leave – offering his thanks for the man's words. As he walked away he stopped and turned and with a weary look on his worn and tired face he added, to the confusement of the secretary man, "The sun-haired boy will be so very disappointed. I won't be surprised at all if the dead Chinaman will now be forced to turn into a forest demon."

Samuel limped his way back to the carriage, intending to thank the Captain for his kindness and say his farewell. The race winner was deep in thought and hadn't a clue what his next step was.

Seeing the concern on Samuel's face – and more and more curious about why the race winner needed to see a Professor so all-fired bad – the Captain finally drew the whole story from his newly-found relative.

At the end of the whole tale, the Captain slapped

his knee and started laughing. Samuel was a little off-put by the reaction, but the Captain quickly explained another coincidence. He was leaving the next day on the *Widgeon* for the Orient, to take an ambassador entourage to visit with the Boy King of China. He was happy to hire Samuel on in some capacity – perhaps as a messenger or an attendant of some sort – and take him to the country where he could deliver the papers in person to the family of the lost man. He could even arrange a private and trusted translator for the documents at the British Embassy when they landed in the foreign port. He even extended his assistance with the offer to hire a guide for Samuel when they arrived in China – to help him navigate and travel that expansive countryside.

With the world open before him – and thinking of his own wide-eyed discoveries of Redwoods, the salty ocean, and other colors of human skin – he quickly decided to make the journey in consideration of the other findings that he was sure to make. He was set on finishing the task asked of him by me on that dusty Klamath roadside, six hundred miles previous and what was beginning to seem like a whole world away.

Chapter Fifteen

Memories of Better Times and Places

"We knew our wounded boys from the fallen enemy before we even saw them. We'd just walk toward where we heard 'Momma' coming from."

– Corpsman Andrew Yates, *USS New Hampshire*

When I made my way out to the back patio of my place this morning – coffee cup, favorite pen, and journal in tow – my eyes caught sight of the slightly overworked and sun-faded Standard flapping defiantly over our Cemetery grounds. I had planned today to write of the adventures I had that summer of 1913 up at the High Springs Pool, but I was annoyed to distraction because I couldn't get the name Harold Jackson out of my head.

Being very old and an admitted Forgetter Of Many Important Things, I decided to sit at my table and wait for any notion connected with that name to recall itself to me. After about an hour of setting there – staring at my journal and the flowers and the crick and the fool sky – my eye caught that waving flag again.

And then I remembered. I remembered Harold Jackson and baseball and writing a letter and the Dominican Republic field hospital and his Mother and Angels with long outstretched wings – and how it all fit together like a dusty and sad puzzle.

I'll write about the High Springs Pool tomorrow – who knows if I'll ever remember all this in its entirety again so I'm getting it down now, while I can.

As a boy – from the time the snow would melt in the spring to the time it would fly in the late fall, I could be found in the woods surrounding our cabin. My dog and I would travel the mountainside on the game trails that latticed through the firs, pines, blackberries, and madrones. We found springs, and caves, and rock outcroppings. We made forts and hideaways in blow-down timber, in rock piles, and in the wide and low braches of hardwood trees perched on the tops of ridges.

We ran the purlieu and the hillsides proper, memorizing every twist and turn in the paths and every watering hole for miles around. A rock crest above our house was the proscenium stage where I acted out plays and dramatic tales with my dog – I, Pylades and she, Orestes – with stage right a grove of live oak and stage left a field of fallen granite. Before a watchful and well-mannered audience of squirrels, chipmunks, skunks, raccoons, and maybe even a fox or a coyote – I set to deliver homage to the long-fallen Globe Theater and a tribute to the amphitheaters of ancient Greece with my rough open-air western stage. My ad-hoc orations resonated through the valley with better and clearer acoustics that those I later heard tested in Belgium's Palais des Beaux Arts or in Egypt's Cairo Opera House.

I wonder, sometimes, if I were to go to those everlasting places of my youth's memory today, would I find the toy army men my friend Zhen Zi and I had placed carefully on a ledge near Flying Rat Cave? Would the pieces of quartz – laid out over eighty years ago to form an arrow on the ground – still point the way to my treasures of marbles and baseball cards hidden in The Old Oak Tree?

If I could go there, now in my advanced age would I find the large rocks I had dragged to the side of the High Spring Pool – to use as a level jumping-in point for my dog and I – still setting in place waiting for a barefoot boy and his black dog who would never return? Even if my body was able, I'm afraid that after all of this time I might not remember how to find any of it.

A lucky few of us have those special environs or outside hideaways in our own history – comforting memories of certain places and certain times in our lives when all was well and the life we were to live was still an unraveled mystery. As a boy I often wondered if other fellas like me had the penchant to retreat into a wooded refuge on occasion. I underestimated, then, the powerful need for most folks to have had one of those special places – when their worries were topped out at seeing if they could skip a rock a little bit farther than the day before and making sure they made it home in time for supper.

I cannot place the proper words on this page to explain what my River Canyon refuges meant to me then, and how I went to them in my mind again and again throughout my life. First, to bolster my attitude when I was lonely and homesick right after I defiantly joined the Navy. Later, I'd fondly think of those special places and times to calm my nerves as our ship – the *USS New Hampshire* – grumbled on and on from one battle to the next during the Pacification of the Dominican Republic.

During that time in my life, which I refer to as my Navy Years – I had the unfortunate opportunity to learn just how deeply important those places and times of my youth really were. Only a few years after I had left my River Canyon to see the world from the deck of that Navy ship, I sat with a young soldier in the field hospital. I recall that day when I had seen my name on the duty roster for the field hospital reconnoiter, I had tried to figure out a way to get another fella to cover for me. It was baseball day, and I wanted to be out on the field and not in some smelly dyin' place. I had had enough of that already, but as it worked out I had to miss the field and found myself – unhappily – trudging from bed to bed jawing with fellas who had busted toes or who were healing from minor scrapes to see when they could be put back on the rotation lists.

I spied a curtained-off corner of the ward, and peeked in. I recognized a fella that played the best short stop I had ever seen – and who was also a double threat with his phenomenal skills at the plate – Seaman Apprentice Jackson, bandaged up and hurtin'. The flies were buzzing about, so I quickly stepped in and shut the hanging screens behind me. I could see the yellow that the weeping burns left on the bright white bandages before I saw the sad and lonely look on the man's face. He stared at the roof, miles away in his mind and deep in the pain of his burns – but he still had tried to move his good arm to salute when I walked in.

I figured that baseball day be darned, and my selfishness be darned too. My required duty time on the hospital floor was just about over, but I took off my hat and unhooked the top buttons of my stuffy shirt and settled in to do whatever I could for the dying boy.

We had once been in the same command group, and we were familiar with each other from playing baseball and residing in the same quarters area on the ship. He was nigh unto all of the way through his eighteenth year, and I was a seasoned veteran of the services at near twenty with two battlefield commissions under my belt. The boy and I talked for hours about where we had come from.

He was dying from wounds given to him by the guerilla-sponsored Dominican revolutionaries, courtesy of a pair of mines placed near an abandoned church. The mines had taken off his left leg, his left hand, and tore out his left eye. He had burns all over from the fire that had happened after, before anyone could get to him. For a short bit, I had a hard time looking at him when we talked – because he was so hurt and burned, but I tried my best not to let him see anything in me but support and kindness for him.

I did not once, that day, let a mention of the game of baseball cross my lips. He'd never play again – probably not live more than the week, by the look of it – and I wasn't going to make the pain of his Great Jump worse than it had to be.

He knew he was in a serious fix, and he looked more relieved than I have the ability to describe to see someone setting in with him. He was scared and quiet and I couldn't imagine what was going through his mind. I wondered to myself what kept him from sobbing as I figured if I knew I was probably going to die I'd more than likely be an awful, wailing mess.

I read a newspaper article to him, and fixed his pillow better, and asked him if there was anything I could do.

"Just stay with me a bit," he answered in his thick bayou accent, adding, "Sir." I made him promise to forget about ranks.

I knew what he meant by asking me to stay there. I explained to him that I'd be there as long as he needed me to be. He knew what I meant, too, and a peaceable look of relief crossed his face for a moment.

We were both quiet for a while and then he asked me to help him write a very matter-of-fact letter to his family, which mainly contained instructions to his brothers to take care of the farm, their Mother, and each other. I had tried to hide my shaking hands, as I wrote, but if he noticed he didn't say anything to me about it.

I read the letter back to him, and he asked for only two additions.

"Write them to please also look after my hounds," he said and I remember he winced as he tried to move a bit in his bed. "And," he added as the tears came on in both our eyes, "write one more time at the bottom to my Momma – that I'm gonna miss her so awful bad."

It was too quiet for a while. I was trying to stop my tears as I made the finishing touches to the letter, introducing myself at the bottom of it as the transcriber, the date, and the circumstances that had brought their son and brother to the care of the hospital. The scratching of my pen on the paper seemed to echo through the strangely silent hospital, and I recalled my own Mother one time telling me a family hand-me-down legend about how when someone is about to die that the sound falls around them. She said it was because of the ring of Angels and their outspread wings, encircling the doomed person in protection and mourning as they waited to bring him Home.

My tears had no business staining that letter or upsetting the hurt man, either. I took a deep breath and kept doing what he needed me to.

I had been in that letter-writing seat a few times before, and I didn't want to be there then, but I suppose it made my heart feel a little better knowing that I helped the boy let his family know – one last time – the deep concern he felt for them. No one should ever have to face their dying hour alone.

How his eyes lit up when he talked about his hounds and the hunting they had done in the tree-lined swamps around his home in Louisiana. He said that the best days weren't necessarily those when he and the hounds took a lot of game – he enjoyed it most when the sun broke through the weather, and he could set in with his dogs on the bank of the swamps, listening to the water and the wind and the trees and the animal life all around him.

He coughed then, and said in his slow and metered way, "You know, I can still remember how it felt when I'd put my hand on one of the hounds' backs after he'd been sittin' in the sun. It was so warm – and I could feel the life inside 'im and the movin' from his breathing." His voice trailed off, and he didn't speak again. He and I both shivered despite the oppressing tropical heat we suffered to breathe through.

His eyes closed, and I could tell his condition was getting worse. I tried to fill the silence and take his mind off the pain that even the rationed morphine could no longer touch, so I started to tell him about the adventures that my dog and I had undertaken in our places in the woods, and for a while he would try to smile when I said something that he knew about too – like when I said I learned how to speak Dog, and that she had loved to eat carrots straight from our garden, and that she had saved my life more than once, and that she was my best friend.

For the rest of his life, I told him all about where I had grown up, and the adventures I had undertaken, about meeting a President, and why townsfolk had called me Trout for the longest time. I told him about Chinese princes and Jade Temples and miraculous coincidences.

I held his hand as I talked about anything I could think of. For those two hours, we were both thousands of miles away from that hellishly hot dying place, me on my well-traveled game paths of Northern California and him in a skiff on the lazy Mississippi River with his best dog at his feet. In those last hours, I wasn't a Petty Officer 2nd Class and he wasn't a Seaman Apprentice – we were just two country boys a long, long way from our mountains. Even after he stopped nodding and smiling, I kept talking and holding his hand until the nurses said that he was gone.

His name was Harold Marchaunt Jackson, and he died thousands of miles from his home protecting the United States and helping to spread Democracy in a troubled world. It's a conflict that most people today have no knowledge of – which is a cryin' shame since so many of our boys fought there and died there. Because of the heat and the diseases that could be had, most of them that died there were buried there as well.

Harold Jackson would never see his nineteenth year, or ever step again across the threshold of his Mother's bayou house to receive the heroic welcome that he deserved.

He showed me that day what I probably already knew. We're lucky if we have those simple and peaceful times in our past to think on when times are rough – whether they happen on the banks of the great Mississippi or tiny Elk Crick.

If there is a Heaven, I think that part of it must look like a swamp on a sunny day – and over the years I've tried to imagine the homecoming Private Jackson got when he met up again, Up There, with his best hounds in what he knew Paradise would be.

Euclid P. Hammarsen

Chapter Sixteen

The Secret of the High Spring Pool

"The whole place is chock full of springs and hidden dales and waterfalls – and mountain lions, giant killer snakes, and vines that produce a devilishly itchy rash."
– Sampson Hutchins, Map Maker
and Surveyor

I recall in that far away summer of 1913, after the Running Indian had left with the copied papers I kept my ear to the ground about his progress. No one knew anything about him, or his foot race, or even if he had crossed the finish line. I was impatient to hear something about the whole business, but it was impossible for me to ask too many questions of folks without giving my secret purpose away in the effort. I resumed my normal activities – as best I could – and tried to think on Dark Knights and Mars-men and

Dastardly Spies and such as I made my way through the hills above my home.

As best as I can remember, it was on one of those hot Saturday afternoons in July when even the shadows of the tall fir and pine trees surrounding my fort couldn't shade the thick heat out of the air. I called my dog, who had been burrowing after some little thing under a nearby log, and we took off up the hill for the High Spring Pool.

The Pool was one of the best secret places that I occasionally visited in my boyhood rounds of the mountains around our home. It was a spring, as far as I could tell, since it had no streams leading to it or from it. It was too far away from our home to be of any use to us, so I never really told Mother about it. I also probably didn't tell her because I was afraid that she'd start in with the whole drowning speech. If I had a nickel for every time a conversation started with, "You know, a full-sized man can drown in a cup of water," I'd be moving in next to the Rockefellers.

For a mountain spring, the Pool was large and deep. It formed itself in a field of granite beside an outcropping of bedrock, and lay atwixt the firs and pines almost at the top of one of the steepest ridges around. I had walked by the spot many times, and I would have never found it if it hadn't been for the wild horses.

It was my very own Clerkenwell, and just as sacred to me as the original water was to those dour London clerics.

As Cinder and I clum the hot and dusty hillside, I thought about that incredible day she and I had stumbled upon it.

Cinder and I had been tracking a raccoon up the

hillside, and I realized that we had traveled higher on the mountain than I probably was supposed to. The tracks were still fresh, so I decided to go a jot bit further. Rounding a large tree, I was startled by my dog. She was stock still in the trail in front of me, crouched low with the hackles on her neck bristling up. She was reacting to much more than a raccoon.

I thought that maybe our luck had run out, and that a mountain lion or a bear was about to eat us. I crouched next to my dog, became quiet, and listened to what was out there.

Shaking my head and closing my eyes, I tried to listen a little harder to the noises I heard coming from below us. I could not place the clacking, a water sound, and animal noises together. All down but nine, curious and cautious, Cinder and I crept over the trail and down hill towards the sounds.

Sitting at the foot of a wide pine, and hidden by some brush, I watched with peeled eyes at what appeared before us.

A large rock field lay among the trees on a bench of the mountainside. Enough sunlight made it through the canopy that grasses, lupine flowers, and cat's paw grew on the forest floor. Since we were on the western side of the mountain, and pretty high up, what lay in the middle of the rocky area shone like glass from the sunlight it was enjoying.

The pool of water was green and blue. It looked cold, and very out of place on the hillside. Cinder was still agitated, but we were upwind of whatever was in the meadow so we crept a jot closer to fetch a better look at some movement in the grasses and beyond the trees. I wished I had brought my trusty .22 along, but instead I quietly armed myself with all I had – my little apple-peeler. Probably would be all right to defend myself with it against a herd of wild carrots or turnips, but against anything that could walk on it's own accord I was looking at a hard and messy fight at very close range with that three inch sharpened steel blade.

I still couldn't make out the noises. They sounded familiar, but very out of place. I crawled around to get a better look from different rocks in our little hiding spot, but when I looked at Cinder she seemed to give me the go-ahead to just stand up and check the whole thing out. On the measure she seemed only coyote worried, not mountain lion worried.

I stood up slowly, craning my neck to its limit to be able to see around the trees that were to the side of us. I rubbed my eyes, not believing what was grazing out before me in that unexpected and magic-looking little valley.

Spread across the little secret valley were the biggest deer in the history of man. I noticed quick that it was odd that the giant deer didn't have one set of horns in the lot of 'em – it wasn't the right time of year for the females to all bunch up.

Then it hit me – they weren't deer at all. With my own eyes I was looking in on the legendary Wild Horses of Happy Camp. I had thought that it had been a made up tale every time I had heard it.

I was so amazed and enthralled by what I saw I would not have been any more surprised if the Lady of the Lake rose in the spring and the horses actually turned out to be unicorns grazing in a fairy valley.

It quickly moved to the top of my list of summer Secret Places. Several times those horses and I would see each other up there, and after many weeks of the chance encounters we were finally comfortable enough to allow the other to go about their business. The wild horses and I were not close – but I had a feeling that they began to tolerate my wide-eyed staring and my overly cautious reigning-in of my dog. Cinder just ignored them, but kept at the ready for a dog-horse tussle if one was brought to her.

If I remembered or planned ahead I'd haul some apples up for them in a small bag and they'd winnie like the devil for them but always shied away. I'd have to end up leaving the fruit and backing off before they'd take any of it.

The beautiful and proud stallion watched close over the bunch of them. I noticed how he played with the little foals and nipped at some of the mares when they seemed to be getting a little horse-naggy at him. He was the undisputed leader of the group, and by the looks of his shiny hooves he was also a proven protector of them as well. No mountain lion was going to win against that horse in a fair fight.

There were many such fitfully hot afternoons when Cinder and I would slip away into the hills after I had finished my chores. We'd scramble through the thick heat, higher and higher up the mountainside. Thirsty and covered in sweat and dirt, we'd descend a bit into the secret valley of the High Spring Pool. Disappointed at not finding the horses wallowing in the field or prancing about, I'd chuck my clothes behind me as I made my way to the Pool, very purt nearly always losing at least one sock in the process. Like clockwork my dog would be way ahead of me, sniffing around the pool and around the little valley making sure that we were safe.

I would jump into the pool, feet first, and upon surfacing I would try to float on my back. Sometimes the water would get into my ears and up my nose as I lay there, and the only things I would hear would be the thick sounds distorted by the pool. Cinder would paddle around me, knocking into me and nudging me to throw her a rock or a stick. And every time, I would.

I'd often entertain the thoughts of showing the place to one of my friends – but I didn't – it was just a place for me and my dog and no one else.

When it was time to go, I'd roll around in the dirt and then lay down in any bit of sunshine I could find making its way through the trees to dry off. Then it was back into my dirty and hot clothes and down the mountainside toward home.

If my Mother had asked me if I'd been up the mountain swimming in the secret pool, I would have told her the truth. She never did ask me that. She did, on several occasions, ask me if I had been out rolling in the dirt, and being a good and honest boy, I always truthfully answered yes.

Euclid P. Hammersen

Chapter Seventeen

The Worst Day of My Young Life

"You never know what – or who – is
gonna come a' running out of these
mountains."
– Elijah Tichnor, Resident

It has been said that you never know what the
day will bring. That early July morning of my youth I
never, ever would have guessed that by sunset I would
have stared down a murderous bear, buried a friend,
and slapped – deservedly – a beloved American icon.

After breakfast I was out the door to begin my
various chores. Cinder came up and brought me a stick,
and I threw it for her a few times. We roughhoused a bit
– me swatting at her and she nipping at my legs. Seeing
my Ma peer out the window at me, I got back to work.
My dog went to her spot on the porch, watching me with
a smart curious look on her face. I had tried to explain
chores and work to her previous, but she didn't seem to
get the whole idea – for her, simply, there was only play

and adventure time and eating and sleeping.

Chopping wood for my Mother to fiendishly fill up the cook stove my mind wandered. I figured that soon maybe I would tire of those domestic duties and join the Foreign Legion. Like my dog, I would forego chores and I would live in a far away country and write to my parents about my adventures. I smiled at the imagined post card I would someday send. "Mom and Dad: Just a note as I am late to climb the pyramids. My camel is touchy, but she is the fastest on the sand. How are you? Yesterday I hooked a crocodile while fishing. No trout yet. Love, your son Euclid Plutarch Hammarsen." I would end my imaginary postcard with, "P.S. I chopped no wood today."

Smiling at the luxury of my anticipated future, I startled back into reality as I thought I heard a few gunshots. They were far away, yet, and were probably just a hunter up across the hill. I set back to finishing my wood chopping.

I looked up from the woodpile when the dog started barking. Mother came to the porch and we both looked down the road at the ruckus in the underbrush.

A large man was being chased by a larger bear. The fella had a rucksack and a bedroll on his back, and a mess of trout on a line strung about him like the decorations on a Christmas tree. He had pine needles and leaves in his hair and in his extremely large mustache.

Now, I had seen a lot of strange things come runnin' out of the woods before that day, but I had never seen anything close to what was barreling toward our house.

In a short bit of time many varied events came to pass. My Mother, seeing the procession heading toward me turned in the house and instantly reemerged with the old shotgun we kept by the door. She lifted it to her shoulder, walking toward the threat and calling to me at the same time.

I looked for Cinder, but she was already spanning the distance between me and the man and the bear. Barking at full force, she wasn't the old, gray-haired lab that had mothered me like her pup all those years. She came alive with a fierceness I had never seen in her before.

The big man, at that point, tripped on his trout string. The bear, breathing down his neck, actually ran over the top of the man due to his sudden stop and fall. The beast, seeing that he had passed over the trout-laced man, turned instead toward the next closest person – me.

My sweet dog, my friend. My *Achates*. I learned to climb the hills around our house by holding on to her haunches as we explored. How many rattlesnakes had she saved me from stepping on over those years? How many hours had we spent fishing and playing in the crick? I've heard it said that a man can give his heart to more than one woman in his lifetime, but there's only room in it for one dog.

As the events rushed around us, I saw my dog turn to me. Her eyes showed concern, and she yapped at me. I heard her warn me and say, "Run, my boy, run! I will protect you! Shin out, now!" No one would believe me later when we talked about Cinder, except for my Dad. When he was a boy he had also learned how to speak Dog. He knew she had warned me. War Sing would have understood, too.

My wood axe still in my hand, I backed toward the house as directed by my dog and away from the bear. My Cinder, with a last look toward me, leapt growling and biting into the black frothing mass of teeth and claws.

The bear, quickly with two cutting swipes killed my best friend. My dog lay dead at its feet. There was no final moment where I cradled her wounded and dying body, thanking her as I held her and rubbed her head one last time. There was no chance to let her know that she was such a good girl for protecting me like she had. There wasn't even a chance for her to know, at the end, that I would be okay. She died violently, and quickly, and alone even though she was only feet from where I stood.

She had died protecting me and trying to buy me enough time to get to a safe place. The black dog safeguarded me like nothing else could have, and she gave her life to shield mine.

Still a boy, I was enveloped in a man's rage without the ability to contain it. My blood soaked and torn dog, dead, was being pulled apart by the bear. I knew what I was supposed to do, and then I did what I felt I needed to do.

I began to run at the frothing critter fast and low, axe still in hand, determined to kill that awful beast – the murderous beast – which had hurt someone that I loved. I had forgotten everything and understood nothing but my need to protect what was left of my best friend.

The beast stood, with a roar, on its back legs welcoming me in its evil and treacherous way. It had my best friend's blood on its awful snout. I was close enough to smell its foul breath. I continued toward it, distracting it from the limp body of my dog, holding the axe like I would have held a baseball bat determined to drive a bloody home run right through its black beastly heart.

I made only two steps before I and my raised axe were grabbed up short by the big man with the big mustache. He had quickly discarded his trout line and righted himself, and seeing the tragedy that had followed him into our yard he was setting about making it right.

I fought with him to let me go, and the bear came closer, walking on its back haunches like a giant man. It roared and roared. Blood rushed in my ears. Sounds had disappeared, except for the roaring bear, my angry yells to let me go, and the heavy loud sound of my dog's blood dripping into the yard.

As the man held me back it was like someone had taken a blanket off of me. I could hear my Mother's yells, the man yelling, me yelling, the chickens behind us all in a flutter, the crick tumbling over the rocks below the house. Above it all, I could hear the shots ringing one after the other into the afternoon.

Like a giant tree being felled, the beast began to lean. Several spots on its chest darkly grew in that moment that lasted forever.

As yet another shot rang out, I finally took notice of my Mother. She had been standing just in front of me, and a few feet to the side, during the whole fray. Later, we would figure by the spent shells and the wounds on the bear that she had shot and reloaded the old shotgun nine times. Each blast had hit the bear.

I can only remember hearing two or three shots, out of all that she had made.

The beast weakly swiped one more time in our general direction as it continued its fall, landing finally with it's snout a mere inch from my Mother's left foot.

She moved back a step, loaded her last shell into the shotgun, placed the barrel three inches behind the beast's left ear, and pulled the trigger one last time. The sound echoed through the hills, going on and on and on until the noise finally died in the far away timbers.

My Mother, who fussed over her hair being just-so in her combs and barrettes, and who prided herself in her seamstress work and our clothing being mended and clean and nicely cared for, absently dabbed at the blood and bone pieces strewn across her apron, face, and hair – pieces of bone and innards which had just moments before been inside the ferocious beast. Looking back to see that I was okay, she promptly fell into a heap where she had just stood, sobbing. I ran to her.

She never did recall that last shot, or even several that she made before it. My Dad said later to me that he had seen strange fugues like hers in the war. Years later I saw it, firsthand, in my men and even once in myself.

I was inconsolable in my loss and my grief. I would not talk and would not move from the side of my killed companion.

My Father came into the yard on our good horse to see quite an awful sight – a giant slumped bear with it's head blown apart, his wife crumpled in a blood-soaked heap with a firearm open across her lap, and me – sobbing, of course – cradling the lifeless body of my dog in my arms. Next to us all, the giant mustached man stood overlooking the disastrous mess with his hands on his hips as the other men from his party were finally catching up with him.

"Ellie," my Father bellowed as he made a running dismount off the good horse – drawing his revolver at the same time, "what in Sam Hill has happened here?"

In a stuttering voice she gave a brief outline of the events, pointing a shaky and bloody hand toward the man who had brought the bear to our yard.

He sat her down on the porch front, and ran to my side. With my dog's blood all over me, I must've looked injured. I recall him looking over me and me not caring much about it – far away inside somewhere I knew that I was going to be safe because he was there to help me – but I couldn't make words in my mouth or my mind. I kept swallowing down the anger rising in my throat, and I was blinking the wetness from my eyes. My hands were soaked in blood, dirt, and dog hair and my hot tears fell into the dusty ground where I kneeled next to my friend.

Weakly, trying to hold back my sobs, I asked him, "Is there anything that can be done for her?" I hoped, but I knew. I knew there was nothing anyone could do.

He kneeled down next to me, and looked her over a bit. He was just doing it to make me feel better, I think, because we could all see that she had been cut too deep and had lost almost all of her blood. Her neck had been broke, too, and my Father moved her head a bit to a more natural angle. He closed her eyes, and brought her legs closer together – giving her finality a little bit of practical respect.

With tears in his eyes, too, he took me by the shoulders and said, "Son, I loved her," and his voice cracked a bit as he pulled me close to him, "because she loved you."

I could feel the hotness of his ears and his neck against me as he held me there, and I let go with sobs and I didn't give a care who or what saw or heard me.

He let me be, then, and stood. I recall he was so

red-eared they were almost purple, and he was clenching his fists so hard his hands were almost bright white.

Turning to the mustached man, my Father let go a string of logger expletives and consternations that normally would have made me blush. He got right up to the mustached man, and believe you me unloaded terms and phrases he had been holding in reserve for a special occasion and I had never knew existed.

The man had his hat in his hand, and looked awful sorry – and the fellas who had come running out of the woods behind the man were all looking at the ground. They all looked a little embarrassed and respectful but also ready to jump in if my Dad started swinging at the mustached fella.

My Father knew my Mother could hear, but that didn't seem to hold him back as he strung together such foulness and threats and degrading language to the man and his entourage. He reached back, readying to smash the man in the face, and his shirt sleeve pulled up a little to show his Kansas 20th Infantry tattoo.

The mustached man boldly but politely interrupted, ducking the roundhouse punch deftly and trying to grab my dad's arm. "My word, Private Hammarsen? Jack, is that you, son?"

My Father stopped his blue streak, and muttered, "Sergeant Roosevelt?"

The big mustached man laughed and slapped my Dad on the back, and they shook hands like old friends. My dad's ears were still deep red. He was acting kind of polite, but even in my state I could tell he was still real upset.

They continued to talk, and I heard words like

"San Juan" and "best enlisted man I ever served with" and "scouting wilderness areas" and even the word "President."

I could barely hear the exchange that ensued. I wouldn't have cared about the conversation even if they were Ty Cobb and Nap Lajoie arguing about their batting records. I didn't care about anything other than taking care of my dog.

In the midst of the conversations and the yelling and the back and forth of the adults, I slipped away like I was good at – becoming invisible to one and all and doing what needed to be done.

I carried the body of my friend around the back of the barn, and laid her gently on the rough canvas litter I had built for a school project the year before. I stole into the house, through the backdoor, and gathered up her favorite coverlid from next to the woodstove – where she liked to nap. I gently put that blanket over her, on the homemade carrier, and put the shovel in beside her.

I pulled the body of my dog to the High Springs Pool on that litter, crying with every step. I remembered all of the times she had made that trip with me, running up in front and back and around me. Protecting me. Warning me of trouble on the trail ahead.

It was a long hike, but it seemed too soon that I was pulling her past the pool and into the flower covered valley where we had spent so many happy hours.

I sat there with her, for a while, before digging a grave for her in the nearby field where we had had so many daisy times. She'd be there forever, among the wild horses and deer and later the elk, in what would someday become a nationally designated wilderness area thanks to the awful man who brought the bear to our dooryard. All I knew then was that I wanted her to be where she and I had been happy, and I'd like to think that if we had talked about it – before – that she would have picked the same place I had.

I wrapped her again in her blanket, and pulled her as gently as I could down into the grave I had dug. I sat there, in that hole with her for the longest time – trying to hold on to her as long as I could. I patted her cold haunches one last time, and kissed her on the top of her broken head.

I couldn't watch as I shoveled the dirt on her, and finally got through that awful task. I found that I was crying so hard that breathing was an afterthought, making sobs escape my mouth in shuddering sharpness.

I piled granite stones around her, and over her, to protect her from being disturbed and only quit as I heard my name being called by my Father from down along the hillside. I couldn't answer him, but he found me soon enough – even in the deepening darkness of the late afternoon – by following the tracks the litter had made behind me.

Without talking – like two folks who knew each other and who had worked together many times before – he helped me move two giant speckled granite slabs on to the top of the rocks I had already placed over my friend.

He didn't ask me about the pool, or the little valley, or anything. With his hand on my shoulder, I knew that it was finally time to go.

As we left in the darkness, I stopped for just a minute and looked back toward the High Springs Pool and the meadow and my dog's grave one last time, knowing that I would never go there again. As I turned to finally go, I spied the stallion horse walk out from behind the copse of trees – he nodded his head toward me, and I nodded back. I never learned Horse, but I'd like to think that he was trying to tell me that his herd would watch over my friend for me.

I finally understood the pain that losing War Sing must have brought to my Father. I wondered for some time if all of the good that comes from caring about someone is worth the searing hurt of eventually losing them – even now, over ninety, I still haint been able to answer that question properly.

I recall that after leaving the grave we moved down the mountain slowly, and I resisted the impulse to run back up to the High Springs Pool to be with my dog. I just wanted all of the awful events of the day to disappear. I was not prepared to be a dogless boy – there were still adventures to have and fish to catch and rattlers to avoid and hundreds of things that I had never done alone. I could not imagine ever smiling again, or laughing again, or going to our special places. I knew that I would never love another dog like I loved her – and I haint – even though she's been at the High Springs Pool for about eighty years now.

When my Dad and I finally made it back to the house, my eyes were red and I was filthy from the blood and the dirt and the sweat of the day still being all over me. We came upon quite a scene in the dooryard, with three or four men surrounding the mustached man who was himself crouched over the foul beast. One man was taking a picture of the whole thing, with a boxed contraption that I had only seen in one of my Mother's send-away catalogs.

Upon seeing me, the mustached man removed his hat and began to speak. In a brash move that I didn't even think of but just did, I walked right up to him and slapped him as hard as I could right across his face. I hit him so hard that his little round spectacles went flying off his head, and I was grabbed up quick by his companions.

"Let the boy be," the man barked out. "This young fella has every right to be angry with me."

I figured he spoke correct, and on that I let another good one fly – this time a right-cross punch that landed pretty much entirely on his left ear. I'd have liked to bust the man in half, but I was exhausted and crestfallen and the fight was purt near out of me, and I had almost broke my hand on the side of his giant and thick head. I was done for a while, and slumped down where I was – set on the ground, head atwixt my knees, and my arms crossed in front to make a poor attempt of covering up the sobbing I was doing.

The big man – still very mobile after the furious beating I had just given him – came up and put his giant arms around me and held on to me with a strength and force that seemed to squeeze the angry right out of me. We sat there for quite a while, like that, and Mother eventually got me to come in the house where she cleaned me up a bit and put me in my bed. As I lay down, I looked at the end of my bed almost expecting to see Cinder there – and just when I thought I couldn't cry anymore, tears filled my eyes as I fitfully fell asleep.

While I slept, my Dad and the mustached man tied a rope around the leg of the bear, and using the horses they drug it off down the road and pitched it into the river. I always admired the fact that it seemed real respectful of my feelings to get rid of that awful carcass – I couldn't imagine butchering that beast and being made to eat it.

I did not know anything about the mustached man even though he had a familiar look about him. My Father had explained the next morning at breakfast that they had served in the Infantry together in the Spanish-American War, and that they had become friends when they were pinned down together for several hours during one of the battles. Even though they were of different rank, my Father recounted how position and title seems to disappear between good men preparing the meet their maker. I was not impressed by the story one bit, and was a little angry with my Father for not knocking the guy's head off for getting my dog killed. I pushed away the breakfast and lit out for one of my favorite trees to climb and get away from everyone.

That event was one of the big coincidences in my Father's life. The man he had served under – Sergeant Roosevelt – had, after serving as President of the United States, traveling the world, forging the Panama Canal to open the international shipping economy, and hunting in Africa, found our front door with a murderous bear in tow as he surveyed possible wilderness areas of the West. Apparently, Mr. Roosevelt had remembered an off-handed comment by my Father about his plans to live in the paradise of the Klamath River Canyon all those years ago while they had both been preparing to die, and as a semi-official field surveyor he had been in the Marble Mountain area when set upon by the bear. With his rifle dropped in a stream, and tangled in his own trout line, his companions and survey party members could only barely catch up to Mr. Roosevelt and the killer beast – and not one was able to fetch a shot off without fear of hitting the former President in the course of stopping the fur-bearing evil.

Apologies were heaped upon me by the mustached man, and I tried to seem to be polite. Deep down I didn't care if he was the King of the World – I didn't like the man and never really did. Even when I was sent a crated blue-tick hound about two months after that by the man, I pitched the "I'm sorry" note in the woodstove and gave the loud dog to the Hawkins boys down the road a ways. I'm sure he was trying to right the wrong he did, but that tear could never be mended. I knew I couldn't give my heart to that new dog, so I found him a home with boys who could.

I think my Father began to feel the same way about the events of that day, many years later in 1931 when the government folks forced him to move from his Elk Crick homestead in order to protect the whole place as a Primitive Area. We were told by all manner of important-acting people that it was a National Priority to prepare it for the impending Designation As An Official Wilderness Area. All the way in 1953 – nigh unto twenty-two years after my Father was forced to move – the folks in Washington, D.C. finally made daisy on their threats and the whole place did become a Wilderness Area. Needless to say, nairn of us Hammarsen's were at the dedication ceremony.

Chapter Eighteen

The Cave Nights

"The Cave Nights have been serious business ever since the Harlin boy was found half-et by the lions. It did leave him with full use of his left arm and hand, but he haint been right since."
– Kel Thompson, Resident

It had been an entire fall and winter and spring and I hadn't heard anything from or about the Running Indian. I had no way to know if he had been successful in delivering my copied papers to the University fella. I was distracted a bit each day, thinking on what my next step was. I felt like there was something right in front of me that I was missing, just past the tip of my mind. With no news, I could only hope that the copied papers were safely on their way across the sea.

My patience had run out about the whole mess – lying to my Father, getting the Running Indian mixed up in the whole thing, and most of all, thinking about the family that War Sing loved and missed never knowing that he would not return. I was sure that in his mess of papers he had a note to his Ma or his Pa or whoever his kin was, in case something bad happened.

About six months after my twelfth birthday, my Father announced that as part of my training to be a man I would finally be allowed to participate in one of the more interesting of the long-standing local traditions – what we called Cave Nights.

I suppose the first step on the proverbial ladder leading to the Cave Nights event was drinking a hard-swallowed mouthful of warm blood from my first deer kill – with the requisite thanks to the critter and to The Maker for the needed meat – but that had happened years before. There had been other, less important steps along the way that proved my outdoorsmanship and my respect of the wildness of the land. It all seemed to come natural to me, as I had always felt at home in the trees and on the winding mountain game trials.

Cave Nights consisted of a young fella staying one or two nights by his self with nought but a knife and the clothes on his back. I'm still not sure if it was a unique practice to our little valley, or if someone had brought it to us when they arrived here. It very well could have been an old tribal tradition we happened upon as well.

While reading about the practice, many years later, I found that exile or hermitages to caves can be found in several religions and cultures – from the Greek *prosphora* event to commemorate the cave manger where Jesus was born, to the *harmolipi* of the monastic monks who sought the silence and the solitude of caves to better forget themselves. I suppose as a race of humans we've been seeking out those strangely awe-inspiring holes in the rocks for more than a little time for secular reasons too – like those of shelter, warmth and safety.

At that junior place in my life, as I have described in other parts of this journal, I was tired of being between the hay and the grass so I was all for anything that could bring me closer towards being considered a full adult. All I knew, back then, that you could've called the Cave Nights ritual just about anything and I still would've wanted to have done it. I had been pestering my Father about it so long, that I had almost given up on it ever happening.

Many of my friends from school had quietly hinted that they had taken part in the Cave Nights. No one really talked openly about it after they had done it. You could tell, though, after a late spring weekend when your pal came walking into school taller and proud of himself, that he had done it on his own hook.

The local custom was very old. Along about nine or ten, boys would be told that they best take note to lessons in hunting and woodsmanship, because as they got older they would have a need to use the skills they learned during their Cave Nights. Most of us thought that our dads and uncles and grandpas were just trying to make us pay better attention, so you can imagine my surprise that afternoon when my Father announced that it was my turn.

I heard a gasp from my ma, and in one of the only displays of anger I ever saw her make, she threw the carrot she had been peeling right out the window and stomped her foot loudly. She looked blackly at us but I did not speak – nor did my Father make that mistake either.

My Mother turned her back on us both, and walked out to the newly-planted summer vegetable garden. The look on her face before she left, directed at my Father, explained wordlessly that she did not approve of his plan and that there may have been other previous discussions about this that I had not been privy to. I didn't need an explanation, since the defenstration of the innocent carrot already told me everything I had needed to understand regarding my Mother's position on the matter.

I knew that my chance to earn the respect of the fellas was at hand, but not wanting to hurt my Ma's feelings, I went to her and kissed her cheek and told her that I'd be fine. I felt like a traitor, and a bit selfish. She did not respond to me, other than sneaking a glance my way as I had embraced her.

Walking to the hitched wagon rig with my dad, I realized that I was going with what I had. Shoes, socks, slightly muddy jeans, a short sleeve shirt, a sweater, a jacket, and thinking on it I was pretty sure I had remembered to also put on underwear that morning. In my pockets, I had a handful of useless junk I seemed to attract to me, as well as my knife – which had gone everywhere with me since War Sing had given it to me two years before.

I figured that I would spend the time thinking some more about War Sing's papers, and try to make sense of the riddles that had been presented in all of it. I could live like a plover for a few days at least.

I heard my Father mutter something about "not having a petticoat government" or some such thing, but I was so excited I didn't pay his under-the-breath comments too much mind.

We set off up the river to the trailhead that led to

the cliffside caves. I waved towards mom as we left, but she seemed not to notice. After quite a while Dad stopped the wagon and we set off up the hillside toward the rocky precipice that held the four ancient caverns.

Trudging through the underbrush to those high rocky holes seemed to take a heap longer than it should have. The hillside was steep and rocky and it was a hard row to hoe to gain a foothold at times.

Finally, the trees opened up before us and the stone wall was fully revealed. Up close, it was rough looking and very, very high. I had looked upon this very same cliff face from the riverside fields below and from the Klamath that snaked next to it, but from that far away it looked smooth and much smaller.

Four caves could be seen above, and I picked the second-down from the top for my two night exile from the rest of the world. It looked to me that the adventure was going to end up being more of the inward-looking *harmolipi* than the fun-loving *prosphora* in that damp and somewhat dark earth hole in the bedrock cliff.

I steeled myself for what was about to happen, and I was finding that even though I had looked forward to this for a spell – I was still a might nervous about it. My wild imagination started right in, always a constant hinderance and distraction in activities during my youth. We scrambled up a deer trail to get closer to the entrance and made the white-knuckled rock-grab over scree and boulders to get to the cave proper.

Other than the death-defying approach to the cave, everything else about it was exactly like I had imagined. Being lightly superstitious, I made sure I entered it with my right foot foremost – since there was no benefit to chance the possible bad luck that would come of entering wrong-footed.

I looked around the rock hole. First and most important, there was no sign of bear or cougar life in the cave – only bat and small critter activity. While a badger or a wolverine could have been inside at some time, it looked pretty cleared out. The inside of the cave, as far as I could tell, went in about twenty feet or so and was about thirty feet wide – leaving enough room for me to feel like I wasn't fixin' to fall off the cliff if I tripped on something. The rear wall, after a cursory inspection, held no secret passageways or tunnels that would allow wild creatures – in which category I naturally included Ghosts, Goblins, Headless Knights, Mars-men, and Ruthless Villains – to sneak up in behind me.

The walls of my little new home sported a few natural benches, and although they were a bit damp I was already considering them as possible sleeping places. The mouth of the cave had a slight overhang on the roof, which I figured would keep most of the rain out if the huge clouds running about the valley gave way on me. A jutting porch-like maw spread before the cave proper and left an area where I supposed a fella could repose and contemplate his life – or at least take a sunny nap without fear of rolling over and off the mountain.

As we sat next to the high cave, swinging our legs over the side of the steep and long cliff-face below us, my Father went over a few last minute details of what he expected of me. I was to stay in the cave area during the day, and to sleep in the cave at night. I was allowed to explore and travel around on the adjacent treed mountainside, where I had already spied a little rock spring on our way in. I would be at the cave for two nights, and after the second night had passed he would return for me and would be waiting at the base of the trail. At all times I was to protect myself, and be wary of my surroundings and any dangers that could or would be presenting themselves to me – day or night. I was to use the tools I had brought with me how ever I could. I was encouraged to make the best of my time, and to use the woodsman techniques I had been taught over the years to make myself comfortable, warm, and well-fed.

My excitement dwindled a bit when he spoke of food – as I had a renowned ability of stuffing my bean-pole frame with a goodly amount of grub that otherwise could usually feed three or four others. I was even known to eat the potato jackets. Sure, I'd miss my bed, I'd miss the woodstove, and I'd miss the companionship of my folks for those two days – but I was sure that I'd miss the pantry and my Mother's cooking much, much more than the other three.

Time came for my Dad to get going, and he shook my hand and ruffled my hair as he left. From my eagle-like perch I watched him go down the hillside to about the treeline, where he turned back to me, cupped his hands up to his mouth, and hollered, "Good luck, boy!"

I couldn't hear the normal sounds of the forest from where he went into the trees – all the birds and squirrels were still and quiet long after they should've picked up their conversations. I figured that he walked into the trees a few feet – where I couldn't see him anymore – and he stayed there a while to make sure I was going to be fine. I almost hollered that it was okay, but after about an hour I heard him cussing when he slid down the hill a bit as he resumed on his way down the trail. I had figured right.

At the time I didn't fully appreciate how dangerous the Cave Nights were and how exposed to mortal jeopardy I was, in the wild lands where grown men had too often lost their battle with nature. The River Canyon could be a mean and unforgiving place, and many a greenhorn had been found floating face down in the cold waters of the Klamath – or never found at all – as all manner of beast and bird feasted upon his carcass. I had even heard of a couple fellas that had been found drug up into the limbs of trees, where mountain lions preferred to leave their kills for a few days before eating them down to the bone – to set the blood and soften the meat, same as we do when we hang venison or beef in the barn after butchering it.

I was confident, even without my trusty old dog at my side, that I could take care of myself as I needed to because I figured my Dad would've never left me in the cave if he thought I couldn't have done all right.

I figured by looking at the sun's position in the sky that I had about five good hours of daylight left, and looking at my sparse dwellings I knew I had about that much work to do.

I set out for the little spring area, always keeping a watch out in front of me, behind me, to my sides, and above me especially as I passed under tree branches that could be hiding a hungry mountain lion. I became very quiet as I walked, picking my steps in the tree duff or old leaves instead of on the crunchy sticks and twigs.

At the spring I took out my little apple-peeler and cut a four foot green pole that had about a three-inch split in the business end. I kept it close, in case I came across any snakes near the spring which was likely since that's where they also caught many of their meals.

With my stomach muscle rumbling already, I hatched a plan to set a few snares around the spring. If I had more daylight I would've weaved grasses together for the long snares, but I figured time was short if I was going to catch some dinner. Instead of taking an hour for the weaving, I started by tearing part of the lining out of my old jacket and ripping straight strips of cloth out of the sturdy material. I made about five little lasso-type riggings out of the pieces and set to placing them. Everyone knows to lay the traps on fresh game trails, but I also set mine in a creative fashion that had paid off well in the past. I looked at the area for a bit and got the lay of the land. I knew that dozens, if not hundreds, of varmints would be approaching this spring near sundown. To the east, a natural opening in the rock outcropping jumped out quick as a must-snare area, and a little sapling that had fallen over the marshy part of the spring got two of my jacket-snares – one on each end. I had seen many critters, going to water, traipsing over little natural bridges like the one made by the fallen tree. A burrow hole in the rocks got the fourth snare, and just when I was ready to move on to my next task I saw the perfect place for a springing snare. I had never placed one, but I had wanted to for quite a long while.

I pulled over a little lissome fir tree – about three feet tall – and laced the long end of the snare around the tip. Stepping my foot on the tree tip and my knot to hold it down, I pounded a small stick, at an angle, into the soft dirt. I wrapped a few loops of the snare around the stick, and gently lifted up my foot. I was pleased to see that the stick loops held the tree bent over, and I tried not to wrap it too tight. I let the snare loop open as wide as it could as I placed it in the game path. I knew that it was more than likely that many of the traps I had set would be tripped without the result of a caught animal, but I thought that it was very unlikely that the traps wouldn't produce at least one critter for my dinner.

Traps set, I leaned down and gulped up a copious amount of the cold, clean water. Trap-setting was thirsty work, and I knew I wouldn't be able to return to the spring until it was time to check the snares around sundown. I tried to stock up on the water, but having no carrier save my own stomach, I had to drink as much as I could.

On my last gulp, I noticed some motion in the swampy grass so I looked up fully from the Adam's Ale just in time to see the thick angled head of a snake looking right into my eyes. I instantly figured that they'd find my dead body laying right there in the spring, face down with a pair of snake fangs stuck in my left eye. I wanted to jump up and shin out, but I knew that the only chance I had was to remain stock-still. I became even more concerned, upon a closer examination of the mean-looking reptile, when I recognized that it was in fact one of our famous local timber rattlers – known, by the way, for their meanness in that they often struck at animals they were not threatened by, nor had any desire to consume.

You can imagine my mounting concern when I saw it drawing back in its coil, readying to strike at me without even a sound from its rattles. Knowing that they push out in a straight line, I tried my best to time my roll to my left and down – and I got away with it, mostly, as the mean creature struck out so far at me that I could feel its long stomach landing on the back of my right leg – making me shiver to my center. Believe you me I hopped up quick enough to be able to pin its head down with my green stick, and I have to admit that I had a great big smile on my face as I cut the thrashing bugger's mean head off with my little knife.

I put small pieces of it, after it stopped wriggling around, near a few of my snares. I buried the head and the rattles off up the hill a ways, as I did not want its mate to track me down. With the remaining five feet of dinner lying limply at my feet, I grabbed it up and fixed to finish my chores.

I made a few trips back to my cave, first with the snake meat and some pieces of wood, and then with several cut pine and fir boughs for my bench-bed. When I was done, I had brought in a baseball-size mound of tree pitch, dry duff I had dug for from under an old pine tree, some Indian Soap shrub limbs, and a whole mess of pieces off a downed tree. My fears of being without fire lessened as I found a tinder fungus conk on a wounded hardwood tree and immediately smashed it free with a rock. I also gathered up several fist-sized chunks of white quartz laying about, a couple handfuls of dry hanging moss, and several plate-sized pieces of thick and wet cedar bark.

I set to making my fire – always easier in the daylight when it isn't needed – and became frustrated at the whole process. I had been successful in the past with the friction drill method and had set out to try it, but looking at the beginning of the night sky I decided to just get it done quick – I figured that I could try more exotic methods of fire-building some other time.

I prepared my little fire area carefully. Setting to making fires in the past, I'd had to retrace my steps in the whole process 'cause I'd forgotten to get one of the ingredients ready. Just about nothing got me more upset than to get a daisy tinder-coal and have it go out for the lack of proper fuel to set it in.

I arranged a nest of the bright-green tree moss, and put the dry pine duff in the center with a good sprinkling of some of the tree pitch. I sat a marble-sized piece of the fungus conk in the nest as well. To the side I made a little bed of the greasy *cianothus* branches, and on top of that I made teepees over teepees starting with smaller and dryer pieces of wood and working my way up so that eventually the outside held some pretty good-sized branches. Readying to get my coal going, I pulled another piece off of the fungus conk and put it atwixt two of the biggest quartz rocks and started smashing them together. I figured I could use my knife against the rock as a back-up plan for spark-making, but I thought that I should try the rocks first so as to not mar up my sharp and shiny blade.

I had about a hundred good sparks between the smashing rocks before the tinder fungus caught on one. It died out quick because I was way too enthusiastic with it, and I started up the rock-smashing-spark-making again.

It took a bit of time to finally get the spark to hold in the tinder fungus, but I didn't have much else to do. I focused my efforts – I knew there were no shortcuts to a good ember – and before long I was successful in placing the cradled, hot tinder fungus piece in the moss nest. After a few gentle and well-placed breaths on the nest, I sat it in it's little fire teepee home, where it caught the oily Indian Soap brush, which caught the dry sticks which caught the bigger sticks and so on. Every time I had the fire making success, I felt like a regular chip-off-the-old-Prometheus giving my heat and light to the world.

My mood cheered incredibly with the success of that particular fire, but in case of any unforeseen fire-dousing events I insured myself by placing a small coal from the fire in the remaining tinder fungus conk and wrapped it in some leaves. Stowed on a little outcropping in the back of the cave, I was sure that my little firebox would hold the emergency ember for as long as I needed it to.

With the fire going steady, but not at a full roar, I put some of the heavy live oak hardwood pieces on – topping the whole mess off with a piece of the thick and wet cedar bark, placed outside-down, with the dressed and skinned pieces of timber rattler sitting on it like a natural-made platter.

The smoke swirled in the cave a bit, and stung at my eyes, but I got used to it soon enough and was glad when it ran the mosquitos away as I had already been feasted upon enough. At the spring I had already dabbed mud on most of my itching bug-vampire wounds, but there wasn't enough mud in the world to fix the itching if those fiends went on unhindered. I was glad that the bats had all lit out on my arrival and I was pretty certain that the smoke and their dinner plans would keep them out all night.

With darkness approaching, I left the cheery fire and the smoky cave and went off to check the snares. I was extra cautious, knowing that the sundown hour was one of the most dangerous for men as all manner of four-legged creatures were up and looking for their breakfast.

Reaching the spring, I was pleased to see that I had snared a fat squirrel and a medium-sized jack rabbit. I dispatched my main course and my entree quickly, reset the snares, and drank up some more water – crouching and cupping the water into my mouth, so I could look around better. The meeting with the snake earlier had left quite an impression on me and had encouraged me to change my water drinking method permanently.

I returned to the cave as the blackness of night was starting to settle down on the valley. The cliffside rock scramble was still hard to negotiate – more so in the dark – but I just took my time and balanced myself real good. I recall that after I put away my armful of wood, stoked the fire a bit, dressed out the rest of my dinner, and cedar plattered it as well – I had quite a good time watching the night come alive in our river valley from my airy perch.

The owls were calling out in the hardwood grove, coyotes were yapping down by the river, and to my right something big crashed through the underbrush – maybe a deer or a black bear. I listened for growls or mewing sounds, and only hearing a snort was still undecided on the species. I figured for every critter I could hear there were probably a dozen more slinking about that I couldn't.

With the damp cedar bark planks heating up in the fire, the meats cradled on them were being roasted and steamed at the same time. I recall that it smelled so good that I was tempted to try to nibble a bit of the rabbit before it was cooked through, but remembering how sick I had got the year before pulling that trick with a piece of venison I was able to remain a bit more patient.

I set to hardening the other end of my green snake pole – I had shaved the top into a spear shape, and I alternately dipped it in the fire coals and then burnished it with one of the pieces of quartz. It hardened up, but not as much as I had expected even though I continued to work on it until the meat was all cooked through.

With my stick I carefully pushed the super hot

bark platters off of the fire, taking care not to tip my dinner off into the flames. The meat cooled a bit – but was still hot enough that when I went to take a bite of the roasted snake, its greasy oil dropped from my mouth and nigh unto burnt my arm.

There are a handful of meals that I've had in my life that I consider the best – and I figure I've classified them not on the taste of the food but from the location in which they were consumed. For example, I recall now the picnic lunch that I shared with Amelia when we both finally made the August-time summit of Mount Shasta was just as fine and wonderful as the white-linen Pullman car dinner we were served as we rushed through the Washington State countryside on our way to Vancouver, British Columbia. That night in the cave, though, was the perfect marriage of view and plate, and at the time I figured nothing would ever match it.

I shaved off most of the roasted meats on to another piece of bark, making a cowboy kedgeree of sorts – missing the rice and eggs, of course. I was in troglodyte heaven, and with great aplomb I even briefly considered staying in my hermitage for longer that just the two nights.

Preparing for bedtime, I pitched all of the varmint bones and skins over the side of the cave entrance where they fell for a full two seconds before I heard the clatter on the rocks below – reminding me how high above the valley floor I really was. Yawning, I stoked up the fire and spread a considerable amount of coals and embers across the entrance way to deter any visitors from coming in while I slept. In a special treat to myself, I scooted about ten good sized white-hot rocks out of the fire with the cedar planks, and placed the flat and round heaters under my benched fir-bough bed on the side of the cave wall. Lying down on the whole thing was a little poky and took some getting used to, but with more fir-boughs covering me I was comfy and warm in the cooling night air. I thought about the Running Indian, and how each of his shoeless padding steps followed the other, over and over and over again to get him from our river valley to a city so far away.

With my snake-stick-spear propped purt near my head, and my little knife opened and close by, I finally set to get some shut eye.

Euclid P. Hammarsen

Chapter Nineteen

The Revelation of
The Ghostly Indian Chief

"The land has always been here, and will remain long after we are gone. Lucky spirits stay close to help others find their way – sometimes in life, sometimes in death."

– Thomas Coyote-Grandfather,
Resident

I was tucked in like a baby in my hot-rock-fir-bough-nest, high above the valley floor in the ancient cave. I had just enough fear in me to be careful, but not so much that I worried instead of slept. With a full stomach of roasted varmint meat, I nodded off after looking at a few of the old cave drawings in the dimness

- the figures almost looked as if they were dancing and moving in the flickering firelight – and then I fell asleep after contemplating the backs of my eyelids for only a short while. The night creature sounds were right – I took comfort in the owl hoots and the coyote yaps, knowing that on the other hand a quiet forest meant something big and mean was crawling about on the mountainside.

I woke after the moon rose, startled a bit by the lunar light that bathed the cave in a white-silver shimmer. I saw that the clouds had passed through, and the night sky was clear. I knew that without the clouds it'd be a colder evening, and I'd maybe even suffer a possible layer of frost up this high by morningtime. I stoked up the fire, had a look about, changed out my hot-rocks for others, and laid myself back on the semi-cozy bench. Once again, the sounds were all right and I began to sleep.

Like memories and sadness often does, I was surprised at a tear that came to my eye instantly as I thought about how that same moonlight might have looked at the High Springs Pool – if it was that beautiful there as well – where my dog was buried. I missed her awful bad, and even though I had begun to venture out of my deep hurt over her being killed by the bear, it was all still close in my thoughts and in my heart and tended to creep up on me when I least expected it.

I don't dream that often, when I sleep, but when I do – and I remember it – it's usually because it was something worth while. I always figured that my sleep-dreaming need was all used up by night time, mostly, by my constant and often distracting daydreams. I'll try, now, to describe what I saw that night – eighty or so years previous to this day and at an elevation gain of about three hundred feet – because it is an important part of this whole story. Of my story.

I may, of course, have gotten some of it mixed up but the vital parts are all here.

In that ethereal place between sleeping and awake, my eyes grew ever heavier as I moved here and there in my warmed fir-bed to get to settle in just the perfect spot.

Far off, I heard a drum pounding – or it could have been the sound of my own heartbeat in my ears. I felt like a bird, tucked in my cliff nest, and I looked out across the great valley open beneath me. The moonlight played tricks with the landscape, making the trees below look close enough to touch and bathing the foamy river in a rich sheen. I saw far, far away, and tried to look into the dark eyes of a man standing in a shadowed forest. I should have been afraid of him, but I wasn't – even when his council fire exploded in green flames, I stood and waited for the Ghostly Indian Chief to come forward, out of the shadow-forest and to his seat near the fire.

First, I saw his hatchet – wrapped in a leather strap and looped to his trousers. It was sharp, and big, and made of the blackest obsidian I'd ever seen. The workmanship was so finely done, that the end-blade was almost transparent well before the edge. I had tried to make arrow heads with a piece of obsidian, a chipping rock, and leather guard so I knew how extremely difficult it would have been to make that terrible precise-bladed hatchet – not even the master teachers of my Indian friends could have made a weapon as perfect as that one.

When the giant ghast approached, the fearsome nature of the legend was gone and I saw only the sage advisor and the night-warrior leader. His arms and legs and chest were a web of scars and old wounds, but his eyes were young and strong and darkly-bright.

He passed by his grand fire-side throne seat, embraced me like a brother and encouraged me to sit down beside him on one of the low rocks reserved for the braves and the warriors. The brilliant emerald-colored fire gave off no heat, but the Ghostly Chief did – a sunny warmth surrounded him that was definitely an odd feeling in the darkness of the shadow forest.

Tightly woven baskets were littered about the seating area, filled with a liquid. Looking past the fire, I saw a high pile of emptied baskets that had been cast away from the Chief. Knowing the legend, I supposed the full ones held the blood of his enemies – or, like Billy McKetter had tried to convince me, perhaps instead it was full of the blood of the last kid who came to bother him.

The giant man reached to one deftly-wound container and poured the thick stuff out and into the green fire – sparks erupted and crackled and the light continued to ebb a bit brighter. A low groaning wail escaped in the whisp of fire smoke.

"*Avuki'i*. Ask me what you need to know, son," the Ancient Father spoke.

I found myself just looking at the man, or ghost of a man, unable to form my words as I needed. He was fatherly and terrible at the same time – speaking with a kindness in his voice that I knew could change to a war battle cry at any moment. My question for him seemed to be on the tip of my tongue, but my lungs felt flat and I couldn't speak. He noticed my distress, and began to speak instead.

"You betrayed your Father's trust, hoping that the

small sin would make a larger wound right. It is a dilemma and many others have sought my council for the same problem."

He stared into my eyes, then, but I still couldn't find the words I needed. I was afraid of his anger and his hatchet, and since I hadn't had much experience talking to ghosts or to dreams I felt a bit out of place.

The Warrior King continued. "You worry Little *apaka-i'pan* Trout that even in your desire to become a man through this ritual, that you face a barrier to that end from your deception."

It was true. I nodded a bit to the Ghostly Chief.

Once again, the giant man emptied the contents of another woven basket into his magical fire. The fire licked higher in the mysterious night air, and what sounded like another moan or a muted war-cry escaped up and away from the fire in a second whisp of smoke.

He looked again into my eyes, as if he was searching for something in them. "You also want to know," he said, "if War Sing's soul can be saved by all of this."

Again, I nodded at the Chief.

"You're also curious where the treasure is – most of all, yes? Is it where the hidden temple lies, like he said, or is it somewhere much more obvious?"

He leaned in toward me, with a look on his face of concern and anger at the same time. He stood and walked around me, as if he was sizing me up for battle or some other horrible end to my short life. He placed his giant hand on the top of my head, turning my view to the sky and the river and the trees beyond the cave. He leaned down and pointed at a spot in the distance that I couldn't quite make out. His hand moved a bit, and I couldn't see where he was pointing to. My frustration got the better of my scaredness, and I tried to speak to him.

Finally, my opened mouth formed words to the Ghostly *Apuruua'niik*. "Sir, I couldn't see the place where you were showing me the treasure is. I'm looking for where the jade temple was built. I've got a feeling that if I find it, all of the other answers will fall into place."

The Terrible Chief grasped his obsidian axe and swung it swiftly over his head, around, and then down right toward me – missing me by nary an inch – landing the hatchet on a rock seat next to me and splitting it open. The halved thunder egg turned out amethyst crystals that glowed violet in the green firelight.

His head shook in disapproval, and his angry face was the last thing I saw as the firelight fell away.

And then everything went black – the fire went out, the moon was gone, and the stars failed to shine.

As I began to stir in my cold cave bed with the morning sun far in the eastern sky, the Chief's voice whispered in my ear, "Little Trout, you already know all that you seek. Your answers are right in front of you. *Ta' mah'iit.*"

Whether it was an oracle, a night-ghast, or simply a dream – the Warrior Chief was gone. Squinting my eyes open just a bit, I saw that he was right in announcing that it was morning. I was out of sorts in that foggy place between sleep and awake, not quite knowing where I was and searching my mind for some way to make sense of what had happened.

The rest of that day I went about the routines of living in a cave – trap setting, fire tending, water drinking, wood hauling, stick sharpening, and varmint eating. I had run up on a sugar pine and found about five great big tight cones full of pine nuts. I sat them in the fire to roast in their own cone, knowing that sooner or later the heat would open the individual scales allowing me to get to the rich nut meat inside. It was a little work, but I figured that I had the time.

Through all of my chores that day, I kept an eye on any predator threats around me – since I supposed that even a blind and deaf mountain lion could've figured I was in the neighborhood from all of my trail walking and meat roasting – and I let the rest of my mind usually reserved for my daydreaming instead go over the dream I had the night before.

Long before I had heard of Freud or Jung, I understood that dreams were probably just a bunch of random thoughts that are still racing around when the rest of the body has enough sense to settle down and rest. I knew that it was possible that my mind was trying to talk to me – somehow – and let me in on something I missed that was probably staring me right in the face.

An uneventful day led to an uneventful evening, and still distracted by the dream I tried real hard to appreciate my last night in the cave. I found handfuls of Miner's Lettuce and hard-got Gooseberries to snack on throughout the day, and at some point had made my hands and trousers purple with the juice of the armfuls of ripe Elderberries I had devoured.

My fire had gone out during the day, so I set up my fire-making kit again and got it going, with the process being shorter using my tinder-fungus-ember stash set away the night before.

With most of my chores all done and with a few spare minutes in the cave, I took a bit of cooled charcoal from the fire and mixed it with a piece of red clay earth, working in a bit of the silvery shale powder from a close-by rock slide and some squeezed Elderberry juice. I drew my story on the cave wall – complete with the Ghostly Chief and His Fire, the Running Indian, and my best try at a likeness of my departed dog. Unless erased by vandals or drawn over by others, the pictures should still remain there today. I suppose I would like to know if they were still there, but I know I would not like to know if they aren't.

I had emptied my snares a bit earlier, and removed them since the morning would find me heading home. I had come across four giant bull frogs in the boggy end of the spring, and quickly dispatched them for an appearance at my supper. I had captured one small raccoon and a little rabbit in the snares but let them go due to the wealth of frog I had encountered.

My spring snare hadn't worked although it looked like there had been plenty of chances for it to give glimpsing at the track activity around it – so I figured that I had wrapped the snare too tight on the holding stick. When I unhooked the spring snare the little sapling managed to slap me across my neck a bit, just like it was really mad at me for being tied over sideaways for two days.

Of all the varmint and critter food I've had I do really prefer roasted frog above all – it's fleshy and has just the right amount of fat and meat to make it cook well. It's also easy to dress out. Paddock stew – frog stew, as it were – had got me through some rough patches throughout my life.

Sitting there watching the frog meat cook, I figured it and I had a little something in common – it was being roasted in a fire, while I was simmering in my own guilt. I kept thinking about the lie that I had told to my Father.

At dusk the cones began to open, and I gingerly swept up all of the super-heated nuts that were being shot here and there. I figured I was too enthusiastic after burning the roof of my mouth – twice – and set to waiting for them to cool off. For roughing it, I was pleased to have topped the evening off with my favorite roasted varmint followed by my favorite wild dessert.

I warmed my bed like the night before, using a few more rocks and a few more fir boughs to ward off the chill. I quieted my mind, inspecting the backs of my eyelids again, and waited patiently for another visit from the Ghostly Indian Chief.

He never came.

I woke a little chilled and a lot disappointed, since I had figured all would have been revealed to me – what with the scary cave and the solitude and the magical cave drawings I had made, it was a Grade-A environment for another ghostly encounter.

I sat at the edge of my cliff-wall bed and resorted to my Chinese vocabulary – I didn't even know if I was pronouncing right – which strangely made me feel a little less frustrated after the uttering. I figured on what the Chief had said to me in my dream, and that my answer was right in front of me. More Chinese words and more thinking later, I left my repose to start clearing up my cave-camp. I was able to toss most of the whatnot over the edge of the cave – like the fir boughs and some of the small sticks – and I left the remaining wood, the quartz rocks and some unused tinder-fungus, my snake stick, and my perfect oval and smooth bed-warming stones all stacked up neatly in the driest part of the cave. We called it a woodsman's tribute – and I've heard it called other similar names as well – which in other circumstances and other weather had proven lifesaving to wounded or lost travelers in the western mountains.

My last step was to button up the fire, to make sure it would go all the way out soon. I set to start kicking the mess apart, and got a shock so hard through me I felt like I was going to pitch myself right off the cliff face to my doom.

Looking below me, deep in the fire, I could see three logs – unburnt and untouched by the scorching flames – that had fitted together just perfectly to form an arrow. I followed the point of the fire-arrow straight out with my eye, across the landscape below me – rocks, river, lowlands, foothills, mountains – until my imaginary line reached the horizon. My mind raced over all that I knew about those lands, searching my memory of having traveled those hills for any familiar spot that would have made the perfect temple building site.

Then a word came to me, and I had to agree that the Ghostly Chief had been right. He had told me that I already knew what I sought. I'd have almost liked to been able to kick myself I felt so chuckle-headed. I smiled and said that wonderfully magic name right out loud.

"Berhai."

I sat down then, and studied the land and the puzzle from a different perspective. Not wanting to know where the land spot was to build a temple, but thinking instead on where a Berhai-like environ held the necessary requirements for the Buddha-statue to be placed. If I only had the requirements of natural beauty and solitude to go on, it could have been any number of places along the fire-arrow line – but adding in the necessities of an earthen Mountain Gate and a natural

Temple Screen, and double-checking the lay of the line, I had a pretty good idea of exactly where the Buddha and his altar was hid.

I finished taking apart the mess I made with my fire, careful to leave the arrow untouched. Trying to accept the magic or the coincidence of how the little logs fell or dismissing the whole thing entirely were all options, I suppose. I had a real tough time thinking of it as a coincidence and dismissing the fire-arrow, since I noticed as I turned to leave that it was made of red-barked dog wood – and I had only brought in live oak and pine to the cave.

It took me a bit to make it over the rock slide and past the spring, and then down into the treeline path. I managed not to slide on the slippery deer trail as my Father had done a few days previous, and my thoughts were full as I had almost made my way far enough to soon see the road.

Coming to the top of a little hill, I looked up into the body of a big-branched madrone tree. Sitting in the tree on a gnarled and wide branch, leaning back on the trunk with her eyes closed, was my Mother. The old shotgun lay across her lap, and her shawls were gathered up around her. I stopped in my tracks and rubbed my eyes a bit.

Afraid of startling her and her shotgun awake after what I had seen her do to the bear that had come in our yard, I quietly retraced my steps back over the hill and toward the caves. Hiking once again toward my Mother's perch, I made sure to make a heap of noise so that she would know I was on my way.

Coming again to the top of the little hill I was whistling and singing and I took a few breaks to chuck rocks at logs and kick twigs and generally be as loud as

I could without giving away that I knew she was there.

It must have worked, because before I got to the tree I heard a rustling commotion and a thud – like someone had jumped out of a tree onto the path below. I thought I heard a hushed curse word, but that couldn't have happened since my Mother had been the only one who could have said it, and I had never once heard my Mother talk like that.

Finding myself at the tree, again, I acted surprised to see my mom walking up the path toward me.

"What are you doing way up here?" I asked her with genuine curiosity. "Where's Dad?"

She stopped, cradling the shotgun in her right arm with her left hand defiantly on her hip, and said, "I got up early this morning and decided to take a little walk and stretch my legs." She had never lied to me that I knew of, but who was I – clandestine Chinese-paper-copier and Nosey Parker and gravestone fouler – to judge her delicate and simple white lie.

"Stretch your legs?" I said, "It's over nine miles from here to the house."

"I know," she replied, "but I was worried about you."

Looking up at the tree, where she had just been, I thought that her story just wasn't adding up. I decided to leave it, then, because I didn't want to upset her and also because I was all-fired hungry.

"Let's go home, Mom." I put my hand on her shoulder, and hugged her, and we walked down the mountain together. I offered to carry the shotgun, and to my surprise, she let me. Just like the Cave Nights taught me to rely on myself and be more responsible, I figure it also taught my folks that they could rely on me more, too. I was closer, at the end of that adventure, to being the man I am now than the child that I had been.

At the base of the hill, at the end of the trail, sat my Father. He was leaning on the wagon, passing time by pitching little rocks against the base of a tree. He glanced up when we came into view, and the sore-worried look on his face let up. He looked glad to see me, of course, but he also looked just as glad to see my Mother.

He patted me on the back and congratulated me for my fine display of courage and woodsmanship. He then put his arms around my Mother, whispered something in her ear that sounded like, "I'm glad to see you, too, you crazy woman." Then we all clum into the wagon and headed home for a great big country breakfast that we all helped prepare.

I had decided that after breakfast I would act like the man that I wanted to be treated like, and finally come clean with my folks about the paper-copying and how I had lied to them about getting into War Sing's belongings. Even just making the decision I felt better about the whole thing, and I figured that one way or the other it'd be behind me sooner than later.

Years and years after that day, when I was taking care of my Dad before he died, I had a chance to talk to him about that weekend. I told him about finding mom in the madrone tree, and how strange it all seemed. He revealed to me what I think I had already known.

The evening before we had left for the Cave Nights, my Mother and Father had had a big argument. It was no secret that my Ma didn't approve of the whole idea, and my Father, putting his foot down, told her that he had decided to let me do it and that he wasn't fixin' to change his mind – no matter what she said. As my Father tells it that was the point where my Mother explained to him – in no uncertain terms – that while she wasn't challenging his paternal authority, she was challenging his right to know where she would be for the next two days. Apparently, on the Saturday morning when we left for the caves my Mother left for it too. She walked all of the way to the trailhead, carrying the shotgun, and ducked behind trees and rocks when she heard wagons moving close in order to miss my Dad seeing her on his return to our house. With only a few gun shells, her heavy shawls, and two wrapped sandwiches in her pockets, she traversed the hilly mountain and finally lit in the madrone tree. There she sat for the next two days and nights, like a wild turkey perched in the forest canopy. I asked my Dad what the heck she did that for, and his answer didn't really surprise me – as I knew her and her depth of love for me.

He told me that she had walked there, and stayed there, to watch over me and to make sure that I was safe – and that even as I grew from a boy to a responsible man and then a husband and a Father, she never once stopped being concerned for me and loving me just as much as the first day she and I had met.

Euclid P. Hammersen

Chapter Twenty

The Thief

"We don't have a lot of repeating crimes happen here – like stealing – since fellas that face shot gun rehabilitation either change their ways or are cured the quick way forever."

– Colly Trinity, Retired Circuit Court Judge

My intention had been to immediately confess to my Father the sneaky exploits I had undertaken, but it was too easy for me to let the days pass without finding the opportunity to talk to him. I told myself that I was waiting for a good time to present itself, but now I know I was stalling to avoid his anger and disapproval. You know what they say about that road to you know where being paved with good intentions – well, then I was on my way to building several miles of that awful thoroughfare all on my own. Before I knew it, all those deferred days had turned into an entire year – and I think I figured that the whole thing was purt near behind me. Nothing harmed, nothing hurt. The Running Indian had not returned, nor had any reports of him or the race he had entered. Not one piece of news arrived in the post or on the pack train for us. I was kept busy helping my Father on our claims and at our little wooded farm.

I did find enough time to venture out over that long year, now and then, along the path shown to me by the dogwood arrow in the cave fire. I spent many weekend mornings hunting and exploring in that area without finding a trace of anything – no trails, claims, or evidence that anyone had ever even stepped foot on those mountains or in those canyons and draws. I dropped veiled questions to Chinese folks I met here and there, and I soon got to figuring that War Sing's temple may have been private to them too. It was like I had two different lives for a while – obsessed with a mythical or mystical temple I wasn't even sure existed, and at the same time considering telling my Father what I had done.

As a boy, I was taught by stories I read and Sunday lessons given by my folks that liars always got caught in the end – usually undone by their own deceptions. I was also taught that there is no such thing as a solitary lie as I had been warned by my Mother and Father that falsehoods breed faster than jackrabbits or field mice. Like most of the big lessons in life, that was one that I had to learn firsthand.

I thought a lot about the fibs that I had told while I was trying to resolve the Chinese writing problem. I figured that when the Professor sent the papers, translated, back to us that my Father would be so happy that I would only get a minor scolding – or at least that's what I tried to tell myself. It had all seemed fairly simple in the beginning, but I was finding it hard to recall all of the different stories and untruths I had told to different folks about the papers. Lying was hard business, and was becoming very complicated.

I couldn't have believed that the whole mess could've gotten worse, but it did. On a Saturday when my Ma and Pa had headed into town to get some supplies and kitchen sundries, I had returned to the dooryard from my traipsing of the hillsides to find the chickens had managed a coop jailbreak, and for about the next hour I was busy trying to get the hens and the rooster back into their pen. I had met up with the neighbor's dog – creatively named Blue, of course – down the road a bit and he had followed me around for most of the morning. I treated him all right, but more like a regular dog and not even close to how I would have treated My Dog. The neighbors took good care of him and the two Hawkins boys wouldn't stop talking about how much they loved him – I was glad it had worked out, 'cause I couldn't have felt that way about him and it wouldn't have even been his fault. When that dog and I occasionally adventured around together, it was different – we were like two fellas who happened to be going to the same place and were walking together. He had his real family for the extra ear-scratching and belly-rubbing and long Dog And Boy conversations – all that still hurt my feelings too much to think about.

My attention was detoured from the poultry I had been chasing around the yard to a loud clatter in the barn. Blue had been helping me try to corral a big old hen, but the floppy-eared mutt lit off to the barn almost before I heard the ruckus. He was baying as loud as he could, and I could see the hackles on his back raised as he went through the barn door. From his barking – and my rusty understanding of Blue-Tick Dog – it sounded like he had whatever it was cornered in the back of the barn, and I lit out to get the shotgun from in the house.

I burst through our kitchen door and grabbed the gun, loading a shell into it quick as I planned to help out the dog – even though it wasn't mine and would never compare to Cinder, I figured it was workin' for the good of our little woodland farm and I needed to work for it too. It was only common courtesy.

I looked up and around for just a moment as I headed back out the door and noticed that something had gotten into the house – all of our cupboards and chests had been knocked about and all manner of items were strewn about the rooms. I immediately thought of raccoons – and that my Ma was going to be really mad. I set off for the barn as fast as I could.

About half-way across the yard I heard the hound – still inside the barn – gnash at something, and then came a big dog yelp of pain. I had almost made it to the barn door, shotgun shouldered and running when I heard something that made me stop in my tracks.

It was a man's voice, cursing at the neighbor's dog as the fella retreated toward the back door of the barn.

At that time in my life, I had faced bears, mountain lions, all manner of forest varmints, and even the biggest fish ever to swim in the Klamath – but I knew that the most dangerous animal on the face of the earth was a human. Especially a human that was sneaking around in someone else's barn and who had tore through someone else's belongings. Instead of dropping the shotgun from my shoulder and calling out, I kept it in place and held it ever more firmly.

I entered the barn just in time to see the back of a

tall and stout dark-haired man, carrying War Sing's box and escaping through the back door. Checking that the loud dog was clear, I let off a shot that peppered the retreating thief across his back forcing him to yell out again. I didn't see his face at all, and by the time I reloaded he was disappeared into the forest.

I waited for the thief to return, fully prepared to defend myself if needed. I waited there for a bit, and hearing nothing more, I backed away from my stand and required the same of Blue.

As I was returning to the dooryard with the neighbor's limping dog, my Ma and Pa raced the wagon in so fast I thought the good horse was going to drop dead right there. Dad had heard the shot about a ways back, and had lain on the whip to get home quick. Ma scooped me into her arms, and I started to sob a bit on accident as I told them what had happened.

After telling them all the details I could remember, my Father's first question was, "You think that you got him?"

I told him that I had heard him yell out, and I apologized for not getting off a better shot. My Mother was squeezing the stuffing out of me, and I had to put on my best wrenched-up "Oh-mom-stop-it" face for the benefit of my Dad– but I really didn't mind her hugging me that much at all.

While being squeezed in my Mother's arms, I spied my Father making his way around the barn to see what the damage was. It wasn't long before he stopped up short.

Dad stood in front of his emptied work bench, with one hand placed where War Sing's box had been. The back of his neck and his ears were turning that warning red and almost a purple color and my Ma took my hand and started to preemptively drag me away from his simmering anger.

I pulled away from her, and she looked at me like I was crazy. I knew what I had to do. I had already decided my path to the truth on the morning I had left the Cave Nights – I just hadn't had the guts enough to have done it.

I figure she thought that I really truly was crazy, when she heard what I told my Father. I said, with all of the courage I could muster, "Dad, I need to talk to you. I have for some time. What happened earlier today – losing War Sing's papers – may have been my fault."

He stared straight ahead, and then looked down at his clenched fists that were resting on his work bench.

Without looking at me once or raising a hand to me, I got a worse blow from my Father than I ever got in the woodshed. He simply said, "I'm disappointed in you. I don't know if I can ever forgive you."

He walked toward the rear door of the barn, with his back still to me. I took a few steps after him, thinking that I could stop him and make everything right if I just had the chance to tell him about what had happened.

As he headed out and away, holding his head down a bit he added, "Uke, I don't want to see you or talk to you."

And with that, he was gone out the back door and into the woods – tracking the thief who had rifled through our house, who had destroyed some of Mother's keepsakes, and who had stolen the last connection my Father had to the man he considered a brother and had given his life so that my Father could live.

Euclid P. Hammarsen

Chapter Twenty-One

The Consequences
of Truth and Lies

"When I was a kid I figured the
only time it was really lying was
when I got caught."
– Lopey O'Brien, Resident

My Father was gone for the rest of that day. Those
were long hours that I sat there on our front porch and
waited for him to come home.

I had helped clean up all of the mess that the
thief had made inside of our house, and tried my best to
get back in my Mother's good graces but I could tell by
the way it looked like she found it hard to lay her eyes
on me that she was really, really mad.

I had never felt any extended disapproval from my
folks, and I figured I would have much preferred to have
got a woodshed trip and just have it all done – but I
knew that this was different than anything I had pulled
in the past. Worst of all, I knew all the while I was doing
it that it was probably a very bad idea. I had talked

myself into making a giant treasure hunt out of my hurt feelings for my Father, rationalizing every little lie I told along the course. I had used the fact that I was trying to find a way to translate the foreign writing as an excuse to create a reason to track about behind my parent's backs.

I was ashamed and I should have been. There was nothing that could come of my efforts that would ever change the fact that I had lied to the two most important people in my life. I knew that everything I had ever told them was instantly suspect to them, and I had no room or reason to expect that they would ever believe me again in the future.

I reflected on what my dog would have thought of me. She would have given me that disappointing look – like when I went in the Grave Shed – and walked away from me too. I would have deserved it.

I pulled myself as quick as I could from considerations of my own hurt feelings to those that I had given to my Father. I still had a sore time fully understanding what a hard thing I had done to him – I couldn't figure that anything I could ever have done could have hurt someone I had thought of as invincible and unhurtable for my entire life.

When night was only a few hours away, I took leave from my Mother and disappeared into the trees. I didn't follow the path my Dad had taken through the woods, but took another – I figured I knew where he had ended up after the whole mess of the day.

I made it to War Sing's gravesite after about a good half-hour of hiking, and sure enough – I saw my Father sitting on the ground, with the big carved stone resting behind his back. He looked like a man who could see a thousand miles, and who could either stand up and give me a bear hug or break my fool self clean in half.

I called up to him, not wanting to startle him.

He said, "It's alright, Uke, I heard you about half-a-mile back crashing through the brush."

I walked up to him and sat down next to him on War Sing's grave. We sat there in the quiet of the forest for a long time. He was watching the last of the sun move on the trees across the draw, and I was watching him.

I had tried to plan out what I was going to say, and wondered if I should try to explain the whole mess to him. In my mind, my explanation was reasonable sounding – but I didn't want it to sound like an excuse when it went from my mind and out of my mouth. I already understood the problems with excuses, and I had known for some time that my Father held no stock in statements that tried to shift the responsibility for a problem from one man to the other. I'd heard my Father talking about men he worked with in the past, from time to time – so I already had a good idea what he thought of folks trying to get out of what they had got themselves into all by themselves with just flowery words and reasons to try to make it all right again.

Now, thinking back on my long life and all of the birthday cakes that have been laid before me – I realize that my Father was a very young man as we both sat on that grave. Purt near as I can figure now he was about thirty-three or thirty-four years old. How I looked up to him and his sage experience and his advice. At that time he already had some white shocks in his darkish beard and on his temple, and the wrinkled and furrowed brow of someone who had lived through some big trouble and seen his share of problems.

I recall that the gravestone was cold behind me – on my back – even in the warm air. When I had found my Father set in there, with his elbows on his knees and his hands draped in front he looked like a man who was purt near tired to his soul. When I sat next to him, I respectfully copied his seated form – because I did not, and still do not, know the proper etiquette for sitting on a grave.

I knew it was selfish of me, but I wanted to confess everything that I had done so that it all would be behind me and I could start to tread down that long road of proving that I could be trusted again. At least I had hoped it would be that easy – but looking at my weary-worn Father in the lengthening afternoon I figured I'd have to put what I wanted behind me so that maybe he could start down that long road of wanting to trust me again. I almost started crying when I thought of how proud he had been of me after the Cave Nights, and now it all seemed soiled and wrong to have even gone to something like that knowing that I was not worthy of being treated like a man when I hadn't been acting like one. I also thought of the night that we had watched the glowing Spirit Lake, and I wondered if he'd ever let me be close to him again after what I had done.

It was nearly dark when we started to talk. I burst in to tears at one point and rambled on and on about Running Indians and races and Professors and newspapers and that I was sorry that I wanted the School House to float away and that I was sure Mr. Roosevelt was a nice man but that I didn't really care for him one bit.

My Father finally interrupted me. "Slow down, Euclid. I'm sure that you've got a lot to confess, but tonight all I want to talk about is the deal with the papers."

When I looked up at him, I had prepared myself to see the anger and dismay in his eyes from before – but those were both gone. He looked at me like he loved me, like he always had, and I felt like crawling under a rock.

He put his giant arm around me, and looking again at the ridge in front of us – as the sunlight was only barely touching the tips of the tallest trees on the top – he asked me to simply begin at the beginning.

I had to tell him first about seeing him in the barn that day when he was sad, and how I felt like I needed to try to get someone to rewrite the papers so that we could read them. I tried to make him understand that at the start of the whole plan, that was the only way I could figure to fix him being sad. I admitted that the whole thing got out of control as I mixed in hunting for the treasure that War Sing had spoken of at the end.

He nodded here and there, and asked a few questions of me when I skipped something I passed over too quickly or didn't explain good enough. When I told the details about copying most of the papers he remarked that it looked like I *had* learned something in school after all. He was starting to be his regular self around me, but I still wasn't even close to thinking that I could be my regular self around him.

He outright laughed out loud when I started to tell him about the Running Indian and what I had asked him to do. I acted like I hadn't heard the laugh, because I didn't much understand what was funny.

I mentioned the argument I thought I had witnessed between Jin and Cho, and how I figured it was strange that I had heard them and other Chinese folk call War Sing the name Yong-Li Jun at times when no one knew I was around. I told my Dad that I thought it was even stranger that I thought the translation of that secretive name was something like *The Honored and Golden Son*.

He nodded, with a look on his face that told me he already knew something about what I had picked up on. I paused in the conversation, hoping he'd tell me what it looked like he knew about War Sing's separateness or difference from the rest of the workers – but he just sat and waited for me to continue.

I explained that I hadn't heard anything about the Running Indian, the race, or the papers at all. It had been just over one full year since I had convinced the man to take the copied papers with him to the university in San Francisco, and I admitted to my Father that even though I still held out hope that the papers were either on their way back to us or on their way across the ocean to War Sing's family – I figured that it was reasonable after all the time that had passed that we would have heard something about the whole affair.

I had even asked my schoolmate, Howard, about the Running Indian and the race on several occasions – each time he responded that his family hadn't heard from him either, and many of them thought that he must have met his end on his way to or during the race he had spoken of.

My Father and I sat there, well after dark, while I explained everything to him – even the dream I had in the cave, and the mysterious arrow of dogwood that I found in my cave-fire. I admitted to adventuring and exploring over the past year through our woods and mountains on that imaginary line I'd figured from the cave that night – trying to find the hidden temple. I even admitted that I was driven on that path mostly by my desire to find the treasure under the temple that War Sing had spoken of.

With all of that information finally out of me I was relieved. I had tried to keep all of my excuses and defenses out of my speech, and I figure I did a right fine job. My Father and I walked back to our house – via the roadway as it was too dark for the trail shortcut – and I was glad that no matter what happened with the undefined outcomes of the papers or treasures or hidden temples, I knew that I already had the most important question already answered. I knew that with my Father's love for me came forgiveness, and even if I didn't get it from him all at once I would eventually – and that he would trust me again as well.

Since that night, I've talked to a lot of folks who never had the chance to learn about the trust and forgiveness that are both parts of caring for others. I was fortunate to have two parents who taught it to me, and who practiced it in their lives with each other. Sure, in the past eighty or so years since that day I had plenty of opportunities to hold my hat in my hand and ask forgiveness from someone – even my Amelia – but not once in a conniving manner or with falseness. I had walked that dark path and had no need to ever return.

I recall that as we approached the house that long-ago dark and starless night, my Father and I had returned to joking about a little with each other and speaking of things not temple or paper related. We did agree to revisit the topic – soon – after my Father had a chance to think about everything I had told him. At that time, I figured it was because he was going to try to help me do some kind of damage-control on the havoc I had created. I found out that he was hatching a plan of his own, after getting some missing information from my reported observations and efforts of the past year. We talked about the local excitement of the upcoming Jamboree and Parade, and on my insistence and in my rambling fashion we talked even more about *my* excitement for the nearing event that hadn't been held for two years.

I figured out soon enough where I got my streak of curiosity and sense of adventure from too. The Euclid apple didn't fall far from the Hammarsen tree, so to speak. As my Father told me goodnight and tucked in my quilted blanket around my feet, I saw a look in his face that I had recognized on my own just about several hundreds of times.

I could tell just by the set of his jaw and the twinkle in his eye that he was up to something. I fell asleep that night hoping and hoping that there was a chance that he would let me be a part of it.

Two days later my Father and I poured over his hand-drawn map of the area, and I explained to him where I had explored over the past year – and basically where I knew War Sing's temple wasn't. After everything that had happened, I had given up almost every hope of treasure at the end of my treasure hunt – I just wanted to help Dad find the temple for the possibility of a hint of where to locate War Sing's kin or why his things had been stolen from our barn. I still felt like there was something that my Father was keeping from me, but I didn't have any room to ask him about my suspicions since I was still working real hard to show him I could regain his confidences.

Over the next month, we lit out whenever we could to explore the area that I had figured everything was pointing me to. We were frustrated, finding nothing trip after trip. We asked the few remaining Celestial miners general questions about temples and such, and even contemplated following a few around at the height of our frustration but decided against it. We were getting nowhere and spending an awful lot of time in our efforts.

We were riding towards home, at the end of one of our explorative outings and the stock were acting a bit nervous – chomping and holding back a bit on the trail we had chosen. Dad and I instinctively stopped the horses just in time to see a buck that looked about double the regular size come bursting out of the underbrush. Most nearly on its tail was a mountain lion the likes of which I had never seen – it looked to be about eight foot long without even counting its tail length. Dad got a quick shot off – I wasn't sure if he was aiming at the buck or the lion – and we were quick in behind the two animals as we chased them through the brush.

We could see them running before us, and when they ducked into the thicker brush we held back a little so as to not be doubled-back on by the lion. They crashed and thumped through the little wooded copse we were going through and my Father let off another shot – hitting the lion with a glancing bullet by the screeching sound it made. We watched it shin out with its tail between its legs and we followed the buck to the left while keeping an eye on where the cat had gone.

I got a bead on the buck before my Dad did, and I stood in my oxbow stirrups to make the shot but my dad's hollering stopped me before I could pull the trigger. Annoyed, and thinking that maybe he was playing a joke on me to ruin my shot so he could take it instead – not outside of the scope of our good-natured competitions in the past – I turned to look for him to ask him what in the h-e-double hockey sticks was so all fired important for me to miss my shot.

I didn't have to say a word, because when I looked at my Father, he was already off of his horse and standing in front of an amazing and beautiful site. Grand carvings and inlaid gemstones and simply elegant architecture seemed to have naturally sprouted from the wooded copse in front of us.

It was The Jade Temple at last.

Euclid P. Hammarsen

Chapter Twenty-Two

The Jamboree

"The fiddler kept poking me in the
arm with his bow as he played –
because we were standing so close
– but I was afraid to move and lose
my footing in the water because I
had never learned to swim."
– Mrs. Rose Nylund, Resident

Our community, back then, seemed to be
connected a little closer than what it is today. We used
to spend some Saturday afternoons at what is now
called the Allen Ranch, up the river, playing baseball
and looking for arrowheads and fishing. My Mother
would always pack a picnic lunch – enough for us and
several more – and in the evening she would also cook
some of the day's catch over the little campfire as we
gathered there. To this day, I have never tasted better
fish. I'd occasionally look up the adjacent hill to the
cliffside caves – with curiosity before my Cave Nights

and with a wry smile and standing a little taller after. I had the opportunity to scramble up the hillside to return to the cave on many of those afternoons, but I never did. Before we left for home, I was always well-fed, happy, and tired enough to fall asleep in the back of the little wagon despite the deep ruts and potholes in the roads. As neighbors, as family, and as coworkers we were more social then, and we depended on each other in ways that don't even exist today.

In late summer the townspeople began to prepare for the yearly Jamboree. There were baking contests and logging contests and a hundred other doin's that a twelve-year-old might find interesting. In the air was a festival spirit. After a hard and hot summer of swishin' the pan or felling timber everyone was ready for a weekend of rest and fun. Spare lumber was rounded up and I found myself assisting my Father and Mr. Tollsen with a Jamboree project. The pavilion that sheltered the nightly dances and reels had needed some repair since it hadn't been used in over a year on account of the drowning of the son of the lead fiddler. I remembered that we had all marveled at the little boy who had played the fiddle like his Father. I think that his name was Joseph but we all called him Joe.

At the graveside service for the poor boy, the Father had played the sweetest and saddest song for his son. He made the boys' fiddle whine and sing like a fine orchestra violin, and as the last notes of the song faded into the tall pines and firs, the man fell to his knees in grief. He placed the fiddle in the grave with his son, along with all of the hopes and dreams he had had for the boy. In my travels in Europe and Russia, I have heard great masters of the violin play before kings and queens in magnificent halls. No notes sounded more beautiful than the ones we all heard that day on the dusty hillside.

Mr. Tollsen recounted that drowning tragedy as we sawed and nailed on the pavilion.

"Hear tell that they found the boy all the way down at Ishi Pishi Falls in an Indian fishnet," he started. "Way I figure is that when he was down by the river he slipped on some of the rocks. Hope the boy hit his head or something before he drowned."

We all nodded at that, and I imagine that I wasn't the only one present that had miasmic nightmares about the terror of fighting the swift and dark waters as breath couldn't be found. I hammered away, thinking on that if the fight between me and the giant fish the summer before hadn't ended right they could've been talking about me and my premature end in their conversation too. I got a chill like a goose had walked on my grave – I laughed to myself then, thinking that it was probably just one of our barn mice running across my headstone.

I could remember at least two people each year that had drowned in the Klamath, and our Mother's stories of warning of the wet death and hounding of the dangers scared us quite a bit. Some of the men present had even helped pull drowned men, women, and children from the waters. I imagine that those men had nightmares worse than mine. We all understood why the fiddler had been too heartbroken to play last year, and us, being decent folk, didn't dare hold the dance in his time of mourning. My family and I were mourning War Sing at that time as well, and probably wouldn't have attended anyway.

It took about three or four hammer strikes for me to squarely sink a nail, but my Father could do it with just one sure-placed hit. With his help and without me messing up too much, we were done with the building before noontime and were able to wander through the doin's a bit before we planned to head back home to clean up and bring Mother back into the dance that evening.

I listened close to the conversations I passed by groups of folks, for any news of the Running Indian and his race – and of course, the fate of War Sing's papers. I found out that Meamber had been meandering again, and the mail service for the entire River Canyon had been waylaid for the past several months. Our community hadn't received any letters, packages, or what interested me most – our teacher's San Francisco newspaper – since the end of the last school year.

My Father and I had patched up quite a bit of our trouble with each other, and even though it seems odd to say so – I had learned a lot from the whole mess about myself, about him, and how a responsible man values honesty and puts stock in trust.

I was distracted by the thoughts of the hidden Jade Temple, and wondering if it would be hard to keep it a secret like my Father had asked. I figured it was the least I could do for him, since I had caused so much trouble. I kept thinking about the riddle of the treasure – trying to understand what War Sing had meant by the "treasure under the temple" phrase as he was dying. I had looked for hours at the Jade Temple grounds and surrounding area, finding that the bedrock slab it was placed on – the same bedrock that jutted up to form an altar for the curious-looking Buddha – was solid and thick and void of any hiding places or potential to place anything under it. Looking at the formation of the hillside from above it and from below it, I figured the bedrock shelf could be ten miles deep for all I knew. It gave me something else to think about – other than the beautiful Penelope or if pirates really still existed or if the moon was really made of cheese like the schoolyard astronomical expert, my friend Greig St. George, had said.

After our walk-through of the rest of the pre-festivities was over, we set out for home to wash and comb our hair and get on button-up shirts for the doin's that evening. Mother was ready to leave when we arrived, and Father remarked at the beauty of her hand-sewn yellow and white dress with the fancy bishop bustle and matching ribbons wrapped through the comb in her done-up hair. After us fellas were all gussied up as best we could, we headed back into town for the dinner and dance.

I jumped out of the wagon as soon as we got close enough, and set to findin' some of my friends in the thick and loud crowd of folks. It didn't take long for a group of us boys to assemble, and as we roamed the grounds in our group we gained more members – we were like a rowdy magnet, and fellas were pulled in almost without thinking about it first.

We loudly reviewed our summers and expounded on the various great adventures we'd had while school was let out. I was unnaturally quiet – boy how I had wanted to tell them all about letting a shot off at a thief or the excitement of discovering the Jade Temple, but when I weighed the importance of the value my Father's trust for me had against the weight held by schoolboy posturing I knew trust won against pride. I recall I mentioned a few things about hunting and fishing, but that afternoon I mostly just listened.

By the time the reels started we were all pretty

much still clean and buttoned, and again as a group we reluctantly moved toward the music and the rest of the evening's doin's.

At the updated dance pavilion we had naturally segregated ourselves by age. The adults were near the stage, and the young men and young women mulled about midstage. My friends and I sat in the back, where we could fetch a good look at all of the foofaraw and escape any chance of being forced to dance. Jostling and joking, we spent a lot of time critiquing everyone and everything.

I took a quick notice that the fair Penelope was in attendance, surrounded with a fortress and a moat made of other less-beautiful and less-interesting girls. Even if I wanted to, I wasn't sure if I could break those defenses on my best attempt.

Somewhere along that celebration evening, a lady from one of the gospel mills bustled through the crowd of revelers announcing that with all of the heathen ways and liquor consumption we were all in short order for damnation and destruction.

Apparently not satisfied with the lack of attention she was getting, she made her way up to the front of the fellows playing in the band. She pulled back her poke bonnet a bit to have a wider field of view to glare at us better, but not too much as to seem improper by showing her head. Clapping her hands roughly, she finally got the attention she had been looking for.

Gathering herself up to the tallest her four-and-a-half-foot body could present – pridefully looking about and waiting 'til everyone was looking at her – she put her hands together real theatrically like she was praying.

"I worry for you – all of you – most of all the little

ones here tonight that deserve to see better of their parents." Looking down her nose, she spat words at us that didn't seem much filled with love, "I will pray for all of you."

There was a little laughter from some of the mine and mill fellows in the background. It sounded like one of them had told a joke that the rest of us didn't hear. Probably was better that way, knowing the rough humor some of those boys had – even in those delicate times.

The church woman pretended not to notice. She glared at each of us like a true and practiced professional guilt-giver. She looked like she was one of the women who had cut their finger-wagging teeth on rougher crowds than ours. Right in front of us she was winding herself up so tightly that I figured if she kept it up her fool head was going to explode like a watermelon that had been stuffed with Chinese gunpowder. Each whispered comment in the crowd or chuckle from one of the boys seemed to prime her even more. By the look on her face, then, you would have thought she had walked over and caught us feeding Christians to the mountain lions or something.

"We all know that dancing is an abomination," she shrieked, "and encouraging that activity is a sin." Losing more of the attention of the crowd, she started to become frantic in her speech. "I insist that you stop this all – right now – out of decency for our community. Shame on all of you!"

One of the mine fellas was overheard, then, talking about what a shame it was instead that he'd be charged with a crime if he picked her up and pitched her in the river, when he'd just be doing the community a service. Laughter erupted through the crowd again.

Possibly sensing her defeat, she bellowed, "You will each one know the blazes of eternal hellfire!" Her poke bonnet had fallen back a little on her head, and was tipped to the side a little matching up her outburst and appearance in the same crooked craziness.

She wagged her long and pointy virago finger at us all, even as the crowd turned away. Painfully outstaying her welcome, she continued to warn us, "There's no leaping from Delilah's lap into Abraham's bosom!"

I knew what she meant from my own religious studies, but the way she had barked it out at the folks it seemed like she was just trying to throw her own knowledge about like a show-off. She hollered a few bars of a hymn that before that night I had been fond of – I figured she could have spoke a Birthday Card to make it sound accusatory and a damnation warning. It seemed to me that she was unnaturally eager to make the Great Jump – when the rest of us were doing our best to keep that Final Breath far, far away.

When Harry McBride finally hollered out, "Either sing or get off the stage," she gathered herself up, and walked down and across the dance floor muttering pearls of wisdom like, "You know better, Mrs. Martin," and, shaking her crooked little finger and uttering, "Really, Mr. Richardson – alcohol?"

The band started up before she was all the way off the dance area, and after quickly setting down his cup of whatever he had been drinking Mr. McBride grabbed the pious woman up and twirled her around the dance floor not once but twice – much to the amusement to many in the crowd – enduring her shrieks and fits the whole time.

After her turn around the floor, she ran off into

the dimness of the late afternoon with her shrieks of "hellfire" and "damnation" following her long awaited retreat. Mr. McBride was overheard saying something about how his prayers had just been answered – and with that, we all continued on with our evening.

It was mostly a good thing to have those doxology works folks around – for the most part they left the rest of us to look to God as we saw fit, but then every once in a while one of their folk would come along so chock-full of the Spirit that there wasn't much room left for common sense. That particular xanthippe was later identified by several as Mrs. Sanderson, a matriarch at one of the local tent-revival type churches. I often wondered after that night if there was such a thing as precognition or adumbration, or if she was in fact a messenger of God. My true feelings were then and remain now that even a broken clock is right twice a day.

I figure that even God Himself tires of incessant doryphores and tattletalers and I can't imagine any degree of Eternal Reward that would include a many roomed palace or a gem-filled crown for the finger-waggers and the self-righteous gossips. I often wondered if they were held responsible – Up There – for every person they ran off from their church due to their nagging and bad example. I'd pay for a ticket to that show, any day.

The musicians had politely stopped playing during Mrs. Sanderson's second tirade also – not so much out of respect for the chuckleheaded woman, but instead because they were laughing too hard to keep time well. When she was finally clear of the festivities they promptly continued their music.

Sitting on a hay bale, I put a piece of straw in my

teeth and leaned back on a supporting pole. The warm river wind jostled my hair, and the sun was gently falling behind the mountain. It was a perfect evening in our river valley – despite the loud cawing of the Sanderson woman.

There are times in our lives that we remember vividly. I looked up from Josh Henderson's new sling shot, to see a sight that I still carry close to my heart. My Mother was busy cooking with a group of ladies, who had joined together to serve dinners to the patrons for a nickel a plate. I watched my Father walk up to her, and sweep her over the table with no trouble at all. She pretended to protest his rude interruption, and then resigned herself to hold his hand as he led her to the dance floor. She paused a moment at the side of the floor, removed the cooking apron and unpinned her bishop to let her skirts flow as she danced. She had patterned, cut, and hand sewn her beautiful dress all by herself – it had taken her nearly four months of her spare time to finish.

My Father led her to the center of the floor, and they began to move in time with the fast reel.

At that moment it occurred to me that I had never seen them dance before. He held her gently and firmly at the same time, and he moved them both gracefully across the dance floor. My Mother's skirts brushed the wooden floor, and then seemed to sail around her as if she was a princess. She leaned back as he held her to turn, and the comb from her tightly wound pinned-up hairdo flew across the floor. Her long, curly brown hair cascaded down her back to her waist, and it also began to twirl and spin in time with her skirts and the music.

It was the first time that I ever really realized that my Mother was not only my Mother. She was a wife.

She was an educated woman. She was once a girl and had fun and played before I was ever born. She was also so beautiful I began to be ashamed that I had never really noticed it before. I loved my Ma, and I still do. Although she's been gone thirty-seven years now, I think of her most every day. It might be strange to think that a man approaching his ninety-second birthday would think often of his Mother, but I had stopped being embarrassed about loving my Mom after being in the war. I saw grown men crying for their Mothers, and held several dying boys who pleaded with me to let their Mommas know they loved them. But at that dance, before my friends and I learned that hard lesson of familial love, I quickly made sure that none of my buddies were watching me, watching my parents dance.

I also realized that it was probably the first time in nearly a year and a half, since War Sing died, that I had seen my Father really smile.

I took a sideaways glance at the beautiful Penelope – shyly standing in the gaggle of girls close by – and I actually started to entertain the thoughts of going over to ask her to dance. I tried to calculate how long it would take me to cross in front of all of the guys, and while crossing what the odds were that I'd be harassed or cajoled by my peers.

My attention turned from devil-may-care thoughts of whirling Penelope around the dance floor to a sound rising over the hill behind us. The musicians stopped the reel yet again as we all turned and looked in awe at the sight before us – almost expecting to see Mrs. Sanderson tirading through the doin's once more.

What made us stop and stand with mouths agape was much more serious than finger wagging or guilt-giving, and ironically Mrs. Sanderson's adumbral words of hellfire and doom were beginning to ring in all of our ears, but for a different and more practical reason.

The trees atop the ridge were backlit by a glowing light. The deep blue of the starry sky was blurred at the top of the hill to a growing yellow and orange. Speechless, we stood as the thundering sound moved to us. The ground shook and the dancing pavilion began to slightly sway. In front of me, I saw Joseph Habshaw pour out the rest of his bottle of whiskey and rub his eyes. I knew the events must've been serious when I noticed that all elbow-bending by those boys was put aside for the more pressing events at hand.

I remember how startled I was when my Father grabbed the back of my shirt with his strong hands, ready to protect me before he even knew what was coming. He pulled my Mother and I close and we began to hurriedly walk toward our old mare and buggy rig. We had never had an earthquake as long as I could remember, and we haint had one here since. The other kids and I were confused and looking around for some direction from the adults. I could see that it wasn't just the young folk who were scared. We heard someone yell that there was a forest fire heading over the ridge and toward us – and it was coming fast as greased lightning. We were all trapped.

Most of us stopped our retreat and everything quieted down for a moment when we first heard the screams. I will never forget the sound that broke my twelve-year-old heart. As we looked back at the ridge, we saw what had caused all of the shaking. The wild horses of Happy Camp, that beautiful herd of proud and magnificent beasts, had been caught in the canyon on the other side of the hill. The fire must've come up on them as they rested, fast and hard. Spooked, some managed to get out of the draw, and now they stood at the top of the ridge. We were between them and the river. Wild by nature, they were stopped atwixt the fire behind them and us in front of them. Then we could smell the fire smoke, and the burning hair of the horses.

I gasped as I saw the stallion make the ridge – the beautiful and magnificent animal from the High Springs Pool meetings was in grave danger as well. He snorted and looked down at our gathered group of folks and then to the river behind us. Beside myself, and knowing how shy the horses were to people, I just yelled out, "It's okay! We won't hurt you!" It seemed the stallion heard me and recognized my voice even in the midst of all the tragedy that was unfolding.

The fire flared up behind them as we watched, and encouraged by the stallion with nips and hoof-swipes and his wordless permission a group of the milling horses finally galloped over the ridge toward us, down the hill and right through our Jamboree. A broomtail bay brought the fire with her in her mane and on her sooty tail to the bushes around us made tinder-dry by the hot summer. Spots flared around us and our friends and neighbors began to panic.

Out of the confusion and the burning horses and the jumble of people, my Father's voice boomed. "Follow the horses! Get your families and follow the horses!" My Father knew that the fire was too quick, and there would be no way to get all of the horse-drawn wagons loaded with all those folks back up the hill and through the fire. By that time, a few men were running from one rig to the next, unharnessing the animals so they could have at least a chance to run to safety too. Instead of trying to make it out in the wagons or on horseback,

Dad urged us again to follow the path the wild horses had made through our dance to the river behind us.

As we ran for the safety of the Klamath, I looked back for a moment for the stallion, expecting him to be coming along to safety too. He stood there still, on the ridgeline with the firestorm around him. In the windy tumult and the blowing embers, he looked back and away from us toward the canyon where the screams of some horses could still be heard over the furor. It was the point where he must have known that no more of his herd would be coming on their own.

I will never forget the sight of that grand and strong horse. His mane and tail were on fire, and the trees near him were beginning to crumble under the heat. With golden smoke behind him, he turned once more toward us and the river where his surviving herd mulled about. He stood on his hind legs and whinnied as loud as I've ever heard, hopping a bit to keep his balance. The horses in the river called back to him. He was saying goodbye.

With one last snort, he turned on his lighting feet and rushed headlong back into the fire, through the steep destruction, to the dying horses below.

The terrible but tragic beauty of that night would haunt my thoughts for the rest of my life – I had no way to fully understand, then, how the death of the wild horses would affect me. It was the beginning of the end of the old days in our river valley, and something others would bring up as a measuring point in our history. Often folk in our community would refer to past events and times as either Before or After the Horses Were Burned.

I remember as soon as the stallion ran back down into the flames, we all turned to save ourselves. My Dad had to pick up my Mother at one point, as her dress was not practical running-away-from-certain-death fashion. Trying to ebb my crying to aid my seeing, I ran with my family the rest of the way to the river. When we were in the water and away from most of the danger, my Father looked at my tears. What he said that day has stayed with me.

"Boy," he said with tears welling in his eyes, too, "that horse, there, well, that's what a man does. He takes care of his family. He'd sacrifice anything for their safety. There's something hardwired inside good men that urge them to choose the right path even if it is a hard one. That horse, there, wild as he was, knew he had to see if he could help out any more of his herd and probably didn't think twice about it."

I looked at my Father, then, and I knew in my heart that the words he said were true. I understood what he said, and I knew that I would try to be a good man too. I knew without a doubt that my Father would always come back for me, just like the stallion did for his dying herd. My Father was a good man. I miss him every day, and I hope that I measured up to the high mark that he set as a husband and a Father.

I can still remember the resolute look on my Father's face and the set of his jaw, as we all stood waist deep in the slow river water waiting for the fire and the danger to pass over us.

What a sight we were. Finely dressed ladies soaked, hair-flattened, and sooty. Men, patting out embers on their shirts and keeping keen eyes on the danger around us. Dozens of wild-eyed and fire-singed undomesticated and stock horses milling about atwixt us. In the center of it all, the musician fellows from the dance decided to forget about the recent reel they had been playing before their escape and instead, standing in the river, began to play some hymn that now I've forgotten – but at the time, with all of the townsfolk singing along and my Father and my Mother holding me close, it was the some of the most moving music I had ever heard. It calmed the remaining horses as well.

Even when the water-logged ladies had to begin removing their water-logged formal dresses to escape the drowning those hundred-pound masses of cloth and bustle posed, we menfolk simply offered our shirts to them to cover their petticoats. We were a practical bunch, and politely regarded and tolerated the societal etiquettes only as long as the silly rules didn't interfere with drawing breath.

The years that have passed and everything that has happened atwixt then and now cannot blur my memories of that night. Watching my folks dance and realizing how beautiful my Mother was is as fresh to me as if it had happened yesterday. I am a good man, thanks to my Father. My pen is heavy now, and the light is low. I'll trade it for the fishing pole, and maybe catch some dinner. Or maybe I'll just dip my old and tired feet in the cool water of the crick, and think some more about my Dad.

Chapter Twenty-Three

The Parade

"I knew that my beau, Tyler Bondbridge, really loved me when I saw him throw himself on that deadly candy-stick."
– Miss June Bunches, Resident

Two days after the Jamboree Fire – which some folks called the Roasted Horse Fire until many objections were raised – as a community we decided to continue with our celebration. It was just natural for us to pick up and move on, and it also served us to have something else to do and to think about. Besides, some of us had been working on parade entries for weeks, and it was a shame to let it go to waste.

The town had been spared of major damage by the forest fire. A few outbuildings and sheds had been lost by folks living up Cade Mountain and Shinar's

Saddle and a few of the stock horses still were missing. Most folks didn't build in the natural firestorm chimney above town, which had burned just the same way so many times no one could count. The afternoon winds, being carried up the giant bowl and canyon only needed to ebb a lingering spark from a previous fire or fan a lightning strike to push the flames up to the very top of the tall mountain – resulting in sand-to-glass melting firestorms and fifty-foot flame lengths near the summit.

It had been a close call for many, especially all of us trapped at the Jamboree grounds. I figured that we'd have to rebuild the pavilion that we'd spent so many hard hours to clean and fix up before.

My Mother suggested to my Father and I at breakfast that we had many blessings to celebrate, with the foremost being that not one person had been killed in the fiery blaze. My Father was quick to add, in his dry and sometimes cynical wit that we should also celebrate some other much overlooked pieces of good fortune.

My Mother and I looked to each other, just waiting for him to say something that would land him in trouble. We could tell by the look on his face and the tone of his voice that he had a controversial comment barely slight moments away.

He continued to tell us about the things that he was personally thankful for in his best I'm-serious-and-not-joking voice. He said he believed that all of the town ladies forced into the water on that burning night needed an opportunity to recover the dignities they had lost after sending their heavy dresses down the Klamath. He surmised that continuing the celebration would also give all of the menfolk a much needed chance to also recover their dignity – through seeing all the women fully clothed once again. He figured that would be the first step to begin to erase the tragedy of the Dress Abandonment. He suggested that many of the ladies should be politely yet firmly asked maybe wear two dresses – and a shawl – to any future event where a Dress Abandonment may be required.

He also added that he was hopeful that those abandoned dresses would find their way, with any luck, down the mighty Klamath to all manner of needy folks.

Holding his hand to his head like he was thinking real hard he said, "Perhaps a few of those frilly and satin-covered items will find their way to shipwrecked fellas in the Pacific, to soothe their spirits and – when properly dried and hung from the palm trees – could be used as shelter for thirty or forty of the marooned fellas at least."

He figured that just one of the dresses would be a great salvation to any storm-damaged ocean vessel – for the Captain could order it run up the main mast, wait to get a breeze up the bustle, and be at home port 'fore the next squall. I tried to stem my giggles so he would continue lampooning the mammoth finery that some of the ladies had been sporting that fiery night – without my laughing interruptions.

He continued with his jocularity even through my snickers, and in fact I think my giggling fueled him a bit. Looking to my Mother and seeing the wrenched up look on her face, I figure he felt his commentary was meeting the mark he had set for his comedy. Walking across the kitchen towards my Ma he grabbed her up "just in case she felt like throwing another carrot out the window" and to my enjoyment he kept on talking.

Switching his tone to a very serious low voice, he moved his hand under Mother's chin so she'd have to look right into his solemn eyes. He said, "I assure you that I am going to celebrate very most of all that every single one of those women had remembered to wear petticoats under their drownable dresses that awful night." With a severe gravity he went on to tell her he was more thankful than his words could ever describe that they hadn't found it necessary to let the petticoats float away too.

Mother responded with her regular fare, staring a hole through his head and then a short time after rolling her eyes. I always figured that was what cultured girls – like my Ma – had been taught to do in society situations when they really felt like letting out a knee-slapping laugh.

Sensing a censure, Father began to sum up his view of the blessings that had occurred – mentioning some that we would possibly never, ever know about. Holding my Mother a bit closer, he postulated that perhaps the most beautiful Queen from India, having all of the jewels and tortoise-shell combs and fine-sewn shoes and crowns and pins – having been given everything she ever had wanted – had for some time been requiring the most beautifully sewn, complementary, and fashionable gown ever created. What if it was possible, at that very moment, that Mother's dress was purposefully floating in a direct path to fulfill that poor rich woman's biggest wish? He asked us to imagine the happiness on the face of that Queen when the ocean gave up Ma's hand-sewn gown.

Then he added, "You know, Ellie, when that Queen puts on that outfit she will never be as beautiful in it as you were that night."

Mother laughed then, with a blush on her face and a smile that lasted for hours. Dad and I both knew that she enjoyed our complements of her sewing, canning, and cooking – and although I never used those complements for my own gain with my Mother, my Father often found his way out of the doghouse with well-placed words. It didn't mean he was making up complements the ease the situation – during those times, he just let them flow a little freer.

We attended the reel that night – held instead on the roadway in the middle of the town – which was blissfully uneventful insofar as burning horses or sermon-filled self-righteous chuckeheaded jackdaws were concerned. Perhaps encouraged by the near-destruction and barely avoided burning death of everyone in our community, when I saw Penelope I marched right over to her – forging right past the moat of girls around her and making my way through the gossipy girl-wall that kept her separate – and took her right out to the middle of the improvised road-rough dance floor. I was in my reeling glory as I promenaded her right by the wide-eyed and open-jawed jury of my peers and friends, and I didn't even look back. She and I danced the night away, and I was the perfect gentlemanly companion in that social situation that my Mother had taken years to teach me to be.

I think I fell in love with Penelope that evening – but only a little bit, and not enough for it to seriously take. She was the most beautiful girl in the town – and I sure enjoyed being around her – but she hardly knew anything about Hamlet or The Lady of The Lake or anything I found very interesting at all. She seemed more ornamental than useful. I couldn't imagine a fella marrying that girl someday, and being forced to talk to her about china dishes or dress hems or hanging curtains and such for the rest of his life. I figured after I left the River Canyon, and saw the world courtesy of the United States Navy or the Foreign Legion, maybe – perhaps I'd call on her when I returned to see if she had got more interesting.

The next morning my Father and I had set to finishing last minute work on the Veteran's Parade Entry – which, like two years before, was basically an assemblage of bunting and decorations for the small fife and drum band that had been put together to follow the Color Guard. The two oldest local veterans who were still able to walk and move about were given the honor of carrying our flags. The oldest fella of those two got to carry the United States Flag, and his junior partner was saddled with the State Standard. The two local veterans most recently returned from duty were always asked to serve as the guards to the right and the left of the standard bearers – and by goodness, back then they sure didn't carry any pretend wooden rifles like I have seen done occasionally recently. I never figured how anyone could shoot memorial volleys with fake rifles, but I'm not going to slip off this topic now and go into that one. Holding the fake rifle to your shoulder and saying, "Bang, bang" only really works in pretend times, not times that sometimes need a bite with the bark.

Anyhow, getting back to the parade of my memories and off my well-worn soapbox.

I recall that some of the local ladies had made jackets and vests for the fife and drum brigade, so the fellas that didn't fit their service clothes or no longer had possession of them could still be dressed up. In the past, only one or two of the field of twenty had used the locally-made jackets – but after the last flood that had destroyed so many belongings, almost ten of the men had lost their uniforms to the stormy waters.

There always had been a specific parade order, and no one was sure who had come up with it but its pretty much the same arrangement that we have today. First, a fella came along announcing that the parade was about to start. The first entry was always the Color Guard – always with Old Glory held high and the State flag lower and tipped forward – and close behind them was the fife and drum fellas, piping and banging out patriotic songs the best they could.

The rest followed behind: the honorary marshall of the parade – at that time, usually a visiting mine owner or a local businessman; volunteer organizations and groups; churches; working outfits – miners, loggers, and visiting folks – who could be counted on to construct interesting and sometimes outlandish decorations for their wagons or horse dressage. My favorite of those had always been the Chinese entries – colorful and exciting at the same time, as they were known sometimes to toss out lit firecrackers at us kids once in a while.

There was a friendly competition between them and some of the other mining outfits – especially Mike Hargrave's group from the *Golden Eagle*. Regardless of who received the prizes at the judge's stand – those of us along the parade route won out just fine, being that their need for parade glory always was run out to us in the form of better and better entries.

The tail end of the parade was a always a couple of guys who had been ordered by the circuit judge to clean up the horse manure and littered items off the roadway, with their reprimand or citation usually resulting from a prolonged fight in one of the local elbow-bending establishments or some other minor crime. There had never been a lack of folks for the judge to choose from when he rode through in August for his yearly visit – but it wasn't usually the same fellas twice, since the public humiliation of their sentences was a real motivating force for them to clean up their own act as well.

The parade would wind through town, ending near the judges' stand in front of the Mercantile. The parade judges took their task very seriously, and I can say that most years folks put their own bias and personal ties aside and tried to make a fair assessment of the presented entries.

The townsfolk and visitors were lined down the parade route, and a great cheer went up as the whole doin's started. Children darted as close as they would dare to the parade path, since some folks riding along in it had tossed out trinkets and treats to us in the past. The kids were like hogs in the trough, bellyin' up for what was to be thrown to them. Their activities got to be right dangerous at times, with wrestling skirmishes between children breaking out over the disputed ownership of a peppermint or gumball – all the while dodging the oncoming wagons, spooked horses or marchers.

Although I figured I was probably a bit too old to be wrestling for the candies with the other kids, I moved up a little closer anyway – figuring that if a stray piece of the thrown treats made their way to me, it was only expected that I'd naturally pick it up.

Each person along the parade route was on their feet with hats off and hands placed over hearts preparing for the approach of the Flag. Salutes were readied by former military folks long before the slowed oldermost fellas brought Our Standard down the way. Shep Anders – well-known for pranks and tomfoolery –

was the unhappy carrier of the State flag. I could almost see the sour look on his face, and he was acting like he was carrying a skunk hide down the road. When the Colors were about twenty feet from where we were standing, he hollered out, "Excuse me a moment," and took off into the crowd. The whole procession stopped up short, and a few of the fife and drum fellas ran into each other in a cacophony of sounds. A few fellas in the band must've known about Shep's little prank plan, as they began to hit drum rolls on their snares. The sound got louder and louder, and they must've had some knowing folks in the crowd too, as some folks around us a started to clap their hands together in a rousting fashion. At the crescendo of the clapping and the drum rolling, Shep gloriously reappeared carrying the State of Jefferson flag instead of the blue and gold California banner. The new white standard held a circle and two x's and proudly sported well-sewn dark lettering that read, simply, "State of Jefferson." We all cheered and the huzzahs bellowed out through our little valley. Some celebratory shots rang out and the fellas took up their parade march again, receiving the same sort of response from folks further along the route.

We clapped for the entries we liked the most – or the ones we had a personal interest in or that threw the best candies – and had a right fine time watching everyone promenade down the street. It looked like the folks in the parade were having a good time as well. Once in a while a horse would spook up, and charge ahead faster than it should have but the rest of the parade would eventually catch up to it.

We all waited breathlessly for the Chinese entry, as well as the entry from the *Golden Eagle* boys led by Mike Hargraves. Their friendly feud had always had interesting results during past celebrations.

Nearing the end of the parade, we all cheered as we saw the Celestial procession coming toward us – the men were all dressed in their finest gold and red silks and aligned in several groups. Some fellas in the front held long poles with what looked like fish and turtles tied to the ends, but as they came closer I could see that the water animals were crafted out of material and soft and shiny pieces of silk – open on one end like the pillowcases my Mother had sewn. I was fascinated how they moved their poles just so to get the little breeze into the tethered air fish or air turtle, making them look like they were playfully swimming through our late summer sky. Following them were the musicians, playing traditional instruments like the round and long varieties of guquin zithers, the paddle-shaped pipas, and even one fella had an erhu that had always reminded me of a meat saw. A contingent of pipes followed behind, with several men playing the colorfully decorated xiaos and dizis.

If I would have known that was to be one of the last times I would ever hear the Chinese folks play their heart-plucking music in our little River Canyon, I'm sure I would have appreciated it much, much more. The musicians stepped past, and their beautiful song drifted away from me on the wind and was gone as they turned the bend in the road.

A few of their fellas following behind the musicians tricked the little kids when they threw out roses to the ladies in the crowd. My Mother was almost buried by the dozens that were tossed to her – but not enough to cover up her big smile. She bowed gracefully to the parade men as they continued on.

A couple of the brightly clothed fellas – right

behind the flower-throwers – made up the unintended slight to all of the children by tossing handfuls of treats to them, making sure that no child was left empty-handed.

I was startled by a large silvery dragon charging down the road at me after the candy-throwers had passed by, until I figured it was made-up – the men's slippered feet sticking out from under it gave it away. As it ran past me, I was thrilled to see the customary fireworks had not been forgotten. Little but loud bangs and pops and whizzy-hopping-things were going off all around. My head was on a swivel and I had a smile on my face as big as a horse's dopey grin – all I could think was that I wished I knew how to fashion those things and what fun I'd have with 'em if I could.

Like most good things, they eventually passed by too – moving down the route with their music and dragon and exploding fun.

I turned my head so fast it almost hurt when I heard the huzzahs and guffawing coming from the last entry. The *Golden Eagle* boys were in full regale, and by all accounts they were having a real hog killin' time. Each man was dressed in counterfeit Chinese silks, and it looked like they were trying to good-naturedly spoof the fellas that had preceded them on the parade route. They also had musicians, but instead of the zithers and dizis, they had fiddles and guitars and were doing a pretty good job picking out a tune and staying together on it. We laughed at their antics and when I looked around, the Chinese folks in the crowd thought the playin' around by Hargraves' fellas was funny too. No one I knew back then was ever offended by some good natured ribbing by friendly folks – that kind of over-sensitivity is a pretty new phenomenon in our country, and one I don't think I'll ever quite get used to.

Not to be outdone by the Chinese fireworks, the *Golden Eagle* boys had hatched a plan. Their whole idea to copy the Chinese fellas was to work in their own explosive entertainment to the parade. The fellas in the back let their musicians go ahead a bit for safety's sake, and then on the call of one of the men in front the marchers formed a circle in the center of the road with their backs to us. From my own experience with mischief, I could almost instantly tell that they were up to something – I'm not sure if it was the hunkering over and the whispered voices that tipped me off, or if as a thirteen year old boy I just had a special sense for emerging monkeybusiness.

When they turned outward toward us I could see that each man had put fire to a piece of explosives –– quarter-sticks and half-sticks of dynamite with fuses lit and sparkling – and were readying to throw them into the crowd.

Panic ensued as my Father pushed us down and back toward the wagons as he readied to charge, and other folks were running this-way and that. The men from *Golden Eagle* mine pulled their arms back, and lofted their explosives into the air toward all of us. I saw the lit doom headed toward us flying just like Joe Hargraves had thrown me a baseball instead of a lit death stick. I tried to dodge it and cover my ears at the same time since the fuse was getting awful short. Mother was grabbing at me and I was trying to get back from it and she tripped and I started pulling her away and just then the fuse burnt in and we could only just look and wait for the explosions. It was awful quiet in that second it would take to ignite itself, as the fuse burned down into the meat of the dynamite. We were all stock still and waiting, and I'm sure many of us were thinking the same thing – thoughts questioning how those fellas got so stupid to use big sticks instead of eighths like we played with all the time.

After two seconds had passed and nothing had happened, we all were looking around at each other. My Dad had made it to the circle of fellas and was throwing back his arm to start and finish the fight in one blow, and I could hear Mike Hargraves quickly holler, "It was a joke! They're paper blanks filled with candy for the kids."

My Dad punched him anyway, and it was the hardest punch I'd ever seen anyone make. The blow had so much force in it that it pushed Mike down after, and I think my Father said something like "I ain't laughing," and walked back toward us. The *Golden Eagle* boys rushed away before they got any more whoopin's, and a couple of the kids – like kids do – threw a few rocks at them as they retreated. At least we thought it was the kids, and thinking later about how good my Ma was at throwing carrots I figure one of them stones could have been from her.

As we regrouped from purt nearly being exploded to shreds, I picked up a few of the offending prank sticks and emptied the candies in my pockets. I smiled at my haul, and figured that was what I had been told about making the best of a bad situation.

Chapter Twenty-Four

The Royal Court of The Exiled Emperor

"Do wonderful things happen because of fate, destiny, or simply just coincidence? Does it really matter?"

– Netterly Habshaw, Resident

Just as we were settling down from the ruckus and readying to head off to the judging area to see who had won the awards, we were all surprised by more parade coming down the street. Of course, we all knew the parade order and we had already seen everybody we could think of go by. Even the judge-ordered litter patrol fellas had already started to make their embarrassed way down the street. We naturally got back into place on the roadside to politely wait for the last entry to catch up.

The group was large and colorful, but in the rising wavering heat of the late morning it was hard to see what and who it was.

I could make out dark green and silver and red, and instantly thought of the colors of the Chinese silks that some of the local men wore on their most important holidays. There were tall horses in the front, like I had never seen. They made our good horse look only half-sized.

As they came closer, I could see that the horse manes and tails were braided and bobbed in a fashion that I was unfamiliar with. I recall thinking that the entry – just from the time it must have taken to braid those giant horse's manes – would have to win at least one award. The other parade spectators – like us – who had reassembled on the road sides were clapping and cheering for that final entry.

The riders, on closer inspection, were Chinese men – but I couldn't remember seeing any of those particular fellas before. I figured that maybe they were visiting from other parts of the County or had just moved in. The riders looked at us with stern gazes, and I could see their horses wore military-like tack – with loops and clasps for the swords and a chain stick and other things I'd never seen before. The horses pranced by in a high-stepped manner, almost like they were dancing. I figured their hooves must've been as big as my head, and I was further intrigued as I saw they were shod with sharp-fronted silver and brass shoes – something I had only read about horses of war being made to wear.

I counted thirty men and horses go by riding three abreast. All of them seemed to be looking for someone in the crowd – and it didn't seem like they were going to be throwing out any gumballs or hard candy from the look on their unsmiling faces. They were a set-jawed group like I had never seen before. Behind them, more Chinese fellas followed in a marching formation – dressed in the same green and silver and red patterns, but also sporting leathery aprons of what kind of looked like armor. The crowd was clapping at the finery of their costumes and the shine of their swords and helmets. They nodded politely at all of us, but looked at the ready to slice us all in two with their glimmering blades if needed.

My Father figured something was strange as well, as he pulled Mother and I back a bit and was readying to get us away from the whole affair. That was the point when one of the marching fellas pointed right at us, and hollered in English, "They're right there. Bring them!"

In the middle of the whole mess, we didn't have time to see that all of the Celestial folks that had been in the crowd were kneeling and bowing toward the road – something that escaped the notice of most all of us, I think.

Instantly my Father and Mother and I were surrounded by giant horses and armed men like something out of one of the books I had read. My Father had reached for his pistol but didn't have time to draw, and the rest of the folks around us who naturally would have come to our aid must've thought it was part of the parade monkeybusiness going on. We were led to the street by the armored men, and I was kicking and hollerin'. Six of the fellas had to escort Dad, and Mother was helpless as she was being carried by two of the shiny-sworded men. In the midst of the clapping by our townsfolk, we were captured and stuffed into a large curtained carriage. Looking up for a second I marveled at the pressed gold and embellishments on the inside of the coach – the cushions looked so rich that I figured I shouldn't even touch them – but we all fell to a seated position as the carriage began to move forward. There were figures of golden dragons everywhere I looked, and I figured it was no wonder they had to have giant horses – it would have killed regular horses to pull that heavy cart around.

I noticed that one of the armored men – the one who had pointed us out, in fact – had also come into the carriage behind us. My Father had placed himself –best in could in those tight quarters – between my Mother and I and the soldier-fella.

I was surprised to see another person in the carriage – he had seemed to blend in to all of the golden decorations by the clothes he was draped with. In the corner of the swaying opulent cabin, sat a boy a little younger than me who I figured had to be about nine or ten years old – dressed in silk finery that I could never have imagined a person could wear. He couldn't have looked any more opulent and polished if he had been dipped in gold and rolled in rubies – but there was something strangely familiar about him.

For just being almost exploded, and then being kidnapped with my family in the middle of the Jamboree parade, we were all a bit stunned.

The armored man reached for his sword, but to my relief he was just moving it so he could change his seat a bit. I studied on him hard, knowing something was familiar about him, too.

He kept an eye on my Father and his hip-worn pistol as he leaned back and whispered a bit to the boy, who nodded and motioned to us. I figured they were about to lop our heads off, or run us through – but it seemed unlikely in the richly dressed carriage because of the mess we would cause by being slain. Looking at my Father, I knew he was mere seconds away from mounting his one-manned assault against all of the fellas, and by the look on his face the armored man seemed to know that too.

The man said something again in Chinese to the boy, who nodded once more, and then he addressed us as he reached his hand toward me.

"Sun-hair-*axva'htaahkoo*, it's been a long time." He grasped my hand as my jaw went slack and my eyes went wide as they could. He shook my limp hand and arm and patted me on the shoulder. I couldn't believe my eyes, and I couldn't speak. He reached out to my Father, then, letting my limp arm fall back into my lap, and clasped his hand in friendship. He seemed to know my Father as well.

"Jack, there is so much to tell you about the past year. I apologize for grabbing you and your family that way but we have to be very careful and vigilant right now. There are many enemies, even here." The armored man took off his helmet then, and I saw that it was indeed my friend, Samuel the Running Indian. I still couldn't talk in my surprised state, and my brain was racing with questions and suppositions and hundreds of things that just didn't match up. My Father and Mother looked to each other, and I could see tears on my Father's face. I couldn't figure why they were so relieved to see Samuel, who I figured they only had ever seen in passing as he ran down the roads and whom they had never really talked to. Father must've made the connection between my confession of the Running Indian's help and the fact that he had arrived back home in such a strange manner. It was beginning to sink in, to them both, that War Sing's papers must have made it to his family.

Mother put her arms around Father. I could tell

then that she was glad to see that Samuel was all right, but I could tell she was most happy to see the unknown shaved-head boy in the carriage.

With the etiquettes of national ambassadorships, kidnappings, and armed hostage-taking brushed aside in one motherly blow my very own Ma leapt across the carriage and grabbed up the little princely fellow.

Apparently she knew more about the whole situation than I thought she had.

With all of the alarm and incredulity gone from her expression, she beamed with kindness and love and peace toward him. She brushed her hands over the richly dressed boy's face, holding him steady so she could look into his eyes.

My Father was unable to talk right then, so Ma spoke softly to the boy instead, holding both of his regal hands tightly in hers.

She asked the small fellow, "Are you the one we were told of – are you P'u Yi?"

Before he could get out the whole word of "Yes" my Father had reached over and scooped him up as well and delivered to him one of his famous bear hugs. I was still putting together everything in my mind, and was really surprised at my Father's reaction as well as my Mother's seeming knowledge of everything I had told my Father about the papers and my dishonesty – and my ears burned for a minute when I figured that he surely must have told her all of the stuff I had done. I'd have to remember to address to her later my apologies as well, regarding my lying.

I should have known that War Sing would have trusted the secret of his past with my Father and Mother. It all made sense, then. It explained why my Father was so fire-lit to get the papers back to War

Sing's Chinese family, and why the thief had come to our house to steal them. It even explained why my Father had placed a carved jade dragon in War Sing's hand before he was buried.

All of a sudden my brain and mouth were set to the same cog and the dam burst – I had about a hundred questions out before Samuel got me quiet.

"In time, in time, little Trout. We have a lot to talk about, but this is not the place."

"Let's start at the beginning," he said to all of us. "Let me introduce everyone." The carriage still rocked along, and I wondered if we were still on the parade route.

He pointed to me, and said, "This is Trout, but his full and proper name is Euclid Plutarch Hammarsen." I nodded to the boy. Samuel pointed to my Mother, and said, "This is Ellie, but her full and proper name is Elanora June Swensen Hammarsen." Ma reached to the boy once more and shook his hand in both of hers, and she reached up to wipe the remaining tears from his eyes like only a woman who is a mother can do. Samuel then pointed at my Father, and said, "The arms that are holding you right now belong to Jack, whose full and proper name is Hjalmer Carl Hammarsen."

Then we all looked at the boy, who was smiling shyly but happily while sitting on the knees of my Father. "This boy," Samuel began, "is known to us as Zhen Zi – it means Treasured Child. His full and proper name is P'u Yi of the Qing Dynasty, nephew of the deceased Dowager Empress Cixidies and Exiled Holder of the Dragon Throne of Manchu."

I was stunned to know that I was sitting in the carriage of a Chinese King, that he was just a boy younger than me, and that my Father and Mother seemed to know him – or at least a lot about him. I was further stunned by Samuel's next comment – but it made everything fit into place.

Samuel looked to me and said, "You would know him by his family, Trout. This is War Sing's younger brother."

With that, the Exiled Boy King was only able to get out, "I'm glad to know you all," before I leaped at him in the fashion of my parents with a great big hug that I didn't know I had in me. He smiled and hugged me back. In perfect spoken English – more perfect in fact than ours – he began to tell me all about his journey to America and how his new friend Samuel had helped him find us.

At that moment, the driver hollered something to Samuel in thick Chinese that I didn't understand at all, and the carriage stopped up short. Samuel grabbed up his sword and helmet, and asked us all to stay put as he quickly left the carriage.

I heard a strange applause outside and a mix of instruments playing, but all I could think of was the hundreds of new unanswered questions I had racing around in my head.

Chapter Twenty-Five

The House of Jade

"I had a rough day hunting. Got stung by a hornet, didn't see any game, and twisted my ankle in a gopher hole. I wandered through what looked like a circle of them Chinese trees – about thirty feet tall – and I felt a peace come over me, like everything was going to work out just fine."

– Army Norecross, Resident

We received the "all-clear" from Samuel, and gingerly disembarked the gilded carriage. It was good to be outside and free again, but the brightness of the day made us all a little sunblind for a minute. I heard the rowdy applause and huzzah-laden hollers way before I could see what was going on.

We had been stopped at the judge stand for the parade. The other folks from the town had mistaken the

Boy Emperor's entourage and coach as one of the entries just like we had. Samuel decided it would be easier to play along than to make a ruckus, but the fellas he was with looked ready for bear if indeed a ruckus did break out.

Community folks and visitors were about fifteen deep all around the judge stand, and as far as I could see everyone was looking in our direction. The Emperor's horses and riders placed themselves in strategic positions – scanning the crowd for trouble from their high vantage points. Many of them had their hands on their sword handles as they monitored the crowd.

The judges had disqualified the *Golden Eagle* boys for the near-panic they had brought to the parade route – and it was just as well since those fellas had lit out to avoid additional rock-tossings by the crowd. The judges and the parade marshal whispered to each other for quite a bit, and then asked entries Number Seven and Number Twelve to also come up to the stand.

Representatives from the two groups – the Lady's Temperance Corps and the local Chinese enclave – moved forward through the thick rows of people and mounted the stage.

Bert Grider, local self-appointed spokesman and unofficial official, awarded the third place ribbon and a bottle of Chinese wine to the Temperance Corps folks – embarrassingly commenting that "Providence had allowed them to take yet one more bottle from the mouths of the local men" among laughter and cheers from the crowd. He awarded the second place ribbon and a knitting set to the local Chinese representative in the same manner, congratulating them for the wonderful silver dragon display and the splendid music.

Grider tried to bow to the Celestial man but only succeeded in knocking off his own and the other man's hat.

Pulling himself up to his five foot maximum, Grider announced the winner of the parade competition.

"We do not know," he said as loud as he could, "who the folks are who entered our parade at the last minute with their imitation of a Royal Chinese Procession – but we're pleased to award the visiting Chinese folks with the bob-haired horses and the beautiful carriage our top award."

He added, "It must have taken them days to braid all of them horses up like that." I nodded my head, approving of his logic. The crowd cheered, huzzahed, and clapped.

Samuel and I walked up to the little stage accompanied by Zhen Zi, and on the face of it most folk would have just seen a costumed man and two children approaching the stand. By the way some of the Celestial folks backed away with their eyes down I could tell that many already knew who my new little friend really was.

The three of us stood by Mr. Grider, and as he handed the first place ribbon to Samuel, Samuel turned and offered it to Zhen Zi. The Boy nodded and Samuel placed the ribbon around the Emperor's neck. The handmade ribbon and medallion looked strangely at home – on the well-dressed boy – resting against the bright field of his silken attire made of cloth that had been spun with threads of gold and copper woven in. Grider handed Zhen Zi a boggy-top blackberry pie and a large jar of canned fish, as the top prizes of the parade day. The judges and the crowd looked to Samuel to say a few words – as the adult in our little misunderstood group – but he deferred to the boy, and helped him make his way to the speaking stand. Zhen Zi thanked him and the rest of the judges very politely, and I heard one of the ladies remark about "what a handsome little heathen boy" he was.

The Boy moved to the front, ignoring the compliment. With an unnamable quality about him – a royal presence, if you will – he began to address the crowd.

"Thank you," he said with a little nodded bow in perfect English, "residents of Happy Camp. I am honored to be in the fabled Gum Shun land, and honored as well with the necklace and the gifts."

Chinese folks who had been a bit confused about Zhen Zi's identity were beginning to understand who he was. Even with a blackberry pie in one hand and a jar of canned salmon in the other, the regal set of the Boy's chin and his ruling gaze were unmistakable. The Chinese folks in the crowd snuck glances at each other and talked in excited whispers.

He took all of the guesswork out of it when he announced something to the crowd in a thick and quick statement in Chinese language. Those folks bowed even closer to the ground while he talked – and I couldn't make out any of it. The guards came in closer to Zhen Zi while he addressed his countrymen with a passion and strength I didn't know a fella that young could possess.

He finished in the Chinese discourse, and turning to all of us once more he added a comment. "Thank you," he loudly spoke in English, "for your community hospitality to the Chinese peoples who have been here."

And with that, we were rushed back into the gilded carriage by the guards and set off for our house amid some pretty strange looks on confused faces of local folks. Samuel and my Father talked in hushed tones in the corner of the carriage, while my Mother held the blackberry pie and the canned fish so they wouldn't fall on the long and bumpy ride. My Father had one or two occasions to glance at the pie – his favorite – to make sure it was safe, too.

I set to talking to Zhen Zi – not enamored of his status and National Rank one bit – but fascinated instead by the fact that he was War Sing's brother. We talked and carried on, and by the time we reached our modest and humble dooryard and home I felt like I had known Zhen Zi my whole life.

Samuel and my Mother and Father went inside the house, and Zhen Zi and I ran around outside for the rest of the day closely followed by his guardsmen. I imagine he really needed to stretch his legs after the long journey. I figured I would ask him about all of the details of his trip – and about Samuel's mysterious involvement – after I showed him around the place a bit.

After the Exiled Emperor almost broke his leg from tripping on his robe my Ma found him some of my old clothes and helped him change in the house. When he came back out to the porch I walked up to him and jokingly said, "Well, I'm not sure what monkey business happens where you're from, but around here only the girls wear dresses."

He turned his regal head toward me, wordlessly and seriously sizing me up, and just when I thought I'd probably stuck my foot in my mouth for good the little fella started laughing so hard and long that tears almost started up in his eyes. He said, "My brother wrote to me that you were a very funny boy." I laughed too, and smiled real big on the inside because War Sing had written that of me.

Apparently used to the boyish antics of their Exiled Emperor, five of the youngest and spryest guards trailed us at all times throughout the hillside running and playing. At the Flying Rat Cave they stopped us, insisting to enter first to maintain the safety of the Boy. We ditched them there for a few minutes, but they caught up real fast and didn't look too happy. Zhen Zi laughed and apologized to them – but they looked like it was a trick he'd tried to play on them several times before.

We found ourselves perched in the Old Oak Tree at one point in the afternoon, and each of us – tired from the play – found a perfect and cool spot to lie against in its wide and shady arms.

"Is it always this fun here?" he asked, leaning back and putting his arms under his head and resting.

"No, this is summer when we don't have school," I replied. "When school is going it's an awful time. I feel like a trapped animal then."

He nodded knowingly. The Boy King sighed, looking around the woods from our perch – not like the King of a country, but like the Boy King of the Woods that all of us fellas were capable of being now and then. "Ever since I can remember," he said, "I've had lessons in languages, history, war strategies, politics and State etiquette."

He turned to me with a strange look on his face. He asked, "Did you know that in some places there are special table forks to eat certain foods with? Or that in some countries, if I visit and my shadow touches one of their people – they would have that person put to death?"

I took a while to respond, since I was busy thinking about what he said. I figured it was a lot harder to be a King than I had thought – I couldn't imagine how bad I'd feel if I caused someone to die just by forgetting where my fool shadow was resting. I told him, as I rearranged my back to avoid a pesky tree knot, "Sounds pretty tough. I'd hate to be the poor guy who accidentally was crossed by the shade of your giant head." He laughed, commenting on the smallness of mind and questioning if there was somewhere else where us Westerners carried our brains – since surely our little skulls weren't suitable. "Unless," he added, laughing, "your brains are tiny as well." We both guffawed at that one.

Thinking on the shadow-death sentence, I tossed a pine cone at him and asked, "What'll happen to someone who cracks you in the skull with something like that?" We both started to laugh once more when a guard below us answered, "Little boy, you don't want to know the answer to that question."

It gave me a lot to think about. I figured no child should have that kind of responsibility – what if he had happened to be a bratty fella like Marty Evart at school? I'd imagine that kind of boy would cause folks trouble on purpose, trying to see how many heads he could get lopped off in a day and such. Looked to me like China had been dealt a good hand with Zhen Zi, and as long as he stayed kind and thoughtful like he had shown us then those far-away folks couldn't do any better for a leader.

Looking back now – from my crick-side table eighty years away from that afternoon – I know the history of that country proved that in fact they never did do any better. Their social ownership of everything from the dirt to each other's thoughts destroyed that beautiful land War Sing and Zhen Zi loved, and crushed the spirit of those wonderful people. I knew of all the death and pain so many of those folks suffered at the hands of the jackdaws that took over that society when they first tried to bend the wills and steal the thoughts of the stubborn inhabitants.

That long ago day, before the fatefully horrible ruination of his countrymen, Zhen Zi and I talked about the great possibilities to be found in the future. He mentioned that his interest in Western medicine would benefit all of the villages, and he and his advisors had planned for a representative government that would give his countrymen more say in the affairs of his nation. Even though he had been forced to leave China for his own safety, he still spoke of it like it was still his.

We tossed a few more pine cones at each other, and after a while both threw a couple near one of the guards. All we got from him was a smile and a wryly disguised comment of "Honored Sir, would you like me to stand closer and in the open so it would be easier for you to hit me?" I had also noticed Zhen Zi's throwing arm was a little weak, while the guard and I snickered a little I prescribed some baseball practice to the Emperor to fix that right up.

With much of the day still before us, my Father rousted us out of the tree after a bit and explained that we were going to take a ride. Zhen Zi looked like a regular boy decked out in my threadbare hand-me-downs. Samuel, four hand-picked guards, my Father, Zhen Zi and I set out on horseback – riding fast and hard through the countryside. I knew after a bit where we were headed.

The Boy handled his mount like a professional rider, controlling his giant horse with gentle but firm commands. Our horses seemed short-legged compared to theirs, and our stock got quite a workout that afternoon trying to keep the same pace and not get stepped on.

We tethered the horses by a stream and even though our little animals seemed dwarfed by the Emperor's giant horses they managed to get along pretty good together. Our stock didn't really have much of a choice, as the war hardware on the Chinese horse's hooves would have made quick work of them.

Zhen Zi seemed to know where we were headed too. He was polite, and understanding that a surprise awaited him, he resisted a bunch of questions. He saw the land we traveled in like he recognized it.

I looked around for the part-shot mountain lion, as I had seen its tracks in the area several times as Father and I had visited that place.

We hiked the last little bit and then right before we reached our goal we all stepped aside, and let the boy go up the rest of the trail first. His guards were close behind ever at the ready. We heard an exclamation from the Exiled Emperor as he reached the ridge top, and by the time I got up to him he was still on his knees – crying.

We stood at the side of the Boy King for a bit, and then my Father couldn't endure his sadness any longer. Regardless of his Kingly status, we all knew that he was also a broken-hearted little fella underneath it all. My Father pushed his way through the stoic guards standing over the Boy and reached down to him and scooped him up. Together they walked up to the Jade Temple that War Sing had made. The deep green of the Indian Crick jade only let the strongest of the afternoon light through, and the images on the sides of the protective structure seemed to have been carved with that in mind. Thin spots which had been worked in to the hard rock let light through to accentuate lilac blossoms and rose bushes and fir boughs and the patterns of cedar and pine bark. Gold had been hammered on the decorations to highlight the breeching salmon and rainbow trout and even the tusks and spine of one giant sturgeon. Flecks of obsidian had been placed near the roofline, and they reflected the light like stars in the sky. Agate, jasper, and opal – probably from the often found thunder eggs – had been carved to resemble bald eagles and osprey and blue heron and were inlaid in the walls as well. There were no lotus blossoms or water lilies or Chinese landmarks to be found anywhere on the structure – the Jade Temple was instead a beautiful reflection and tribute of the countryside where it was created.

We gave Zhen Zi all the time he needed inside the small structure, as he paid his respects to the Buddha resting there and made his prayers. We waited for his men to do the same, and I thought on the Berhai story a bit. Like a lot of things I had been involved in during those two or three years, the discovery of the Jade Temple didn't accomplish the goals I had set out with. It didn't reveal where to contact War Sing's family, where untold heaps and heaps of gold were stored, or answer any of the mysterious questions I had once had about War Sing's past. When we had found it, I was excited beyond belief – remembering my Father's words, that day, set me straight though. The treasure War Sing had spoken of was displayed on the intricately carved walls and uprights of the Temple. The treasure wasn't hidden under the ground of the Temple. It was the ground – and the land – itself.

As we returned to our house that day, we were

careful to hide where we came out of the brush. The Temple wouldn't last long in the hands of some – I couldn't bear to think what would happen if the wrong people found the priceless place or the ancient Buddha housed inside. It was a worry that my Father and I shared. Zhen Zi was quiet on the entire ride home, and I could only imagine he was thinking on his brother.

Returning to the dooryard, we helped put up the stock and then lit out again for the woods. We jumped into Elk Crick for a bit and swam around, splashing at the guards a few times, and then raced back up to the Old Oak Tree to recline once more in its expansive crown.

We talked until the supper call from my Ma about his travels, Samuel's visit to Chinaland, what the Emperor thought of our country and River Canyon so far, and how glad he was to finally be here. We talked about the Temple and War Sing's craftsmanship and his mirroring of our wildlife and our countryside. The Boy Emperor seemed to hang on my words about his brother, and by the time we descended that tree I'm sure he knew that with all of our differences there was one great big thing that he and I had in common – our fondness and care for the departed Prince of China and Honored Heir of the Dragon Throne of Manchu, who we simply called War Sing.

After dinner, many groups of the Chinese folks from town visited our dooryard – each one had offerings of food and clothing and boxes of items for the Emperor. He gracefully received all of the folks and their tribute gifts under the watchful eye of the guards.

Samuel had returned from visiting with his family – who were amazed to see him upright after all of the time that had passed – and we all sat to listen to the

Chinese musicians gathered on our front porch to play for their Exiled King.

My Father later would tell my Mother and me that he counted over four hundred Chinese folks in our dooryard that night. There were ribbons and silks and musicians and all manner of celebratory items here and there in the clearing around our house. Traditional food and drink were set out and all told it was a full-on celebration. Lanterns sprung up around the yard and after a bit, so did some fireworks. Rockets shot into the night sky, exploding in streams of purple, gold, and silver – spraying cascades of sparks over Elk Crick like waterfalls of diamonds.

The Boy King, who had changed into his gold and copper woven silks at some point in the evening – stood to address the gathered folks. Acting as the Emperor once again, his formal manner and speech were displayed to his expatriate subjects. Samuel translated the foreign talking to my Father and Mother, and I listened in as well.

"Welcome, countrymen and subjects of the ruling hand of the Dragon Throne of Manchu.

"I am honored to be here with you in the fabled Gum Shun land. It is true, that the streams and rivers here hold great golden treasure. The people who live here in this River Canyon have been very welcoming to us – our people here have not suffered the injustices, the jealousies, or the abuse that some of our countrymen have endured in other places in America.

"You may be aware of trouble in our home country. There have been several battles and uprisings around our nation against warlords and outsiders set to do away with our long heritage and peaceable religion.

"I, Exiled Emperor P'u Yi of the Dragon Throne of

Manchu, have come to America to finish a family obligation. Out of duty and my responsibility to our blessed country and to our blessed people – I will return to our homeland to finish the fight that I did not begin. I am asking that you, the golden sons of beautiful China, return with me to help aid in the defense of our country and people."

At that point, the visitors to our dooryard bowed their heads in a reverent acceptance of the boy King's request. I looked to my Father and Mother, as they looked towards each other. I suppose they had made the same mistaken assumption that also had crossed my mind – that since he was alone and without any other family the boy King would naturally stay and live with us. We had no idea that he had intended to return to his country.

The boy kept talking, and Samuel kept translating, but I couldn't take listening to any more of it. I lit out for a bit down one of the game trails, and ended up sitting for a while next to the Old Oak Tree. I knew what I heard, but my mind raced to try to find some words or reasons that I could use to change the boy's mind.

At some point, tired of being upset and getting a little hungry as well, I returned to the celebration in our dooryard and tried my best to put all my hard feelings behind me. I couldn't help but wondering here and there why anyone would leave our peaceful home and valley to return to a country at war – where an almost certain death waited. I took it personally, since I couldn't really understand the real reasons behind that choice.

I found my way to the side of the Boy King once more, and we continued to pal around the festivities –

but I acted less familiar around Zhen Zi when his subjects were around.

Eventually, in the lateness of the evening, my Mother found us in the crowd and took the Emperor and I indoors to wash off a little of the countryside found behind our ears and dress for bedtime. She didn't seem to mind that she was mother-henning an exiled ruler of an entire country, and Zhen Zi didn't seem to mind it either. I imagine it had been a long time since someone looked him in the eye and told him what for – like only a mother can do. Although the Emperor didn't understand why she said he may have potatoes growing in his ears before too long, he figured it out pretty quick when she took a washcloth and the bar of soap to him. I couldn't understand why he was smiling the whole time he was being looked after, but later my Dad told me that since his aunt – the Dowager Empress Cixidies – died when he was only two years old, and being the only one of his family still left in China he was placed on the Dragon Throne while he was still purt near a baby. In the course of only a few years, the boy suffered the loss of his own Mother and Father, his Empress Aunt, and then his oldest brother died on that ship to America. He remarked that all of it was awful for him, but the only relief he got was knowing that War Sing would return to China one day. He had been alone from those he loved for a long, long time, and although he had advisors and guardians and teachers and appointed playmates no one had ever probably treated him like he was a regular fella.

We bunked down camping-style in my room – even though I offered my bed to the Emperor he seemed excited to use the canvas shakedowns he had read about in a cowboy novel he'd been given in Sacramento.

As we were drifting off to sleep after that incredibly long day, I asked him why War Sing had come to our country if he was a Prince or somesuch thing in China. Zhen Zi explained to me that when War Sing and his other brother left China, they were members of the Royal Line and that no one could have forseen the tragedies that would befall his Aunt Cixidies family or his own to eventually place someone so far removed from the Royal Court on the throne. Because of the great distance between China and America – and the several years of mischief some of the palace advisor folks had made with letters Zhen Zi had tried to send – the Exiled Emperor figured that War Sing had probably only found out about the coronation a few weeks before he had died.

In his last letter to Zhen Zi, War Sing had apologized for being absent and promised to return as soon as possible to protect his small brother from the politics and the trouble of the country that they both loved dearly.

The Boy told me a little of what War Sing's papers had held. There had been essays on American mining techniques, plans to build a home, and poems about the Klamath River Canyon and the beauty that it was made of. My ears perked up when Zhen Zi told me of his favorite letter – the one that described War Sing's American family. He had written of us in glowing terms and in what Zhen Zi described as "deep affection."

Hearing a noise outside then I started to get up and see what was going on, but Zhen Zi waved me off. "It's only my sworn sentries," he said. "At least one will stand guard outside of the window all night, and one will stand in the doorway, inside the house."

It was strange to know that those men – trained

killers and professional soldiers – were merely feet away from where I was going to be sleeping. My last thought about that strangeness as I found myself contemplating the backs of my eyelids, I recall, was a half-smile on my overly-washed and tired face as I figured that I could just add it to the list of the odd and fantastic things that had already occurred that day.

I briefly wondered what excitement the next day would bring.

Chapter Twenty-Six

Grave Diggers and the Exodus

"It was like they all just vanished into the thin Siskiyou air."
– Mrs. Marybelle Hickham, Local
Merchant

The time for Zhen Zi to go came too quickly. I did my best to encourage him to stay with us as my Mother and Father had offered – but he was steadfast in his need to return to help his people survive the civil war that was raging in his homeland. He was the last of his line, and he had been trained from near birth to step up to help his people. His national responsibility outweighed his personal interests.

I had begun to understand some of his responsibilities. I knew that if he had a choice, he would've stayed with us instead. I know that's what War Sing would have wanted for his little brother, but on the same hand I also knew that War Sing would have understood his brother's decision to return home.

I took advantage of the time that I had to spend with Zhen Zi – we ran about on the hillside whenever we could get away. We talked at great length about our interests and what we wanted the future to hold. I introduced Zhen Zi to the great game of baseball, and he made all of his guards play along. It was a pretty odd game, actually, because the guards fielding weren't very motivated to tag out their Emperor. They didn't seem to have any problem at all, though, chasing me around the bases or laying the tag on me instead. It was probably the worst game I've ever played in, but I always figured that even the worst day playing baseball is better than the best day doing chores for my Mother or any day spent imprisoned in the school house. It was all a matter of perspective, I guess.

I can honestly say that the time I spent with Zhen Zi – in our hillside travels and adventures – was one of the best times I can remember in my childhood. Even then, it was hard to enjoy the time that we had to play and run about because it felt like there was an invisible sword hanging over all of us – a sword that we knew would eventually fall, regardless of what we wanted or how we rallied against it or how unfair it was.

My Mother and Father also tried to make the best of their time with the boy. At that point we all knew that our invitation to him to stay with us would never be taken up, but we hadn't quite accepted it yet.

He learned me the recipes for most of all of the wondrous fireworks we had played with – but I wrote them all down just in case I forgot a step. That was when I still had all my fingers, and I was pretty interested in keeping it that way. I was very intrigued by the way he could aim most of the homemade rockets, so that they didn't light trees and brush on fire. I didn't have to be a fortune-teller to know, around those dry mountains, that was a skill I'd have to learn.

We went hunting and fishing and climbing and swimming and horse-riding and lizard catching. We had a great time at the rock slide down the Klamath a ways, too. I showed Zhen Zi how to use a stick as a lever to push over the man-sized boulders at the top, giving them the nudge they needed to start to make their bounce-filled downhill run to a forceful loud and splashing finale in the river water. That never got old or lost it's fun, but when the Emperor got a little too enthusiastic and sent one of the rocks off sideways into the Douglas fir stand – breaking one of the trees clean in half – we figured we had better move on to something else. I don't know if an Emperor can get in trouble, but I knew real well that I sure could.

I understood that he had announced to the Chinese community that he was asking them to return home with him. I had heard they had all agreed to go – every last man – when he had explained to the weary and the homesick fellas what was happening in their country. He told them how much they were needed to help end the destruction of their family homes, their temples, their cities and their country by ferocious warlords and a few other foreigners with strange ideas about creating societies that stripped the religion and the beauty and the very spirit of the people. A date was set for their Exodus, and still I hadn't wanted to accept it. They planned to leave the River Canyon when the moon was full again.

With the cheese-filled planet showing a waning crescent in the night sky – later when I double-checked it – I knew it was only a few weeks before they planned to leave.

I didn't fully understand, at that time, what was about to happen. I knew what had been said but I couldn't imagine that all of the Chinese folks would just up and leave their community, their claims, and their homes here to return to that far-away country. I underestimated their love for their homeland – being that far-away foreigner a few times in my own life since then I understand their national obligation and fondness for their peril-bound country and way of life much better.

Zhen Zi and I spent every extra moment of those last days taking advantage of what fun the countryside offered – always with at least one of his guardsmen in tow. I asked one fella, as he was watching us swimming about in my favorite deep and clear Elk Crick pool, why he guarded Zhen Zi so closely. "Like his family was born to be Emperors and Empresses," he replied, "mine were born to be palace guards. In the beginning of time, his family was made godlike – and my family was made just after, to keep them safe."

He was a very serious fella, and as I did my best to float on my back without getting water in my nose I figured that seriousness was a good trait to have if you were to spend your whole entire life watching out for someone else's.

I went with Zhen Zi several times to the Jade Temple, accompanied of course by my Father and a few of the most trusted guards. To hide our trail to it, we never entered the area from the same way twice – always going into the woods on a pretense to anyone outside of my family or his entourage that we were hunting.

Zhen Zi took rubbings of some of the carvings and said that after the civil war in his country was over, he would commission an artist to try to build a complementary likeness in his home town in the Kwangtung Province – knowing an almost identical-looking place in the mountains to the north of where he and War Sing were born.

We promised to meet again in Cairo in the far-away year of 1925 – always with the unsaid caveat of "if it all works out" – and spent hours in the Old Oak Tree outlining our plans to visit all of the interesting and exciting places of the world together when we were older. Every night I looked at the increasing size of the moon above us, wishing and hoping that somehow it would just stop progressing.

I had been cheated of a brother when little Thorin had died. Zhen Zi had been cheated of his brothers when they died as well. I wanted him to stay with us, hoping all the while that in a twist of fate – like in Shakespeare's plays or Homer's legends – the universe or God or The Fates would decide that some possibility of a chance to fill the loss of our brothers could be given to both of us. It wasn't a perfect solution, but it seemed to fit under the circumstances.

Samuel, who had been a close advisor to the Exiled Emperor and his troops for almost the whole past year, was still consulted on many occasions and regarding many details of the secret Exodus. I had cornered him at one point, asking him about the race and how in the world he came to understand the Chinese language and how he had come to know the Emperor – but in his classic and straight-forward manner all he said was, "No time now. We'll talk later." He had decided to stay in our land, knowing by the example set by the small Exiled King that helping his own people was the most important thing he could do with his life.

As the Exodus day approached, Samuel was often at our house – included in the motley group of kitchen table advisors to the Exiled Emperor. He continued to take his place beside the Boy, and hash out plans and strategies with my Mother, my Father, and three of the specially picked guardsmen. I listened in quite a bit, but I never said one word during those councils.

I did sit and talk with Samuel much later, and he told me all about meeting the British Captain, and the coincidences that occurred on his first trip to the Orient. Apparently, he had found a translator he could trust to work with the papers on the ship, and he was able to figure out where the documents were supposed to go and what most of them meant. Overhearing the Ambassador's Secretary speaking one afternoon about the recent changes in the Chinese rule, Samuel was finally able to piece it all together. He tagged along with the Ambassador and his entourage with his own secret purposes when they finally reached China, and skillfully made a request of the Boy King in open court to the amazement and embarrassment of the folks he had been traveling with.

Everything after that, as they say, is history. Zhen Zi decided to travel to America, with one of his stated reasons to rally support among the quarter-million or so of the Chinese folks whom he needed to return. The Boy King enlisted Samuel as his guide to the West and then had arranged for his training in the language and in the skills needed to be a guard and a court familiar. Samuel was moved by the Boy's predicament, and signed right on to help him.

I recall that on that long-ago evening I was upset to see that the moon was in the first quarter, and I couldn't hide my angry feelings about Zhen Zi leaving any longer – so I went to the barn to find something to smash on or kick around. I just ended up sitting on a hay bale with tears in my eyes, and I didn't even jump when my Dad seemed to appear out of the dimness behind me.

"I never understood how important a place a barn is for being sad," he said trying to get me to cheer up with a reference to my previous accidental spying on him. I just put my hands under my chin and slumped over a little more, trying to will myself invisible. His giant arm found my shoulders and even if I wanted to escape his trademarked bear hug I couldn't – I was jailed-in by his care for me.

We talked for quite a while about what could have been, what we wanted the future to be, and how life more often than not seems to push out rocky obstacles into even our best laid plans.

We sat there for quite a while, and my Father answered almost every one of the questions that I asked him. I found out how little I really knew about my Father and Mother's involvement with War Sing's secrets, and their knowledge of everything that had been going on in War Sings home country. A lesser boy would have been upset to have been kept out of that ring of knowledge, but I had no legs to stand on as far as that was concerned because I had already shown my Father – through my deception with War Sing's papers – that I had a bit of trouble in the trust department. I was still working on getting all that back.

I got a better understanding, talking with my Father in the barn, about how close I actually came to putting our family in danger by exposing War Sing's family papers. Luckily, the references to treasure and the cached gold in the papers were so hidden and obscure that most folks would never ever be able to figure them out.

I apologized to him again, and he continued to explain to me that sometimes things are a lot more complicated than they appeared to be on the surface. He didn't need to tell me that twice, since I figured that out on my own on several occasions. He also explained to me that he had worked before with Samuel, and even though they'd never talked about the Chinese mysteries he could tell by the way that Samuel had held responsibility that he was a good fella. He said also that he had held out a good hope that Samuel had got the papers translated after I told him about what I had talked the Running fella into.

I had about a thousand other questions for my Father, but he explained to me that we'd have years and years and years to hash all of those out – and that right then the most important thing I could do was to spend time with my new friend.

With a playful slap on the top of my unruly head of hair, my Father simply said, "Go play," and pushed me toward the door. He didn't have to tell me twice.

I tried to fit months of fun and running through the woods with Zhen Zi into the next three days or so. By goodness, I couldn't change the constant hands of time but I did my best to slow them down. We went to the Flying Rat Cave and both stood some tin army men at the entrance to guard it until we both could return. We lit up into the Old Oak Tree one last time, dropping a handful of green-glass marbles into a squirrel's nest. Always playing the clown, I said, "I'd like to see his face when that chirping squirrel bites into those this winter instead of those acorns," and the Emperor almost fell out of the tree he was laughing so hard.

Looking down, I saw one of the guards appear out of nowhere – ready to catch him. That made both of us laugh even harder.

Although they didn't say so, I knew it was finally time for them to leave. It was the last day before the full moon, and my trained and keen observer's eye could see all of the preparations being made in their community. Grocery and hardware bills were being paid off, and mine deeds were signed over and plans were made to quietly leave them tucked into the front doors of deserving and friendly locals all across our River Canyon.

My Mother was teary-eyed all day, and also sensing the imminent departure of the Boy she had almost scrubbed all of Zhen Zi's skin off behind his ears and on the back of his neck that morning. I knew she was trying to get a little extra cleaning in before he left, since there would be no mother – ever again – for the poor little Royal Boy. For about three seconds I contemplated running off with him to China, but looking at my Ma I knew instantly that was the most horribly wrong decision I could ever consider.

Zhen Zi – in his Emperor's way – had a few decrees for his subjects and his armed men. The guards and about twenty of his trusted local brethren traveled to the Jade Temple that morning, and after Zhen Zi had completed his prayers inside and walked back a ways, he gave the signal to everyone to begin to bury the whole thing. He knew that the shrine would not last –

especially if there was revealing fire in the area – and covering it would keep it safe until he returned in the future. The work was done quickly and without complaint. He placed six arimantus seedlings in the ground – in a large circle – in the dirt covering the temple, to reveal it's location to him on his next visit.

We ran the purlieu that afternoon, ending up on the granite "stage" above the house. Neither of us mentioned anything of the great possibility he would be killed as the last surviving member of his Royal Lineage. I knew why he had those guards with him – and so did he – and they were a constant reminder that bad people were planning bad things for him, maybe even as we sat there.

He told me that two of the family guards had been sent with War Sing and his other brother when they had left China for their adventures in America, but that one of the local Chinese men and told him that those two fellas lit out after War Sing was buried. I thought he must have been talking about Jin and Cho – and I figured their overheard argument at War Sing's funeral had probably been about what to do with War Sing's belongings. At that time, they were the only ones – besides my Mother and Father – who knew all of War Sing's real story. They also knew, it seemed, of the trouble raising in their homeland and the disappearance of little Zhen Zi from the throne – because in the end they did leave the items with us.

After an early supper, we loaded up our wagon with as many shovels and picks we could find and led the folks to War Sing's grave. It was the first time that Zhen Zi had wanted to go, even though we had offered it several times. I was beginning to wonder if he was ever going to go at all.

I wasn't quite clear on what was going on, figuring they were going to remove the ornate headstone and take it back with them. My Father's face belied a grimness and sorrow from the set-out, and just like most things at that time I just buttoned my lip regardless of my curiosity.

My Mother had a bleak and severe look on her face as she stood on the porch and watched us leave into the night.

As we neared the grave area a few guardsmen and local Chinese folks were set out here and there to watch for anyone coming along, and the whole thing started to take on a sneaky tack – I was sure none of the local folks would have been upset to see someone removing a headstone so I figured something else must've been in the works.

We let Zhen Zi be alone for a while at the graveside of his brother. I watched as he came back to the wagon, with his head hanging so low that it hurt my feelings to see him. He walked straight to our stacked piles of tools and grabbed a pick axe almost as tall as he was. And then he returned to the grave.

I thought he had split his gourd when I watched him start to lift up then sink the pick-axe into the ground where his brother was buried. It made me mad, a lot. I cared for War Sing too, and that was too much to take. I started to go forward to stop him, but my Dad grabbed me by the collar and took me around the other side of the wagon.

"It's not for us to stop," he whispered to me.

"But Dad," I said, "he's fixin' to mess up War Sing's grave! Aren't you going to do something to make him quit?"

Hanging his own head, then, and sighing long

and deep my Father wrapped his arm around me and looked me in the eye. "No, Uke. I'm going to gather up all my strength and care for War Sing and his little brother there, and I'm going to help him because I know in my heart that it is what War Sing would have wanted."

He left then, picking up a shovel from the back of the wagon. He walked to War Sing's grave, gave the Boy Emperor a great big hug, and started digging too. Others in the crowd picked up their tools, and spread out over the hillside at each of the graves and set into free the bones of their countrymen from our hard, rocky, foreign soil.

I stood there, next to the wagon, with my hands on my hips and sporting a furrowed-brow mean-faced countenance that I am sure let everyone there know how fully disgusted I was.

Sure, I had heard the legend that for the Celestials to make it to their Heaven they had to be buried in the soil of their homeland. I knew that in theory it was probably a good idea, but for cripes sake I sure didn't figure it was necessary to be digging up graves – secretly at that – in the near-darkness of that late summer night. Normally, I would have thought the whole affair a mysterious adventure – like in one of the pirate stories or something out of *Macbeth* or more appropriately, *Hamlet* – but when the whip hit the horse, so to speak, it was a different race entirely.

It was near full dark when I heard the first shovel hit wood. A tap, then tap-tap again from the shovel-wielder to make sure of the sound. Lanterns were then briefly lit and held over the coffin. In short time the wood lid was pried up, with the coffin nails screeching as they were pulled from their home. That whole chain of events happened over and over and over that night as all forty-six graves were opened. After a while, I helped dig a bit and hold tools for fellas and light lanterns when asked. I didn't want to help at all, but I figured with an extra set of hands maybe it would all go a little faster.

We had a few close calls – at one point a wagon of mill boys was coming up on the road, and the lookouts warned us in time to douse all the lanterns and shin out behind some trees. There were about sixty of us hiding here and there on the hillside, and a few men crouching down in the dug up graves – and we all held our breath as the wagon passed. Their stock horses whinnied a little, sensing us on the hillside, but the wagon occupants just went on past without looking up. I wonder what that cartload of fellas would have thought if they had seen all of those grave holes opened in the hillside on that dark night, and all of us filthy with grave-dirt, holding shovels in the darkness, with a wild look in our eyes.

We resumed our awful tasks when we were sure the wagon had passed through the little draw to the west.

A real old Chinese fella was walking from grave to grave handing folks large velvety bags. They were about three foot by three foot, and had characters sewn into them – and on the other side was the symbol of the Dragon Throne of Manchu. A fierce chill went up my spine as I guessed the bags were for putting the bones of the dead folks in.

One by one the bags were filled. Zhen Zi, out of tribute to the Klamath land and the people, ordered a shovel-full of our earth be placed in each bag too. When each man was reburied in China, the dirt from our

River Canyon would be reburied with them as well.

All of the bags were marked, filled, and tied and then gently placed in our wagon, save one. The men all gathered around War Sing's grave, and little Zhen Zi climbed back down into the earthen hole. When his feet landed on the wooden lid, a thump like someone hitting a drum rang through the hillside. I figured he was the strongest person alive – that little boy – as he set to prying open the coffin lid of his brother. He had traveled across an ocean and half of a country to finish the task set before him, and I wondered if he was scared under his tough outside.

I figured it was probably his duty, as his kin, but as the Exiled Emperor I was sure he could just ask someone else to do it for him. My Father was crouched down at the graveside, ready to help or grab up the boy if needed. He held the velvet bag meant for War Sing in his big hands, absentmindedly twisting it and bunching it in his nervousness.

I thought that burying folks was the hardest thing to do. I can tell you from experience – actually – that digging them up is twice as bad.

The moon – the horrible, unwanted full moon – was beginning to peek over the mountaintops to the east of us, shimmering the ghostly silvery light over the crowns of the trees around us. Zhen Zi bent his head again in prayer, and then continued in working. The men on the hillside began to softly hum a low and sad temple meditation song.

The Boy – with a set jaw and a peaceful look on his face – pried the lid off in just two or three tries and stumbled back as the top was moved away.

The meditation song was forgotten, and a thick silence covered everyone.

Zhen Zi stood staring down at the opened coffin at his feet. I heard my Father gasp in surprise or anxiousness – and he bowed his head, bag forgotten, and looked like he was saying a prayer hisself. Calling for more lanterns, Zhen Zi motioned for everyone to come closer forward. We respectfully moved in, forming a circle around the partially unearthed grave of the man who should have been the rightful Emperor of China.

When folks got closer to the grave, and peered in, they fell to their knees one by one. With heads bowed, they started back in with their low chant that got louder and louder until it moved through the ground under our feet and through all of us. I figured the practical side of the death had got to them – surely a gruesome sight awaited me as well, as poor War Sing had only been in our ground for just over a year. I figured it wasn't even close to the time needed to cure the body to just a bone state – but I couldn't hardly let my mind think of that at all.

I approached, weaving my way through the chanting and kneeled folks, watching keenly the look on the faces of my Father and Zhen Zi. They simply just stared in the lantern-lit hole in the ground.

I figured I would look in quick, out of respect and custom – it seemed required of all of us there that night. I fixed in my mind the last time I had seen War Sing, as my Mother had helped wash and dress him and place him in the wooden casket my Father had made. He had been there on our kitchen table, lying peacefully in that death box – dressed in white funeral silks – with his hands resting together on his chest. Father had put a carved jade dragon under War Sing's clasped hands – at the time I supposed it was a trinket from the foreign-born man's youth. War Sing's long braid had been combed out and rebraided by my Mother, and she had gently placed roses and lilacs and Christ's Cross flowers – what we call dogwood – all around the dead man. I had watched my Father kiss War Sing's forehead right before fixing the wood lid to the coffin and nailing it shut for what we thought was to be forever.

With that picture of War Sing in my mind, I took a deep breath and peered over the side of the dirt bank. What I saw took all of the air out of my lungs and brought me to my knees as well. I couldn't believe what was right before me – it didn't make any sense at all.

I was glad of the darkness I sat in, so as all of the tears racing down my face had a bit of privacy. I peered in again, not believing what I had seen – yet there it was.

War Sing, heir to the Dragon Throne of Manchu and older brother to the Exiled Emperor of China – and our dear, dear friend – lay in his temporary grave perfect and beautiful. It looked like he was just resting there – eyes closed and hands brought together on his chest – and there was even a little hint of color in his face and on his hands. No notice of the natural ravages of death lay upon him, and absent also were all of the distasteful results those unavoidable natural ravages usually produced. I rubbed my eyes, not fully believing my sight. Looking back to the grave a third time, I noticed what I had overlooked before.

Even the roses and the delicate lilacs and the dogwood flowers my Mother had so gently placed around War Sing, over a year previous, were as fresh and as lovely as if they had been cut that afternoon.

Since that night – over my long life and my travels across the world – I have heard about other people who were found that way and whose bodies did not become less after their deaths. They were called Incorruptables by the Catholic Church, and most were sainted – but at that time I had only ever heard of it happening to Saint Bernadette, the girl who claimed to have seen and talked to Jesus' Mother in Lourdes, France. Later in my life, during my travels I saw the very body of that woman in a church in France – laid out in a wondrously gilded glass coffin. I also happened on a Buddhist monastery in eastern Siberia – quite near Lake Baikal, in fact – and looked upon the face of the long-passed Khambo Lama, who had been setting peacefully in the lotus position for decades after he had drawn his last breath. In the local custom, I pressed his scarf against my head and made a few prayers, but I was distracted in my mediations there as my mind kept returning to the same peaceful look I had seen on War Sing's face on that darkened grave-digging night of my youth.

Regardless of my rational scientifically-based reasoning methods, I still believe that War Sing's earthly body benefited from the unexplained enchantment of the earth-dirt that was for the local Indians the cradle of the life of the world, as well as from our prayers to our God with our faith that War Sing would live in Heaven. Our land and our beliefs had worked with War Sing's Chinese mystical harmony of nature and Buddha that he had held close. I figured that all of those magic-laden forces had obviously mixed together to preserve the body of the man who had given up a Kingdom to save the life of his friend. I was sure that the love he had shown to us had surrounded him in death like a bright and shining barrier, and would let nothing else harm the Lost King.

I recall that the moon was lifting higher in the gol durned black sky as we all reached in to raise up War

Sing's casket from the ground and into the back of the wagon. Men reached up to touch the wood of the casket once more before it was covered in a traditional and ancient tapestry by the Boy King.

We all helped to fill in the empty graves, first throwing the handmade wooden temporary grave markers in the holes first – apparently so other well-meaning Chinese folks wouldn't try to dig there to remove their countrymen, thinking it was still a grave. We left War Sing's carved stone where it had always been, finding out it hadn't been a headstone after all. It had been a present that he had made, and right before we left the empty graveyard Zhen Zi translated it for us.

My Father and I stood close to the Boy. At that point none of us were trying to hide the swells of tears that afflicted everyone.

"The stone was carved by my brother – who you call War Sing. He writes on the side that it is a gift to his American family, on the occasion of his long-postponed return to his brother in China. He has signed the piece in the name our Mother called him, Yong-Li Jun."

Pointing to different symbols, he recited to us what they all meant.

"Beautiful wife of my friend-brother, in your long life may you find peace for the sadness that all women who love must someday bear." He was talking about my Ma, and my Father and I memorized what he said – Mother had not come to the grave digging, and had not wanted to.

Zhen Zi continued, pointing to the next ring of script, and looking to me briefly before he started. "Adventurous son of my friend-brother, in your long life may you find safety in your travels but most of all find the path that leads back to your true home." I listened to the words, and memorized them, too – but for a different reason.

Pointing at the last ring of script, and then smiling up to my Father, the Boy King continued. "My trusted and loyal friend-brother, in your long life may you find wealth, happiness, and contentment and also a smile remembering the piece of our life path when we traveled together."

We left that place then, walking behind the drawn wagon like a ghostly funeral procession bathed in the silver moonlight. We were quiet, and thought filled, and tired from the hard work and our heavy hearts.

The rest of the thousands of Chinese graves – in our countryside and out of it – would have to wait a little longer. The Emperor had taken as many as he could.

Nearing the dooryard, I was shocked to see the gilded carriage and the various wagons and teams drawn up, loaded, and ready to leave. If the night hadn't already been bad enough. I didn't think I could deal with the grave digging and saying goodbye to a boy who I felt should stay and be my brother, all in the same evening. I tried to see past it, but having my heart broke was something I never took easy.

Zhen Zi approached me and simply said, "The full moon will light our way out of the River Canyon, and we can leave in peace. We have a long journey to the boats that will take us home."

I gave him a giant hug – trying to replicate the hugs my Father gave – and I didn't even try to ask him to stay. I knew he was leaving, and that all I could do was say goodbye.

My Mother was hovering nearby, and gave the

Boy King a few more last minute orders like, "make sure to eat greens as well as those sweets you're so fond of," and one I'd heard a thousand times, "for goodness sakes remember to wash behind your ears."

I ran into the house real quick, and grabbed up a few things. I sprinted to Zhen Zi, handing him my canvas shakedown he had liked so much and my dog-eared copy of Sir Walter Scott's finest works. He smiled and thanked me.

My Father almost squeezed the stuffing out of the kid, and he knelt down to look into the Exiled Emperor's eyes. "Remember that you are always welcome here, no matter what happens or when you can return." Hugging him again, I heard my Father say, "War Sing would have been so proud of you."

Dad picked up the small boy and carried him the rest of the way to the gilded carriage, and seeing that he was safely inside, he returned to hold on to my Ma and me as we set to watch them leave.

With that, the procession of the Exiled King started to move away followed by every last one of the Chinese folks who had lived in our River Canyon. I almost couldn't bear to see them all go, and I almost couldn't actually see them all go 'cause of the multitude of tears that filled my vision.

At the bend in the road, Zhen Zi leaned out of the carriage window, waving and yelling, "Goodbye American family! I love you." As the driver set to dim the carriage lanterns, my friend stuck his head back out, one last time, and yelled to me, "Euclid, remember our plans to meet in Cairo!"

And then they were gone.

Euclid P. Hammarsen

Chapter Twenty-Seven

The Treasure of The Klamath River Canyon

"When I opened my front door that morning, the deed to Chun's *Constitution Mine* fluttered out of the screen and right into my hand. My widow prayers had been answered."
– Mrs. Nellifer Jones, Resident

Now, dear reader, if you think that the string of events I have described in this journal – all of the coincidences and luck and misluck – are just a bit too fantastic and far-fetched, I'll have you look back on one of the magic times in your very own life. You and I both know that the past is what it is, and that only in looking back are the connections laid out clearly. When we're in those magic times, it's awful hard to recognize it is happening.

On that tear-filled Exodus night of long ago, we stood waving to the very last man in the long line of leaving Chinese. We retreated to the house and found ourselves standing once again around our kitchen table. It looked like it was near-ready to bust under the parcels it held, and my Father spied an envelope on the very tip-top of it all.

Mother hadn't seen anyone place the boxes in our house while she was helping load the wagons, but she admitted she had been very distracted.

He opened the envelope and read ahead in the letter a little bit, until my Mother elbowed him in the ribs and he started over – from the beginning – reading it out loud. It was from Zhen Zi.

"Dear, dear wonderful Hammarsens of the fair Klamath: My hurried words here will never come close to attempting to describe the care I have for your family and my gratitude at your care for me and mine. My brother loved you all dearly, and I am consoled in my sad heart that you were the ones who he had here, at the end.

"I have been taught that the path I need to take is before me, and that other paths I wish to take – like staying with you in your River Canyon – are barred to me through duty and responsibility. I do wish that I could have stayed and had a chance to be a son and a brother again, but my wishes and needs are last as long as the people of my country are being killed and starved." My Father's voice crackled a little at that point, and his eyes were full.

He continued reading the written words, after clearing his throat a few times and looking away from Mother and I. "I trust you all like my dear brother did, and I ask that you help me one last time. Charged with keeping the heritage items of my line, and being too young to have an heir and facing years of battle and an uncertain future when I return to my Kingdom, I have directed three of my trusted guardsmen to place my most treasured possessions in your wonderful barn house, to keep for me until I return to retrieve them. They are the only ones who know of this, and they have sworn their secrecy to me." At that, Father looked up at both of us with a puzzled look on his face. He kept reading the Boy King's words after a moment. "In the case that I am unable to return for them, I will send an emissary who you will know by the letter they carry. Do not entertain any requests from anyone regarding the items that are not sent by me. The objects are not the property of my country or those who are trying to take my country, but instead are the property of my family and have been handed down as such for the last 3000 years. I trust you to do what you will if necessary. I look forward to the time when we can meet again. With great affection and esteem, Emperor P'u Yi, Holder of the Dragon Throne of Manchu and Rightful Ruler of the Kingdom of China, September 14, 1914."

My Father looked real close again, searching for some explanation of the parcels on the table. He found a scribbled note on the bottom of the document.

Unable to read it out loud, my Mother took it from him and read it instead. "P.S.: Upon your table, where my brother was cleaned and carefully placed in his coffin with your loving hands, please find payments for the rental of the portion of your barn and considerations for your careful keeping of the treasures of my family until I can return. The rest of the payments and considerations can be found stacked in your pantry, the bedrooms, and near the woodstove where the floor was thick enough to hold the weight of the boxes. Take care until we can meet again, Zhen Zi."

I opened one of the parcels on the table, and gold nuggets came spilling out at me. I couldn't believe my eyes.

Stunned and heart-sore, we went up to our rooms, making our careful way around the columns of stacked boxes. Each of us was tired of the long and hard day and all that it held. We slept deeply and soundly and woke only when the next morning's late sun came through the windows to fall on us.

That day we started an inventory of all the items in the barn – being responsible caretakers – and crated them up to wait for their owner to return. We also started moving the gold from the house, putting it in caches here and there like any good miner knows how to do. We were hard at those two tasks for several weeks, and I think all three of us were glad to have something to do to keep our hands busy in our sadness at the leaving of Zhen Zi.

Every box that had been placed in the barn caused a wonder-filled gasp from the three of us as we opened it for our inventory list. Each one held a different sort of treasured item. I was amazed at the workmanship of what was left behind. I figured it was a good idea to stow all of those items with us, considering the decreed goal of some of those folks who were warring in China to take everything from everyone. I agreed that no one had any right or claim to Zhen Zi's family possessions – just like no one had a right to my baseball cards or my Father's picture of his family.

Zhen Zi's Chinese treasure was much more than the riches he had directed stacked in our barn. It was more valuable than the boxes and boxes of gold nuggets that were left on our dinner table and stacked throughout our house, and worth more than the ancient crowns, ruby-encrusted scepters, the carved and crafted vases, golden rings and jewelry, or the boxes and boxes of cut emeralds and sapphires and differently-colored diamonds that the Exiled Emperor left in our care. He knew that the spirit of the people he loved – the people he was charged to care for and was returning to – and their land and their lives and their hopes and dreams and their love for one another all mixed together to form his real and true Treasure.

As you have probably discerned by now, observant reader, that the Treasure of the Klamath River Canyon is also much more than the jade, the silver, or the rich veins of shiny and brilliant gold that run through our hillsides. We had all found the same Treasure that War Sing had spoken of under his jade-carved Siskiyou temple. It was and is the amalgam of all of our beauty, all of the kindnesses of the folks who have lived here and who continue to live here, as well as the natural richness that the land holds of undefineable value. Our gems are hidden wildernesses, rugged peaks, quiet mountain trails, ghostly lakes, and star-deep nights.

Our Treasure also is, in a large part, how much we care about others and what we do for them when they need us.

I figured out, much later, that the Ghostly Indian Chief wasn't pointing me towards the Jade Temple or mountains of treasure and hidden gold as he directed my gaze out from the cliff cave – instead, next to his ghostly council fire he had been trying to show me that the treasure was right in front of me the whole time. It had been all of the land and the community I could see from that lofty perch. Even the mystical dogwood arrow in the fire had pointed me toward it.

Our Treasure is more than something that can be touched. It's a helping hand and a hot dish at a potluck after a funeral. It's finding someone's mowed your lawn for you while you were in the hospital. It's a clothes drive at the school for a family who lost everything after a house fire. It's looking each other in the eye and saying hello at the post office, and taking time to really listen for the answer when you ask, "How're you?" It's celebrating when the high school team wins a game, and everyone turning out for the June graduations. It's pulling together to send Gold Star mothers back to D.C. to see The Wall, or to send a dying woman and her sons on a vacation for a chance to make one last memory before the sickness gets too bad. It's knowing families and their children and their parents and their grandparents and who married who when. It's following newlyweds through town after their ceremony, driving and honking car horns along the way to announce the grand event. It's good natured ribbing and back slapping and friendship. Most of all, it's a sense of community and the proud and strange way we all say, "I'm from Happy Camp," when we're asked – or from Seiad, or Somes Bar, or Forks of Salmon, or Willow Creek or Hamburg or any of the thousand other communities that make up our tough-as-nails proud-as-punch River Canyon population.

We know what mill wigwam burners were, and we've seen them lit off and blazing in their glory. We know why one side of the mountain is fir and pine and the other one is oak. We know where the secret Scorpion Caves are, and also where another entrance to those caverns is that isn't blocked off with a locked government grill and gate.

Our Treasure is also the way we smile when we

try to explain our curious community names and the often curious River people. It's the way we're familiar with the stories about Bigfoot and U.F.O. lore as well as being pretty certain that D.B. Cooper was the real name of a crazy fella that lived up on Greyback for a while in the '80s. It's how we rally around each other in the good and the bad and all of the in-between times. It's how we always take off our hats and cover our hearts when the Flag goes by.

I'm certain that most of us here understand the full measure of the treasure that our community was or that it still is. I am the first one in the crowd to recognize how important it is to go Out Into The World to gain perspective and life experience and an appreciation for the mostly-quiet little forgotten River places where we usually all eventually come home to.

I've pulled solid gold nuggets out of the Klamath as big as a man's fist, and believe you me I was in high spirits those days – but those feelings never compared with the important things. Like thinking about sitting on that felled log next to Spirit Lake with my Father. Or seeing that my Mother had lit up in a madrone tree during my Cave Nights to watch over me and see that I was safe.

Much of the history of our place here is lost forever. Hopefully this writing can help it live again – if only briefly. Everyone ever touched by the true Treasure of the Klamath River Canyon knows the rich magical nature of the unnamable force of human spirit and kindness that our land and our community – almost a hundred years after the Exodus – still holds.

Euclid P. Flamen...

Chapter Twenty-Eight

The Kissed Page

"Roses are for the young courting folks. Lilacs are for the sweetness of growing old with someone you used to give roses to."
 – Mrs. Alice Fenway, Resident

My hand is finally steady after this morning's events, but my heart and mind are lost thinking of a lot that has happened over the last eighty or so years. I had got so used to the burdens I carried, that at my advanced age I had almost forgotten the sweetness of the life I had once. I had almost forgotten all of the wonder of the woman who had married me.

My Amelia. My love of my life. I grieve for her every day, and I miss the surprises that she brought to me.

It took me a while to start writing in this journal this morning – at my preferred garden-side picnic table – and even after I was seated and thinking about my first journal entry of the day and how I would sum up the Treasure adventure of long ago, I decided to put down my pen when my desire for another cup of coffee outvoted my muse.

As I returned to my seat with my warm coffee in my favorite cup the crick breeze moved the pages of my project. I muttered something best left out of this entry. The journal lay open to the very back of the book. Annoyed that my place had to be found again, I impatiently grabbed the journal and before I turned back the pages I looked down.

I felt like I had been hit with a thunderbolt. My face and hands grew ashen and my fingers began to tremble. My breath was short, and my heart raced. I dropped my favorite coffee cup into the grass, and my much needed coffee was forgotten as it spilled onto my pant leg, my shoes, and the ground. I couldn't even feel the burning heat of the coffee on my skin.

On the corner of the page, the bright red lipstick caught my eye first. Someone had kissed the page – far in the back of my long forgotten journal – and then wrote beneath it.

I immediately recognized Amelia's handwriting, and I pondered the three separate entries that appeared below the kiss.

The first was lettered in a strong hand, with formal curves and beautiful spacing. Amelia wrote,

"Sunday, July 5, 1936. Dearest Uke: Yesterday you married me and made me the happiest woman in the world. As you are at the river fishing us breakfast right now, and as I am supposed to be baking the bread, I have but a moment to leave you this note in your beautiful journal. When you reach this page, during your writing of your adventures, come to me and kiss me again, and let's sit in the garden and remember today, when all of this was new to us. My love to you, A."

Needless to say, the tears were welling in my eyes as I thought about that day. I even found myself thinking that later when I go into the house I may pretend to be sore at her for writing in my book before I give up the ruse and laugh about her sneaky woman ways. Then I'll gather her up into my arms and kiss her and indeed, sit with her in the garden to talk about those first days that happened years and years ago. Then I remembered that that would be impossible. She was not here.

The second entry, below the first a little, was also in her beautiful, metered handwriting.

"Tuesday, September 23, 1941. Dearest Uke: Five years have passed my dear since I first opened your book. What amazing adventures we've had! Remember how the old woman in Morocco blessed us? Remember dipping your toes in the Ganges and jumping away because you thought you saw a crocodile? I know that you will have time one day to fill these pages with your stories and maybe even of our traveling adventures, but right now it may have to wait. I will tell you later today that you, my dear husband, are soon to be on another adventure. Before summer our child will be born. We are going to have such fun! I am scared but terribly happy. I hope that you will be happy too. My love to you, A."

And I was happy that day. I remembered every moment of that evening. I had nigh unto choked on my own tongue with surprise, and awkwardly stood wanting to hug her until my little Amelia convinced me that holding her in my arms would be just fine. I spent the next six months from that day alternately treating her like she was made out of glass and also planning all of the fishing trips and baseball games and camping outings that my soon-to-be-born son and I would enjoy together.

I wondered how many years I had walked by her secret notes, hidden away in the otherwise empty bookshelved journal.

It had been so long since I had thought of those times. I had showed her Morocco and India and Italy and her favorite – the islands in the South Pacific. She had enjoyed our adventures.

I stood there and soaked in the warmth of that love and the whispers of memories that blew through my mind. Were she and I ever really that young? Were we really as happy as I remembered?

I also knew that I was avoiding reading the last entry – as I had already glanced and noticed that the writing was faint and a bit shaky. I was savoring the healthy and vibrant, the lovely and mischievous Amelia. I already knew how the story ended. I knew that reading the last entry was fixin' to hurt. I could already see that the date on her final entry was about a year before she died. Amelia wrote,

"Tuesday, November 28, 1975. Dearest Euclid: My hand shakes and we both pretend it doesn't. I am old and wrinkled and gray, but you still look at me like you always have, with the love and care in your eyes. This morning I forgot your name, and all of your nicknames, for several hours. I know in my heart that my journey here, with you, will end soon. I will always, always love you. You spent so much of your life loving and laughing with me, it seems no time was set aside for this poor book! I am afraid that soon you will have a lot of time for your book. Thank you for loving me, for marrying me, for our son, and for how well you will take care of me until I am gone. Just in case I forget to tell you. I have, and always will, love you. Yours, A."

She had told me, at the end, that she loved me. I did take care of her, every minute of every day of that last year until she was gone. I've missed her every moment that has passed in the last twenty-two years.

I'll never quite be convinced that those pages opened only because of the morning wind. I'm going now to take some roses and lilacs to Amelia's grave.

I can write no more today.

Euclid P. Hammarsen

Chapter Twenty-Nine

The End of My Journal

"Old Man Euclid? He has a
standing order for fishing line from
a place in Indiana, cat food and .22
shells."
                    – Harry Langfield, Grocer

I get visitors here once in a while, and I get the
opinion that some of the townsfolk must have
volunteered to come and check in on me under the
guise of a friendly visit. I've been that secret volunteer
before, and I was always relieved when I found the little
old man or little old woman still breathing when I called
on 'em. I've also found a few not breathing, too. There's
an unspoken tradition of taking care of our own here in
the river valley, and we step up to the plate the best
when no one else is left to take care of our old ones.

I'm afraid that one of these days someone will find

me in my big chair, with a neighborhood cat chewing on the toes that I have left. I used to joke about keeping a big bowl of cat food in the laundry room just in case the cats found me before the secret volunteer did, but I guess at that point it won't matter to me anymore.

One of the boys that my son had been friends with – Stevie Ammon – now has sons of his own. They're in high school and they're both good boys. They come over and help with the yard work and take me to get groceries once a week. I give them some extra money for their trouble, but I always have to insist that they take it.

I asked Steve, a few years ago, if he would take care of my final arrangements when it came time for it. He agreed to spread half of my ashes over the graves of my Mother, my wife, and my son over in the Cemetery, and to hike the other half up to Spirit Lake to be with my Father.

Steve doesn't know it and doesn't expect it, but for all of his trouble I've made sure that my estate will pay the way for his kids to make it through college. It won't be a hand-out, since he'll have some real work to do to button up my affairs.

My library books are on the counter next to the old refrigerator, and the rest of the boxes and boxes of gold nuggets are appropriately hidden here and there where I'm sure no one will ever find them. There's a certain poetic justice to that, I think – since most of it went back into the ground that it had come out of. We never had to use much of it to get by through the years. My Father was known to be a bit extravagant now and then with the riches Zhen Zi had left us as pay to caretake his possessions – sometimes buying a whole new shovel-handle when the old one broke or getting me a baseball glove and a woolen baseball hat one Christmas by trading some of it. We made our way just fine, and had to dip into the gold caches only a few times in all of the years. I believe that my Father had intended on just giving it all back to Zhen Zi when he returned. After we found out that Zhen Zi would never be able to return to our River Canyon, we used some of the gold for charity purposes in the community.

Our life was just fine with or without all of that gold.

I think pretty often about the giant treasure hunt I had undertaken – so long ago, now – and the unintended consequences that it had. If I had understood that the Treasure that War Sing referred to was our beautiful land and community all along, would the Running Indian have won his footrace and traveled to the Orient and back on a British ship? Would the exiled Chinese prince – who happened to be War Sing's younger brother – ever have set foot in America, meeting with folks who wanted to help him with his resistance effort and his return to power? Most important, would War Sing's bones and the bones of the other forty-five men ever have been taken back to their homeland so they could finally be at peace?

I spend a lot of time thinking on events that have happened here since the days before the horses were burned, too.

Here the summer evenings fall quickly. The sun heads to the sea, and the mountains cut short the warm glow. The canyon darkens. High above us, we can watch the progress from our shaded homes – the tree tops on the high ridges glisten and glow in the lessening light. The grass hoppers sing, and the heated wind rushes up the river bringing the sweet and damp smell that we river folk know as home. These are the hours that the sweethearts and the old ones hold dear.

This is the place that I compared all of the others to in my life. Looking at steep, fir and pine lined mountainsides all across this world, I've thought the same thing – that they either did or did not bear a resemblance to the mountainside that stood out of my bedroom window as a child, the first thing I saw when I woke each morning and the last thing I would see at night for all of those good, good early years.

To make it easier for any kid who happened to read this all for a school report – I suppose that the moral of this story, of my story, is that our lives are connected by the details and fondnesses that make us what we are. The people that we love. The way we care for each other. The spirit that we all carry to make us daring, adventurous, and young at heart no matter how old we are lucky to become.

It is ironic to me, as I look back over the adventures I've placed in this book, that I've chosen ones that don't really have much to do with what most people would have considered to be exciting about my life.

No mention at all of the two years I spent in the Hawaiian Islands after the war. Absent also are any details of my first near-fatal summit attempt of Denali – where most of the ring finger on my left hand and two of my toes still remain to this day – or of my triumphant return to that pile of icy dirt and successful summit seven years after. I've even left out the almost unbelievable story of the time that I met the Dalai-Lama at an actual llama and cattle ranch when our paths crossed in Argentina.

I've been around the world at least three times,

and although each of my trips lasted much longer than a fictional eighty days, I did, in fact, employ some very exotic modes of transportation on my journeys.

I did visit Egypt – and was employed there a while. Yes, I did go fishing, and yes, I did send my parents a post card purt nearly identical to the one I had imagined sending as a boy during my woodcutting daydreams. In 1925 I waited for several weeks in Cairo – just as Zhen Zi and I had planned for our meeting – but he never showed up. I found out later that the poor little King had bravely met his end trying to save the country and the religion that he loved. I wonder if any of those people ever understood everything they lost when they gave their country, their religion, their daughters, and their thoughts to a revolution that had no respect for any of those things. My heart tells me that they didn't deserve Zhen Zi fighting for them, seeing how quick they gave in after he was gone – I'm sure that he would have done it anyway, out of respect for his family and the glory of the past. I miss him, too, and often think about what could have been if his story had a happy ending.

I've also left out most mention of my son's death and the tragedy and loss that it brought to our lives. While the pain of losing him still hurts me every time I breathe – fresh even after nigh unto fifty years – I have no words for that soul-crushing wound or the emptiness left in our house after the accident.

It was through my travels that I found what I had been looking for, for so long. Almost a hundred years after sealing my fate by placing my name in the Bear Man's guest book and igniting my desire to leave and explore the world – I also discovered that the hard-found road that leads out of the small hometown can most definitely lead back to it.

I hit upon the same treasure that War Sing did, under his temple. I found my treasure in my community and in the land itself – hidden under the rock I like to sit on at my favorite fishing hole. My friend, Samuel, said that he had found his on a peak that overlooked our River Canyon. My Amelia always told me that her treasure was split between the Marbles' Green Granite Lake and Ukonom Falls. We all knew that we had riches that couldn't be bought with gold.

Amelia, dear, I have now filled this journal front to back with many of my favorite adventures, just as we had talked about. The only regrets I bear on my shoulders now are those that I had no power to change, and that I didn't find your kissed page sooner.

Euclid P. Hammarsen

Afterword:

Regarding Euclid

Estate Executor Steven Ammon's Final Report Summary
August 12, 2007

Having been asked by Mr. Hammarsen to help with the final disposition of his body and his belongings, and being named as executor of his Last Will and Testament, I found it important to try to explain the circumstances under which his journal was published and the hundreds of historic items and, well – treasure – found in his home and in his property were parsed out to different organizations.

My sons and I had discovered him missing from his home on June 3, 1996 during one of our regular visits. Looking closer at the whole situation, we noticed a business card from the County Social Services Senior Ombudsman shoved into his screen door – and we later found out that one of the well-meaning busy-body ladies from that office, seeing his age on some list of theirs, had decided to check on Euclid to make sure he was being treated all right.

We called in the Highway Patrolman, Ray Dalton,

and we set about trying to find Uke. The hospital bag the little old man had packed years before and always had sat next to the bookshelf was missing, and under the open bathroom window was a smudge of a footprint. Checking the large and well-stocked gun cabinet, we saw that his old .22 was absent from its normal spot in the rack as well a few boxes of shells.

Patrolman Dalton suggested that possibly some kind of foul-play was involved, but after we found the journal and skipped through it a bit we all figured the adventurous old man lit out to avoid the pushy Ombudsman.

We mounted a community search – with the Forest Service helicopter, their fire crews, about forty men from town, and local packers – but weren't able to find him even though we looked for almost two weeks before the search was called off. Knowing his love of swimming and fishing, we searched the stream side and riverbanks all around. I knew that with his knowledge of the area that if he wanted to escape and had the energy for it there was no telling where he would end up. I'm certain that he knew none of us ever would have tried to make him leave his house, and it's a common sentiment that the next Ombudsman who arrives in our town had better just keep driving right through.

For the past ten years my family and I kept his house and yard up, waiting for him to return – as he had asked in his Will. It wasn't much work, since we'd been trying to help him already. And it was the least we could do, as the two checks that fell out of his Will when the Judge opened it – each for $75,000 – were made out to my boys. In the memo line for each he had written in his shaky hand, "for college."

As directed by his unusual and interesting last

document, on the tenth anniversary of the date of his disappearance we set in to close up his house and get his belongings to where he had wanted. My wife and I had our truck full of cardboard boxes from the market, ready to label and send away what he had inside. When we opened the little envelope the Judge had given us from the stack of legal papers that Old Man Uke had left, there was only a numbered list. We were a bit unprepared for what his little house really held.

He had written, "1. If my library books have not been returned yet, please return them and send the County Library the past due monies for the ten years." *Done*. We had brought the books back to the Library about three weeks after he had gone missing on the annoying insistence of the local librarian. They had been sitting, neatly stacked and in order, on the kitchen counter next to the refrigerator when he had disappeared.

"2. Please contact the County Historical Society and ask if they want any of the papers in the nineteen boxes, in the attic." *They had*. In those boxes were historical documents from our own founding in the River Canyon as well as thousands of pages of truly ancient Chinese documents and essays. They figured it'd take years and years to actually understand everything that had been left.

"3. Please send all of my books, except my journal, to the County Library in Yreka. Let them know that some of them should be put on reserve since two of the titles are first-run rare copies that were appraised at over $921,000 in 1978. The appraisal papers are in the binder with all the legal documents. It's okay with me if they sell or auction my old books, but only to buy new books for the river kids." There had been such an interest in Euclid's story and his journal, that my wife typed it up and sent it off to be printed – including in the manuscript several of the pencil drawings he had done. We figured Uke would have wanted that and maybe had those plans himself before the Ombudsman butted in.

"4. Please set aside $5,000 from my bank account in a trust for the Cemetery Board to use to buy a new United States Flag to replace the old one whenever it needs to be done."

"5. Please contact the Archaeology Department at Oregon State University to see if they would like to be in charge of the collecting and cataloging of the items in the back bedroom, garage, and basement marked 'Antiques.' Have them mind the swords – they're real sharp. I understand they have some pretty smart folks up there in Corvallis, but what tipped the scale for me was their baseball program – it's good to see a school that still respects the importance of The Fine Game. Whatever the University doesn't want, the Smithsonian can have second call at."

That last item on the list caused the most uproar. Folks from the Chinese Embassy in San Francisco came up as soon as word had got out as to the items Uke had stored away and bequeathed to the University. The Chinese officials laid claim to the items, but while the papers that Uke had left were a jot vague about who the rightful owners would end up being they were perfectly clear on who the owners weren't. The local judge who had been administering and overseeing the strange estate of Euclid Plutarch Hammarsen for a decade was very steadfast in his decision to be shut of those interloping folks from the Embassy, and he took special care to admonish their submission of a claim at all.

The Embassy folks dragged out the proceedings for almost a year, and one day the judge had seen enough and closed the whole show down. He quoted from Euclid's journal on several occasions in his court judgment, and only permitted the University to possess the items under an agreement to never give them back to the Chinese government folks. The judge, in his summary at the packed Siskiyou County Court House, chided the Chinese officials for trying to mix up the whole process and not respecting the wishes of poor disappeared Euclid. His famous final words on the matter were given as he stood up behind his bench, took off his dark robe and rolled up his shirt-sleeves. In a statement that would have made old Euclid proud he said, "Deputies, give me a hand to get these chuckleheaded jackdaws out of my court." He grabbed a fistful of the folks, dragging them out of their chairs, out of the courtroom, down the staircase, and right out the front door – followed by our fine deputized fellows hauling out the rest in the same manner. After the last one was tossed down the front steps into the street, the court staff returned to work.

The whole thing caused a pretty big ruckus and brought a lot of outside people into our community. The judge got reelected, and most of us figure he has that job for life if he wants it.

Some folks on the television called what had happened an International Incident, but we didn't pay much attention to any of it. About a month after all of the cataloging and collecting was completed, and when all of the television news crews had finally left, I got a phone call from Officer Dalton regarding Euclid.

A group of hikers from McCloud, California – headed into the Marble Mountain Wilderness area – got lost on their way to the trailhead and trying to find it instead found the body of what was thought to be Mr. Hammarsen high in the remote mountains above Sulphur Springs. A team from Yreka was brought down to identify him because he had been passed away for so long, and I went with them to find out what had happened.

From reading his journal, I immediately recognized the strangely beautiful place where they found the skeleton of the sweet old man – wrapped in his canvas shakedown sleeping bag with an old-time woolen baseball cap on the top of his skull – next to a long pile of rocks. They figured he had probably died close to the time he went missing ten years previous.

He was found in a dale with beautiful and sparkling water to one side, set in a granite field – and a flower-filled meadow to the other, surrounded by tall and straight firs and pines just as he had described in his journal. He had made it to the High Springs Pool of his youth that he had written about, and I'd like to think that he went to his reward in his sleep. I'd like to think that the last thing he saw was the diamond-twinkles of the millions of stars above him, set in our deep-black night sky.

I found his tennis shoes – worn by the sun and the rain of forty season changes – still on a rock near the pool. I could imagine him sitting there on that long ago sunny day and taking them off right before he jumped in for that last swim.

His campsite was pretty much intact – a fire ring, some cedar planks, his .22 and a rusty knife were found close-by him. The folks from Yreka were curious about the whole scene, since it was rare to find a body virtually untouched by the forest animals after all that time had passed. They also remarked on the high number of horse hoofprints found in the little valley since no one had seen wild horses in those mountains in almost fifty years.

It looked like he had made it to some of his other special places before he ended up there – namely the Flying Rat Cave and the Old Oak Tree he also had described in his writing. In the hand that wasn't draped over the grave of his beloved Cinder, the folks from Yreka found several toy army men, a smooth white heart-shaped piece of quartz, and four green-glass marbles.

Not more than a month after that, my boys – home from college for the summer – hiked with me to Spirit Lake to give Uke the send off he had asked for. With half of his ashes spread over the graves of his wife, son, and Mother, we took the other half with us on our trek to the Ghostly Lake.

I figure we sat on the same felled log that he had – first with his Father ninety years previous, and then alone fifty years after that as he let his Father's ashes go.

It was a beautiful night, and with my sons setting close we admired the reflection of the stars in the black water, and saw the mysterious glow that Uke had described turning the starlight an emerald green right in front of us.

Even after we let the rest of Uke go to be with his Father and the Ghostly Indian Chief at their Council Fire, we quietly sat on that log until the moon rose – full and bright – over the rocky cliff to the east.

Steven Ammon
Estate Executor of Euclid Plutarch Hammarsen

A Few Words From

The Author

Dear Reader:

As a work of historical fiction, I've taken author's license and creative liberty with just about all of the names and facts and events that are found in this book. I used that beautiful and wonderful River Canyon setting to show my sons the magic that can be found in the mountain lands and in the waters of the Klamath and in the people who have called Happy Camp and the Klamath River home. I wanted to try to explain to them a bit about the curiously-named small town and I wanted them to know what it was like to grow up wild and free and safe in a community and land that taught respect, self-reliance, and compassion for others.

Much of what I've put between the covers of this book was inspired by events in my life, my families' lives, and from community stories handed down over the years. I believe my upbringing on the river made me the independent and sure person I am today. I've spent hours and hours quietly fishing the Klamath with my

Father, or tagging along with him and my grandfather while they prospected. I've gold panned until my hands were near frozen in the Klamath and in the mountain creeks. I've hiked the Marbles trail that leads right past the real Spirit Lake. I've even worked as a logger and a loader operator for a helicopter show. When I shot my first buck near Tannen Lake, like my Father and Grandfather before me I put the warm blood in my mouth and thanked the animal for the food it was going to give to my family. I am the proud descendent of the fair and noble ocean-faring Alanders from the White Sea, and the granddaughter of the pioneering River Canyon man that Johnson's Hunting Ground was named for. In fact, my family homesteaded in that beautiful place before it was a Wilderness Area.

My own eyes were opened to the world, like Euclid, when I also wrote my name in a gilded guest book of a local man who was very much like Old Epharim. I was fascinated by the lists of foreign names, and worried about the bears outside at the same time.

It's been said that long ago Mr. Roosevelt did frequent our area, and was rumored to have owned a riverside home on the Klamath. Hundreds of Chinese folks used to live in our River Canyon at one time, and most of the bones of their dead brethren were taken back to China when they left, long ago. We have a rich tribal tradition, which continues today – and luckily for the rest of us, the World Renewal Ceremonies are held faithfully each year.

In this book I also wanted to pay a tribute to the folks that still have managed to make their lives in the other little towns – like Hamburg, Scott's Bar, Sawyer's Bar, Etna, Fort Jones, Seiad, Somes Bar, Orleans, Selma and Cave Junction. For those of you who have managed to stay, know that River Canyon expatriates like me think of you often and we consider the hills where you live as our home as well. One day, hopefully, we can return.

There are plenty of resources to use if you really want to know the hard and true facts about the place, the settlement of the area, and the brave people who charged head-long into new lives in the Klamath River Canyon.

Above it all, remember that like Euclid I am a fisherman too.

Trisha Johnson Barnes
June 18, 2008

Unconventional, Foreign, Hay-Seed and Old Word

Glossary of Terms

A

Ab ovo: literally, before the egg; in the beginning

Abacus: traditional Chinese tabulating instrument

Academic Work: term used to refer to what enlightened and educated folks do instead of working with their hands or backs

Aces high: term regarding holding something good; from card-playing vernacular

Achates: In Virgil's *Aeneid*, Achates was always a faithful friend and companion

Adam's Ale: water

Adumbral: forecast the outcome

Airtights: items that had been canned to preserve freshness

American Inn: historic Happy Camp building and former inn and mail drop

Anti-establishment chuckleheads: one of many terms for dumb-acting environmental protestors

Aplomb: self-sure

Apple-peeler: small knife

Apuruva'niik: local tribal term for ghostly demon

Arimantus trees: commonly called The Trees of Heaven;

foreign species brought to Siskiyou County by Chinese miners beginning in the 1850's

Athithu'uf: local tribal term for Indian Crick

Atwixt: between

Auric: relating to gold

Avuki'i: local tribal term for boy

Axva'htaahkoo: local tribal term for blonde-haired person

B

Banausic: routine or mechanical

Bar, The: nickname for Murderer's Bar

Bellerophon: in mythology, the man who tried to ride Pegasus to Heaven

Belly-through-the-brush escape: retreating in a quick and stealthy manner

Bert's Super Service Station: downtown gas station used often as a meeting place for loggers and fishermen in the mornings; closed up shop some time ago

Better Part of California: the part of the State from about Red Bluff northward to the Oregon border, extending from the Pacific Ocean eastward to the Nevada border

Big find: gold discovery

Big Show, The: major league baseball

Bigfoot: big hairy creature that roams the woods between Arcata, California and Happy Camp, California

Bishop: large and fashionable hip bustle on formal dresses

Bivouac: to camp out, usually work-related

Blacksmith: man who shod horses and fashioned metal work for carriages and other items; could be counted on to fashion miner's innovations from a rough explanation

Blue streak: using more than one cuss-word in a thought out series

Boat dance: part of local tribal world renewal ceremony

Boggy-top pie: any pie made without a covering crust

Bothahrayshun: a big bother

Bragging rights: what you get when you won a contest or were proven tight

Broom-jumping: wedding ceremony

Buddhist temples: house or building where Buddha was honored; Chinese community center and meeting hall

C

California wave: a rude gesture made with the hand
Cat: big piece of logging machinery; in skilled hands, it can almost be driven upside down
Caterwauling: effeminately carrying on like a cat; wailing
Cat skinner: the crazy fella in the driver's seat on a Cat
Central Pacific: rail company with service to California area in the early days of the Northern California Gold Rush
CB radio: citizen's band radio; communication tool in the logging industry
Celestial: local pioneer term for the Chinese-born residents of the area
Celestial district: area in our community where most of the foreign-born miners lived
Chinaman: local pioneer term for the Chinese-born residents of the area
Chinese coins: often found in the silt and riverbanks of the Klamath Canyon, the old trading pieces are round with a hole in the center and bear embossed Chinese character writing; holes were used to string the money together for safe-keeping
Chinese Exclusion Act: formal movement to keep ownership of businesses and land from Chinese possession
Chuckleheaded: with wood for a brain
Cinder: best dog in the whole world
Claim: piece of land registered for mining
Claim improvements: required work that needed to be done to prove that you hadn't abandoned a claim
Clerkenwell: a holy well found in London
Clum: climbed
Clym of the Clough and Adam Bell: do-gooding adventurous outlaws of the forest; characters in Percy's *Reliques*
Colossus of Rhodes: one of the Seven Wonders of the World; Chare's sculpture of the sun god Helios
Conniption fit: a real kicking and hollering ruckus
Coon's age: a long, long time
Cowboy kedigree: stew of what is on hand, usually made with fish, rice, vegetables, and eggs

Crick: creek
Cut stick: leave really, really fast

D

Da Yao Yu: fabled and legendary giant fish of the Klamath River
Daisy: term used for good or sweet
Defenstration: act of throwing something out a window
Del Rio Theater: Happy Camp movie house and theater; burned down some time ago
Dirt worshippin' atheists: one of many terms for environmental protestors
Dog: language of words, barks, and nonverbal cues that lucky and observant children learn to communicate with their canine friends
Dogwood: mid-size spring flowering tree, said to have magical properties; rumored to be the wood Jesus' cross was made from
Doryphone: a person who enjoys pointing out small errors made by other folks
Downriver: referring to any land, person, or item found down stream from a certain point
Doxology works: churches
Divvy up: divide item equally between two or more parties
Dynamite: explosive used in mining and logging; often set with a leading thread-like fuse; occasionally used to expedite lake fishing by stunning all of the fish
Dragon Throne of Manchu: lineage right of the Qing Dynasty to rule in China
Dredge: float-mounted gas-powered mining machine used to bring gravel, dirt, and rock from the stream or river bed through a mounted sluice box; usually operated by a submerged diver
Dredging: mining with a suction dredge
Drift boat: a river fishing boat with high sides, pointed bow, and wide water displacement to navigate rapids as well as low-water areas; usually rowed backwards against the current to allow the bow fishermen to use the river current to make their lures move

Eddy: calm places in rivers an stream where large rocks or other debris block the swift currents

Elderberries: bluish-purple fruit of the shrublike tree; highly sought after by bears, jam makers, and hungry boys

Environmental hypocrites: any of the folk common to California and Oregon who have vacationed on the picket lines of our timber sales before returning to their wood-framed homes, which are usually well-stocked with toilet paper, books, and such

Ethereal: heavenly

Fallers: term for 'fellers' that outside folks often use in error

Farriers: horse tenders and trainers

Fellas: fellows; refers to group of men

Fellers: tree sawyers

Final Breath: death

Foreign Miner's Tax: a fee of $4 per day, levied by the State and Local governments against any foreign-born miners; used to begin to limit mining competition

Forks of Salmon: historic outpost, mail stop, and grocery on the Salmon River

G

Ghast: like a ghost, but shimmery and see-through

Ghostly Indian Chief: spirit warrior who is an adversary or an advisor as deserved; said to live under the depths of the glowing Spirit Lake

Gold: precious metal naturally found in the rich Klamath River Canyon and surrounding lands

Golden canyon: the Klamath River Canyon

Gooseberries: sweet but hard-got fleshy berries that are surrounded by thorny spikes

Goosey bumps: small skin bumps appearing when scared or suddenly chilled

Great Jump: death

Great Master: supreme being; God, if you're so inclined

Greenhorn: miner with no experience and little common sense

Guquin zither: traditional Chinese stringed instrument, resembling a neckless guitar

Gum Shun: Chinese term for the Golden Mountains rumored to be found in Siskiyou County and down the Klamath River Canyon

H

Hale: Hawaiian term for house

Handle: nick-name of a person

Happy Camp: Northern California town with a rich history and beautiful setting

Hard-hat area: work zone requiring use of safety equipment such as hardhats

Harmolipi: the hermitage of certain monks in isolated cliff caves

Hay-seed: local pronunciation or translation

Hebetudinous: dull and slow-minded

H-e-double hockey sticks: childhood term for 'hell'; used in conversation to avoid cursing

Helgrimites: a crick insect that fashions a cylindrical home from small bits of sand and pebbles

Higuamo River: fresh-water tributary located near San Pedro de Macoris in the Dominican Republic

Huckleberry above a persimmon: really, really good

Human pine cone: fella falling out of a tree

Huzzah: exclamation of celebration; hooray!

Hydraulic mining: using the force and pressure of water, as with a water cannon, to force minerals and rocks through a pre-made sluice system

I

Independence Crick: tributary to the Klamath south of Happy Camp; site of one of the longest held patent mines in the River Canyon

Indian Crick: tributary to the Klamath River; runs southward from the Greyback and Cade drainages

Ishke'esh: tribal name for the Klamath River
Ish'xikik'ar: tribal term for Klamath River sturgeon

J

Jackdaw: idiot or fool
John Tamson man: henpecked husband
Johnson's Hunting Ground: area near Sulphur Springs where a small boy faced off a giant black bear with a shotgun and won
Jot: a little bit
June Lawson: local Gold Star Mother and patriotic supporter of soldiers, veterans, and the community

K

Ka-am: local tribal term for 'upriver'
Katie-bar-the-door: to keep out
Klamath River: the 268-mile-long Northern California River that winds from south-eastern Oregon through the Klamath River Canyon and eventually empties into the Pacific Ocean south of Crescent City

L

Lady of the Lake: In Arthurian legend, Lancelot's Mother Vivian
Landslide: earthen avalanche
Lethogic: unable to remember the correct word
Lex non scripta: followers of an unwritten law formed by their common sense attitude
Lilac: tall deciduous flowering shrub bearing fragrant purple groupings of blossoms; favored by married folk
Lissome: bendable
Litter: pioneer structure used to carry or move items; two poles lashed with a cloth or hide and pulled behind a person or stock animal
Logger: any person who works in the timber cutting, retrieval, or removing process
Logger-talkin': ability to wind expletives in sentence form

and create expletive phrases on the cuff

Lois' Café: long time Happy Camp restaurant; burned down some time ago

M

Meamber: to roam aimlessly with no plan or timeframe
Miasmic: poisonous
Miner: someone who searches for gold, silver, or gems in the Klamath River Canyon or surroundings; includes placer, dredge, and other types of mining
Miner's Lettuce: a delicate and delicious plant with heart-shaped leaves found in marshy areas
Misanthropic: hateful acting toward people
Montague: rail town located near Yreka
Mount Shasta: Northern California resting volcano over 14,000 feet high; said to be the home of a race of magical people
Mountain gate: part of the temple providing a defined entrance to the sacred interior
Murderer's Bar: original name of the Happy Camp settlement

N

Nairn: none
Nancy-Boy: derogatory term for a silly, good-for-nothing, girl-acting boy
Ned Kelly: an Australian desperado who was popular in the countryside but was eventually caught and hanged
Nigh unto: almost

O

Obsidian: glass-like opaque dark rock; sharp chips used as weapons, knives, arrow-heads, and scrapers
Old Log Schoolhouse: Happy Camp's historic former one-room schoolhouse; used as a meeting hall
Old sourdough: miner with a lot of experience and a little common sense

Orestes: tragic Greek mythology figure, tormented by family ruin; his name, loosely translated means *mountaineer* or *man of the mountain*

Oriental: local pioneer term for the Chinese-born residents of the area

Outfitters: shops that sold everything a greenhorn or old sourdough might need on their mining journey

P

Pacification of the Dominican Republic: U. S. military effort from 1915 through 1918; Marine and Navy presence was sought to quell revolutionary uprising

Paddock stew: soupy meal made of boiled frogs

Patent mine: a special type of claim wherein the Federal Government has given title of the land to the claimant; has the rights of private property, not just mineral rights

Pegasus: the mythological winged horse

Placer mining: any type of mining that includes panning, sluicing, or hydraulics; usually a placer miner is going after deposited gold, not tunnel vein lines

Pick-Yer-Wish: local mispronounciation of the Pikyavish area and ceremony

Pikyavish: local tribal name of certain ceremony and area along the Klamath River

Poison oak: brushy and viny plant with three-lobed oily leaves; produces an itchy rash when touched

Poker Flat: high valley area north of town in the Greyback Mountains

Poultice: mix of medicinal herbs and natural items placed directly on or in a wound

Proscenium stage: the formal front-piece of a theater stage; where many soliloquies are recited and narratives given

Prosphora: a Greek traditional celebration to commemorate the cave-manger birth of Jesus

Ptolemy: an early astronomer and scientist from ancient Alexandria

Pullman car: a special rail car with exceptional meal service and sleeping quarters

Purlieu: area of woodland approaching and surrounding the full forest

Purt near: pretty near; close by
P'u Yi: exiled child Emperor of China, holder of the Dragon Throne of Manchu

Q

Quartz: white rock found near gold veins; sparks when hit by another quartz
Quay: wharf or harbor-front
Qui vive: alert and vigilant; secured by sentries or guarded

R

Raccoon: mischievous forest creature renowned for its curiosity and cleverness
Rattlesnake: coiled death; venomous fanged snake
Reel: form of dance or bringing in a fish on a pole
Resenar: Swedish term for 'traveler'
Ribaldry: rough humor and language
Right foot foremost: old taboo against entering a situation or new residence with the left foot
River eel: long, snake-like water creature that attaches itself to fish, boy feet, or whatever it can
River foam: once thought to be evidence of river pollution, the mounds of white foam floating in the Klamath have been determined to be a by-product of the churning vegetable material in the water
River guide: hired person that shows others to fish on banks or from drift or jet boats
Rosebushes: bushy flowering plant favored by young lovers

S

Salmon River: tributary to the Klamath River; a beautiful and wild stretch of the best rafting waters in the world
Sam Hill: term used in place of rough cursing
Scree: loose rock and gravel field
Secret name: private tribal handle given to members or friends

Shakedown: sleeping roll or bag, covered by a canvas sleeve to protect from water and cold

Shasta Butte City: former name of Yreka

Shivaree: Midwest tradition of carrying the bride and groom through town on chairs and roughly serenading them through the night

Siskiyou: name of the county and the mountain range north-east of Happy Camp

Sluice box: mine equipment that traps gold in base slats; used with running water

Sound on the goose: raise an alarm

Southern Pacific: rail company with service throughout the west; connected Oregon to The Other Part of California

Spotted owl: small nocturnal wood bird that's not too good for eating

State of Jefferson: area that includes part of Southern Oregon and Northern California with a southern border near Redding, California; officially created by armed revolt and establishment of government in 1941

Sugar pine: large variety of pine tree with heavy cones regularly up to fourteen inches long

T

Tattle-tale: a person who reports misdeeds of others

Temple screen: part of the temple providing a respectful separation of the altar area

Thompson's Dry Diggin's: area near Yreka made famous as the first big Northern California gold strike

Thunder egg: a geode; a naturally occurring egg-shaped mineral ball, often containing sought-after gems or minerals

Tinder fungus: a thick and dense tree conk; renowned for holding embers over long periods

Trap: device used to catch nuisance, food or fur animals

Trapper: any person who sets, checks, and clears a trap or a trap line

Tree-sitter: timber sale protestor often found in the canopy of a tree scheduled to be cut

Trees of Heaven: the spire-like, deep green arimantus trees planted by Chinese pioneers

Tree spike: metal shaft driven into trees by cowardly

protestors; causes mill saws to break and explode, sometimes killing the mill workers

Troglodyte: cave dweller

Twenty-two or .22: a small rifle; common caliber in varmint hunting

U

Upriver: referring to any land, person, or item found up stream from a certain point

V

Varmints: animals usually not used for food, such as mice, rats, coyotes, and snakes

Victuals: food items

Virago: loud and bad tempered woman

W

Water cannon: large and heavy metal end piece used in hydraulic mining

Went south: something bad occurred

Western Valhalla: heaven for Viking-descended fellows dying outside of their homeland of Sweden, Finland, Denmark, Holland or the Aland Islands

Wild horses of the River Canyon: herd of horses that had been abandoned by miners and pioneers over the early years of the community

Whoopin': spanking with a belt, stick, or willow switch

X

Xanthippe: nagging or harping woman or wife

Y

Yarded decks: piled debris after timber cutting and removal activity

Yarder: piece of logging machinery used to pull logs and debris out of cutting areas

Yreka: Siskiyou county seat; formerly Shasta Butte City until a bakery tent sign was misread and the community was renamed

Yu'ruk: local tribal term for 'downriver'

Z

Zither: one of a family of Chinese instruments resembling a many-stringed, neckless guitar

The Klamath River Canyon

Dear Reader: Although this book is a fiction work, the
setting for the exploits of young (and old) Hammarsen is
a very real and wonderful place.
Consider visiting us on your next vacation!

Happy Camp Chamber of Commerce
P. O. Box 1188
Happy Camp, CA 96039
www.HappyCampChamber.com

Happy Camp Ranger Station
P. O. Box 377
63822 State Highway 96
Happy Camp, CA 96039

Siskiyou County Museum and Historical Society
910 South Main Street
Yreka, CA 96067

Klamath National Forest
1312 Fairlane Road
Yreka, CA 96097

River Canyon Press

Book Order and Information

☐ Please send me _____ copies of *The Klamath Treasure* at $18.52 each, plus $4.00 shipping per book.

☐ My check or money order for $_____ is enclosed.

Please visit us at www.RiverCanyonPress.com for credit card orders.

Name _____

Organization _____

Address _____

City/State/Zip _____

Phone _____ Email _____

River Canyon Press respects your privacy.

Mail your order to:
River Canyon Press
P. O. Box 70643
Eugene, Oregon 97401

10% of Publisher's Profit of This Title Will Go To Siskiyou County Charities

3310715